"DO YOU HAVE ANY IDEA." Jepp told the Traveler " you? I mean everyone? No one knows ' Everyone believes that you would just as .... even thinks about getting in your way. And everyone believes that there is nothing you fear anywhere in the whole Damned World. That must be nice, not to be afraid of anything. I can't imagine that. I'm a human woman. There were times in my life that I felt like I was afraid of everything.

Suddenly she lunged toward the Traveler, her face twisted in fury, her fingers outstretched like claws. The Traveler flinched back, even bringing up his arm to ward her off.

Jepp stopped a foot short of him and slowly lowered her hands. "So you are afraid of something," she said. "You're afraid of me. Why is that? What is it about me that you fear?"

The Traveler made no reply.

Crazy Eight Press is an imprint of Second Age, Inc.

First edition

THE HIDDEN EARTH

BOOK TWO

HEIGHTS OF THE DEPTHS

PETER DAVID

CRAZY 8 PRESS

TO ALL THE FANS WHO NEVER STOPPED ASKING WHEN THIS BOOK WAS COMING OUT.

THE COLONEL HAD NEVER EXPECTED that humanity would survive. He had not anticipated that he would be proven correct in quite this manner.

He takes no pleasure in the imminent extermination of mankind. His foresight offers neither satisfaction nor solace. After all, who in his right mind desires bragging rights about the end of his race?

But the colonel could never have guessed the manner in which this tragedy would come about. Who could have? Who could have imagined such an insane, nightmarish turn of events that even now, at the end, he cannot comprehend.

All around him there is smoke, blinding him to his surroundings. He stumbles, falls to his knees, and mutters a string of profanities. It is the exact sort of reaction for which he would have excoriated his troops. He has trained them to be focused at all times. To expect nothing while anticipating everything. The colonel would have expected them to remain focused rather than wasting energy in shouting imprecations or demanding that an uncaring God damn this, that or the other thing. Yet now he falls prey to the same weakness of will and spirit that he would have found so unacceptable in his soldiers.

Perhaps it stems from the fact that all his soldiers are dead.

All his superiors are dead.

Everyone. Everything. Dead, dead, dead.

They are all dead, and he is in hell, consigned there because he was unable to lead them to victory.

There is no reason for the colonel to take the failure of his forces onto himself. Four branches of military service, hundreds, thousands of officers who outranked him, governments worldwide that acted with confusion or bewilderment or denial when confronted with an enemy beyond any measure of human understanding.

And yet he does, because that is simply the way the colonel's mind is wired. He cannot help but feel personally responsible for the outcome of everything in which he is involved, even when nothing he could have done would have changed the way things turned out.

In the thick underbrush of the jungle through which he is running, he lies in the moist dirt, sweat streaming from under his helmet and down his face. His breath is rattling in his lungs, despite his best efforts to rein in his gasping lest he alert those pursing him of his whereabouts. He is clutching his machete, the only weapon that he has left available to him.

The weapons.

What the hell had they done to the weapons?

When those creatures of myth had intruded so forcefully, so insanely, into the colonel's world, they should have been easily dispatched despite their considerable number. And dispatching them had been the only option available since their immediate actions upon arrival had left no question as to their purpose or priorities.

It had been an indelible image, seared into the consciousness of every man, woman and child on the planet. That moment when, all over the world, the skies had turned purple and swirled as if vast whirlpools had opened in the heavens. There had been cries that the Rapture was occurring, that Jesus was about to descend upon a golden chariot, or that it was heralding the arrival of the Prophet. Scientists attempted to analyze it and some were pointing accusing figures at a new superconducting supercollider that had been activated underground and yet supposedly had managed to open up a spate of black holes in the upper atmosphere.

They had swirled above the Earth, appearing in succession, one every hour until there were twelve of them. People huddled in churches, or in laboratories, or in their homes or home made bomb shelters, while others set up camps so that they could gaze upon the phenomenon and watch and wait and see the glory that *they were sure was to unfold.*

The colonel was on alert at Fort Bragg with the rest of his squadron when the moment came, the moment that would be referred to subsequently as the Burst.

The holes had been churning in the skies, and suddenly every single one of them came to a halt. It was a sight to see, all those energy whirlpools slowing, slowing and then stopping. It was as if nature itself was holding its breath.

Then there was an explosion that was without noise. The first thought was that the light would be visible and the sound would follow shortly, like thunder after lightning. It never happened. The Burst was, as some wags dubbed it, silent but deadly.

No one was laughing minutes later, however.

Astronomers watching through telescopes were the first ones to see the vast containers hurtling through the holes. At first glance they appeared to be vessels of some sort, but they did not seem to have any manner of propulsion or guidance. They were just gigantic shells, ejected from the vortices like bullets from a gun. They hurtled toward the ground, and there was not just one or two of them, but thousands upon thousands. All over the world they spiraled down, at which point the sound finally came. It was the whistling sound typically associated with bombs dropping.

"We're under attack!" came the screams from some, while others brushed off such sentiments as alarmist.

The whirlpools in the sky collapsed in on themselves and vanished moments after their contents had been disgorged. Down came the vessels, and although the world was three quarters water and thus random chance would have dictated that most of them would have had water landings, in fact only a relatively small percentage of them did. All the "bullets" that had erupted from one hole plummeted into the Atlantic ocean. The remainder came to rest on land. In every instance they managed miraculously to avoid major cities. Instead, without exception, they hit on deserts or forests or other areas that were unpopulated by human beings.

They came in at angles, not smashing straight down but instead skidding to a stop, leaving trenches dug up behind them that were miles long, crisscrossing each other like a gigantic hatchwork.

The first contact was made in the Nevada desert. The sun had set, the last fingers of orange light disappearing from the horizon. Army troops moved in, of which the colonel was still not a part. The gigantic shells lay there, smoke still wafting from them, and frost covering their surfaces. There was no hint of movement, no sound of engines powering down, no nothing. The soldiers approached carefully, their rifles out, believing they were ready for anything. Attempts to take readings of anything within the shells were thwarted by the vessels' exteriors. It was as if they weren't even there.

Suddenly there were sounds like guns going off, except none of the soldiers had fired at anyone. They were the sounds of the shells cracking apart, gigantic gleaming metal oblongs as if laid by an enormous mutated chicken. As one the troops stepped back, leveling their weapons. From the back, the commanding officers observed carefully, constantly reporting progress to the White House.

The shells broke wide, and a creature emerged from within that seemed to be stepping out, not from some manner of spaceship, but instead a book on mythology and legend.

It was a Cyclops.

It was gigantic, well over ten feet tall, shielding its eye and blinking against the fading light. Another Cyclops stepped out from behind it, and then more of them. There were audible gasps from behind the squad leader, a battle-hardened master sergeant. He told his men to shut the hell up and then, slinging his rifle, slowly advanced upon the foremost of the Cyclops. The creature looked down upon him with a single brown eye and a brow that seemed arched in mild curiosity.

There was someone of more normal, human proportions standing just behind the Cyclops, but it was also clearly not human. The master sergeant hadn't noticed it at first, which was odd because it was standing right there. Its skin was sallow, its face triangular in shape, its ears long and tapered, and shoulder-length, purple hair fluttered around it in the breeze. The being fixed its gaze upon the master sergeant and there was nothing but contempt in its eyes, which should have been the master sergeant's first warning.

He willfully ignored it.

"Welcome," said the master sergeant, "to—"

The Cyclops stepped on him without hesitation. Before the master sergeant could react, the Cyclops simply took two vast strides forward, the ground thundering beneath him, and then it slammed its foot down on the master sergeant, crushing him with a sound that was oddly like a balloon popping. Blood spread from beneath the Cyclops' foot. It lifted his foot and scraped it on the dirt as if it had just entered someone's home and was availing itself of the welcome mat.

There was no hesitation as the assembled armed forces opened fire.

The Cyclops, looking positively stunned, went down in a hail of bullets. So did several behind it. Then the purple haired being waved its arms, gesturing widely, and just like that the weaponry ceased to function. More specifically, it functioned in reverse, as the rifles proceeded to backfire, exploding in the hands of the young men and women aiming them. Faces were ripped off, bodies blown backwards. Those that had mouths left went down screaming; the rest just went down. Any who attempted to throw hand grenades had them explode in their hands. Mortar shells detonated within the launchers.

As the human beings staggered around, bewildered, disoriented, unable to comprehend what was happening and how this amazing first contact scenario had gone so wrong, so quickly, the Cyclops charged. They came pouring out of the ship, a vast wave of them. Scientists who would later study video of the event would conclude that the number of Cyclops emerging from the ships far exceeded anything that the ship should reasonably have been able to contain. It was like watching a real life version of a clown car, except no one was laughing.

They continued to pour out by the tens of thousands, and then the hundreds of thousands, all from those same fallen shells of ships. And when the planes came swooping in with bombs, a goodly number of the monsters were blown to hell, indicating to most observers that there seemed to be a range involved in what the obvious magic-wielding creature could accomplish. (The scientists disliked the term "magic" intensely, preferring to substitute the phrase "Arcane physics." None of this mattered as, over the long period of annihilation that followed, almost all the scientists were killed.) But many more of the creatures were not killed at all, and they swarmed across the face of the United States, up into Canada, down into Mexico.

Had that been the only arrival, humanity might have been able to cope. But there were eleven others, and all around the globe humanity found itself under assault. Minotaurs, satyrs, vampires, two-legged dragons and more. The attack was relentless, and merciless, and eventually, it was successful.

The colonel was witness to it all.

Now he runs and stumbles through a jungle, the branches tearing at his uniform, bites from random insects pock marking his skin. He falls back as something hisses directly in front of him. For a heartbeat he thinks it's one of those dragon creatures—Mandraques, he believes they call themselves—and then he realizes it's a homegrown snake. He whips his machete around and severs its head from its body in one clean slice. Then he keeps going.

He hears pursuit.

The speech is gutteral and booming, and the trees are crashing down behind him. It is unquestionably the creatures.

They are coming for him. Not enough that his entire squad had been wiped out; they want to be sure to take them out to the last man.

He wonders if he is indeed the last man.

He has lost contact with headquarters. He has seen no other humans in days. For all he knows, the entirety of humanity has been destroyed and he is the last man standing. The final and only defender of the human race.

Your race is run, he thinks bleakly.

Suddenly there is a triumphant roar directly in front of him. It is a Mandraque, looming before him like a miniature dinosaur. It says something incomprehensible, and its forked tongue snaps out. It wields a double bladed sword that is as big as the colonel's arm. The Mandraque whips the sword around, and the colonel ducks under it, slamming forward with the machete. It drives home, and the colonel has the opportunity to see close-up what a Mandraque looks like when it is startled. The Mandraque reflexively tries to lunge toward the colonel, but the action only serves to drive the machete deeper into its own chest. The sword slips from the creature's now nerveless hand and it falls over. The colonel yanks out his machete, spits on the carcass, and then tries to lift the creature's sword. It is impossibly unwieldy. The colonel is not a weak man, but he can barely clear it from the ground. It is useless to him.

He hears more snarling, more shouting. He knows that he is doomed, but he is not going to go quietly. Leaving the sword and his enemy's body behind, he continues to run.

A creature drops from overhead. It emits a hellacious screech. Without looking he swings the machete and gets lucky, beheading the pale skinned monstrosity. Its head falls directly in his path, its lips drawn back in a frozen sneer exposing twin vampiric fangs. Its body flops around for a few seconds, clawing at the air, and then lies still. By the time it ceases thrashing about, the colonel is already gone.

He hears the sounds of his pursuers growing. They're getting closer, and they are making no effort to hide their progress. They do not care if he hears them or not. That is how confident they are in their eventual triumph.

And they are converging. The sounds are not just from behind him now, but from all around. They are cutting him off, using a pincer movement. It seems like a good deal of effort for one man. He should, he supposes, feel honored to some degree.

He does not. All he feels is anger. Anger and impotence.

He trips over an outstretched root, scrambles to his feet, keeps going, and bursts out into a clearing. There is a small rise up ahead. High ground. Go for the high ground, he thinks desperately as he sprints toward it.

He is halfway to the rise when his pursuers emerge, running, from the forest. Two Minotaurs, another Mandraque, two more of the vampires who are sprinting on their feet and knuckles. They converge upon him and he scrambles up the rise, hoping to lose them, knowing that he is doomed to failure. The magnitude of his failure is evident when he reaches the top of the rise only to see more of them coming from the other direction. "Get him!" *shout the Minotaurs, which surprises him because he had been unaware that any of them speak English. Obviously they learn quickly, or at least the Minotaurs do.*

The colonel braces himself, drawing his arm back, trying to see all around him at once, his head whipping back and forth. They know they have him now. They slow their approach, none of them interested in making a precipitous rush, because the machete is blood stained and they recognize that it is the blood of their fellows upon it.

Then slowly, carefully, they advance, with a combination of snarling and hissing and spitting and stray words of English that are doubtless hurled at him as epithets. And as they draw near, he holds his machete high in the air and bellows at the top of his lungs:

"Get off my damned world!"

And then he leaps upon them.

THE OUTSKIRTS OF FERUEL

KARSEN FOUX HAD ABSOLUTELY NO idea what his destination was going to be, or how he was going to reach it. All he knew was that he was getting there as quickly as he could.

The Laocoon had never quite been the tracker his mother was. Zerena Foux, the leader of their hodgepodge clan of Bottom Feeders, had always had the true nose in the family. Many had been the time when she would stop the jumpcar dead, hop out and land deftly on her cloven feet, and sniff the air with endless patience. She would turn in a slow circle, as if she were listening to what the gentle winds of the Damned World had to tell her. Her nostrils would flare a bit, and then she would turn to her fellows and inform them in what direction a battle had just occurred and where dead bodies were lying, ripe for the picking. She had never been wrong, even though in some instances the site had been miles away.

Karsen came to the conclusion, however, that it wasn't that his olfactory prowess was so much less than his mother's. Instead it was simply the fact that he had never needed to employ his own abilities. Mother had always been there to take charge. Since Karsen had struck out on his own, leaving his fellow Bottom Feeders behind, he was in the unusual position of having to rely on himself for everything. On the one hand it was daunting. On the other hand it was exhilarating, even liberating.

He was on his own. Really, truly, at last, on his own.

It had not been an easy endeavor initially. When he had departed the jumpcar, his fur-covered legs had been quivering. He wasn't certain if his mother or any of the others noticed. He certainly hoped they did not. At a moment in his life where he was trying to appear as strong as possible, he was appalled by the idea of seeming weak even in the slightest. He steadied his jangling nerves, however, gripping tightly the strap of the supplies-filled sack he had slung over his shoulder. A second strap, crisscrossing his bare chest, kept the war hammer that he had taken from a dead Mandraque fixed solidly on his back.

He remembered the look on his mother's face when he had made it clear that he was really going to depart their oddball tribe. That was what the group of them had become, even though—aside from he and his mother—no two of them were of the same race. An aged Mandraque named Rafe Kestor who, even on his best days, scarcely seemed capable of stringing thoughts together; Gant, a perpetually depressed shapeshifting pile of ooze who purported to have once been a member of that eldritch race called the Phey; and Mingo Minkopolis, member of a race called the Minosaur, whose formidable intellect seemed at odds with his massively powerful build. They had been as close to a family as Karsen and his mother, Zerena, had ever known.

And he had left them. For a Mort. He could almost hear Zerena's voice dripping with contempt. A godsdamned Mort.

Karsen stopped.

He'd been walking through grass, but it had been thinning over the last few miles and now it was gone completely. Instead a field of mostly rock stretched out before him. It was going to be harder on his hooves, certainly, which were already showing signs of wear and tear. But that was secondary to the fact that his quarry was going to be that much harder to track. Draquons left a distinct trail when they were moving through grassy plains and such. Everything from the bend of the blades to the faint smell of sulfur that accompanied them all acted as easy indicators. Everything became far more problematic on a rocky surface.

But Karsen didn't see any other choice.

He got down on his hands and knees. His legs were protected by the thick, matted fur that thoroughly covered him. His hands were scraped up in places where the rocks were a bit jagged, but it wasn't anything he couldn't live with.

Karsen lowered his face to the rocks and started sniffing around. As long minutes passed, he fought to keep down his fear. He wasn't picking up anything.

The image of Jepp's terrified face was etched in his mind. The Travelers had shown up out of nowhere, their long black cloaks flapping and their faces eternally hidden beneath their hoods. Astride their draquons, they had plucked the frightened young woman from within their midst. Karsen had been barely conscious when the attack had occurred, having been flattened by a punch to the head by his perpetually dyspeptic mother. When the Travelers had first arrived, credit Zerena with at least attempting to provide some manner of resistance. She hadn't realized that they had been coming after Jepp; she was just trying to defend herself and her tribe. Had she realized that their target was the single human among them, she likely would have stood aside and told them to do with her whatever they wanted.

Karsen had barely had enough strength to lift his head when Jepp was carried away, his eyes narrow slits rather than open. Nevertheless he saw Jepp reaching toward him, screaming, trying to escape the firm grip of the Traveler who had ensnared her. Her screams seemed to echo in the still air long after she was gone.

As he continued his attempts to track her across the rocky surface, he remembered his mother raging at him, "That girl has done something to you!" as he prepared to take his leave of them. It hadn't been his first choice. He would have far preferred the Bottom Feeders to come with him. The task he had set himself was indeed daunting and he could have used his long-time allies along with him, watching his back.

But that had never been an option. His mother was too intransigent, too disapproving of Jepp and too determined to keep her clan as free from trouble as possible, even if it meant allowing her only son to head off into the wilderness on his own.

That girl has done something to you!

The damning thing was, he knew his mother was right. He knew perfectly well that Jepp had done something. And it wasn't even a matter of his not caring. He had, instead, embraced it.

So caught up was he in his musings that he almost missed it. But then his head snapped back and he retraced his steps a few feet.

There was a chip off a small section of stone, such as might have been left by a passing creature. The draquons had extremely hard feet, judging by the thunderous sound they made as they galloped across the land and their fabled imperviousness to injury of any sort. It was possible that the passing draquons had caused it to chip away.

And there. A second piece, also broken off. He held the chip closely to his nostrils. The faint but distinctive acrid aroma of a draquon wafted from it.

He continued to move a few yards more, and then his incredibly sharp eyes perceived a thin strand of hair lying on the ground. He picked it up delicately and he didn't even have to take a whiff of it to know that the black strand had fallen from Jepp's head.

Jepp and her abductors had come a long way by this point. Was she still struggling in their grasp? Was she screaming for help? Her throat would be raw and she'd probably have no voice left. But the mental image of her writhing in their grasp, trying to break free and not even coming close, drove him on.

He began to run again, convinced that he was moving in the right direction. His hooves beat a steady tattoo on the rocks as he sped across the barren plains, spurred on by the hope that he might somehow catch a glimpse of them. That was all he would need, a glimpse. And when he saw them, then pure adrenaline would enable him to overtake them.

And then . . .

Then what, you idiot?

It was his mother's voice, sounding in his head. The disdain, the contempt for him was so realistic that she might well have been right beside him, rather than riding along like an unwanted passenger in his imagination.

Then what are you going to do? Zerena's voice persisted. You're going to fight a group of Travelers? Travelers, the good right arm of the Overseer here on the Damned World? You're going to challenge them with that hammer on your back? How stupid are you? Or, more to the point, how stupid has that girl made you? The absolute worst thing that could happen to you is that you in fact catch up with them. Because you will, in your dementia, stand up to them and try to fight them. I attempted that, only because I thought they were attacking, and they brushed me aside as if I was nothing. So can you imagine what they will do to you if you actually try to pick a fight with them? No. No, I don't think you are imagining it, because if you were, you'd realize that you have no business doing something so monumentally stupid. They will kill you, Karsen. They will kill you and whatever is left of you will be food for carrion eaters, and I will never see you again.

And he thought grimly, Good. That would probably be for the best.

It was at that moment that he realized he had lost the scent again.

He fought down panic once more as he methodically began to check around some more.

The shadows lengthened as the sun moved relentlessly across the sky, underscoring the passage of time, and still Karsen could find nothing.

Finally he backtracked, trying to pick up the scent yet again. Still nothing. It was as if they had vanished off the face of the planet.

Had they, in fact, done so? These were, after all, Travelers that he was trying to track down. The full extent of their powers was unknown. Could they have simply disappeared into some sort of hole in reality?

Or perhaps they had boarded a vehicle that had gone off in a completely different direction.

Or perhaps they had gone straight up . . .

He looked skyward, scanning the heavens. It was possible. He had never beheld a Zeffer at anything more than a great distance, but he knew they existed and knew what they were capable of. And even the Zeffers, or at least as they were commanded by their masters, the Serabim, would be as obliged to follow the dictates and demands of the Travelers as anyone else. So if the Travelers had issued commands—by what means they would convey their desires to the high flying Zeffers, Karsen could not even guess—then the Zeffers might well have airlifted them from their current path. Why? Had they detected Karsen's following them? No. No, that made no sense. If they wanted to discourage pursuit, they would likely have just turned back upon him and attempted to run their draquons right over him. The act of going airborne, courtesy of the Zeffers, would simply have meant that they were attempting to reach someplace that the draquons couldn't take them. Some high mountainous point, perhaps, or maybe over the vast ocean.

Karsen didn't even realize his legs were buckling until suddenly he was on the ground. A long, ululating scream ripped from his throat and he pounded the ground in impotent fury with his fists.

It couldn't end like this. It simply could not. What the hell kind of quest was this, to come up so miserably short? What was he supposed to do now? Return to the Bottom Feeders as a complete failure? After he had set off with such high-flown words and certainty that nothing in the world would stop him from finding Jepp and rescuing her from her captors? There was no question in his mind that they would welcome him back, but he would feel small, diminished. Puny and pathetic.

He lost track of how long he expended energy in the pointless pursuit of venting his frustration. Eventually, though, he flopped on his back, gasping for air, his throat raw from bellowing his fury. Karsen was relieved that his mother couldn't see him now. She would chortle at his relative helplessness and the absurdity of his predicament.

Karsen stared up at the blue-tinged skies. Thick clouds were crawling across them, not threatening with rain but covering the skies nevertheless. Then, for a moment, some of the clouds parted, and a stream of sunlight filtered through. In Karsen's imagination, it was as if one of the gods was staring down from on high, the light issuing not from the sun but from the deity's own orb.

He had never been much for praying. Karsen was reasonably certain that as far as the gods were concerned, everyone down there was on his or her or its own.

Yet now, frustrated, hungry, thirsty, and convinced that short of divine intervention, he would never see Jepp again . . . Karsen prayed.

"Gods," he whispered to the nameless deities. "Gods, please, if you're listening: Help me. Help me, because I . . . I need her. I'd love to tell you that this is all about her, and saving her from the Travelers, and rescuing her, but it's not just that. It's about how she makes me feel when I'm with her. It's about having some sort of purpose in life instead of just being this . . . this creature who shows up on battlefields after it's all over and picks up valuables and supplies and trinkets. When I'm with her . . . when I see how she looks at me, and looks up to me, and sees me with such love as no one else in my entire life does . . . she makes me happy to be alive. I've never felt that way, and I don't want to go back to feeling the way I did before she showed up. Because I never realized before what a pointless and empty existence that's been. So please, I'm begging you, gods on high, please . . . no matter how many cycles around the sun it may take, I will wait. I will wait however long you require, even if it seems endless, I—"

He heard a low moan from a short distance away.

Karsen sat up, confused and distracted by the noise. He knew instantly that it wasn't Jepp; it was a male voice for starters. A Traveler? Possible, but not likely. Even if somehow a Traveler had been injured in some manner, they always rode in groups and would never leave one of their own behind.

There was a short cluster of rocks about three hundred feet

away. It was a scattering of boulders that looked as if someone had dropped them from the sky in a random manner. The moaning was originating from behind them.

Slowly Karsen got to his feet, dusting off his legs. His instinct was to call out to whoever was obviously in some form of pain. Something made him restrain himself, though. It was nothing more than his normal caution, honed from many years of trying to make himself unnoticed by bigger, stronger members of the Banished (as the Twelve Races collectively referred to themselves)

His situation with Jepp was certainly not forgotten, but he was intrigued by the timing of hearing someone in distress just when he was in the midst of praying for divine intervention. The gods were renowned for moving in ways that were not only mysterious but also downright incomprehensible. As unlikely as it seemed, perhaps there was some chance that whoever he was hearing now, might somehow be sent as an avatar of the gods as a means of aiding him in his quest.

Is this how desperate you've become? Karsen thought. That you would grasp at the flimsiest of possibilities? Karsen Foux, the grand adventurer, embarking on a journey to save his lady love, reduced to praying for intervention and hoping that someone who is clearly in even worse shape than you are might be of some aid. You've been stinking of the road and your exertions for some time, but now you're beginning to stink of desperation as well. And at what point did you suddenly start sounding like your mother?

He approached the boulders, not liking the fact that his hooves were clacking on the ground. It was impossible for him to make any sort of stealthy approach. Nor did he know for sure who or what he was going to be encountering on the other side. He could well be walking straight into some sort of ambush. At that moment, however, he really didn't care all that much. His concern was so focused upon Jepp and his inability to find her that his own fate was of no relevance to him.

Whoever was on the other side of the rocks must have heard his approach, because the moaning abruptly ceased. When it did,

Karsen froze in his tracks. He was unsure of what to do next. The entire concept of it being a trap returned to him once more. On the other hand, it was possible that whoever was there, presuming they were as injured as their pained voice made it sound, had lapsed into unconsciousness.

To hell with it, thought Karsen. He straightened up and boldly strode toward the boulders, no longer caring how much noise his hooves made.

Just before he reached them, an uneven voice came from behind the boulders. It sounded as if was trying to be threatening but didn't come close to succeeding. "You just . . . just stay back," it said with a growl. "Or I'll kill you."

Karsen hesitated. There was something about that voice that was extraordinarily familiar. He'd heard it not all that long ago, in fact. That voice, like several small rocks being rubbed together and slowly being crushed—

"Gods almighty," he said with a gasp. "Eutok?"

"What?" The voice changed, sounding startled. The belligerence had vanished almost immediately. It even sounded a bit afraid, as if the mere mention of the name had robbed him of his power somehow. "That . . . who . . . ?"

"It is!" Then he grew abruptly cautious. "Throw your axe out where I can see it!"

There was a pause and then the voice came with a great deal less belligerence. "You are an idiot," it said. "I'm not going to hurt you. I'm hardly in a position to hurt anyone."

There was every reason for Eutok to be lying about it, but Karsen decided to take the chance. He vaulted the remaining distance, his powerful legs propelling him through the air like coiled springs. He landed atop the boulders, prepared to leap back instantly if the situation required it.

He looked down.

"I'll be damned," he said.

Looking back up at him was Eutok of the Trulls. "I can only

hope, Bottom Feeder."

The short, barrel-chested, hirsute underground denizen looked as if he had been battered nearly to death. His beard was stained with what Karsen was quite sure was blood, although whether it was his own or someone else's was impossible to determine. His already squat nose had been broken. One eye was swollen shut, while the other was halfway closed, although his pupil was visible through it, gazing hatefully at Karsen. His swollen lips pulled back in a sneer and several teeth was visibly missing.

"You've never looked better, Trull," Karsen said with excessive cheer.

"Shut up."

"As you wish," said Karsen with a shrug, and he turned to leave. Before he could do so, however, Eutok suddenly growled, "Wait."

There was no reason for Karsen to obey him, and yet he did. He turned back to the Trull and regarded him with open curiosity. "What am I waiting for?" he said when Eutok did not speak immediately.

"I am . . . injured."

"No! Really? I hadn't noticed."

"This would be a great deal easier," he said, his breath rattling in his ribcage, "if you could spare me what passes for wit in a Laocoon."

"Spare you? Your people wanted to kill me and my clan."

"And then I was the one who got you out of the Underground! My mother and brother would have annihilated you for your trespassing and your theft if it hadn't been for me!"

"You are rewriting an interesting version of history, Trull," Karsen said. He wasn't angry. He was having far too good a time staring down at the helpless creature. "You helped us because you wanted us to slay your mother, the queen, so that you could take over as ruler of the Trulls. A fascinating little plan. The last I saw of you, your brother, Ulurac, was endeavoring to kill you. I see he did not succeed."

"Not for want of trying." Eutok tried to sit up but then winced, grabbed his chest and slumped back again.

"How did you get here? In one of your handy underground cars?"

Slowly he managed a nod. Even that action seemed to cause him pain. "Barely. I got away from my brother . . . barely."

"And not without cost." He craned his neck to get a better look. "I believe you've lost part of your right ear."

"It's not lost. I know exactly where it is. It's inside Ulurac's stomach."

"I doubt that it was your brother's intention to swallow it."

"Ah. Well, that makes everything all right then, doesn't it."

Karsen put his hands on his hips. "What would you of me, Trull? We have no business 'tween each other. You aided our escape in the hopes that we would dispose of your mother for you, you power-grabbing wretch. We left you and your cursed brother to your mutual attempts at destruction. You're lying there in your sweat and blood and stink, and it couldn't happen to a more deserving individual as far as I'm concerned. Why are you even up here on the surface? Your kind abominates the light."

"Because if I'd stayed below, they would have found me. Found me and . . ." His voice caught for a moment and then he simply repeated, "They would have found me." He paused and then added, "And it would not have gone well for me."

"An attempted fratricide, matricide and regicide all rolled into one? Hard to believe you wouldn't have been the most popular Trull in the Underground. You still haven't told me what you would have of me."

"Your aid."

Karsen laughed curtly. "Good luck with that."

"I'm serious."

"As am I."

"It is said that Laocoon have . . ." He coughed violently for a few moments. It didn't sound good. Karsen suspected that there might be some fluid in the Trull's lungs. When he recovered himself enough to speak, Eutok said, ". . . have a certain talent for the healing arts. Is it true?"

"It can be," Karsen said judiciously. Unconsciously his hand strayed to the sack he had slung over his shoulder.

"Do you possess this knowledge?"

"What if I do?"

"Thunderation!" bellowed Eutok and then he started coughing again, this time even more violently than before. Karsen felt as if there was no reason for him to be standing around watching Eutok suffer, as enjoyable as the experience might have been. Ultimately he decided there was no reason not to stand around watching Eutok suffer. "Stop giving me vague questions in response to my questions! Can you—?"

"I have some knowledge of it, yes," said Karsen. It was true; he had some. As was usually the case, he was not quite as proficient in such things as his mother. But he had basic healing knowledge, and an assortment of medicines and powders derived from certain plants were in his bag. However, he had brought them along to tend to whatever wounds he might sustain during travel and, if necessary, in combat. He had no reason or desire to waste his supplies on a Trull. "What of it?"

"You can help me."

"I can minister to your wounds. Facilitate and expedite the healing process. But why would I want to do that?"

"Because I can help you."

"Oh really." Karsen made no effort to hide his skepticism. "First, I assume that you are lying. And second, I don't need your help." This time he turned away, determined to waste no more time on an encounter that was accomplishing nothing.

He froze, though, when Eutok said, "You seek the girl, do you not?"

Very slowly, deliberately, he turned back and stared at Eutok with open suspicion. "What do you know of these matters?"

A smile spread across Eutok's face slowly. It was the single most unpleasant smile Karsen had ever seen on any being, ever. "I have your interest now, do I?"

"I said—"

"I heard you." He took a deep breath and let it out to steady himself. "I have been here for quite some time. I saw a pack of Travelers go past. The girl was with them. The one that fought like no human I've ever seen. Like no person I've ever seen. They had her. They went past here. I saw which direction."

"I lost their scent," Karsen said. "I thought perhaps a Zeffer had . . ."

Eutok waved off the notion dismissively. "There was no Zeffer, you idiot. They flew."

"Flew? Who flew? What are you talking about?"

"The Travelers on their draquons. Draquons can fly."

"What? Since when?"

"Since always, I would surmise."

"Then why don't they fly all the time?"

Eutok shrugged. "I imagine conditions aren't always optimal."

"I don't understand—"

Grunting, Eutok said, "Actually I suppose that 'glide' is the more accurate term. They have great flaps of skin between their arms and legs. If a sufficient wind arises, they are able to take to the air and glide distances. How far I could not say. I saw them take off and they were still airborne when they went beyond my sight line."

Karsen sank into a crouch, amazement on his face. However much he thought he understood the rules and parameters of the world in which he lived, there always seemed to be something new thrown at him. Draquons could fly? Who knew?

And more importantly: Now what?

He looked toward Eutok, sudden hope on his face. "You saw which way they went?"

"I told you, they went beyond my sight line."

"Yes, but you know what direction that was."

Eutok managed a nod, even though he grimaced as he did so.

"Which way did they go?"

"And what possible . . . ?" He stopped, braced himself, and then continued, " . . . what possible reason is there for me to share that information?"

"All right, fine!" said Karsen in exasperation. He hopped off the rocks and landed next to Eutok. Yanking his bag off his shoulder, he began rummaging through the contents. "Just lie still."

"Ah. And here I thought you were going to require that I get to my feet and dance for your entertainment."

Karsen didn't even glance at him. "You are aiding no one, least of all yourself, wasting breath talking to me. If you have something of use to say, by all means, speak out. But if all you desire to do is enjoy the sound of your own voice, then indulge yourself at the risk of your own health. Or, more accurately, what little of your health remains."

Eutok's mouth opened but then snapped shut. He glowered at Karsen, who neither noticed nor cared.

Karsen set about pulling out what he hoped was the right combination of leaves and berries to attend to Eutok's wounds. He pounded the selected leaves into a paste and the berries into a juice. As Eutok lay there, regarding him with hate-filled suspicion and obvious frustration over his helplessness, Karsen spread the paste on Eutok's more prominent wounds. Air hissed between the Trull's teeth. "You bastard . . ."

"The burning sensation is how you know it is working."

"Then it must be working beyond your wildest dreams. Gods damn it!"

"It will only last for a few minutes."

"You had best hope so, or—"

"Or what? You'll breathe heavily on me and fling drops of sweat at me?"

Eutok didn't respond save to glower once more. As the minutes passed, though, his breathing regularized as the healing properties of Karsen's ointments began to take their affect.

Karsen, in the meantime, finished preparing the juice, adding a few more ingredients. He wasn't thrilled about being in such proximity to the Trull. He'd applied the paste with a brush so as to keep some distance, but Eutok was still too weak to lift his hands. Karsen crouched next to him, his nose wrinkling from the Trull's pronounced body odor, and brought the juice to Eutok's lips. "You aren't going to be happy with the taste, I'm warning you right now."

"I am a Trull. As a rule, we don't do particularly well with the concept of 'happiness' even on our best days, which are never much in abundance."

"I'll remember that."

"How do I know you're not trying to poison me?"

"You don't. Now shut up and drink." Before Eutok could say anything else, Karsen shoved the juice, which was in a small wooden cup, between Eutok's thick lips. He poured it down Eutok's throat, and the Trull coughed violently several times but still managed to keep it all down.

"You were not understating it, Laocoon, I'll give you that much." He gasped a few times and then said, "Water."

Karsen stared at him and then said drily, "You could at least make the most minimal effort to be courteous."

For a moment Eutok looked as if he hadn't the slightest idea what Karsen was talking about, and then it dawned on him. With a look of derision, he grudgingly said, "May I please have some water? I have a water skin on my belt; I simply haven't the strength to reach it."

"Yes, you do."

"Idiot!" he said with a snarl. "When I say I have not the strength to—"

Even as he spoke, his arm moved as if on its own and brushed against the brown water skin that hung from his waist. He looked down in surprise as if the arm wasn't his but rather someone else's. "I'll be damned."

"One can only hope," said Karsen.

Eutok ignored the comment, pulled free the water skin and was about to drink from it when Karsen said, "Take only as much as you need to minimally slake your thirst. If you drink too much, you'll dilute the juice's healing properties and make the process take longer."

He expected Eutok to respond with some dismissive or irritated comment, but instead Eutok simply nodded. In fact, he went him one better. He took a small swig, rolled it around in his mouth, and then spat it out. Karsen hated to see water wasted on principle, but had to admit that Eutok's way was the most sensible.

"How long before I can move as of old?" said Eutok.

"A day. Two. Your body needs time to fully recover."

"I'm not going to keep lying here, exposed to the elements or potential enemies," he said.

To Karsen's surprise, Eutok forced himself to a sitting position. Karsen was about to caution him to take it easy. Then he decided that it really wasn't his place to worry or his problem to worry about. He had other, far greater, concerns. "All right, then. I've fulfilled my part of the bargain. Tell me which way the draquons went."

"How would I be doing you any favors?" said Eutok. "She is a human. You're a Laocoon. Consorting with her will bring you to no good end."

"Your opinion would mean a great deal to me had I asked after it. Again: which way—"

"I heard you the first time. Again, how do I know you did not poison me?"

Karsen's eyes widened with incredulity. "You're still alive, aren't you?"

"For now, yes. But Laocoon are crafty, and Bottom Feeders have no scruples. You are both and thus doubly a threat. You could have given me something slow acting that temporarily energizes me but, after a time, kills me."

"I have no knowledge of a drug that would accomplish such a thing, much less how to prepare it."

"So you say." Slowly he hauled himself to his feet. He swayed as he did so, gasping for air at the exertion.

"We had a bargain, Trull!"

"Yes, we did, and I intend to stand by it. I will take you in the direction I saw them go."

"You cannot be serious! You can barely move!"

"I become stronger with each passing moment."

"I am hemorrhaging time, Eutok! I keep falling further and further behind!"

"You are on hoof while the Travelers are astride flying draquons. If you seriously thought you ever had any chance of overtaking them, then you are completely delusional. And what did you think would have happened even if you had managed to sprout wings and catch up with them? Eh?"

"I would have found a way," he said, but he sounded less than convincing, even to his own ears.

"You would have found a way to oblivion, is what you would have found," said Eutok with a sneer. "You must know that your only chance was to pursue them to their destination, wherever that may be, and then try to rescue the girl from them at that point."

Karsen hated to admit that what Eutok was saying made sense. Unfortunately, it did. "All right," he said reluctantly. "Let's admit that is the case."

"Then time is not of the essence."

"They could be bringing her to some place for the purpose of killing her!"

"Don't be ridiculous. If that was their intent, they would have already disposed of her. She's a Mort. A human. Why ride away with her if they didn't have some use for her?"

"I don't want to give them time to put her to that use, whatever it might be."

"Well, you're not really going to have a choice about it. The only choice you're going to have is whether you are going to have the chance to catch up with her, and that opportunity in turn is going to rest on me. I will bring you to her. In return, if my health lapses, you will be able to attend to it. I want to remain in a position where you need me alive and well."

"That is unacceptable to me."

"And undesirable to me. Yet here we both are. What do you intend, then, to do about it?"

"I—"

His voice trailed off as he realized he really didn't have any choice.

"Very well. But this business goes two ways, Trull. If I see any flagging in your cooperation . . . if I believe even for a minute that you are endeavoring to trick me or prolong our association beyond the point of necessity . . . then the last thing you see will be my back as I walk away from you while you're in your death throes. Do we understand each other?"

"I believe we understand each other better than you think we do," said Eutok.

Karsen considered that. "I have no idea what that means."

"Worry not. You will."

THE SPIRES

NICROMINUS HAD GENUINELY NO IDEA what to expect from the Overseer when he had put forward his admittedly radical theories.

The aged and wise Firedraque—arguably the finest mind of his people—had been taken forcibly from Firedraque Hall in Perriz and relocated here to the towering city simply referred to as the Spires. A lesser Firedraque would have been overwhelmed by the scope, the architecture, the sheer magnificent achievement of the Mort population in constructing this admittedly awe-inspiring city. But Nicrominus was who he was, one of the greatest and most senior Firedraques in the history of his people. There was very little that he was unable to take in stride.

However, even for all his experience and wisdom, Nicrominus had found himself in a situation that went far beyond anything he had ever known.

The Travelers, the right arms of the Overseer himself—the ultimate power in the Damned World—had come to him and given him a mission. They had demanded that he come up with a theory to explain why the hotstars, the primary power source of the Banished—not to mention of the Elserealms from which they had been banished—appeared ,to be slowly diminishing in power. Eventually, after much research—not to mention some notions put forward by his gifted albeit fainthearted disciple, Xeri—Nicrominus had developed a working theory. At that point he had been whisked away via Zeffers to the Spires, and had found himself addressing none other than the Overseer himself.

Nicrominus had never before laid eyes upon he who had been

placed in charge of the Damned World by their home dimension. He did not, in fact, know anyone who had. Certainly no one aside from the Travelers had done so, or at least lived to tell the story. Yet here had been Nicrominus, finding himself standing in what seemed to be a vast theater, with none other than the Overseer listening in silence. It had always been Nicrominus's assumption that the Overseer was a member of one of the races who had dispatched the Banished to this enforced planetary prison. But the design and build of his armor was such that it was impossible for Nicrominus to determine which race he belonged to. For that matter, Nicrominus had no reason to conclude that he was in fact faced with a male of any kind. The creature in the encompassing armor could have been male, female, or anything in between.

The Overseer had been lowered from overhead in a massive throne, down to the proscenium at the front of the amphitheater. There he had remained in stony silence as Nicrominus had resolutely ignored his own uncertainties and laid out for him what he felt were the reasons for hotstars slowly losing their effectiveness and puissance.

The idea of responding to a physical problem with a metaphysical solution was preposterous on its face, and yet Nicrominus had put forward a reasoned argument for that very thing.

"To understand our present situation . . . one has to understand the previous occupants of what has been named the Damned World. I am speaking, of course, about the humans. It is undeniable that humans possessed a spectacular arrogance regarding their own status. According to our studies and their own histories, they took it upon themselves to befoul this world as they saw fit, with pollution and filth. They deforested entire sections, heedlessly slew other life forms into extinction, without caring how such actions would affect the cycle of life, and life interaction. That arrogance carried over into subspecies interaction, as different subspecies believed that they, and only they, were the right and true rulers of the Damned World. They would often endeavor to hunt one another into extinction as well.

"Even more intriguingly," Nicrominus continued, "the humans had a tendency to be . . . how best to put this? 'Human-centric' in many of their philosophies. At one time they believed that the sun moved around the Damned World, rather than the other way 'round. Their answer for life on other worlds was to dismiss the notion out of hand since no planetary neighbors had made a point of coming by . . . as if the universe considered them anything other than one single mote of dirt in a vast universe of similar, undistinguished motes.

"In short, Overseer . . . humans foolishly believed themselves to be the center of everything in creation.

"The thing is, Overseer . . . what if the humans were right?"

He had waited for some sort of response and got none. Resolutely he had soldiered on.

"It's . . . this way. This realm that we're residing in right now . . . it's just one of many. Infinite realms there are, infinite dimensions. We know and understand that, even though most humans did not. And each dimension works in different ways, has rules that enable it to function. Rules that were put in place by the gods, blessed be they. Rules that are not handed to us, but instead we are expected to discern as we go.

"Different dimensions align more closely with some than others. As it happened, the Elserealms aligned closely with this one. 'Neighbors' is the way that the humans would have put it. When individuals are neighbors, that which happens in one realm can spill through to, or affect, what happens in the other.

"Part of the 'spill through,' in our case, are the hotstars. They were rare here, but commonplace in the Elserealms. What we did not realize, I believe, is that the source of their energy was here, in this plane of existence.

"I believe that the source of that energy . . . was the minds of humans. Which may on the surface of it, sound ludicrous. Then again, I should point out that it is documented fact that humans used, as their own source of energy, the fossilized remains of long-dead animals. So I don't think that one is intrinsically more ridiculous than the other.

"Say what you will about humans . . . but they relentlessly used their imagination, their dreams, if you will, to shape this world to their liking. They thought, in their limited way, that this was simply a measure of their ingenuity. But it was more profound, much deeper than that. This plane of existence, for whatever reason—whim of the gods, if nothing else—was, and is, entirely shaped by the conscious and even unconscious desires of human beings.

"They thought that form followed function. They were wrong. The truth was the exact opposite: Function followed form. Humans would develop in their collective, dreaming minds, the sort of world they desired. One that did not exist. This unconscious desire would then sit in a type of 'between' state, a 'limbo' or transitory condition. And so it would remain until enough humans dreamed the dream, at which point they would then . . . through bursts of industrialization, or visionary philosophers and leaders, or even wars . . . bring the unconscious desires to reality. They would think of it as ideas waiting to happen, and in a sense, they were right. They just didn't understand that there was an actual, metaphysical structure behind it. The concepts would develop a nebulous form, and then the functions would follow to actualize it.

"In any event, Overseer," Nicrominus had continued, "here is the situation, and the problem. The human race has largely been purged from the Damned World. And if my theory is correct, those humans who do remain are remarkably dangerous. For energy cannot truly be destroyed; it simply changes form or concentrates elsewhere. Which means the pure power of dream and imagination, rather than being diffused over millions of humans, is now concentrated within the minds of a mere handful. Of course, they don't know it. They know of a time when humans dominated, but accept the status of their environment for what it is. But if they dream of greater things . . . if they take to imagining things not as they are, but as they could be . . . it could be disastrous for us. Through means we cannot begin to guess, they could set events into motion—affect probabilities, develop devices—that could spell the end of the Twelve Races.

"But we cannot simply destroy the humans in self-defense, because therein lies our quandary. You see, naturally this sphere, this plane of existence, far pre-existed human beings. It was, however, chaotic. Unformed and void, almost unrecognizable. Humans were created to help bring it into sharper focus. They began as primitive specimens, but evolved over time. As they evolved, this sphere likewise evolved from the chaos that reigned to the relative order that now holds sway. The calamitous depopulation of humans has thrown this plane of existence out of whack. We are seeing, in the diminishment of the power of hotstars, merely the first step. If my theory is correct, if the few humans who are left should die off completely, the hotstars will not be the first things to give out. This entire plane of existence could come completely unraveled. It could well descend into the chaos that existed before humans were developed to hammer it into shape through their imagination, their will, their hopes and dreams and aspirations, and their odd obsession with ascribing names to everything. They even gave a name to the phenomenon: Entropy.

"Nor will it necessarily end here. The nearness of the Elserealms, its dependence upon hotstars, and the effect the current energy depletion is having, indicates that the deleterious effects may ripple through to the Elserealms as well. Both the Banished, and those who banished us, may well share the same fate.

"The depopulation of humanity may well be the single greatest calamity the Twelve Races has ever faced. There is only one solution that I can see: We must locate what humans there are and find a way to repopulate the species, all the while holding their dreams in check or turning them to serve us, lest they wind up—through sheer force of will—creating a series of circumstances that could lead to our utter destruction."

For a long moment, the Overseer said nothing.

Then had come an explosive sound, like a crack of thunder. Lights had flickered on and off, and the very air seemed to crackle as if a storm were building up within the structure itself. Nicrominus had fallen to his knees, whimpering like a hatchling in the face of the unfettered wrath of the single most powerful being in the Damned World.

And for the first time since Nicrominus had shown up, the Overseer had spoken.

"You," thundered the Overseer, "Have *got*. To be *shitting me*."

II.

NICROMINUS. DURING HIS RELATIVELY LEISURELY voyage over courtesy of the Zeffer's vast, dangling tentacles, had had a good deal of time to try and figure out just how the Overseer was going to react to his admittedly extraordinary theory.

You have got to be shitting me wasn't it, or even remotely close to it.

For starters, although Nicrominus understood the basic words being uttered, he suspected there was some sort of vernacular twist that he wasn't entirely grasping. Furthermore, it simply didn't sound like something that the single greatest power in the Damned World might say. It was so startling, so bizarre, that for a moment Nicrominus suspected that perhaps he had been fooled somehow. Perhaps this was not, in fact, the Overseer at all. An imposter, maybe? Someone who had been sent to test his mettle? Except who would have sent this individual? The genuine Overseer? Or unseen warders from the Elserealms?

All manner of possibilities rattled around inside his head as he simply stood there and stared at the armored figure.

The Overseer vaulted from the proscenium. When he landed, the sound echoed through the vast theater, the thunderclap-like impact of his previous bellowing reaction only having just died down. As he moved, Nicrominus could hear a series of faint whirring noises coming from the armor. He had no idea what they were. The armor was unlike anything he had seen before. It had an air about it, something that made him think of the Elserealms, clinging to it lingeringly as did the scent of, say, a female's scent to one's clothes on the morning following a night of passion. But there was also something about it that smacked of Damned World technology. The Banished had very little use for such things, but still, Nicrominus could spot it when he saw it.

He strode right towards Nicrominus and didn't slow as he approached him. Nicrominus's bones may have been old, his muscles might have been sore, but he was still capable of getting out of the way of an oncoming behemoth when the need arose. He did so at that point, stepping aside and almost falling into a row of seats to his right. He stood there and watched as the Overseer strode past him.

Left on his own, Nicrominus was uncertain of what he was supposed to do. The Overseer had not issued any instructions, or even really acknowledged his existence in any way save to listen to what he had to say. What was he supposed to do now? Stand there and wait for further instructions? What if none were forthcoming?

Nor was it his nature to simply stand around and wait for other people to tell him what to do, even when one of the other people in question was the Overseer himself.

But he couldn't very yell out, "Wait!" to the Overseer. The Overseer did as he willed, when he willed it, and answered to no one. Or if he did, he certainly didn't answer to an aged Firedraque.

Nicrominus folded his arms, tasted the air with his forked tongue, and then shrugged and started off after the Overseer. His tail moved aimlessly in mild agitation, an outward reflection of his inner worries. The Overseer was making no obvious effort to leave him behind, but neither was he taking his time. He was simply walking, and so Nicrominus followed him.

There was a large set of double doors at the back of the theater. The Overseer swung wide his arms and knocked them to either side. He passed through them and they almost slammed shut back into Nicrominus's face before he caught them and stepped through.

There was a large lobby with broken mirrors and faded gilt lining it. The Overseer kept going, heading towards the main doors that led out into the street. Nicrominus continued right after him, wondering if at some point the Overseer would turn, notice him, and obliterate him with but a gesture.

Nicrominus considered that possibility further and came to the realization that the prospect did not bother him particularly. He had led a long life, seen many things, had mates, eaten them, spawned children, eaten them, allowed one of them to live almost on a whim and found the experience to be, on the whole, rather uplifting. There were still things he wished to see and goals he wished to attain. He had no overt desire for death. But if the next few minutes were to result in his being a red and green splotch on the streets of the Spire city, well . . . it wasn't as if he hadn't had more than his share of experiences.

He also wondered just how far he was willing to follow the Overseer before he gave it up as a pointless exercise.

The Overseer strode out into the street, his armored feet clanking beneath him. Nicrominus, following, heard a cessation of noise and wondered if the Overseer had simply vanished into thin air. It didn't seem possible that he could do such a thing, but then again, this was the Overseer they were talking about. Who knew what was and was not within his capabilities?

But no, he could see him through the large glass doors that led out. The Overseer had stopped dead in the middle of the street and he was just standing there. Nicrominus had been hurrying after him, so much so that he was getting out of breath. Now he slowed and then stopped, standing on the sidewalk and just staring at the armored figure.

"You should have seen it," the Overseer said abruptly. It so startled Nicrominus that he actually jumped, and his tail whipped around as if seeking to dispatch a foe that had snuck up on him hoping to catch him unawares. "Back in its hey day, I mean. What I'm doing here . . . standing out here on Sixth

Avenue . . . you couldn't do it back then. Far too many cars, packed with people honking their horns, on their way to God knows where. Like so many hamsters sprinting on their wheels, spinning and spinning and thinking they're getting somewhere when they're really not. Still . . . New York was just about the only city in the world that I could tolerate for any period of time." His voice trailed off and then he turned and looked directly at Nicrominus. "You have no goddamned idea what I'm talking about, do you."

Slowly Nicrominus shook his head. "I have . . . some goddamned idea, Overseer. I assume you are talking about this city at some point in the past. But . . ." He had no clue what else to say, and so said nothing.

"What the hell was your name again?"

"Nicrominus."

"Nicrominus. Hunh." He seemed to be considering it. "Good name. Sounds similar to Nicodemus. You wouldn't have any idea who that is, would you?"

"No, Overseer, I would not. Should I?"

"A Biblical judge. He helped prepare the body of Jesus for burial after the crucifixion. I don't suppose you know about any of that, either."

"I know of that, actually. I have done a good deal of reading into Mort philosophies and history. I know of the Bible. It was a book of mythologies that the Mort appeared to set great store by. This Jesus was one of the central characters. There are a number of pictorial representations of him back in Firedraque hall."

A strange noise came from the Overseer's armored figure and it took Nicrominus a moment to realize that it was actually laughter. It seemed a strange thing to hear the Overseer laughing. Nicrominus wouldn't have thought such a thing likely or even possible. The Overseer was like unto a god. Why would he be laughing? Then again, it had been the opinion of Nicrominus that the gods had been looking down upon the Banished and laughing at their fates for quite some time. So it made a certain kind of twisted sense that their representative in the world would likewise enjoy some merriment at their expense.

"Notre Dame cathedral."

"I'm . . . sorry, Overseer?"

"The place you call Firedraque Hall. Its true name is Notre Dame cathedral. I saw it when I was twenty-two, when I was stationed in Paris."

"You mean Perriz?"

The Overseer had not been looking at him directly, but now he did. He turned and when he spoke his voice was tinged with anger. "Paris, goddammit. You could, at the very least, say it right. It's pronounced 'Paris.'"

"Pah-ris," Nicrominus said carefully.

"Incredible. Earth was crawling with idiots, and then the idiots are damned near wiped from existence, and who replaces them? More idiots." The Overseer was now walking back and forth, pacing, moving a few feet and then pivoting and walking back the other way in agitation. "They say that hydrogen is the most common element in the universe. But I disagree. I think it's stupidity. I think that if the entirety of creation were left to fester and drown in the filth of its own ignorance, then that would be a good thing. Instead you're telling me that I'm supposed to find the remaining humans and encourage them to breed so that we can make more and repopulate the Earth in order to save the whole of creation? And that's supposed to be my job, is it? Well . . . what if it's not? What if my job is to make sure that creation succumbs to the entropy it so richly deserves, and the first step along that path is to watch all life on Earth vanish?"

"With all respect, Overseer . . . I might better be able to answer that question—presuming it actually requires an answer—if I knew what 'Urth' was?"

"You know of the Bible, you know of Jesus, but you

don't know 'Earth'?"

"If it relates to Mort history or mythology, my readings and understandings are limited due to language barriers."

"It's the name of the planet you're standing on, Nicrominus. It's the name of the planet that fell to the Twelve Races."

"Is it?" Nicrominus found that extremely surprising. "I had repeatedly come across what I thought was an old Mort name for it: Ee Arth. But nothing called 'Urth.'"

"Ee Arth is Earth. It's pronounced Urth. Ee Arth would be how you said it if you didn't know how to read it properly."

"I see." Nicrominus shrugged. "Truthfully, Overseer, I—as do most of my people—have always simply referred to it as the Damned World."

"Yes. I know. Are you aware of why that is?"

"Well, the story may be apocryphal, but it is said that the last of the human defenders of the planet, when confronted by those who were about to destroy him, took a final stand and shouted something to the effect of 'Get off the damned world.' And that was taken by those present to be the name of this sphere."

Again the Overseer made that same strange noise that almost sounded like a laugh. "It is not apocryphal."

"With all respect, Overseer, how do you know? Were you there?"

At first the Overseer didn't respond. Then, slowly, he reached up to the wide collar that encircled his head and touched either side. There was a hissing sound, and white mist floated up from the connection point. He reached up and twisted the domed helmet. There was a loud "clack" as something disengaged and then he removed the helmet, lifting it off slowly.

Nicrominus trembled, so much so that he was almost unable to stand. He would have indeed fallen had his tail not managed to balance him and keep him upright. *This is it. I am going to die. To look upon the face of the Overseer is to die instantly.* He had no idea exactly how that death was going to occur. Some said that beholding the face of the Overseer would result in bursting into flames. Others claimed your head would melt. Some even contended that not only did you yourself die, but any and all of your descendants would likewise be struck down instantly, prompting a brief surge of regret for the catastrophe he might inadvertently have visited upon his daughter, Evanna. *Look away! Look away! It still is not too late!* But he could not look away. His curiosity got the better of him.

He could not quite fathom what it was that he was looking at.

The face that stared back at him was lined and wrinkled and haggard and looked for all the world as if it would be perfectly happy to just shut its eyes in final repose but never, ever could. Those eyes were a dark green, and only one of them appeared to be functioning. The other, the left one, was nearly milky white, with only a hint of a pupil. A mass of gray hair clung to the head, sopping, like a lion that had been caught out in the rain.

It was the face of a Mort. A human. A gods damned human.

"It wasn't just that I was there," said the human. "I was the one who said it."

THE LAND OF FEEND

I.

THE CHILDREN'S CRUSADE OF THE Ocular huddled for mutual warmth and protection deep within the woods. They were cold and tired, and they could not stop staring at the distant green glow that emanated from the far off city.

The children were looking to two of their own for guidance, the two oldest. One was named Turkin, a young, strapping Ocular lad. The other was a female, Berola. Berola had always been a precocious sort, and had far preferred to run with the males than associate with the females. Defying Ocular custom, she had actually shaved her head, which had infuriated her parents and made her quite the talk of the town.

Now she and Turkin were sitting a short distance from the others, and Berola was muttering, "This is ridiculous. We should just head back to the city, that's all."

"While it's glowing?" demanded Turkin. "Don't be ridiculous."

"So it's glowing. So what? A glow never hurt anybody."

"The captain said we wait here for him to get back," Turkin said firmly. "And here is where we wait. Did you all get that?" he raised his voice so the others could hear him. "We wait here until the captain returns." Then, once they nodded, he lowered his voice so that only Berola could hear and said, "Between you and me . . . I think this is all part of the training mission."

"Eh?" Berola looked at him skeptically.

"Yup. They keep coming up with all sorts of ways to try and keep us off balance. Why, earlier the captain had me follow the high adviser himself, Phemus."

"Really." Berola now seemed impressed, which pleased Turkin

no end. "Did you find out anything interesting . . . ?"

"He was talking to a Piri."

"No! You lie!"

"Gods' truth," Berola said fervently. "I told the captain, and that's why he went and left us here: to go back and tell the king himself."

"But why? Why would he have been talking to the Piri?"

"No idea. Not my job to—"

"Look!" one of the youngsters suddenly called out. "It's the captain!"

He was right. The captain of the guards was coming through the woods toward them. Berola and Turkin, who had been sitting, were promptly on their feet, shoulders squared, trying to look like capable members of the Crusade.

And then the captain began to stagger.

"Captain?" Berola said. "Is something wro—?"

"Stay back," said the captain, his voice thick and raspy. He'd been standing in the shadows of the trees, and the moon was covered by a cloud, but now it emerged from hiding and the children gasped. Even from the distance they were at, they could see his skin was blackened and peeling and falling off. His teeth were gone, and his eye looked like it was cracking.

"Don't . . . go back," he managed to say. "Nothing for you . . . everyone dying . . . all of them . . . all . . . dying . . ."

"Dying?" gasped Turkin. "Of what? Why? From what?"

"Humans," the captain of the guard managed to get out, and then he collapsed. Several of the children cried out as he fell, and they started to move toward him.

"Don't touch him!" shouted Berola, and the children froze.

They heard the captain wheeze horribly for long seconds, and then there was an ugly rattle, and then nothing.

"Is he okay now?" asked one of the children, and another one hit the first child upside the head and said, "No, he's not okay, he's dead, stupid!"

And then came wailing and sobbing and cries from all the

children that they wanted to go home, that they had had enough, that this was all too terrible. "Shut up!" shouted Berola, putting her hands to her head. "We . . . we just need to think!"

"Think about what?!" Turkin was clearly starting to panic. "You heard the captain! We can't go back! Everyone . . . everyone is going to be like him—!"

"I want my mother!" cried one of the children and they started crying all over again for their parents, and Berola and Turkin looked helplessly at one another. Because, really, all they wanted to do, deep down, was break down and start sobbing as well.

And that was when a voice shouted over all of them, "You don't have mothers, you don't have fathers, and you're not going back!"

They turned and stared, and Berola felt a surge of fear bubbling up in her throat. Turkin tried to control a similar sensation. It was all he could do not to bolt and run. Collective gasps were ripped from the throats of the remaining children.

A female Piri was standing there. She was tall and elegant, but had a haunted look. "All you have," she said softly, "is me."

"You?" said Turkin, trying to sound confidently arrogant. "You're . . . you're a—"

"I know what I am," she said. "But you don't know what I am. I'm your salvation."

"You're not serious," said Berola.

The Piri nodded. "If you come with me, now, I will protect you from the others of my kind. I can do this for you. And I will train you and help you . . . and, in time, you will help me. We will be able to protect each other."

"Us protect you?" asked Berola. "Why should we?"

"Because," said the Piri, "like it or not . . . you're the last of the Ocular. And you're in trouble. And I'm in trouble."

Berola studied her, tried to get some sort of sense of her. She noticed the Piri's left hand. "What happened to your little finger?" she demanded.

"Nothing. It's fine. It's just not on my hand."

"What's your name?" asked one of the younger Ocular.

"Don't talk to her!" Berola ordered.

But the Piri ignored her. "My name is Clarinda. What's yours?"

"Kerda."

"Kerda . . . will you come with me?"

"Will you hurt me?" Kerda asked guardedly.

"No. Never. I swear."

"All right," said Kerda.

Clarinda nodded, and started to walk off into the dark of the forest. Kerda followed her, and the others started to as well.

"Are you insane!" shouted Turkin. "We were being trained to kill her kind! You can't . . . this is crazy! Berola, tell them they're crazy!"

"You're crazy!" Berola called.

But the youngsters didn't stop, following Clarinda. And as the last of them disappeared into the woods, Turkin and Berola exchanged nervous looks, shouted as one, "Wait for us!" and sprinted off after them into the endless night of Feend.

II.

YOU ARE OUT OF YOUR mind.

The thought kept flitting through Clarinda's head as she led the Ocular children away from their ancestral home without the faintest notion of where she was leading them to. The only thing she knew that was important was that she had to get them as far away from the immediate area as possible.

She heard huffing and groaning from the children after the third hour of the rapid pace she was maintaining, and she turned and looked at them with obvious annoyance. "I thought," she said tersely, "that you were all supposed to be warriors. What is all this whining I hear? This complaining?"

"We're tired," moaned one of the younger males. Clarinda hadn't taken the time to learn all their names. There were several dozen of them. Chances were she would never need to know. As soon as they had gotten her clear of Feend, beyond the reach of the Piri, she would take her leave of them and that would be the end of that.

Before Clarinda could chide her, however, the younger female, Kerda, cuffed the complainer on the side of the head. The complainer stopped and looked balefully at Kerda with his single eye. He was at least a head taller than she, but she wasn't the least intimidated by him. "Stop it," she said. "Clarinda is doing the best she can."

"How do we know that?" he said, rallying. "How do we know what she's doing? She's a damned Piri! A ground-dwelling, blood-sucking Piri! Are we so desperate for leadership that we're following our enemies into who-knows-where?"

"Leadership? You think I give a damn about leadership?" said Kerda heatedly. "Right now I'd just be happy to be with someone who knows what she's doing! Who knows something about the world!"

"And you think she knows aught of the world? She lives underground, for gods sake! What is someone who roots around beneath the dirt supposed to know about anything above it?"

Clarinda hated to admit that it was a perfectly valid question. She had been to various places in the Damned World, but consistently had remained underground. Even when she had wandered so far afield that she had wound up in Trull territory, she had remained safe within the cooling confines of subterranean lairs.

When her mind wandered to her explorations in the land of Trulls—the Underground, as the residents had so dubbed it with the characteristic Trull lack of imagination—naturally her thoughts turned to Eutok. As they did so, her hand drifted to her belly. There was not yet any telltale bulge or swelling as a result of the tiny half-breed dwelling within her. The only reason she knew for certain that his issue was growing within her was what her mother, Sunara Redeye, Mistress of the Piri, had told her.

Sunara had known. No shock there; Sunara always knew.

Clarinda had paid dearly for the knowledge that Sunara had acquired through simple observation. Sunara had tied her up, beaten her so badly with lashes across the back that Clarinda would have collapsed to the ground had ropes not bound her tightly to an upright rock. And then, in order to coax the name of the father from her, Sunara had bitten off the little finger of her left hand and assured her there would be more dismemberment if the name were not forthcoming. Clarinda had screamed then, louder than ever before, and she had howled, "Eutok! Eutok of the Trulls! We met and he was my lover and I did it because I hate you, mother! I hate you! I hate our race! I hate this life! I hate living in fear of mating and being mutilated and turning into a sick, twisted, perverted *monster like you and why not just kill me now and get it over with!*"

In that moment of heat and passion and livid fury toward her mother, she had meant it. The life of the Mistress of the Piri, the title and rank that was hers because of her birth, was not one that she coveted. For the Mistress of the Piri was supposed to be all things to all her people, and thus was required to be turned into some . . . some asexual thing. Once it was her turn to take on her birthright, she would have her breasts removed, and her nether regions would be burned away, leaving nothing but a scarred and desensitized mass of flesh. She had wanted no part of that, and if her dalliance with Eutok was a means of rebelling against it, well, so be it. She hated her life, she hated her people, she hated the fate that awaited her.

And yet, insanely, for all that, she still didn't hate her mother. Even though she had said it at the time. Even though her mother had beaten her and maimed her.

What the hell is wrong with me, she wondered, *that even after everything she did to me, part of me still wants her approval?*

The young Ocular were still arguing and the noise brought her attention forcefully back to their situation. "Shut up," she said tiredly. "Just . . . shut up."

To her surprise, that brought the young Ocular to a halt. They stopped their arguing and stared at her expectantly.

They want you to say something. They're an aspiring army and you're their leader, and they're waiting for you to rally them.

She spoke without actually knowing what she was going to say.

"You're all tired. You're all hungry. I understand that. We have no shelter. Get used to it. For the time being, we're going to be living under the stars. As for food," and she paused and then continued, "which of you is the best hunter? Or at least fancies himself as such?"

Turkin's hand immediately shot up. A couple of the others were more tentative but joined him in claiming that dubious title.

"All right, then," she said. "You three head off into the woods. Stay together; this is no time to separate from each other. See what you can find in terms of game for the rest of us."

The young Ocular had spears and wooden swords, the simple weapons that they had been given by their trainers who thought they would have a lot more time with them before meeting their demise. But they also had bellies that were becoming more familiar with the pangs of hunger with each passing hour, and Clarinda knew that that could be a superb motivator. They headed into the woods, disappearing with as minimal sound as giant beings could make.

"What should the rest of us do?" said Kerda.

"Make yourselves comfortable. We're going to be here a while."

"Why here?"

"Why not?" she said reasonably. "Have you a better idea as to where we should be?"

"Back home," one of the Ocular males said. There was both challenge and frustration in his tone.

Clarinda was in no mood for arguing. "If you wish to return home, feel free to do so. You should be able to find it without too much difficulty. There. You can see the glow in the distance."

"The Captain said not to," Berola said firmly. "Or have you forgotten that, you great addled fool?"

"What if he was wrong?"

"You saw what happened to him. You saw how sick he was." Berola strode toward him and stood there with her hands on her hips, her single eye glaring balefully at him. "You want to end up like him? Do you?"

The male met her glare for a time and then lowered his gaze. He did not respond. He didn't need to.

Clarinda felt the eyes of the Ocular upon her. Furthermore, she was feeling as hungry as any of them, but she knew that—presuming the others found any game—it would very likely not satisfy her. She had neglected to tell them to bring it alive, and she was not ecstatic about the notion of drinking blood from something dead. The blood of dead creatures, even if the source was only deceased for a few minutes, had a rank and bitter taste to it. Cold blood held no allure for her; she needed warm blood.

And even if they did indeed bring something to her alive, she was not comfortable with the notion of eating in front of the young Ocular. She knew that many of them were still uneasy with the fact that one of the predatory Piri was now in a position of leadership. They might well start to worry that she would turn on them in their sleep and feast on their blood while they lay helpless.

For that matter, she had no more reason to trust them than they had her. She could no more do without sleep indefinitely than they. All that was required was one suspicious Ocular—and there were quite a few to choose from—who would take the opportunity to dispatch her while she slumbered, figuring that it was wiser to take their chances with the evils they didn't know than with the evil they did.

Taking all that into account, Clarinda felt that at the very least it would be wise to hunt and eat separately from the rest of the pack.

"Stay here," she said to Kerda. "I will be back."

"Where are you going?"

"I have matters to attend to."

"What sort of—?"

"Gods' balls, girl, stop asking questions and learn to do as you are told! If you do not, then rest assured that I will put my back to you and you can just as easily tend to your own needs for the rest of what will assuredly be your short lives! Do you understand?"

Although she was still a child, Kerda was a head taller than

Clarinda, and she was one of the shorter ones. It was a ludicrous sight, the pale Piri bellowing at creatures that towered over her as if she could somehow physically dominate them. Yet they recoiled from her and Kerda said meekly, "Yes." The others bobbed their heads in unison.

"Good," said Clarinda, who momentarily felt sorry for snapping at them. They had, after all, been through a hell of a lot. They had lost their parents, their homeland, everything in one stroke and were still trying to cope with it. But then her regret passed as quickly as it had come. She had her own problems to worry about: She was hungry, she was pregnant, she was tired, and she had left her people behind for an uncertain future.

She turned away from the Ocular and headed into the forest.

III.

HUNTING WAS A NEW EXPERIENCE for her. As a privileged child of the Mistress, obtaining sustenance was never anything that she had needed to concern herself over. There were others in the tribe who attended to such things. But she had every confidence that she would be more than up to the task.

She penetrated deep into the forest, further and further until she felt that she had left enough distance between herself and the Ocular. She felt no need to mark the trail, confident that she would be able to find her way back.

Clarinda believed she could count on the fingers of one hand (*even my left hand,* she thought ruefully) the number of days that she had spent outside. The vast, vast majority of her existence had been underground, hiding away from the upper world with dirt just everywhere. Dirt under her fingernails, dirt permanently staining the bottoms of her feet, the smell of dirt so pervasive that she felt as if she could smell nothing else.

She stopped and looked toward the skies. The stars glittered down at her.

They made her wonder.

Her mother seemed unable to understand that Clarinda aspired to so much more than Sunara's view allowed for. She wondered if perhaps that was because of the circumstances under which they lived. Dirt in and of itself was not the end of things, because it was possible to cultivate the dirt, grow things on it, bring life from it. But beneath the dirt was indeed the end of things. The dead were buried beneath it, and when you lived in Subterror, there was darkness and limited vision. You couldn't look up. And when you couldn't look up, that was somehow, in some way that Clarinda could not articulate, the end of aspirations. The skies were limitless, and represented equally limitless possibilities. They were the beginnings of dreams. They practically cried out, "What if?" and dared you to aspire to them. A perpetual roof of dirt over one's head was antithetical to dreaming.

It was nothing short of remarkable that she had encountered another soul—Eutok—who seemed to feel the same way. Trulls were as loathe to engage the surface as Piri, although the sunlight wasn't as damaging to the Trulls as it was to the Piri. The great burning orb in the sky was hurtful to Trulls' eyes, whereas for the Piri it was painful head to toe. Still, Eutok likewise dreamt of more than the life that he led dwelling beneath the ground. She knew that his goal was to become leader of the Trulls so that he could in turn lead them to a greater and glorious destiny than was available to them as permanent cave dwellers.

At least that's what he tells you. Who knows what is truly in his heart?

Suddenly a scent wafted to her, causing her to salivate and driving all other thoughts from her mind. She wasn't accustomed to hunting, but she certainly knew the range of animal scents since hunters brought food to the colony. She quickly identified it as a creature known as a bir. It was big, covered in brown fur, and absolutely filled to the brim with blood. Birs were huge favorites of the Piri since, even when they had been dragged down into Subterror and were half dead, they still tended to put up a struggle. That naturally made the feasting all the more worthwhile.

Best of all, she was downwind of it. The breeze was bringing its scent to her, but it was unaware of her presence.

A tall tree stood nearby. It was the Piri way either to attack in numbers, or else hide below and try to pull the prey down to them. Neither option presented itself to Clarinda, and so she chose a third option: Height.

She leaped upward, light as air, gripped the lower branches of the nearest tree, and quickly gained some altitude. Then she crouched there, immobile, cloaked in shadow. She heard a distant growling and her fingers wrapped tightly around the branch. Poised in a feral crouch, she remained unmoving. Clarinda was amazed to discover just how much she was enjoying the sensation of the hunt.

She heard the bir drawing ever closer and slowed her breathing so that she wouldn't be rushed. She knew she had to time this perfectly. Birs were big monsters with impressive strength. Once she had seen one on the edge of death, and yet a random sweep of its paw had been sufficient to crush the skull of a Piri that had gotten careless.

Closer . . . closer . . . all the time in the world. That was what she kept telling herself, and yet it was difficult to maintain that degree of levelheadedness as her growing hunger try to compel her to be precipitous. She realized her legs were shaking and she stilled them with effort.

The bir was growling low in its throat; she could hear it even from her perch. Then the bir stopped moving. She became concerned that it had caught her scent somehow, even though there was simply no way it should have been able to. There was a long pause that seemed to stretch out forever, and she was about to cry out in hunger and frustration when suddenly the bir was moving and it was there, right below her, lumbering into view. Padding forwarded on all fours, it stopped dead again, looking around, sniffing the air as if certain there was something in the vicinity that posed a danger but unable to determine precisely what.

Perfect, she thought, and Clarinda released her hold on the branch. She descended, straight as a perfectly thrown spear. The bir must have had a second or two warning caused by the air rushing past her as she fell, but she couldn't do anything about that. It wasn't going to matter, though. The bir was big and slow moving and there was no way that it was going to be able to dodge her.

She was right.

Clarinda landed on the bir's back. The bir roared and tried to claw at her, but she had her arms wrapped around its throat so that its flailing claws couldn't reach her.

To her astonishment, the bir suddenly reared back and stood on its hind legs. *It can stand on two legs? Shit.* She hadn't known they could do that. She had only ever seen them down in Subterror where the ceilings were so low that the bir standing upright had never been a possibility. Even as she processed this new and distressing bit of information, she dug her fingers into its fur to prevent herself from sliding off. Her legs wrapped around its midsection and then Clarinda, baring her fangs, sunk them into the creature's throat.

The bir roared and threw itself backward against the nearest tree.

Pain ripped through Clarinda's body, the sheer weight of the creature nearly being sufficient to crush her. Originally she had intended simply to take enough of the creature's blood to satisfy her hunger. That was rapidly becoming no longer a possibility. If she released her hold on the bir and it was still alive, the thing was so fearsome and full of power that it would turn upon her and rip her to shreds. This was no longer simply a meal. This was Clarinda fighting for her survival.

Howling, the bir staggered forward from the tree. She braced herself for another impact, drinking quickly, greedily, blood dribbling down the sides of her mouth and onto the creature's fur. The bir did not repeat the maneuver, however. Perhaps it was just too damned stupid to realize that it had hurt her and that repeated impacts of that nature might well be sufficient to—at the very least—shake her loose.

Instead the bir dropped to all fours and then threw itself to its side. Clarinda barely had time to yank her leg clear, repositioning herself. Had the creature landed with its full weight upon her, she would have been permanently crippled.

Even as she shifted her position atop the bir, she never lost the solid hold of her fangs in its throat. As the blood flowed from the creature and into her, the bir became weaker while Clarinda became progressively stronger. Toward the end, as the bir writhed in her grasp, it became less and less aggressive and she knew that she had it. The danger was past and she had provided sustenance not only for herself but for her unborn child.

Suddenly, with no warning at all, something grabbed her by the back of the throat and flung her clear of the bir. She sailed across the space and slammed into a tree, rebounding from it and hitting the ground. She had enough time to get her hands and feet under her and she landed, in a crouch like a wolf preparing to spring.

"Bartolemayne," she whispered.

That was indeed who was standing in front of her. It was Bartolemayne, the most formidable and dangerous of all the Piri. He had taken advantage of her in the same manner that she had managed to catch the bir unawares; he had approached her from downwind. And she had been so engrossed in her meal that any sounds Bartolemayne might have made as he approached on foot went completely unnoticed.

Bartolemayne was rarely seen around Subterror. He was considered the right hand of the Mistress, and because of that, he best served Sunara as a ranging spy. Bartolemayne came and went as he wished. None were more adept at hunting, fighting, or accomplishing whatever Sunara Redeye required.

Unlike most of the Piri who were wiry and lean nearly to the point of desiccation, Bartolemayne was massively built. Not on par with an Ocular, but a head taller than any other Piri and as wide as three of them. His hair was long and flowing rather than a stringy mess as was the case with most males, and his eyes burned a pale green, which was a most unusual color for a Piri and an indicator at an early age that Bartolemayne was destined for achievements far beyond those of most Piri.

That, and the fact that all his teeth were fangs. Not just tucked in neatly on either side, as was typical for Piri, but every single one. When he grinned, which was often and never good news for the individual he was grinning at, they were frightening even to a Piri.

A half dozen more normal Piri were clustering in around Bartolemayne, jumping around excitedly, their knuckles dragging on the dirt. They were whispering her name, "Clarinda, Clarinda," dodging and moving as if she were attacking them.

The bir was lying nearby, trembling. It tried to get to its feet and fell over, still too weak to move. The Piri noticed it and looked hopefully to Bartolemayne. He gave a single nod and they sprinted toward it, covering the poor suffering creature like army ants. The bir howled as the Piri bit down wherever on its body they could, seemingly not even caring if they hit veins. They just wanted to feast.

Bartolemayne did not bother to join them. He was far too superior to the rest of them to engage in such a group meal. Instead he returned his attention to Clarinda, who was frozen in the defensive position she had assumed.

"Your mother misses you, Clarinda," he said softly. That was how he always spoke, sometimes so quietly that it was barely above a whisper. "She misses you ever so much."

"And that's why she sent for you." It was all clear to her now.

He nodded slowly. "Of course. To bring her wayward child home."

She knew it was a waste of time to try to appeal to Bartolemayne's sense of mercy. It was well known that he had none. But she needed to do something, just to buy herself some time. "I have no future with our people. You must know that." She had to raise her voice to hear herself above the slurping of the Piri and the dwindling and pathetic moans of the bir.

"Your future is of no interest to me. All that matters is that the Mistress warned you what would happen if you ran."

Clarinda slowly crawled across the ground toward him. She smiled up at him with as close to a look of seduction as she could manage under the circumstances. There was blood visible on her lips, her cheeks, her chin. She hoped that would serve to make her more alluring. "Come now, Bartolemayne. That cannot be all that matters to you. Certainly there are other things of equal importance." She drew close enough to run her hand along his bare leg, straying up to his knee. "Those others," and she inclined her head toward the Piri who were finishing their meal, "will do as you command. Command them to return home. Then it can be just you and me, and together we can . . ."

"Together?" His double row of fanged teeth drew back in derision. "Together?" He lashed out with his foot and caught her on the side of the head. Clarinda fell to the side, hitting the ground heavily. "You are damned lucky that I am sworn to do you no serious harm. Not as long as you are with child. Still . . . do you seriously think there can be any 'together' with one who has defiled herself with a Trull, no less? A Trull? Or do you think your mother neglected to tell me that?"

"Lies, Bartolemayne," she said desperately. "She lied to you. Or she was mistaken. Either way. You cannot believe that I would do such a thing."

"Tragically, I can believe it all too readily. I know you of old, Clarinda. You always had nothing but contempt for your own people. And every Piri male and female knew that, and tolerated it because you were daughter of the Mistress and heiress to the title. That is not going to continue to be the case, however, and I assure you of this, Clarinda: As much as I journey this land, I will take time to return and be there for when you are finally made to pay for your arrogance and smugness. Once you have pushed that child out through your nethers, then there shall be a reckoning.

The hybrid freak will be destroyed, and as for you—"

Clarinda did not wait to hear. Instead she abruptly lunged forward, hoping to catch him unawares. Perhaps sink her teeth into the tendons behind his ankles, rip them out, hamstring him, render him helpless.

She had no chance. Bartolemayne yanked his legs clear, deftly stepping out of her way. He grabbed her by the nape of the neck, yanked her to her feet and twisted her around so that she was facing away from him. He was handling her so effortlessly that one would have thought her a child having her parent's will forced upon her. She tried to drive a foot back at him, but he caught it and lifted her off the ground as if she weighed nothing. He started to bend her backwards and she cried out.

"Have you had enough?" he said patiently. "Are you through fighting?"

Seizing bravado as her only option, she grunted through her pain, "You have absolutely no idea how much trouble you're in. All I have to do is cry out and my army will descend upon you."

The other Piri, having sated themselves on the bir, were moving toward her and chuckling to each other.

"Very well," Bartolemayne challenged her. "Summon them. Let us tremble in fear at your army."

He could have throttled her, preventing her from drawing breath. He did not do so. That was how confident he was that she was bluffing, which of course she was.

Nevertheless she filled her lungs and cried out as loudly as she was able, "To me! To me, my followers!"

Nothing. Dead silence, save for the snickering of the Piri and a soft, almost disappointed sigh from Bartolemayne.

"All right, Clarinda. Now it's time to—" Suddenly Bartolemayne's head snapped around. He looked bewildered. "What the hell—?"

He had detected the scent first, but even if he had possessed no nose at all, the steady trembling of the ground that made it seem as if an earthquake was approaching would have alerted him. The Piri were looking at each other in concern as trees were heard crashing in the near distance.

I'll be damned, thought Clarinda.

With a roar of pure fury, Turkin smashed out of the underbrush.

He had a bir in either hand. The birs were smaller than the one that Clarinda had attacked, but they were still wild and furious and looking for someone or something to attack.

Turkin was perfectly happy to accommodate them. He hurled the animals at the Piri, first one and then the other. The first of the birs landed atop two of the Piri, crushing them beneath its paws and roaring so loudly and furiously that the other Piri immediately backpedalled. The second bir had not been quite as well aimed, thudding to the ground and spinning toward the nearest of the Piri. It opened its mouth and roared so loudly that the Piri were falling over each other to get out of its way.

Bartolemayne looked annoyed. "A child, Clarinda? Your army consists of one Ocular child? Do you seriously . . . ?"

Then he heard them. More thundering of huge feet stampeding their way, and the noise of the approaching Ocular was combined with the bellowing of the birs and the terrified cries of the Piri. Piri were perfectly capable of bravery when they significantly outnumbered their prey and could overrun it with minimal risk to themselves. This was not the situation they were being faced with now, and they had little taste for it.

Clarinda saw the concern in their faces, and cried out over the oncoming thundering, "And that is simply the first wave! Call them children if you wish, but how do you plan to stand up to a hundred of them!"

"You are bluffing," said Bartolemayne.

"Try me."

Bartolemayne hesitated and then, with an angry snarl, threw her down. The Piri were busy trying to keep away from the two angry birs, both of whom were doing their best to take down whatever Piri they could get their teeth on.

"If you fancy yourself the head of an army, Clarinda, know that I will raise up an army against you," said Bartolemayne. He did not sound the least put out by this reversal of fortune. If anything, he seemed pleased, even excited by the prospect of having to rise to a challenge. "And we will take you and your children down, and feast on their carcasses for many months."

He called out a brisk command to the remaining Piri, who would happily have fled earlier if anyone save Bartolemayne had been leading them. But they were relieved to have the opportunity to vacate the area, and they did so without any further urging.

As a result, more of the Ocular hunters came pouring into the clearing just as the Piri vanished into the shadows. Bellowing their anger over the disappearance of their intended victims, and wanting to have nothing to do with the Ocular if they could help it, the younger birs charged away into the shadows of the trees.

Berola came running up behind Turkin, with several more Ocular behind her. "You're letting them get away! Those birs were our dinner!"

"They're serving us well enough sending the Piri scattering," said Clarinda firmly. "Let's take advantage of it. Gather the others. We need to leave."

"But we haven't eaten—"

"Better that than being eaten!" Clarinda shouted at him, having no intention of discussing the matter at length. "We haven't gotten far enough from my people!" She didn't add that she wasn't sure it was possible to get far enough. The reach of the Piri seemed very long indeed. "If you value your lives, then we need to distance ourselves!"

"We were being trained to fight them," said Turkin heatedly. "We're not afraid."

"Nor are you ready. And you're going to need time to get ready, and that's what I need to provide you now. Not another word! We go or you die! Make your choice and be prepared to live with it, or not!"

IV.

HER VOICE HAD BEEN SHARP enough and her attitude clearly brooking no argument from them, so Turkin, Berola and the others fell into behind her. When they had returned to Kerda and the others, there had been questioning looks and attempts to discern what had just happened. Clarinda had shut it all down and led them away from the immediate area.

They continued to move through the darkness, and it seemed to Clarinda that every shadow from every outstretched tree hid an enemy. Every branch was like a giant outstretched hand with long, wooden fingers, threatening to grab them and hold them.

The Ocular continued to run as quickly as their huge legs would carry them. Hour passed into hour, and darkness continued to hold sway as was typical for the land of Feend. They were, however, heading steadily south, and Clarinda knew that sooner or later they would leave the land of perpetual darkness behind them. When that happened, travel would become more problematic. Ocular were damned near blind during the day, and Clarinda would likewise require shelter from the sun's rays lest it threatened to burn the skin from her body. Meanwhile Bartolemayne, less daunted by the sun than average Piri, would not be likewise constrained. He would no doubt lead the Piri in continued search of her, finding passages, caves and the like in which they could hide while they mounted their continued pursuit. There would be no place to rest. She had told the Ocular she would train them, mold them into a fighting force. The truth was that she had little concept of how to do such a thing, and no time in which to do it. The Piri had them on the run and there was no end in sight, unless one considered the Piri falling upon them during an unguarded moment, killing all the Ocular and stealing Clarinda back into the depths of Subterror to be an end. *I suppose it is. It simply isn't an end that I would welcome.*

Yet that was very likely the end that awaited them, unless they could find sanctuary.

Sanctuary.

"I know where we have to go," she said abruptly. "I know where we will be safe from the Piri."

This brought the entire squad of Ocular to a halt. They grouped around Clarinda in a manner that could only be considered protective. She found it honestly to be somewhat sweet. It surprised her that she was thinking of Ocular in that manner. These brainless children who had only been a means to an end, to be used and disposed of when it was convenient. Yet now she thought it almost charming the way they were clustering around her as if to shield her from any harm.

"Where?" said Kerda with hope in her voice that she almost seemed afraid to acknowledge was there.

"Perriz."

The Ocular looked at each other, their single eyes blinking rapidly in both awe and amazement. "The home of the Firedraques? Really?" said Berola.

"Yes. Really. The Firedraques are the great peacemakers. They always have been. If they agree to take us under their wing, we will be safe."

"And if they don't?" said Turkin.

"They will," Clarinda said with a firmness that she did not feel, but at least was able to sound convincing over when she said it. "I know it. And if I know it, then you can know it, too."

"My mother always wanted to see Perriz!" said Berola. "Apparently she read about it a great deal in her youth! She told me all kinds of stories about it! But isn't it far?"

"Very," said Clarinda. "But we will move as much as we can without resting, and find food along the way, and we will make the journey faster than any others possibly could. And we will find safety there, and sanctuary, and a home."

"Home," the children whispered to each other, and that was all the incentive they required to keep going.

She just prayed that she wasn't leading them astray.

FIREDRAQUE HALL, PERRIZ

I.

ARREN KINKLASH DID NOT ENTER Firedraque Hall so much as he was propelled into it. The infuriated Mandraque, his skin even greener than usual and his forked tongue flashing out, yanked his arms away from the trio of armed guards who were escorting him, if forcing someone to go somewhere that they were not remotely interested in going could be defined as "escorting."

"Keep the hell away from me!" he snarled at them, and the guards backed off.

One of them stepped forward, looking nervous and fidgeting slightly. "Lord Kinklash, please understand. We are Mandraques, as are you, but we are in service of the Firedraques and had no choice. We were merely following orders—"

"You were ordered to treat me as if I were nothing more than an enslaved Mort?"

"We were ordered to return you here, whether you wished to come or not."

Arren had a leather carrying bag slung over his back. It contained all of the supplies he could quickly gather and collect on short notice. He unslung it now and dropped it to the ground. "Whether I wished to come or not? How is that even an issue? Of course I did not wish to come! That should be obvious considering that," and he indicated the leathers he was wearing, "I am dressed for the road and am carrying supplies for a journey! What did you think was going to happen when you caught up with me and dragged me off the road to return here?"

And a sharp female voice broke in. "They were not required to think. They were required to do as their duty commanded them."

A tall, imperious female Firedraque strode in, her head held high, her maw outthrust, her long and elegant tail twitching in anger. "For that matter, they did as I commanded them. At least some around here understand that which is required of them. And in case you haven't figured it out yet, Kinklash, these good soldiers are concerned that, as head of the Clans, you are going to seek some manner of retribution against them. Or worse, against their family."

Arren looked at them. "Is that true? Is that a concern to you?" When he saw them glance at one another, each of them clearly hoping the other would say something, he rolled his slitted eyes. "You and your families need not worry. You did as Evanna, daughter of Nicrominus, instructed you to do. There will be no retribution taken against you, now or ever. You have my word."

"Satisfied?" said Evanna. When they nodded, appearing distinctly relieved, she gave them a leisurely gesture and said, "You may go." They backed out of Firedraque Hall, bowing and scraping as they did.

Arren waited until they were gone, the huge doors of the cavernous hall shut behind them, and then said angrily, "What the hell did you think you were doing?"

"Kinklash—"

"What the hell did—? Damn it all, Evanna, what gave you the right—?"

"Nothing, Arren! Nothing gave me the right! Are you happy? Nothing gave me the right, and so I took it. And the reason I took it was because you were tossing it aside because you wanted nothing to do with it! Except I didn't feel like giving you that option!" When he did not respond immediately, Evanna made an angry growling noise and turned from him. She strode away, heading toward the cavernous inner hallway. Sunlight beamed through the vast multicolored windows. It was as if a rainbow had taken up residence within the building.

Arren's impulse was to turn around and bolt from the hall. He knew that would do him no good, however. She would simply dispatch guards to haul him in and return him to Perriz, and it would be even more humiliating than it had just been. And that had been pretty damned humiliating. Arren Kinklash, leader of the Clans, being escorted shouting and frothing like a lunatic through the streets of Perriz while other Firedraques looked on in amazement and perhaps even pity. He was not particularly anxious for a replay of that mortification.

So instead of going with his instinct, Arren reluctantly followed Evanna into the main hall. She stood there, bathed in the prismatic light, staring up at one of the large decorations left from the days when Morts ruled over the Damned World.

Arren stood next to Evanna and glanced sidelong at her. "Are you taller?"

She stared at him. "Excuse me?"

"You seem taller. A couple of inches."

"Oh. Yes. That. I've gotten into the habit of slouching. When I'm with Xeri, when I'm with my father. I slouch. Otherwise I tower over them and they have to look up at me to make eye contact, and they find that disconcerting. So I compress my spine a bit. Salves their egos and it is no consequence to me. But when they're not around— or when I'm yelling at idiots," and she looked pointedly at him, "I tend to stand upright."

"Ah." He switched his gaze to the large monument mounted at the far end of the hall. Carved from some sort of wood, it was a representation of a scantily clad human male who was resting with his arms outstretched upon a cross.

"What do you think he represents?" said Evanna. "Xeri and I debated about it at length. My father believed it to be religious iconography of some sort."

"It's possible. On the other hand, it could also be agricultural."

"Agricultural?"

He nodded. "Morts used to mount similar constructions made of straw or such like materials in their fields. They were designed to keep scavenging birds away from crops by making them think that a human sentinel was standing guard."

"Did it work?"

Arren shrugged. "The birds likely ignored it and the humans felt they were being proactive, so I suppose everyone benefited."

"So that statue," and she indicated the one in the hall, "is intended to keep birds away from here?"

"Are there, in fact, any birds here?"

"No."

"Then obviously it's working."

Evanna smiled at that and then slowly shook her head.

He regarded her for a moment and then said softly, "How are you holding up, Evanna?"

"How do I look like I'm holding up?"

"You look terrible."

"That's your answer then."

"Evanna—"

"Everyone is looking to me for solutions, Arren! My father was kidnapped by a Zeffer! The bell tower has been shattered! There was rubble and debris everywhere! We have no spiritual leader, Xeri has crawled over to a corner and curled up into a ball . . ."

"Literally?"

"Metaphorically, but the principle is the same. And everyone is looking to me for solutions! Me! I have no idea what I'm supposed to tell them. I've no clue when, or even if, Nicrominus will be restored to us. The only ones who might know are the Travelers, and they are long gone, and even if they were standing right in front of me they would still tell me nothing. With all of that happening—with all of them hanging upon me—you go running off!" She swung a hand around and cuffed him on the side of the head.

Arren let out a cry of pain and clutched at his earhole. "You didn't have to do that!"

"Apparently I did! Apparently you have to be reminded of your responsibilities! No one forced you to become head of the five clans, Arren," and she waggled a finger in his face. "You maneuvered yourself into that position of power all by yourself. And you did it by dropping a gods damned giant bell on your closest competitor for the title. You have no one to blame but yourself for having responsibilities here."

"I have responsibilities to my sister as well!" he said. "In case you've forgotten, the same Zeffer that made off with your father also took Norda with it!"

"Of course I haven't forgotten. Except if I know that addled sister of yours, the Zeffer didn't take her. She doubtless grabbed on thinking it would be entertaining to—"

Arren's hand clenched into a fist and he brought it snapping around toward her head. But he was slow and Evanna caught it before he could connect. They stood frozen there for a moment, glowering at each other, but then Evanna slowly released her hold on him. "I beg your pardon," she said formally. "I should not have disparaged Norda in that way. Whatever else she may be, she is also your sister and worthy of respect."

"Thank you," he said, still offended but otherwise opting not to push the issue. "And frankly, knowing Norda, if she did grab onto the dangling tentacles of a Zeffer, it wasn't out of whim or caprice. She was quite fond of your father. She spoke of him often. If she saw him being threatened and being carried off, that would have been more than enough motivation for her to grab on."

"If that's the case . . ." Her voice trailed off.

"What? What were you going to say? If you have a thought, finish it."

"If that's the case—if she thrust herself onto the Zeffer—then there's every possibility that she is beyond saving. Your impulsive rescue mission, for which you would have abandoned your responsibilities as head of the Clans, would be for nothing. The Zeffer would be taking care to transport my father safely to wherever it is that the Travelers wanted him taken. But it would have had no such responsibility for Norda's well being. She could have lost her grip—"

"No."

"—fallen asleep, perhaps, or—"

He shook his head and repeated firmly, "No. Norda did not lose her grip. Not ever. You never saw her bounding around the rafters of this place. Heights are her second home. There is no one more confident, more sure footed. Norda does not lose her grip. I have come upon her up in the bell tower . . . when there was a bell tower," he added ruefully, "and found her sound asleep hanging upside down, dangling from her tail curled around a beam. I admit that Norda can be flighty. Difficult to understand. Bizarre, even. But if she did indeed grab a ride on the Zeffer in order to accompany Nicrominus—and I have no reason to believe that is not the case— then wherever he is, she is."

"And perhaps, upon her arrival, the Travelers or even the Overseer dispatched her since she was not supposed to be there. Or do you think that Norda would be capable of surviving the wrath of the Overseer as well?"

"I think Norda can survive anything she . . ." Then his voice tapered off and he looked downward. "No. Unlikely."

"Very unlikely."

"But we can pray to the gods. Pray for both your father and my sister."

"And we can agree," said Evanna, "that you will not be embarking on any more foolhardy rescue missions? The five Clans, given the slightest opportunity, would go to war with each other in a heartbeat. The Firedraque treaties seem to mean nothing to them. And with Nicrominus gone, they will doubtless consider our people to be at a low ebb, and would not be far wrong to do so. The only thing keeping the Clans in line is you, and if you are gone—"

"All right. You have made your point."

"Have I? I have not heard you foreswearing any further rescue attempts."

"When would I have done so? You have not ceased your yammering."

"Very well," she said. She folded her arms and waited.

"If I may ask: how did you know about this one? Soldiers were waiting for me when I was on the road, before I'd even left the city limits of Perriz. How did you dispatch them?"

"You were hardly subtle about it. You stormed about your keep, yelling that you were going to go after your sister. And the Firedraques have eyes and ears everywhere."

"So my mistake was in my own yammering."

"Yes. Which means that there is naught to stop you from trying to go off on another such fool endeavor and this time eluding detection through the simple method of keeping your big Mandraque mouth shut. Nothing save your word of honor, which I am still awaiting."

He growled. "I will not," he said, "go running off on my own to try and save Norda."

"Good," said Evanna with visible relief. "That is what I needed to hear."

"And that is what you have heard."

"It was a stupid idea to begin with. Where did you think you were going to go, anyway? How were you going to find her? You had no means of trailing her. She was airborne and long gone."

"Well," said Arren calmly, "I was figuring I would find a Traveler and beat the information out of him."

"Brilliant plan."

"Thank you."

"I was being sarcastic."

"I know. But I know that you have disdain for most Mandraques, and so will take my compliments wherever and whenever I can get them."

"As you wish. And by the way, Kinklash," and she stepped in close to him and further straightened her spine so that she was practically a head taller than he. "If you ever raise a fist to me again, I will shove it up your bung hole. Is that clear?"

He inclined his head slightly. "Abundantly."

He bowed deeply to her and took his leave, knowing all the

while that his word of honor be damned, and the rest of the Clans be damned, he was going to go after Norda. If all the Mandraques left in the Damned World embarked upon a great war to end all wars and annihilated each other, leaving nothing behind but scorched ground, then Arren Kinklash—who had spent so many years manipulating situations to gain the amount of power he currently enjoyed—would not have cared.

Norda was all that mattered.

All that mattered.

THE VASTLY WATERS

I.

JEPP HAD NEVER SEEN THE Vastly Waters. Not really. Not in anything save her dreams. Naturally she had wondered how it was possible that she could see something in her dreams that she had never experienced in real life and have that dream imagery be anything remotely accurate. In fact, she had assumed that whatever the Vastly Waters did look like, it was somehow very much removed from her dream image of it.

As it turned out, she was right.

The Vastly Waters were far greater, far more amazing, than anything she could possibly have dreamt or even conceived.

First of all, the water seemed to go on and on forever. She knew that most of the Damned World was water, but the knowledge of that didn't begin to approximate the astonishment of seeing it for herself. She had seen great plains, true, stained with Mandraque blood. But even plains had features to them, mountains and shrubs and holes. The Vastly Waters, on the other hand, were featureless. The surface wasn't smooth. There were steady waves that caused the ship to bob constantly. For the first two days, Jepp had had a difficult time adapting to the unusual sensation. She had staggered around the deck of the ship, gripped the rail, vomited violently and repeatedly, and kept falling over. Any food that she had attempted to eat and keep down wound up being evicted back into the waters. By the third day, though, Jepp was managing to keep down simple broth, and by the fifth day she was walking around the deck with confidence, matching the swaying of the vessel with a rolling gait that enabled her to keep her feet. She was rather proud of herself, having developed that particular skill set.

The second thing that was amazing to her were all the physical sensations. The salt air stung her nostrils and yet also invigorated her. And the wind, gods, the wind was amazing. She loved standing at the front of the ship and just let the wind blow her long black hair around while droplets of water sprayed in her face and that wonderful smell would just pervade her senses.

Jepp became aware of the presence at her shoulder and turned to look.

The Traveler was standing there. It was her Traveler. She wasn't quite sure how she knew he was hers, but she did.

There were three of them on the ship. Two of them seemed involved primarily in the running of the vessel. One was operating a wheel that appeared to control the direction in which the ship was going. The other tended to sails and occasionally engaged in activities that appeared related to navigation. They never spoke to each other, or at least if they did, they did not do so when Jepp was around.

The third Traveler had the sole responsibility of attending to Jepp.

He had not spoken to her. For that matter, knowing that he was, in fact, a "he" was more conjecture on her part than anything else. He had simply stayed right nearby her the entire time they had been on the ship. Perhaps he had feared that, given the slightest opportunity, she would throw herself into the Vastly Waters rather than endure one more minute in their presence. It actually had been an option that she had considered. Even the Mandraques, in whose company she had spent much of her life—even the inestimable Mandraque known simply as the Greatness—had spoken of the Travelers in uneasy whispers and talked about how certain death waited for anyone who looked upon them for too long, or at all. So Jepp, a mere human woman, would be a very likely candidate for suicide rather than endure the sustained presence of even one Traveler, much less three. And she was on a sailing vessel where, aside from the sparsely decorated quarters below where she slept, there was nowhere to hide from them.

Jepp had, in fact, been utterly terrified when the Travelers had first descended upon the Bottom Feeders and snatched her from their grasp. On one level their timing could not have been better. Her presence among the Bottom Feeders had reached a flashpoint. The clan's leader, Zerena Foux, was insisting that she be forced to leave immediately while Zerena's son, Karsen, was squaring off against his mother and demanding that Jepp be allowed to stay. As if Zerena's prayers had been answered, the Travelers had suddenly come riding up on their draquons and whisked her away. She had screamed and kept screaming until her throat was sore. She also came to the conclusion that the screaming wasn't doing her any good and she was starting to feel a bit foolish making all that noise for no return on her expended energies. Obviously the Travelers had no intention of harming her; otherwise they simply would have done so and gotten it over with. And so she had quieted down and decided to wait and see what happened next.

During the entire journey to the boat, not a single Traveler had spoken to her. When they had stopped, it had been briefly and apparently for her convenience rather than theirs. They seemed to have no need for sustenance or sleep. They had provided her with some sort of food that she had never seen, wafers that one would have thought would not be remotely filling and yet miraculously when she ate one she wasn't hungry for many hours after. There was a stockpile on the boat that they were now on.

She had peppered the Travelers with questions. Why did they want her, where were they going, what was the purpose of all this? On and on, and none of them afforded her an answer to any of them.

On occasion they would speak to each other, but they did so in a language she could not begin to comprehend. It didn't even sound like a language; it sounded more like winds whispering through trees. It was low and subtle and not meant to be understood by mere humans, or perhaps even mere mortals.

Once they had her on the boat and were heading off toward wherever their destination was, Jepp tried to keep track of how many days passed but lost track. All she knew was that they were heading west.

At one point she thought she spotted a Markene floating not far off. He paced the ship for a brief time, keeping up with ease, and then he submerged and she didn't see him again. She felt that was a shame. She would have liked to talk with him. She would have liked to talk to anyone.

"Is it all right with you," she said wistfully to the Traveler standing near her, "if I talk about Karsen some more?" She hadn't been looking at him, but now she did turn to regard him thoughtfully. "I mean, I know I've talked to you about him a lot in the past days. I tend to go on and on and on and on and all you have to do to stop me is tell me that I should be quiet. That's it. That's all. Just speak up."

The Traveler said nothing. She couldn't even tell if he was looking at her because the hood enveloped the Traveler's head and face, casting a shadow so encompassing that it almost seemed as if the darkness was alive and aiding him in keeping his features hidden.

"Okay. That didn't work. I admit it. I was hoping it would, but . . ." She shrugged.

A long silence followed, broken only by the lapping of the waves and the rippling of the sails as the stiff wind propelled the ship across the Vastly Waters.

"Do you have any idea," she said at last, "how afraid everyone is of you? I mean everyone? No one knows why you do what you do. Everyone believes that you would just as soon destroy anyone who even thinks about getting in your way. And everyone is even more afraid of the Overseer. So since you work for the Overseer, that's double the fear. That's a lot of fear. More fear than I think anyone should have to live with."

Still nothing.

"And everyone believes that there is nothing you fear anywhere in the whole Damned World. That must be nice, not to be afraid of anything. I can't imagine that." She looked down at her feet. "I'm a human woman. There were times in my life that I felt like I was afraid of everything. I was trained as a Pleasurer, you know. I can bring pleasure to just about every one of the twelve races. But then I bonded with Karsen, and that changed everything. And then—"

Suddenly she lunged toward the Traveler, her face twisted in fury, her fingers outstretched like claws.

The Traveler flinched back, even bringing up his arm to ward her off.

Jepp stopped a foot short of him and slowly lowered her hands. "So you are afraid of something," she said. "You're afraid of me. Why is that? What is it about me that you fear?"

The Traveler continued to make no reply. She didn't know what to make of him. For some reason she suddenly felt a chill. Jepp was wearing far more than she had been when she had been with the Bottom Feeders. During that time she had not been dressed in much more than scraps of cloth, which was typical attire for one such as she whose main reason for existence was to provide pleasure for partners. On the ship, though, she had discovered more clothing, none of which fit her especially well but was more concealing and also warmer. At this point she was wearing a simple white shift that hung to below her knees and a cloak around her her shoulders. Her feet remained bare; she found that she preferred them that way. Now she drew the cloak more tightly around herself.

She squared her shoulders, her spine stiffening. "I am tired," she said, as much to herself as to the Traveler. "I am tired of being afraid of the world, and uncertain of my place within it. During my time with Karsen, his mother did nothing but berate me, and the rest of the Clan never fully accepted me. They were, at best, indifferent toward me. But for you, they had very strong feelings. All do. All fear the Travelers. And you could have killed me, yet here I am, and you retreat from me. I am important to you. And not in any way related to providing pleasure. You have, in many ways, elevated me. Lifted me up above every other race, every other individual on the Damned World. Some say the Firedraques do not fear you, and perhaps that is true. But everyone else does, and not living in fear of you when so many others do . . . my gods, it's more than elevating. It's liberating.

"These Vastly Waters . . . they suggest things to me that I never imagined before. Vistas to be explored. Endless possibilities. I have never pondered endless possibilities before because mine were so limited. I looked to the skies but can never touch the stars. But I can touch the water below. I could leap into it, sink below it. That would be the end of me, true, but were I to die, I would die free. There are worse fates, are there not?"

As if to match deed to word, she abruptly put a foot up on the edge of the prow.

Instantly she heard those soft, eerie whispers between the Travelers, and the one closest to her started quickly toward her, noiseless as he moved. But he was not quick enough and suddenly Jepp was straddling the prow. It would have been a simple matter for her to throw herself over the side.

"It's your own fault," she said. "You backed up when I approached you. So you placed yourself too far away to stop me from doing this. Return me whence you took me. Return me to Karsen. Return me or I shall throw myself over the side and drown, for I cannot swim, and whatever greater purpose is connected to your desire for me, it will never be fulfilled. Do you fear that prospect too, I wonder? Shall we find out?"

For the first time, the Traveler spoke. It was soft, so much so that she could scarcely hear him, especially above the crackling of the sail and the splashing of the water against the ship.

"Don't," he said.

The simple word froze Jepp where she was. Her hair blew in her face and she brushed it away. "Why not?"

"You'd be quitting."

"I'm not quitting. I want you to take me back."

Although she could not see the movement of his head, the hood that covered his head slowly shook back and forth in the negative.

"So I have no reason," she said, "not to do this. Not to kill myself."

"One reason."

"And that is?"

"Karsen," said the Traveler, "is not down there." He spoke with what sounded like weary patience, and perhaps even the slightest touch of sympathy, which she most certainly would not have expected.

The damning thing was that he was right. She knew that what she wanted more than anything was a reunion with Karsen. But Karsen did not wait for her below the waves; only death did. Death was the end of hope, and as long as she was alive, hope remained that she would be reunited with him.

"You're not going to turn the ship around, are you." It was not a question.

Again the Traveler slowly shook his unseen head within the hood.

"Aren't you concerned over what will happen to you if I die and you fail in your mission."

"No mission."

This caught her off guard. She tilted her head, studying him, wishing that she could see some hint of expression so that she might get at least a glimmer of what was going through his mind. "No mission? You mean . . . the Overseer didn't send you to get me?"

He shook his head.

"Then why? Why did you capture me?"

"Have to."

"But why?"

"Cannot tell you."

"Is it a secret?" When she saw him shake his head again, she persisted, "Then why?"

"Do not know."

And with that, as if she no longer mattered, he turned and walked away from her. His long, encompassing cloak swept noiselessly around his feet. The unspoken message he was sending her was clear: It was up to her to do what she wanted. If she was resolved to pitch herself over the side and sink to a briny doom, then it was to be her choice and hers alone. He was not going to hover over her and force her to keep living.

Jepp felt slightly deflated over that, and even a bit embarrassed. She had spoken proudly, defiantly, made a threat that she was fully prepared to carry out. And now she was supposed to . . . what? Meekly withdraw herself from her precarious perch and go back to staring out at the water? How would the Travelers take her seriously if she backed off from her ultimatum?

On the other hand, if I go through with it, then they'll take me seriously but I'll be dead and so will hardly be in a position to appreciate it.

With a sigh, she eased herself back onto the deck and stood there, arms folded. The Traveler who had been walking away from her stopped, turned, and looked back at her.

"I hope you're happy," she said.

"Never," whispered the Traveler and walked away from her, leaving her alone at the prow.

II.

SHE DREAMS OF A FAR off land, and although she has never seen it before, she knows it as well as she knows the shape and feel of her own body. She is having a memory that is not hers, cannot be hers. It is impossible, and yet it is more real than she herself.

Jepp has never seen a city such as this one before. She is walking through it slowly, and the streets are deserted, but the buildings, gods, the buildings are beyond description. They tower so high that it seems their uppermost pinnacles must assuredly be caressing the very sky.

She is naked as she walks down the street. Her nudity does not bother her. It never has in the past, and the unreality of her surroundings only add to the surreal aspects of the experience. Although she wants to think that this place in which she finds herself cannot possibly be real, she nevertheless comes to the realization— even in her dream—that she does not possess this level of imagination. She could not possibly have fabricated this on her own. She was never clever enough by half to conceive of buildings so tall, especially when common sense would seem to indicate that . . . once a building gets above a certain height . . . it would most assuredly have to topple over. Structures such as this should not be able to exist. It was physically impossible.

Wasn't it?

But because of her lack of imagination, how could she have come up with this when left to her own devices?

Then she hears a distant rumbling. It is not coming from the skies, though, as an oncoming storm might prompt. Nor is it originating from the streets around her, as would result from an oncoming army.

It is coming from below the street. Tunnels, perhaps, such as Trulls built, along which high speed cars called Trullers ran. But the sounds being generated are much louder, suggesting that whatever is causing them is proportionately bigger. What, Jepp wonders, could be so big as to cause such noises?

Hot air is blowing up from below, and she sees large rectangular entranceways into the ground. She has seen hard ground like this, not grass or dirt but instead some sort of gray material that is incredibly solid. "Paved" is the word that now comes into her mind, and "sidewalk," but she has not heard these words before and so does not comprehend how they could be coming to her now. They are things left over from humans, from that race of which Jepp is a part, but about which she knows little and understands less.

There is movement from the entranceways. It is a human. One. He is dressed head to toe in blue cloth with a scrap of fabric hanging from around his throat, pointing downward like an arrow toward his loins. Perhaps it is symbolic, to remind others that he is a man and has a man's equipment. Or perhaps he is simply addle minded and could not find his equipment unless he had an article of clothing that reminded him of where it is situated.

Then another man emerges, dressed in different colors but in the same general sort of attire, also with a loin pointer. And then more, some dressed similarly, some not, and now women as well, wearing far more clothing than Jepp has ever seen any female human wearing. It seems, oddly, both constraining and yet liberating.

None of them are moving at normal speeds. Instead everyone is moving very quickly, so much so that it is becoming nothing but a steady blur. She can no longer distinguish one from the other. She cannot determine if she is moving slower or they are moving faster, or whether time has any meaning at all anymore. All she knows is that there are human beings, hundreds of them, thousands of them, perhaps millions. They are coming up from below, and all around her, moving past her in a steady stream of humanity that causes her eyes to well up with tears.

And other objects are moving past her now. They are vehicles that remind her a little of the jumpcar driven by the Bottom Feeders. But again the number of them is staggering, coming in all colors and varieties and moving far more quickly than the clunky jumpcar could ever hope to go. Jepp remains standing in the middle of the street which in turn is in the middle of the city, and she raises her arms and stands there with them stretched toward the sky, thanking the gods for this vision. And she cries out, Oh gods on high, is this a vision of things that have yet to occur, or things that have been but will never come again, or things that were and can be once more? She waits for the gods to reply and at first there is nothing. No sepulchral voice, no guiding spirit, nothing to explain to her the full parameters of what she is seeing or telling her what to do with this information now that it is being presented to her.

Then she sees something.

It should be impossible for her to perceive it because it is simply *too far away. And yet she does. There is a tall building, one of the tallest around if not in fact the tallest. There is a huge spike projecting upright from the top, and wrapped around that spike, holding tightly against a steady wind that threatens to dislodge her if she should ease up on her grip, is a female Mandraque. Jepp has no idea how the Mandraque could have wound up in such a position, but the Mandraque does not appear afraid. If anything, she seems intrigued by the position that she's in, and genuinely eager to discover what's going to happen next.*

They are separated by an incredible distance, by miles of both geography and altitude, and yet the Mandraque is now looking right at her. Again, it should not be possible, and yet it is, and the Mandraque tilts her head in curiosity, apparently as surprised to see Jepp as Jepp is to see her.

Together, says the Mandraque, together we can accomplish this. And here is how. Ludicrously she leans forward slightly as if that will somehow bring them closer and then—

"Wake up! Now!"

Jepp was jolted from her slumber, sitting up so quickly and in such confusion that she banged her head on the low hanging ceiling. She was completely disoriented, thinking at first she had awoken in the tent of the Greatness, and then the jumpcar of the Bottom Feeders.

A hooded figure was leaning in toward her. That was when she remembered where she was and, more importantly, who she was with.

The Traveler was close to her, very close, his black-gloved hand on her shoulder, prodding her to awaken. There was mostly darkness in her room, and yet she could not resist seizing the opportunity. Had she given it a second's worth of thought, she never would have done so. But she did not; instead she acted entirely on impulse as she reached up and shoved at his hood.

It fell back for just a second, and in the darkness of the room, in the extended shadows, she should not have been able to see him, just as she should not have been able to see that Mandraque female in her dream.

And yet she was able to, thanks to the Traveler himself. When his hood was knocked away, a glow emanated from the Traveler and filled the cramped room. It happened so quickly that Jepp only had the time to get a brief impression rather than a good look. That impression was of silver. Silver suffused with light. And there was beauty. She hadn't seen the Traveler's face clearly, and could not have described any details. All she had was an impression of intense beauty combined with astounding sadness.

The Traveler yanked away from her, pulling his hood back into place. Jepp rose from her bed, fascinated, her hands reaching toward him as she said, "Let me see . . ."

His hand whipped around and caught her in the side of the face. Her skull snapped so quickly that her neck would be sore for hours. Jepp let out a startled cry and fell back onto the bed. The Traveler loomed over her and this time when he spoke, there were no whispers, no brevity of sentences. There was just pure anger and it was all directed at her.

"Are you out of your mind?" he demanded. "Do you have the slightest idea what I can do to you?"

There was a young woman within Jepp who was cowering, who wanted to shrink away and beg forgiveness and ask if there was anything she could do, anything at all, to assuage the wrath of this formidable creature. But then, as much to her own surprise as the Traveler's, she got to her feet and said defiantly, "Then do it. Do it, if you dare. I'm tired of your talking and your whispering and your . . . your ominosity! You made a huge mistake kidnapping me. Because being taken away by the Travelers was the absolute worst thing that could happen to anybody. All the others just shake at the very idea of it. And here I am, and I was taken, and I'm still here, and instead of doing anything to me you're just being threatening! Well your threats aren't working anymore! Either do something about it or get the hell out of my room!" And she pointed defiantly toward the door.

He took a step toward her and loomed even more. "You have no idea—"

She waved dismissively. "You keep saying that. Do something, don't do something, but stop threatening me because it's tiresome." His silence and the fact that she was still alive and unharmed emboldened her. "You know what the problem is? I don't have anything. I never have. I own nothing. I'm not allowed property. I have no home. I have no freedom. My life has always been at the disposal of the Twelve Races, so even my life is not my own. And it took your snatching me away from Karsen's side for me to come to one simple realization: To have nothing is to fear nothing."

Then Jepp felt as if something was beginning to build up within the small room. Energy, escalating toward a detonation that would wipe her from the face of the world. Once, she would have screamed and begged and pleaded. Now she stood there with her shoulders squared, confident that he would do nothing, uncaring if he did.

Very slowly the energy subsided. The Traveler turned away from her then, paused in the door, and then rumbled, "'Ominosity' is not even a word."

"It is now! How's that for an idea?"

He moved through the door and it slammed shut behind him.

III.

WHEN THE TRAVELER EXITED JEPP'S room, one of his brethren was standing there waiting for him.

"'Ominosity?'"

"Shut up," said the Traveler.

"Seriously, Graves: omniosity?"

"I told you to shut up, Trott, and I mean it."

Graves bolted up the stairs and onto the deck of the ship. Pulling back his hood, he looked to the skies and wondered, as he always did, whether those who had exiled them were looking down upon them. He suspected they were not. He suspected that they were not giving the Banished the slightest thought.

The starlight glittered against his face. It was a sensation he usually enjoyed, although less so now since he had much on his mind.

Trott, as always, made no noise as he came up behind Graves. None of them made any noise when they walked. Graves found that irritating. It made it seem as if they weren't quite there. When Trott said nothing for a time, Graves finally sighed and said, "We should really just throw her over the side, you know."

"I know."

"But we cannot."

"I know."

"Except why can't we?"

"I don't know."

Graves looked at Trott with undisguised disdain. "You are being less than helpful."

"I wasn't actually trying to be helpful. And in that, I can assume, I have succeeded."

"Indeed you have." Graves shook his head. The soft tinkle of bells accompanied the movement. "I hate this, Trott. I truly do."

"Hate what?"

"This. The entire situation. The knowing but not knowing."

"It is the way we are and the gift with which we have been endowed."

"It is a gift that none of us has asked for and that I could, quite frankly, do without."

"Your preferences in the matter are of little consequence, Graves. You know that. Things are what they are because they must be that way."

"That's entirely too circular an answer for me to find even a modicum of solace."

"I wasn't saying it to give you solace."

Despite his generally bad mood, Graves actually snorted in amusement. "That is what I love about you, Trott. You consistently aim your sights low and thus always succeed in your endeavors. It must be nice."

Trott shrugged. He went over to Graves and draped an arm around his shoulders in commiseration. "It has its moments, I suppose. By contrast, I don't think you're truly happy unless you are truly miserable. Neither of us is perfect, but I will take my lack of aspirations over your lack of cheer any time."

"You are probably right."

"I generally am."

Graves leaned his head on Trott's shoulder and looked out into the night. It was so dark that it was impossible to see where the water met the sky. Although the stars twinkled overhead as a general guide to directions, the small sliver of moon that was out tonight had hidden behind a cloud. They were cloaked in blackness as black as the capes which enveloped them. "What do you think she was dreaming of?" said Graves.

"How would I know? You were the one who chose to awaken her."

"No. I was the one who was chosen to awaken her, just as such things always happen with us," Graves reminded him. "I do not understand why this girl is important. I do not understand why her dreams are important. Of what significance can they possibly be?"

"I wish I knew. Sadly, I do not."

"We will take her to the Overseer as planned," said Graves with a sigh. "We will take her to him, and he will know why she was brought to him and what to do with her."

"Do you believe that, Graves? Do you really and truly believe that?"

Slowly Graves shook his head. "Not for a moment."

"Nor do I."

"Just my luck," said Graves, "that we select that, of all things, to be in agreement upon." He paused and then called to the remaining Traveler who was standing at the wheel of the ship, "Ayrburn! Our good friend Trott here believes we are in a world of trouble, with no clear direction and no obvious end in sight. He believes transporting this girl to the Spires is a fool's errand and that the Overseer will be of no use at all in determining her fate, ours, or that of the Damned World's. What say you?"

Ayrburn shrugged.

"Well spoken," Graves said drily. "Very well spoken."

The ship continued into the night.

THE UPPER REACHES OF SUISLAN

I.

PAVAN RUCAPHONOUS WAS IN TROUBLE.

The youngster sprinted down through the narrow, mountainous trail, slipping at one point and nearly falling. His padded feet managed to catch themselves before he tumbled, though, and he righted himself quickly before moving on. A stiff wind was blowing through the pass, but that was fairly normal for the regions in which his people, the Serabim, dwelt. Pavan was no more bothered by it than he ever was, for the white fur that covered him from head to toe provided him more than enough protection against the hostile environment in which he resided.

He gasped for air as he continued to run, small mists puffing from his mouth as he did so. Just ahead of him he saw that there was a gap in the path, which opened down into a yawning cavern. One misstep and he would plunge into it and, by extension, into a huge pile of difficulty. Yet Pavan did not slow. Instead he sped up, his legs scissoring, his arms moving quickly to help gain him velocity. When he hit the edge of the drop he sprang with legs that were like coiled steel. They propelled him over the gap and he landed on the far side. Snow puffed out from beneath his feet in little clouds as he continued to run.

Pavan's face was flatter than most of the Serabim, looking for all the world as if someone had smashed it in with a skillet. What made him distinctive, though, was the crest of black fur that covered the top and back of his head like a hood. The fur marked him for his destiny. When he was much younger, he had been of the opinion that such demarcations seemed terribly arbitrary and not even fair.

Since then he had come to accept it, along with his status.

Mostly.

"I'm sorry I'm late! I'm sorry I'm late!" he said, almost sliding past Akasha's cave. He caught the edge of the cave with his fingers, the claws sinking in and preventing him from going any further. "I'm really, really sorry!"

No answer came from within the cave.

This caused Pavan some concern. "Akasha?" he called, more cautiously this time. "Akasha? Is there a problem? Are you all right?"

Still no response.

Pavan was unaccustomed to entering Akasha's cave without any sort of invitation. The ritual of Pavan's visits and time with his mentor was very specific. Pavan would announce his presence. Akasha would acknowledge it, typically with some cutting comment designed to make Pavan believe that he was hopelessly inept. Not that Pavan required such negative encouragement from Akasha, because he already believed it and was disinclined to accept that the destiny awaiting him was anything to which he was truly entitled.

Now, though, no invitation was forthcoming. There was nothing but silence.

A chill moved up Pavan's spine, and it had nothing to do with the stiff breezes that were blowing past and through him. His furry body was flecked with snowflakes but otherwise the weather continued not to be an issue for him. Indeed, the Serabim had settled in the Upper Reaches of Suislan all those turns ago specifically because they found the climate attractive and comfortable. Serabim could survive outside of the environs of the Upper Reaches well enough. For a while, at any rate.

The chill that was moving through Pavan came from growing concern over his mentor. "Akasha," he called once more, with greater firmness of voice than before, and this time when no response was forthcoming, he steeled himself and strode boldly into the cave. He had no idea what he would find.

He found nothing.

There was no sign of Akasha. There were signs that he had eaten there, and toward the back of the cave was defecation that seemed relatively recent, although it was hard for Pavan to be certain. He had virtually no possessions, because Akasha disdained such things. "Keepers need nothing other than themselves," was his oft-stated philosophy, repeated so often in fact that it was all Pavan could do not to roll his eyes in impatience every time he heard it.

He called Akasha's name and this time his voice echoed as he did so, bouncing around within the confines of the cave.

Pavan was becoming more and more disturbed. This wasn't like Akasha at all.

His mind started racing back over all his recent interactions with his mentor, and gradually a most disturbing, even disconcerting thought occurred to him. There was a grand tradition among the highly exalted rank of Serabim called the Keepers that Pavan would never, for one moment, have thought that Akasha would embrace. Yet here was Akasha, nowhere to be found, and he was getting up in years, and what other possibility could it be?

Pavan knew he had to tell someone, but he wasn't sure who to tell or what to tell them. He had nothing more than vague suspicions, nothing that he could really report to others with any sort of certainty. Still . . .

"Someone must be told," he said with certainty. He pivoted to head back for the mouth of the cave and let out a startled yell of alarm.

Akasha was standing directly behind him, staring at him with his head cocked and a look of amusement on his wrinkled face. He had a crest of differently colored fur around his head, as Pavan did, but his great age caused it to be shot through with gray.

"Pay attention!" shouted Akasha. His right hand whipped around before Pavan had time to react and struck Pavan on the side of the head. Pavan went down, landing hard on his rump, his skull ringing from the force of the blow. It was hard to believe that one as aged as Akasha still had that much power in his arm, but clearly he did.

Akasha stood over him, his face now the picture of calm. "You were not paying attention," he now said calmly. "You need to. You need to pay attention all the time. I will not always be around to protect you."

"Protect me?" said Pavan, rubbing his head. "Right now the only thing that I need protecting from is you! Damnation, Akasha! You nearly took my head off!"

"I could have taken your head off," Akasha said. He walked slowly past him, leaning against the wall for extra support. "If I had a blade in my hand, your head would be lying on the floor, lonely for its neck. Except that won't be their aim."

"Whose aim?"

"Our enemies."

"What enemies!?" Pavan felt as if he had wandered into the middle of a conversation, spoken in a foreign language no less. "We have no enemies! We are Serabim!"

"Everyone has enemies," Akasha said patiently. "You are a fool if you think otherwise. How is your head?"

"Still ringing."

"Good. Perhaps it will knock some sense into you."

"I was worried! About you!"

"The one you need to worry about is you. There is no one else to do it for you. Your parents are gone and our noble Chieftains are suspicious of you, as they always are of the Keepers. They mistrust that upon which they depend. You cannot trust them. You cannot trust anyone save yourself and me, and even I cannot be depended upon, for I am old and my time will be done ere long."

"That is ridiculous, Akasha. You still have many turns before you will leave us. Ow!"

The cry of pain resulted from Akasha having struck him on the side of the head again, just when his head had nearly ceased throbbing from the previous cuffing. "Will you stop that!?"

"Do not tell me things that you yourself do not believe," Akasha said to him. "When you were running about in alarm, calling out for me, you thought something had happened to me. That I was dead."

"I did not think that, but," he added hastily, seeing Akasha readying his hand for another blow, "I was worried that you had done something foolish."

"What sort of foolish thing did you think I had done?"

"Well, I . . ." He hesitated.

Akasha sighed heavily. It sounded like rocks rolling down a side of a mountain. "Out with it."

"I had heard that Keepers, when they become old enough . . ." He paused once more and then said, "that they dispense with themselves."

"You mean we kill ourselves?"

"That's what I had heard."

"For what end? To what purpose?"

Pavan shrugged. "No one knows."

"Does that make any sense to you?"

"No. Not really."

"Then why would you believe such a thing?"

"Because," said Pavan, "you are the only Keeper that I have ever known, and in many ways you are as much of an enigma to me as when I first became your disciple all those turns ago. And because . . ."

"Because what?"

"It's ridiculous. It's selfish."

"One's concerns for oneself are never ridiculous." Akasha's voice was surprisingly soft. "What's going through your mind, Pavan? I have many talents, but the ability to read thoughts is not among them. So what—?"

"People leave me."

"Leave you?"

"My parents left."

Akasha moaned softly. "Pavan, that was a very long time ago. You cannot still be dwelling on—"

"They abandoned me, Akasha. When my coloring came in, when

they saw me, saw my crest, saw this," and he pulled in frustration at the hood of black fur on his head, "they abandoned me. Left me to the care of you, and of others, and went off to find another tribe of Serabim. I think about them, and think about that, and all I can think of is that people don't seem to care about me enough to stay around."

"So your fear that I dispatched myself had less to do with me than it has to do with you."

Pavan looked uncomfortable. "It sounds even worse when you say it than when I thought it."

"It doesn't sound bad. Desperate, perhaps, and pathetic, but not bad."

"Well . . ." Pavan cleared his throat. "Anyway . . . you're here . . ."

"And you're here, and this conversation has gone as far as it can go. So we must take it in a different direction. Have you been practicing your singing?"

"Every day. Sometimes it seems every minute of every day."

"Then it's high time you put it to use."

Pavan's eyes widened. "Seriously?"

"I always speak seriously," Akasha informed him imperiously. "Come along." He turned and headed out of the cave, and Pavan followed behind him, his mind racing. Was this really it? Was this the time? Pavan had fantasized about it, dreamt about it, and also been afraid of it. Afraid of what would happen if he failed, and even more afraid of what would happen if he succeeded.

II.

IT SEEMED TO PAVAN THAT the wind had picked up as they approached the edge of Zeffer Point. Perhaps nature itself was trying to tell him that this was a bad idea, that he was not remotely ready. All of his practice didn't seem to mean anything, because he felt his throat tightening up as he contemplated what was being asked of him.

He remembered legends that he had read about how would-be

Keepers had hit a wrong note in their first attempt to commune with Zeffers, had been picked up in a tentacle, and thrown carelessly off the mountain, screaming all the way down and never heard from again when the scream eventually stopped. He didn't know if such stories were true, or were merely designed to intimidate anyone who aspired to such high position. Either way, in his case, it was working.

Akasha stood on the Point, turned and gestured impatiently for Pavan to approach. Pavan stayed right where he was and touched his throat. "I . . ."

"You what?"

"My throat feels scratchy," he said as his fur rippled in the wind. "This may not be the best time. I should be in good voice, should I not, if—?"

"Get your furry white ass over here," said Akasha, never one to suffer fools even on his best day.

Not wanting to seem like a coward to his mentor, Pavan approached slowly. He felt as if his feet had boulders tied to them. Akasha's look of annoyance made it clear that Pavan's sluggish approach was not merely subjective perception on Pavan's part. Pavan did his best to hasten himself and what seemed an age later, he was standing at Akasha's side. Akasha made a sweeping gesture as if taking in the entirety of the view. "Go ahead, Pavan. Impress me," he said.

Pavan drew in an initial breath, and the cold air stung his chest. He sang the first several notes of the song, and they were crackly and off pitch. Akasha raised a paw and Pavan quieted.

"Calm down," said Akasha in a voice that was surprisingly sympathetic. "Steady yourself."

"It's just . . . it's hard to breathe. The air—"

"It has nothing to do with the air. It's hard to breathe because you're nervous and your chest is tightening up. Relax."

"I don't know how."

"Take a deep breath in through your nose and let it out through your mouth. Do it slowly and three times. That should be enough to clear your head. And by the way, no Zeffer ever threw a would-be Keeper into the abyss."

"Really?"

"Really."

"If it had, would you tell me?"

"No."

"I do not find that to be particularly reassuring."

"Just do it, Pavan. I tire of this and I tire of your cowardice."

Pavan bristled, the fur on the back of his neck standing up. "I am not a coward."

"There! Right there: The emotion you displayed there. That is what you need to do in order to have a proper Communion."

"I need to be annoyed with you?"

"You need to take all your strongest emotions—all of them—and focus them. They will be both the sustenance for the Zeffers, and your shield lest they take too much from you."

"But annoyance isn't really a strong emotion. What if . . . what if I don't have any?"

"When the time comes, I assure you that you will. But that is an issue for another time. For now, do as you have trained to do."

Displaying an assertiveness that he did not feel, but hoping that he would draw actual inspiration from acting as if he did feel it, Pavan strode right to the edge of Zeffer Point, opened his mouth, and began to sing. His voice wavered at first, but then he found his proper pitch, and his training and practice took over. His song began to build. The words were ancient, so much so that their original meaning had been lost and were the subject of spirited debate among many tribal elders. But Akasha had told him that it was less about the specific meaning of the words so much as it was firmly believing in the sincerity of one's intentions. Zeffers thrived on sincerity.

The wind took Pavan's song and caused it to rebound throughout the High Place. He heard his own words, his own chant, coming back to him. They sounded pure and good and wonderful, and Pavan stretched wide his arms as if welcoming his wandering spirit back to himself. It grew colder and colder, but Pavan took no notice of it. He sang with growing confidence, as if it was something that he had been doing not only for the entirety of his life, but since before he was born. He had practiced his songs repeatedly throughout his training, but never before had he felt connected to those Keepers who had preceded him.

For the first time in his life, he did not feel alone.

The wind began to shift and at first he didn't realize why. He thought it was simply a natural turn of the weather. Then he realized that something was coming, rising from below. The realization excited him so much that it almost threw him off his song, but he managed to keep himself together and maintain the steady strength of his tune.

Slowly, majestically, a Zeffer rose in front of him. Its surface undulated and the tentacles dangling beneath it swayed in the wind. It was massive, as Zeffers always were, taking up the entirety of Pavan's field of vision.

A second Zeffer appeared behind it, and then a third.

And they sang back to him.

No one was sure exactly how it was that Zeffers managed to accomplish their songs. They had no vocal apparatus that anyone was aware of. Then again, there was much about Zeffers that remained cloaked in mystery. No one knew how they mated or reproduced, or how long they lived. The only thing that anyone knew for certain was how they derived sustenance, and from whom.

His voice slid up the scale and he was fascinated to see that the Zeffers responded physically. They titled on an invisible axis, first one direction and then the other as he shifted the tones almost playfully. On one sustained note he even got them to turn completely over, which he had not thought Zeffers were capable of doing.

For the first time, however, he began to feel that he was capable of shouldering the responsibility that was to be thrust upon him, once he had reached the proper age and circumstances dictated that it was time.

An arm rested gently around his shoulder. Akasha was at his side, and was smiling in approval. "Well done, young Pavan. Well done," he said. It was the first time in ages that Pavan could recall receiving unqualified praise from his mentor.

"Thank you, sir."

Then Akasha cuffed him in the back of the head and said, "Do not become overconfident. That can lead you to ruin."

"Yes, sir."

The Zeffers were swaying with much more agitation than they had previously been displaying. Akasha looked at them and then back to Pavan. "Why did you stop singing?"

"Because you were talking to me, Master."

"And you let yourself be distracted by someone else?" He cuffed him once more and then said, "Get back to it."

Pavan did as he was instructed, and the Zeffers and he serenaded each other with songs that were ancient. They did not Commune, for Communion was only for the Zeffers and the Keeper. But this was a first and necessary step toward that time when the Keeper would be the sole means of sustenance for the Zeffers, and the survival of not only the magnificent creatures, but the Serabim themselves, would depend upon him.

For the first time in his life, Pavan began to believe that he might well be up for the task.

THE SPIRES

I.

NICROMINUS COULD SCARCELY BELIEVE WHAT he was looking at. The face of a human being was staring back at him from within the armor of the Overseer. It seemed ridiculous, a grand joke somehow, as if a human had found the armor lying around and had climbed into it, commandeering it. And that human would most certainly die for such effrontery, because the Overseer would never tolerate such an action, never . . .

"Never wondered?" said the Overseer. "Never wondered which member race of those who sent you into exile would be the one overseeing you all?"

"Of course I have wondered, Overseer," said Nicrominus uncertainly, still trying to process the warped reality being presented him. "Of course I have. We all have. The, uh . . . the most oft repeated theory was that it was one of the Magisters. They are the oldest known race, and so it was assumed by many that—"

"I'm sure there were a lot of theories, Nicrominus. Out of curiosity, how many theorized that it was a human being?"

Nicrominus didn't even have to think about it. "None."

"That's the beauty of it, isn't it."

"I do not understand. I have some familiarity with the life spans of Morts . . ."

"I hate that term."

"Humans," Nicrominus quickly corrected himself. "The Third Wave was long enough ago that any humans who might have survived it would most certainly have succumbed to the ravages of old age."

"Do I look like a spring chicken to you?"

"I . . . do not know what that is." Nicrominus was weighing

every word, eager not to give offense. "So I cannot accurately state whether you look like one or not."

The Overseer didn't appear to be listening. Instead he was staring at the helmet he held in his armored hands. "Been a long time," he said, "since I breathed the fresh air. Or at least what passes for fresh air in Manhattan."

"Man—?"

"—hattan. New York City. The Big Apple."

"Big Apple?"

"It's a nickname."

Nicrominus looked around and saw no indication of any sort of fruit. "Why is it called that?"

The Overseer considered that and then shrugged. "You know, I have absolutely no idea. Maybe there used to be orchards around here. I honestly couldn't tell you."

"Were any other cities referred to as 'big' anything?"

"New Orleans was the Big Easy."

The name "Orleans" sounded familiar to Nicrominus. In his readings of human history back in Perriz, he had seen myriad mentions of a "Maid of Orleans" and thought they might be related somehow. "Why the 'Big Easy?'"

"Not sure. Perhaps the women were all sluts. Actually, I was stationed there for a few months, during Mardi Gras, and they damned sure were easy then." He studied Nicrominus's reaction. "You have no blessed idea what I'm talking about, do you."

"I am afraid not, Overseer."

"Stop calling me that. It's a stupid name. Stupid title. Never much cared for it. The Travelers call me that, but you're not a Traveler and it sounds ridiculous coming from you."

"Very well. How would you prefer I address you then?"

The Overseer appeared to ponder that. "I haven't been one for a long time, but I kind of miss 'Colonel.' 'Colonel' would be nice."

"Colonel is your name?"

"Colonel is my rank. Colonel Elijah Dunn. I won't bore you with my serial number. Can scarcely remember it, actually." He frowned. "Lot of things I have trouble remembering from my previous life. Would you like to see the best view of the city there is, Nicrominus?"

"Very much so, Colonel."

"Right this way, then. It's a bit of a hike, but worth it."

Nicrominus was having trouble believing that all of this was happening. It was like living a very strange dream. The Overseer was taking great strides but then appeared to notice that Nicrominus was having trouble keeping up with him, and so slowed, allowing Nicrominus to catch up.

"You should have seen this in its heyday, Nicrominus. So many people. So much life. Although frankly I'm still not certain if it was a good thing or a bad thing."

"Overs—Colonel. My apologies. You sound rather ambivalent over the status of your own race."

"You picked up on that, did you?" The Colonel smiled ruefully. "I'm not even sure I think of them as my own race anymore. In many ways, I feel as if they were just this aspect of me that I've since outgrown."

"You said that 'Colonel' was a rank. A rank in what?"

"United States Army. Special forces. I could go into greater detail, but it wouldn't mean much of anything to you."

"I suppose not. If I may ask . . ."

"How did I get this way?" The Colonel tapped his armor. "How did I wind up in this tin can? In charge of everyone and everything on Earth?"

"That was more or less what I was wondering, yes."

"Can't say as I blame you. Frankly, it's all a bit of a blur to me as well. The last thing I remember was facing off against the assembled forces of the Third Wave. And I shouted at them, well, pretty much what everyone says I shouted. Told them to get off my damned world. Obviously I had no idea that I had just dubbed the entirety of the planet with a brand new name."

He stopped walking. Nicrominus looked at him questioningly

and then the Colonel shook his head, appearing abashed. "Sorry. Red light. Force of habit, really. Stupid habit, too. Nobody in New York gave a damn about red lights even when there were people and cars here." Nicrominus had no idea what he was talking about, but then a glowing red circle set above the intersection caught his attention. As the Colonel walked under it, the red circle was extinguished, only to be replaced by a green one. Nicrominus had no idea what significance that might hold, but resolved to ask the Colonel about it at some later point.

"And then the hordes descended upon me and I figured, you know, that was it. I was done. And the next thing I knew, I was gone."

"Gone?"

The Colonel nodded. "There was just nothingness around me. Blackness. And a distant glow, except I couldn't make out the source. I wasn't in a room or anything like that. It was more like hanging in a void. I was sure I was dead. A goner. And then I heard this voice."

"What did it sound like?"

"Like not one voice. It sounded like a chorus of them, actually. A dozen, a hundred. Hard to say. But they were all talking together using exactly the same words. And they told me what was going on. See, I was thinking like an army man. I just assumed—as everybody else did, really—that this had been an invasion. An attempt to conquer us. Except that wasn't what the Third Wave was at all. You know what it was? Australia."

"Aus . . . tralia? What is—?"

"It's a country. Or a continent. I'm a little hazy on that. We'll say a country."

"All right," said Nicrominus, wanting to be reasonable.

"And it had plenty of indigenous life. People who had been living there for thousands of years. And then, in the eighteenth century, the British decided to set up shop there and began dumping their criminals into newly created colonies."

"The 'British'—?"

The Colonel waved off the question. "Don't worry about the

specifics. Basically one nation decided to send its cast offs and unwanted to Australia so they wouldn't have to deal with them. And this practice continued for, oh, seventy-five years or so. The result was that the people who were already there, the natives, found their population dropping thanks to diseases and such that they weren't prepared to deal with. For that matter, the history of this country right here isn't all that much different, except in our case it was unwanted religious elements as opposed to criminal elements. As far as the natives were concerned, it was all the same, I suppose."

"I suppose," Nicrominus said, doing his best to keep up with the conversation.

"So basically you lot were criminals and we were Australia."

"With all respect . . . Colonel," he said, trying to remember the new, preferred means of address, "we were not criminals. There was a war for the hearts and minds of the residents of the Elserealms, and the Twelve Races sent here lost."

"Again, the specifics don't really matter, do they? All that matters is that you got sent here, and we were already here, and so you had to get rid of us."

"It was not the desire of the Firedraques to dispense with those who were already residing in this sphere. We would have been perfectly content to craft treaties that would have guaranteed our living in peace with humans."

"I can believe that. My ancestors upon arriving here crafted treaties with the natives to ensure that all would live in harmony."

"There, you see—?"

"We broke all the treaties, took their land, and nearly obliterated them all."

"Ah," was all Nicrominus could think of to say.

By that point they were approaching a building so tall that Nicrominus could not even begin to make out the uppermost reaches. "This is it," the Colonel said. "This is what I wanted to show you. It's called the Empire State Building. Constructed back when skyscrapers had a modicum of style. This way," and he walked in through wide glass doors, bending slightly to avoid banging his head since the armor built up his height beyond normal human proportions. Nicrominus followed him.

"Anyway," said the Colonel as he pushed a small button inset into a wall, "once I understood what was going on, well . . . I couldn't say I was happy about it, but at least it made sense. It was sort of a vast symmetry. That which members of my race had done to others throughout our history was now being done to us. I'm a big believer in actions generating consequences, and having to live with those consequences. And the Third Wave was the ultimate extension of that.

"So there I was, hanging in this sort of void between life and death, being made to understand the vastness of the situation, and this voice—these voices—offered me an opportunity. A chance to be put in charge of the entire world. To oversee it all. Act as a sort of ultimate power who was designed mostly as a figurehead to keep the Twelve Races in a state of fear."

"Fear of what?"

"Of each other. Of the Banishers. As long as the Twelve Races continued to focus their attentions elsewhere, they could not mount any sort of counterattack against the Elserealms."

"Was that ever truly a possibility?"

The Colonel gave him an amused look. "Of course it was."

There was a faint "ding" noise and the doors opened. Nicrominus looked at it suspiciously. "I rode in this earlier. I am not entirely sure I understood its function."

"It's called an elevator. It's perfectly safe. Well . . . as safe as a small room suspended by cables over a drop of hundreds of feet can be, I suppose. Come." He entered the elevator and gestured for Nicrominus to follow him. The Firedraque did as he was bidden, although he was nervous as the doors closed him in. The room began to move and Nicrominus staggered slightly as it did so.

"How was it a possiblility? That we could mount a counter-attack? From this realm, of all places? Does it have something to do with the hotstars?"

"It doesn't matter."

"With respect, Colonel, it does to me."

"This is your home, Nicrominus. All your homes. The sooner you come to terms with that, the better. I know I did. Just as, when I was floating in that void," he said, "I came to terms with what my role in life was to be. I'll tell you, those moments as I was just drifting, helplessly, in the darkness . . . they were the happiest of my life. And then the voices made me an offer, and I debated for a long time what to do. Well . . . it seemed like a long time. Probably just seconds, subjectively speaking."

"You accepted their offer."

"Obviously. And I wound up here, in this armor that they provided me, that keeps me alive long past the time when I should be worm food. And with the Travelers to aid me as the long arm of the Overseer to help keep the Twelve Races in line."

"And what are the Travelers?"

"They are what I need them to be."

"Meaning?"

He did not answer.

They stepped out of the elevator and switched to another. Nicrominus experienced that same momentary disorientation and fluttering of his stomach before settling in.

"You have to understand something, Nicrominus," said the Colonel wistfully. "I was never any great fan of the human race to begin with. I didn't wish death on them. Hell, I swore to defend them, and I kept that oath for as long as I could. But it reaches a point where you just wind up saying to yourself that maybe it all turns out the way it does because we have it coming. That we don't deserve to survive. And if that's really the case . . . if we don't deserve to . . . then who am I to get in the way of our deserved extinction?"

"I do not understand how you can have such a dim opinion of your own race."

"Why not? Do your kind hold that much higher an opinion of

humanity? Hunting us near to extinction, keeping the few remaining of us as slaves. It must be staggering for your frame of reference to know that a pathetic human being is the dreaded Overseer."

"It is . . . revelatory, Colonel. But my opinion of humanity has not been as dire as all that. I have been impressed by what your people were capable of accomplishing."

"That is because you didn't know us as well as I did." He spoke with a grim sadness. "I knew us as only one who has fought for our preservation could. Ah. Here we are."

The elevator had slowed and now the doors opened. They stepped into a large room with light flooding in. Nicrominus had literally lost track of time. Dawn was coming up, the first rays of the sun spreading tentatively across the city.

There was an observation deck outside and the Colonel walked out onto it, Nicrominus following. A large set of curved metal bars reached around the perimeter, obviously designed as a safety measure.

"You think that the Twelve Races are warlike," said the Colonel.

"I know they are. Were it not for the Firedraques, and the authority we carry in the name of the Overseer . . ." His voice trailed off.

The Colonel smiled at that. "Yes. Your precious authority, devolved from me and enforced by the Travelers. Imagine a world devoid of that authority, as would be the case were the Twelve Races to know that the Overseer were a lowly human."

"It could well be chaos."

"Yes, indeed."

"Or," said Nicrominus thoughtfully, "it could establish the foundation we require to re-create the human race. That would seem to be a necessity, if you believe the theory that I have put forward in regards to the very essence of reality that they provide."

"I am not entirely sure I believe it, although I'll tell you this, Nicrominus: It's just insane enough to be true. Except here's the thing: I'm not convinced that resurrecting the human race is a necessity, or even a good thing."

Nicrominus was dumbfounded to hear such a notion. "How can you possibly say that, Colonel?"

The Colonel leaned against what appeared to be some sort of viewing device. "I won't lie to you, Nicrominus. When the voices first offered me this—job—I saw the possibilities of payback for what they had done to us. I figured I could find ways to manipulate the Twelve Races into obliterating each other, and sit back and laugh on behalf of my demolished race. I was going to enjoy watching the Twelve Races crash and burn. However the more I thought about it, and the more time I had to ponder it—and obviously I had more than enough time—the more I was forced to the conclusion that not only were the Twelve Races no less deserving to survive than humanity, but that they were in fact more deserving to survive."

"I don't understand, Colonel. Look at that," and Nicrominus gestured toward the entirety of the city that lay sprawled beneath them. "Look at what your people accomplished! We have nothing like that in the Elserealms! Nothing! Your achievements—"

"They mean nothing."

"But Colonel—"

"It's soulless, Nicrominus. They're just buildings, just architecture. The things that we did . . . they're just things." The Colonel sighed heavily and there was great sadness in his voice, in his face. "They're just a vast, elaborate façade to cover up the fundamental emptiness in our souls. Hell, I couldn't say for sure that we even have souls." He turned back toward Nicrominus. "You haven't seen what I've seen, my friend. You haven't seen the great evils that humans are capable of perpetrating upon each other. At least with the Twelve Races, you were attacking someone other than yourselves. Beings to whom you by rights had no emotional or spiritual attachment. But the things that we've done to each other . . . that I've seen us do to each other . . ."

He stopped talking. Nicrominus waited and, when the Overseer did not speak immediately, he prompted, "Colonel—?"

"Sometimes," said the Colonel so softly that Nicrominus had to strain to hear, "I think the reason humans have such limited life spans is that, if we're around for too long, then we have too much time to think about what we've seen. What we've done. In my case, what I've seen us do, and had to do, and been ordered to do. I killed women, Nicrominus. Women and children, and the types of people I swore to protect, and I was given medals for it and awards and a high rank. And the things we've built to destroy each other, from the smallest virus to the biggest bomb. The inhumanity, the brutality that became the hallmark of our day to day existence . . . it would stagger your imagination. And every time I would encounter yet another example of what we were capable of doing to each other, I would die a little more inside. And now I've had years and years to dwell on it, more years than any human should rightfully have. And all I can do is think that, considering what we were doing not only to each other, but to the very planet itself . . . considering all that . . . perhaps our extinction is the absolute best thing that could have happened. Your people may have done us a tremendous service, annihilating us and saving us the trouble of slowly drowning in a vast cesspool of our own making and quite possibly taking the planet down with us.

"And now you're telling me that resuscitating our race has become an imperative? That it's necessary not only for the survival of this sphere, but the Elserealms . . ."

"And possibly the entirety of reality, yes,"

"Then maybe reality doesn't deserve to exist. Maybe humanity is the litmus test, the yardstick by which we're supposed to measure just how worthwhile the universe is to save from entropy. And if we're going to judge reality by that standard, then I think the solution pretty much presents itself, don't you?"

"With respect, Colonel, I do not think that at all. Nor, if I may be so bold, do I think the gods believe that. Or do you place no more stock in the reality of gods than you do in the right of your race to exist?"

"I did," said the Colonel with a sigh. "Once upon a time, many long years ago. I believed in the notion of a single great being looking down upon us, having a master plan and with our best interests at heart. But now?" He shook his head. "Now I very much doubt it."

"I do not," said Nicrominus firmly. "There are forces in the universe that we cannot comprehend—"

"More in heaven and earth than is dreamt of in our philosophy?" said the Colonel, chuckling slightly.

"Yes. Very much so. There is order in the world, and there is chaos. Two factions that are capable of butting against each other," and he thumped his fists together, "or," and then he interlaced his fingers, "working together. Order and chaos, if they act in an obstructionist manner, can inflict great destruction. But if they work with each other—if they ally—they can accomplish anything."

"I can see that," said the Colonel. "This world, born out of chaos, and then cooling and becoming . . . ordered, I suppose."

"Yes. And it was the hand of the divine that brought order out of that chaos. I believe that hand remains in existence to this day. Beings infused with the spirit of order and chaos walk among us, touching the world, influencing events."

"Fanciful."

"Perhaps. On the other hand, I would submit that this very conversation we are having is proof of His divine hand."

"How do you figure that?" The Colonel sounded genuinely interested.

"Why else would we have been brought together if not for a particular reason?" said Nicrominus. "You have trusted me with a great many secrets this day. Secrets that none others save, I assume, the Travelers know."

"Not even the Travelers," said the Colonel. "I have never spoken to any other living being as I have spoken to you."

"There, you see? Further proof of trust. Here we are: I, the person who has come to believe he knows why the hotstars are dying, and you, the person who holds the power to reverse the trend. We need humans. We need to repopulate the species. At such a time, who better to lead us in our efforts than a human?"

The Colonel stared at him, looking incredulous, and then started to laugh. He laughed so hard that tears began to well in his eyes and he had to wipe them away. "Is that what you think is going to happen? That I'm going to be Adam and we're going to trot in a series of Eves so that I can singlehandedly regenerate the species with my mighty seed? Is that what you believe is God's plan? Because if it is, then it's a pretty damned stupid one."

"I would not presume to know God's plan."

"Well," said the Colonel affectionately, and he rested a hand on Nicrominus's shoulder, "that makes two of us."

"I assure you, Colonel, I wish I did know what His plan was."

"Good news in that regard, Nicrominus. I believe I can help you, by arranging for you to ask Him."

It was only at that moment that Nicrominus realized his danger, but it was too late. The Colonel's hand swung quickly and struck Nicrominus in a nerve cluster just below his shoulders. Nicrominus felt all power of movement vanish from his body, and before he do anything, say anything, the Colonel had lifted him off his feet. His strength was astounding, although it might very well have been powered by his armor.

"I'm sorry, Nicrominus. But the last thing this planet needs is more humans. Or any humans."

And then Nicrominus was flying, up, up, up and over the metal rails that served as protection toward anyone who might fall from such a tremendous height. He would have reached out to snatch at it, but he remained unable to move.

A vast drop yawned beneath him, and he had just enough time to realize that he'd never had the opportunity to ask what the purpose of those flashing lights at the intersection were. Then visions of his daughter and Xeri and Norda Kinklash all spiraled in front of him. They seemed to be saying good-bye.

He fell, slamming into an extension of the building, and there was the loud crack of his back snapping as he rebounded from it and tumbled out into midair. The last thing he saw was the sun rising, and he wondered how he had never noticed just how beautiful it was, and then the pain from his shattered back finally caught up with him and caused his brain to shut down.

By the time he hit the ground he was already long gone.

II.

NORDA KINKLASH WAS SURPRISED TO discover that she was waking up in exactly the same place as she had fallen asleep.

This caught her off guard for several reasons. First, for Norda, the division between reality and fantasy was always a shaky one at best. To her they coexisted nicely with each other. So if something was happening to her, she was never entirely certain whether she was dreaming it was happening or it was actually happening, or for that matter if she was dreaming it while she was awake. It was, as far as she was concerned, an exciting way to live, presuming she was actually living it. She might have been dreaming all of it. No way to be sure.

Second, Norda had been absolutely positive that, presuming what she thought had happened had actually, in fact, happened, that Arren would be along in short order to rescue her from her predicament. That was, after all, what Arren did. He made certain that he was there for her at all times, which meant that she had the luxury of being the way she was and not having to worry about the ramifications.

Consequently, she had hitched a ride on the very same Zeffer that had absconded with New Daddy (as she had come to refer to Nicrominus, having only the vaguest memory of her original father) and had done so with impunity. She had given no thought to her action other than that it seemed like a wonderfully good idea, and if she got into too much trouble, Arren would find a way to rescue her. She had clung to that notion in the exact same manner that she clung to the tall spike atop the building.

Norda had been getting extremely hungry for a while, but a few passing birds that got too close to her, doubtless out of curiosity over never having seen anything like her before, had enabled her to attend to that problem. She had snatched one right out of the air with her hand while ensnaring another with her tail, crushing both of them to death in an instant. Then she had devoured them hungrily, feathers, bones and all. The feathers tickled as they slid down her gullet, and every so often she coughed up another small cluster of them. But they had at least satisfied her hunger, although she still remained powerfully thirsty. To allow herself some rest, she had sung herself to sleep with a gentle song that she found particularly relaxing.

She dreamed of Arren saving her with such certainty that, when she awoke, she was genuinely surprised to discover that she was still atop the spike. She was also surprised to discover that she had some fleeting memory of a dream that didn't quite seem to fit within her own head. There was a human, a female she was reasonably sure, in the dream, and she could have sworn that the human female was looking right at her even though they were in fact nowhere near each other. It didn't make a whole lot of sense to her, but then again, most things didn't.

Norda blinked against the rays of the slowly rising sun, and that was when she heard something from below. The sounds of thumping, something hitting something else. She looked down and saw a man in the strangest suit of gleaming metal, and he was holding New Daddy over his head. She couldn't fathom why. Perhaps New Daddy wanted to have a better view of the city and the metal man wanted to help him by providing him an improved vantage point.

And then she watched the metal man throw New Daddy high in the air, over a fence, and New Daddy fell and fell and at first Norda still did not understand what she was seeing. When she finally did comprehend it, when she realized that she was watching New Daddy being thrown to his death, her impulse was to believe that what she was seeing was not, in fact, happening. That it was just another dream, another fantasy from the fevered mind of Norda

Kinklash that bore no resemblance to the real world.

At some point, as a stiff wind blew across her face, she realized that this was not so. What she was seeing was actually happening, and what was actually happening was terrible beyond belief.

She had never witnessed anyone's death before. She had been the cause of it. For instance, she had released a gigantic bell from a tower that had crushed an enemy of her brother into paste. It hadn't bothered her in the least, and she had applauded herself over her cleverness and resourcefulness.

But this was different, because this was New Daddy. New Daddy, who had found her adorable and pleasant to talk to and was quite obviously charmed by her. He was going to fill the void in her life that Arren could not, no matter how much he tried. He was going to teach her things and care about her and the notion that she might be witnessing his death was so overwhelming that she had no desire to believe it. She wanted to believe that he would somehow manage to slow his descent and land gently upon the ground, and she would be waiting there for him and they would have a good laugh together over it and at the silly man in metal who thought that he had killed New Daddy.

Norda loved games, loved fantasies, loved to live in her own head, and that was where she wanted to remain rather than deal with what she was seeing.

But she could not.

This was too big, too monstrous, too unjust, and as much as she wanted to run away deep into her head and not deal with it, the enormity of it pulled her out of herself and squarely into the real world.

Norda Kinklash felt something breaking within her and realized belatedly it was her heart.

Then she felt something else, something black and powerful forming around that same broken heart and mending it and darkening it and making it a fearful and frightful thing.

Never in her life had Norda Kinklash hated anyone before. She didn't have the capacity for it.

That all changed when she witnessed the death of Nicrominus.

The metal man was still standing there, staring down toward the street. From the angle she was perched, she could not see his face. She didn't know if he was smiling or sad. She didn't care. All she wanted was to see him dead.

Her impulse was to leap down upon him, to tear into him, rip his head off, send his body tumbling down into the street so that he would be able to keep Nicrominus company. But before she yielded to that impulse, she found herself wondering what Arren would do in a similar situation, because he was ever-so-clever at figuring out ways and means to dispose of people.

And Arren, in her imagination, said to her gently but firmly, *Wait. Not now. Not yet. You have to wait.*

She stayed where she was. She stayed there and watched as the metal man reached down, picked up his helmet, and placed it back upon his head. He twisted it and it slid into place with a slight "click." Seeing this caused Norda to curse herself that she had made no move, because he was now effectively impervious to whatever harm she might be able to inflict upon him.

It was a new sensation for her, wanting to inflict harm. That time with the bell, when she had conspired with Arren, it hadn't been personal or stemming from any sort of enmity. It had just been part of a grand game of power that Arren had put together. That was how he had explained it to her.

Not this time, though. Not anymore. This time she was seized with cold, implacable fury. But fortunately the words of Arren the Schemer, Arren the Planner, were wisely counseling her and preventing her from meeting a demise as quickly and as assuredly as had New Daddy. Whoever and whatever this metal man was, he was clearly formidable and could not be readily dispatched with a frontal attack, no matter how fueled by righteous fury it was.

She had to wait.

But she knew that there was one thing for which she could no longer wait: her brother. Perhaps Arren would eventually show up, or perhaps not. Perhaps she would find him, given time, or perhaps she would never see him again. The latter notion would have overwhelmed her with grief at one time, causing her to curl up into a ball and become inconsolable.

Not now. Not this time.

Fortunately she felt as if she had Arren in her head, right there with her, instructing her, telling her what to do. Sadly, he wasn't telling her how to go about it, save to counsel caution. That she could do.

The metal man had turned away from the observation deck and disappeared from view. She was actually able to hear a faint clanking from his armored feet that receded until he was gone. The wind continued to buffet her and the chill had worked its way into her bones. As a result when she made her first efforts to move, her muscles protested and her joints ached. She overcame such discomforts, though, because ultimately they were minor and nothing for her to concern herself over.

Slowly she made her way down the spike. She had no fear that she was going to fall. She had no fear of anything, really, because all other emotions save anger had been washed away from her upon witnessing New Daddy's demise. When the wind tried to pluck her from the spike and send her tumbling to the streets far below, she simply wrapped her tail around the spike and steadied herself until the winds subsided. She had no idea quite how long it took, because she had never been much for keeping track of time's passage even during her best periods.

Finally she had drawn near enough to the observation deck that she was able to release her hold and drop down to it. She landed in a crouch and her forked tongue flicked out and sampled the air.

"Mandraques do nothing in half measures," she whispered. It was the mantra of her people, the truism that caused other races to tremble at the merest mention of Mandraques. She had never had much reason to care about such matters, because she'd never really been much of a Mandraque. She had been far too busy living in her own world. "Not anymore," she continued to whisper. "Now I'm going to live in this one. But the metal man won't. Because I'm going to take him out of it."

THE OUTSKIRTS OF FERUEL

I.

KARSEN HAD NEVER SEEN SO many whores in one place, but he knew that managing to get one between his legs would solve a lot of his problems.

Eutok drew close to him, hiding behind the same rock that Karsen was. The smell that wafted from the Trull was still fairly powerful, and Karsen would have far preferred it if Eutok had been several yards downwind of him. But he decided that it wasn't worth saying anything or starting an argument over.

The whores were magnificent animals, Karsen had to admit that much. There were about a dozen of them in various colors, sizes and shades. Native to the Damned World, they were four-legged and tall and moved with an undeniable grace even though their hooves made a curious "clip clop" sound. Their eyes displayed a remarkable native intelligence. Every so often one of the whores would toss their heads and their great black manes of hair would flip around. It was so beautiful that Karsen almost wanted to cry.

"Amazing, aren't they," he murmured.

"They are . . . impressive," said Eutok grudgingly. "Why are we watching them?"

"Because they can be of benefit to us."

"Good eating, are they? That would be fortunate since the game has been slim."

"No, not for eating."

Eutok looked from Karsen to the whores and then back again. "How else then? Are you that starved for sexual congress?"

"What . . . ? No!" Karsen hadn't understood at first, but once he did his face twisted in disgust. "How could you think that?"

"You're half animal. I don't know where your preferences lie."

"Yes, you do! You know that I am doing everything I can to find Jepp!"

"And she's a Mort. Obviously your interests lie toward species other than your own. How am I to know where you draw the line?"

"I draw it at them. I do not have sex with whores. No respectable creature would. It's a beastly notion."

"Fine," said Eutok who clearly had lost interest in that aspect of the conversation. "What did you have in mind, then?"

"We ride them."

"Ride them? I thought sex was not an aspect of your interests . . ."

"It's not! In the name of the gods, Eutok, focus your attentions elsewhere!" He pointed at the animals, who remained oblivious to their presence. "Humans used to sit astride the creatures, balanced atop them. They are responsive to commands and can move very quickly over vast distances. Much faster than we can move on either foot or hoof."

"How do you know that is what humans used to do with whores?"

"My mother told me. And she is usually right about things having to do with humans."

"My mother is usually right about everything, and even when she is wrong, she makes certain that we know her to be right," Eutok said ruefully.

"I believe it. I met your mother. You knew your mother. Hell, you wanted me to kill your mother, an action I still consider reprehensible."

"If you truly knew my mother, rather than simply claiming to, you wouldn't find the action quite so reprehensible."

Karsen Foux shrugged. "That may well be."

Eutok grunted at that and rubbed just under his ribs. There was still visible bruising there, but the bruises and cuts were in the process of healing. "All right, then. What is the plan?"

"If humans can ride whores, so can we."

"That's not a plan so much as it is a statement. A statement I've no reason to believe is true, by the way."

"Then I think it's time we find out. Here's the thing: I need you to roar."

"Roar?"

"Yes. A loud noise that will ideally freeze them in their tracks long enough for us to get close."

"Why do you not roar, if you think it's such a fine idea?"

"I don't do well with roaring."

Eutok gave him a confused look. "Why not?"

Karsen stared down at his hooves, suddenly self-conscious. "My roars tend to sound more like bleats. They are not particularly useful."

"I see how they could paralyze an opponent by causing him to fall down laughing."

Grunting impatiently, Karsen said, "Are you going to help me or not?"

"Fine, fine. Make your move."

Karsen sprang from hiding, opting to move quickly and thus gain the element of surprise since the herd of whores were sufficiently far from their place of cover that sneaking up on them was simply not an option. As he did so, Eutok was right behind him and unleashing a Trull sized bellow that was so terrifying, it almost backfired and caused Karsen himself to freeze in his tracks.

The whores reared up but otherwise looked confused, uncertain of what to do or which way to go. Karsen had had his eye on a large brown one and now he leaped through the air, propelled by his powerful legs, and landed squarely on the back of the one he had selected.

The whores let out a high pitched whinny and attempted to throw Karsen off its back. Karsen clamped his powerful legs together and grabbed onto the sides of the whores' neck to further brace himself.

Eutok was not remotely as spry as Karsen, nor as tall. But he was not without his own resourcefulness, and when he approached a smaller black whores, he grabbed it by the tail and yanked down, hard. His intention was to force it to bring its rump down to his level so that he could then clamber up the back and mount it as Karsen had. It was a good notion in theory but failed in practice as the whores lashed out with its hooves, smacking Eutok squarely in the chest and knocking him back.

This so infuriated Eutok that he bounded to his feet, yanked his battle axe from its holster on his back, and swung it as hard as he could. It slammed into the whores' midsection, crushing its ribcage and collapsing its lungs. The creature went down and Eutok proceeded to pummel it long after life had fled the unfortunate beast's carcass.

"Eutok!" shouted Karsen. "Nothing is to be served by beating dead whores!" His own whores was still trying to throw him off its back, spinning in a circle and bucking single-mindedly. But the more it tried, the more Karsen held on.

Realizing that Karsen was right, but also aware that he was going to require a different approach, Eutok selected it. There was another whores that looked as if it would serve Eutok's needs, but it was a distance away and starting to gallop even further. Eutok picked up a sizable rock, hefted it once to get a feel for it, and then let fly. The rock sailed through the air with precision and struck the whores in the head. The whores went down to its knees, the world no doubt whirling around it. Eutok took the opportunity to trot briskly over to the whores—a large black one—and clambered aboard. The whores offered a whinny in protest but wasn't in condition to do much more than provide token resistance. Moments later the whores got to its feet, staggering a bit as it did so, disoriented both by the blow and by the unaccustomed weight it was bearing.

"Your knees!" Karsen called over to Eutok. "Use your knees to guide it!" He was already finding that he had some control over the whores' direction by applying pressure from his knees, a fact that he was discovering through—he hated to admit it, but it was true—the animal side of him that was represented by his lower half. He was still keeping a firm grip on the base of the whores' throat, but the whores was working less and less to throw Karsen off.

Long minutes passed. The rest of the whores had backed off to a safe distance, watching Karsen and Eutok master the creatures while snorting and whinnying and probably imploring their fellows to toss these interlopers from their backs. But the Laocoon and Trull would not be so easily disposed of, and soon they had the steeds fully under their control.

Eutok actually sounded pleased, which was unusual for Eutok. "This is marvelous!" he said with a chortle. "I've never been this high up before! It . . . it is exhilarating! To see the world from this level!"

"It's a heady notion, to see things from a different perspective, isn't it, Trull?"

"Aye, it is."

So in control of the whores was he, and confident of his position upon it, that Karsen was able to maneuver it toward Eutok with only the lightest of touches upon the beast's neck. "All right, then, Eutok. I trust you haven't become too turned around during this bit of business."

"I know which way we're going, if that's what you mean." He pointed with confidence. "That way."

"That way would be in the general direction of Murako."

"Yes."

"Very well, then. I suggest," and he patted the whores on the shoulders, "that we take it slow to start out. These are still powerful beasts and I have no desire to be thrown from one. Nor, I suspect, do you."

"If it throws me off, it will die for such effrontery."

"In which case you will wind up walking while I ride, so I suggest that you strive to keep your temper in check."

Eutok growled at the reasonable nature of the statement but otherwise kept silent.

They began riding the whores at a brisk trot. It remained a

challenge initially because the whores would want to wander off if they spied something that seemed of particular interest, such as something to eat or a stream of water from which to drink. Karsen and Eutok found that they had to assert themselves, which was slightly challenging for the milder-mannered Karsen but no problem at all for Eutok. As a result, Eutok—after a slower start—transcended the learning curve faster than Karsen did.

Soon they had developed sufficient confidence in their own whoresmanship to bring the animals up to a steady gallop. They covered a far greater distance on the backs of the whores than they could conceivably have done on foot, and even developed a compromise position wherein every few hours they would stop and allow the beasts to refresh themselves by grazing on available grass or drinking at a water source, the water being no less important to Karsen and Eutok than it was to their rides.

Concerned that the animals would wander away, Karsen took some rope that he had in his satchel and affixed them around the whores' necks. He would then tie the other ends around trees, thus guaranteeing that the whores would have no opportunity to take off. After a while it seemed less of a concern. The whores appeared to appreciate their company, and it made Karsen wonder if at some point the animals hadn't actually been domesticated.

The other reason they needed to stop, aside from allowing the whores to rest—because, as Karsen pointed out, "There's only so long you can ride whores before they get worn out"—was Eutok's well being. Although he was responding well to the medicines that Karsen was ministering, he still became tired far more easily than he ordinarily would have. He was far too proud or even stubborn to admit when he was having difficulties, and so Karsen grew accustomed to keeping an eye on him as they rode and deciding when it was time to stop, more for Eutok's benefit than the whores or Karsen.

He resented the necessity of having the Trull with him, but Karsen had still failed to pick up any additional scent of Jepp or the draquons. Eutok, however, claimed that he was able to see places in the rocky surface or barren grounds that they galloped across where the draquons had briefly touched down before gliding again. "Here a small piece of stone was chipped away" he would claim, "definitely as a result of a draquon's claw," and Karsen could not gainsay him because he couldn't be sure it wasn't true.

Doubt continued to gnaw at him, though. The Trull had been injured, possibly on the verge of death, or at the very least slipping into extreme helplessness. He had seen Karsen as a means of avoiding such a fate. Karsen wouldn't put it past Eutok to say or do anything to maintain his hold on Karsen, even if it meant keeping him hoping for a reunion with Jepp that could never be.

Night had fallen, and Karsen and Eutok were both exhausted, although both of them were too stubborn to let on to the other. They had found a passable encampment by a lake, and Karsen had even managed to lure in several fish that he and Eutok had greedily devoured. The whores had been tied off by nearby trees. There were some caves that might have provided shelter, but it was a pleasant enough night and Karsen saw no reason to shut themselves off from the night sky.

Eutok regarded him thoughtfully for a time and then said, "You think I have no idea which way your little human was taken, don't you."

"It concerns me," Karsen admitted.

"I wouldn't do that."

Karsen had been lying on his back, staring heavenward, but now he sat up and stared with bemusement at Eutok. "I'm supposed to take your word for that?"

"I am the son of the Trull Queen."

"A queen whose death you attempted to arrange."

"That does not in the least diminish my status or rank."

"I actually think it does somewhat," said Karsen. "I think that anyone who would take such an action is unreliable and not to be trusted and sacrifices whatever . . . I don't know . . . 'integrity' that might be accorded to one of higher rank."

"Yet you trust me to lead you in your little human's direction."

"Yes, I do. Because I am just that desperate and just that pathetic."

The Trull just stared at him for such a long time, in such silence, that finally Karsen said impatiently, "What? What is it?"

"You are many things with which I could take issue, Laocoon," said Eutok with surprising softness and a distinct lack of his typical surliness. "But 'pathetic' is not one of them. You are not pathetic. Some might find your actions laudable. Even heroic."

Karsen laughed bitterly at that. "Yes, well . . . my clan would not be among them. Particularly not my mother."

"Mothers," said Eutok with a resigned shrug. "What can you do?"

"In your case, you can try to strike a bargain with some Bottom Feeders to end her life."

"Are you going to keep throwing that back at me?"

"It's rather hard to ignore if one is going to keep bringing up mothers."

"Fine. That," and he stabbed a thick finger at him, "is the last time that I endeavor to express sympathy for you."

"Is that what you were doing?" Karsen's face was a study in amazement.

"Shut up."

"No, seriously. I had no idea that's what you were trying to do."

"I told you to shut up."

Karsen was about to speak again, and then he saw the angry glare that Eutok was firing at him and his mouth closed again. Instead he sat there, contemplating the Trull, running the conversation back through his mind. The Trull was not lying down, but instead staring upward at the sliver of moon that was hanging high above. He seemed . . . what? Saddened? Wistful? But why? Why would he be like that? Trulls were relentlessly obnoxious and constantly scheming, claiming that they were neutral and aiding all sides—

except the Piri, of course, who were universally reviled—while on the other hand no doubt trying to manipulate everyone to keep the Twelve Races in a constant state of warfare. Yet there had been something in Eutok's voice, something in his manner, that seemed to stem from something else, something . . .

"No," said Karsen softly.

Eutok fired him an angry glare. "I said no talking."

"I was talking to myself." He hesitated and then said, "But . . ."

He didn't follow up, and the hanging silence clearly annoyed Eutok. "But what?"

Taking a pure shot in the dark, Karsen said, "Who is she?"

The question had the exact effect that Karsen was hoping for. Eutok's spine stiffened and he still had that annoyed look to him, but there was something else as well. Something that almost made him look like a wounded animal. "I don't know what you're talking about," he said, at which point Karsen came to the startled realization that Eutok the Trull was a stupendously bad liar.

"I think you do. I think the actions that one takes on behalf of a female seem ridiculous and benighted to just about anyone except someone who himself has a woman for whom he would do anything, take any risk—"

"Healer or not, I am going to come over there and throttle you if you don't—"

A flash of inspiration exploded within Karsen's mind. "And it's not a Trull female, is it. That's why you're not repulsed by the notion that I'm in love with a human. There's a female for whom you have strong feelings, and she's not one of your own kind. That's it, isn't it?"

"You have no idea—"

"—what I'm talking about, yes, you've said that, except I think I do." He had moved from where he was and vaulted over to the other side of the narrow stream. Eutok's eyes narrowed and his hand strayed toward the battle axe that lay next to him. Karsen ignored it. "Who is she, Eutok?"

"That is none of your concern."

"So you admit there is someone. Some female that is not one of your own. Which is why," and now everything was coming together in his head, "you were so interested in finding a way of disposing of your mother. It wasn't about attaining power. You knew that as long as she ruled, she would never allow you to take other than a Trull as a mate. But if you disposed of her, then the way was clear for you."

Eutok stared off into empty air. He took a deep sigh and let it out in a slow rumble. It seemed as if Karsen's questions had taken some of the energy from him. "The way would never have been clear for us," he said finally. "It was foolishness even to conceive of it. Even with my mother gone, my brother would never have accepted it. And even were he gone, and I were supreme ruler of the Trulls, her presence would have guaranteed insurrection. We would not have survived. Or at the very least, she would not have survived, and that is all that matters."

"Have you considered the possibility that you are underestimating your fellow Trulls?"

Eutok actually seemed to find the notion amusing. "No. I have never considered that possibility."

"But why? Would they be so averse to your interest in a human that—"

"It wasn't a human."

"Oh." That brought Karsen up short. "I just . . . my apologies, I simply assumed that—"

"It wasn't a human. Isn't. She isn't a human."

"Then what—? I mean, if you don't mind my asking . . ."

"I do, actually, but I very much suspect that isn't going to stop you." He hesitated and then said, "I lived my life underground. How many non-Trull females do you think I am liable to encounter?"

Karsen frowned. "I don't understand what you . . ." Then he lapsed into silence, unable to disguise the shock he felt at the very notion. "No."

"You see—"

"A Piri?"

"—this is exactly what I didn't—"

"A Piri?"

"—want to have to deal w—"

"A gods damned Piri?"

Before Karsen could move, Eutok's hand lashed out and clamped around his throat. Karsen's eyes widened in fear as he tried to draw in breath and failed to manage it."

With a low, furious snarl, Eutok said, "You don't know her. You don't know what she's like. So don't act as if you do. Because if you continue to act that way, then you're not going to act in any way, ever again." Making no attempt to hide his disgust, he shoved Karsen aside, allowing him to thud to the ground. Karsen lay there, gasping hungrily for air, clutching at his chest, trying to pull himself together.

Eutok turned his back pointedly to him but remained sitting. "You don't know her," he said again, under his breath, seemingly as much to himself as to Karsen.

Karsen was caught between his strong desire to know how in the world Eutok could possibly become involved with something as repulsive as a Piri and an even stronger desire to purge his mind of what little knowledge of Eutok's assignations he already possessed. Deciding that saying nothing would be better than saying the wrong thing, Karsen pulled himself over to the other side of the narrow brook and lay down to sleep. The large brown whores stared down at him with sympathetic eyes.

Can you believe it? Karsen asked the whores silently.

He lay back, stared up at the stars, fell asleep, and awoke to someone about to kill him.

II.

WHY DID YOU TELL HIM?

Eutok kept going over it and over it in his mind. Granted there was no denying that the Laocoon was extremely intelligent, and had figured out for himself Eutok's secret. Still, Eutok had practically taken him by the hand and led him down the path.

Even so . . .

You didn't have to tell him. You didn't have to tell him or acknowledge that he was at all right. You could have said nothing. Hell, you could have beaten him into silence. But you didn't. And he reacted exactly the way you expected him to.

Except . . .

Why shouldn't he? After all, when you first lay eyes on Clarinda, your intention was to kill her. You wanted to bring her head back to your mother as a trophy. You didn't think of the Piri as anything other than animals. It took ages, and Clarinda's influence, to make you come around to another point of view. So doesn't it make sense that the Laocoon would react with the same disbelief that you initially displayed?

Which brings you back around to why you told him, or allowed him to figure it out, considering that all you could reasonably have expected from him was revulsion.

Maybe it's because you've been carrying this inside you for so long that you wanted to have the opportunity to talk to somebody about it. You couldn't talk to your own brother. The bastard hated you, and you despised him, and if he found you now then things would certainly be no better between you considering all he wants to do is kill you. If my lover is a Piri, then why shouldn't I wind up becoming friends with a Laocoon . . . ?

He stared at Karsen, whose chest was rising and falling in a steady motion. The whores also appeared to be dozing, although curiously they were doing so while standing. He considered that to be very strange. Who or what sleeps standing up? Still, he had to admit that it was handy in case someone tried to sneak up on you while you were asleep. It meant you could start running the instant you realized that there was danger bearing down upon you.

A friend? Is that what you've come to? Have you fallen so low that you are actually worried about acquiring a friend? What do you need with a friend?

He realized he had no answer to that. Having never actually had a friend, he wasn't sure what his life would be like with one. Nor could he entirely comprehend why his thoughts had turned in this direction.

Maybe, he thought, *it's because you have no one and nothing else anymore. You don't even have a brother to hate you, or a mother to despise you, or soldiers to look up to you and obey you in your authority as—*

"Chancellor?"

The voice was nothing more than the softest whisper, and yet Eutok heard it and was immediately on his feet. Karsen, sleeping deeply thanks to sheer exhaustion, did not react. If anything, he snored slightly louder.

It had come from one of the caves. He squinted, trying to see clearly, and then two shadows separated themselves from the shadows within and approached him cautiously.

Trulls. Two Trulls, and even in the dim light that the sliver of moon was providing, their astonishment was evident. "Chancellor?" one of them said again.

Eutok did not recognize them immediately. "Fokor . . . ?" he said uncertainly to the slightly larger of the two.

"Vokar, Chancellor."

"And Tobis," said the other.

"Yes, Vokar . . . Tobis . . . of course." He had his axe in his hand, preparing himself for their inevitable attack. He was, after all, a traitor and a fugitive.

"What are you doing way out here, Chancellor?" said Vokar. He looked with obvious distaste toward Karsen. "And with that?"

It was at that point that the Trull's voice caused, not Karsen to awaken, but the whores. The whores took one look at the new arrivals and, apparently deciding that they were not to its taste, produced a loud and protesting whinny. The other whores did as well, and this was more than enough to awaken Karsen. Upon seeing the other two Trulls, he was immediately up on his hooves.

He kept his hands relaxed at his sides, making no sudden moves, but he was understandably cautious considering he had no clear idea of just what sort of situation he was facing. He looked questioningly at Eutok as if silently asking him how exactly they were supposed to deal with the newcomers.

As for Eutok, he could not quite comprehend why Vokar and Tobis were not attacking him immediately. "He is . . ." His mind raced, trying to come up with an explanation that would seem reasonable. "A spy. A spy on my behalf on Mandraque activities."

"Mandraque activities, Chancellor?" said Vokar. He didn't sound skeptical; merely curious and eager to learn more.

Still they made no move to attack. Instead they were treating him with all the deference that would be required when interacting with the Chancellor of the Trulls.

"Yes." Eutok cleared his throat, trying to sound confident rather than tentative, as if he were still Chancellor rather than a fugitive. "And it would appear that they have acquired weapons from someone other than us. This spy is leading me to a weapons cache that we believe to be somewhere in the vicinity of Murako."

"Really," said Tobis. "Then obviously we wish to assist you, Chancellor."

"Yes, Tobis speaks truly," said Vokar. "In our capacity as long-range scouts, it is not very often that we have the opportunity to be of direct aid to you and the interests of the Trulls."

Karsen's face was carefully neutral. "Long range scouts, you say."

"Yes, Chancellor. We are gone for many turns at a time, and so have very little access to any news from the Hub."

"That is true. We never have any idea what is transpiring. In fact, we are very much looking forward to news from home."

They were now walking toward Eutok with that swaying, slightly waddling stride that Trulls typically had. Eutok felt a flood of relief rushing through him. If he could keep these two Trulls with him, have them watching his back, then that would provide even more safety for him. Of course, they didn't have whores available for the newcomers to ride upon, but perhaps more mounts could be found. Or maybe—

And suddenly Karsen had his war hammer in his hands and he said grimly, "They're about to attack."

"What?" Eutok couldn't believe what he was saying. "What do you mean they're—?"

With a roar that was remarkably similar to that which Eutok had displayed when he and Karsen were charging the whores, Vokar and Tobis came straight at Eutok. Vokar was wielding a massive spiked club, and Tobis a sword carved from stone. They moved quickly, converging from either side.

Eutok was caught completely flatfooted. He had moved away from his battle axe and was empty handed. Vokar whipped his club around and Eutok barely avoided it. He tried to grab at his axe, but Tobis swung his sword around and down and Eutok barely yanked his arm out of the way. If Tobis had connected, it would have shattered Eutok's forearm.

The whores were leaping about, trying to yank free of the ropes that were keeping them affixed.

Karsen vaulted over the brook and swung his war hammer. Vokar, who had been about to take another swing at Eutok, spotted the assault at the last moment and switched targets. He blocked the swing of the hammer with his club. The impact was so violent that it ran the length of Karsen's arms and caused him to lose his grip on the hammer. He leaped to one side as Vokar slammed down his club, which barely missed connecting with Karsen. Karsen lashed out with a hoof and caught Vokar's right wrist, which snapped under the impact. Vokar screamed, dropping his club. He bent to grab it up with his left hand, and then looked up just in time to see the head of Karsen's war hammer sweeping through the air right toward him. He started to shout, "No!" but he didn't have the time, nor would it have made much difference as the head of the war hammer buried itself in Vokar's face, smashing it flat. His brains seeped out of his ears and the Trull collapsed. Karsen had to yank hard to extract the hammer since he had virtually buried it in there.

He turned just in time to see Eutok catching the blade of the stone sword between his massive palms. Tobis blanched as he realized he was unable to free his weapon from Eutok's grip. Furthermore, he saw the Chancellor's face and realized his death was written in Eutok's expression. He released his hold on his sword, backpedalled, and then turn and ran straight for the cave.

Tobis didn't make it. Eutok threw the sword like a javelin and it drove through Tobis's back and out the front, impaling him. Tobis looked down, never more surprised, as he saw the blade sticking out his chest. He tried to grab at it as if he could somehow push it back out the other way and thus survive the fatal wound. Then he lost all feeling to his legs and tumbled forward.

Eutok strode toward him and crouched next to him. "You knew," he said. "The entire time, you knew. And you tried to catch me off guard by acting as if you hadn't heard about what transpired."

"Not tried . . . ," Tobis managed to say. "Did . . . catch you . . . would have . . . if not for damned . . . Bottom Feeder," and he tilted his bearded chin toward Karsen.

"I'm pleased I was able to disappoint you," Karsen said.

Tobis's chin twitched violently, and then before Eutok could move, a wad of bloodied spittle flew from Tobis's lips and landed on his face.

"Traitor," growled Tobis, and then his head slumped to one side and his eyes glazed over.

Eutok reached up, wiped the spittle from his face, and then smeared it on Tobis's beard. For good measure he kicked the dead Trull. Then he reached back around, placed one oversized foot against Tobis's back for balance, and yanked hard. The sword came free with a loud splutch and Eutok studied it. "Decent enough weapon," he said.

"You want it, you're carrying it," said Karsen. He had placed the war hammer back in its strap on his back.

"A warrior should be well armed."

"I'm not a warrior. I just do what I need to do and take no relish in it."

"Nor do I."

"I don't believe you."

"It's true," said Eutok, who knew that it was not. Karsen knew as well but chose not to make an issue of it. Eutok took the sword belt off Tobis's body, fastened it around his own waist, and slid the sword in. "How did you know?"

"Know? That they were simply trying to get close enough to you to kill you?"

"Yes."

Karsen shrugged. "It was obvious. The way they carried themselves, looking ready to leap upon you at the first opportunity. Their fists were clenched. Their words were laced with lies. They tried too hard to sound as if they had not heard what had transpired with you. I know not if Trulls as a race are bad liars, but these examples certainly were."

"We have to hurry and keep hurrying. They will know we are here."

"How will anyone know? We've just dispatched these two."

"They are scouts, true, but scouts report back regularly. They are as expert in navigating Trullers as anyone else," he said, referring to the high speed underground means of conveyance. "When they do not report back, it will be assumed that something has happened to them. The further assumption will be that I was involved, considering that the only thing that would have lured Trulls out from underground would be me. The Trulls will converge on this area, and trust me, Trullers can move far faster than whores."

"I know," said Karsen. "I rode in one, remember?"

"Yes. It seems a lifetime ago, but yes, I remember."

The whores had settled down with the demise of the attacking Trulls. Now Karsen and Eutok remounted, knowing that further attempts at resting in that area would be far too hazardous. "Out of curiosity: Do Trull tunnels reach all the way to Murako?"

"Of course they do. Our digs reach from one end of the land to the other."

"What about to other lands? Other continents?"

Eutok paused and then shrugged. "Not to my knowledge."

"I suppose we have to hope it doesn't come to that, then. Come. We have a long way to go before we dare rest again, I think."

"Aye, we do. By the way . . ."

"Yes?"

Eutok appeared as if he were about to vomit up something truly foul that had lodged in his chest, and then he managed to cough up two words: "Thank you."

"For what . . . oh. For saving your life, you mean."

"For warning me," Eutok said quickly. "You did not save my life. I saved my own life. You simply warned me that my life was in peril. I did the rest."

Astride his whores, Karsen bowed slightly. "I never meant to suggest otherwise."

Moments later they were riding across the plains while birds, as if sharing some manner of psychic link, converged upon the fallen bodies of two Trulls and prepared to feast.

EN ROUTE TO PERRIZ

I.

THE HIDING HAD BEEN THE worst part of the trip.

Initially Clarinda would have thought that it was going to be the constant state of paranoia. The certainty that, at any moment, more Piri would descend upon them and attack them, led by the implacable Bartolemayne.

But it hadn't happened. It had not happened, and she could not begin to guess why that might be. Her mother, Sunara Redeye, had sworn to her that she would be pursued by the Piri no matter where she tried to run.

Why would they stop, she wondered. *They wouldn't stop. That's the only possible answer. They wouldn't stop, which means that they are continuing to pursue us except we're not seeing them. Why are we not seeing them? There must be some reason for it. Why would they hide themselves from us? It must be to lull us into a false sense of security. Which means we cannot relax vigilance for a moment. But that's going to wear us down until we're in no shape to fight or even string coherent thoughts together. What is their plan? Is it possible they don't actually have a plan? Maybe they're not out there at all. Maybe my mother simply decided to let me go, and to hell with me, because if I didn't want to be part of our race, then why should my race go to such lengths to get me back? Maybe she did it out of love. Gods, I hate her.*

Night by night as they trekked, she kept going over the same things in her head. The problem was that the further they got from the land of Feend, the longer the trek took. She had known that was an inevitable result of their putting distance between themselves and their homeland, but it had seemed the only possible means of survival.

The young Ocular had damned near panicked the first time that the sun's rays peered over the horizon. They had not been expecting it, for they were accustomed to the lengthy nights of Feend. Their miles-consuming pace had brought them a healthy distance from Feend in fairly quick time, but now they were paying for it.

Fortunately they were near some burned out city at the time. Clarinda had no idea which one it was. There was so many leftover Mort cities scattered around the entirety of the continent. The more intact ones had been taken over by various tribes and clans and races, but the ones that weren't worth salvaging were left to deteriorate. The smallish city was one of those, and so Clarinda had them take refuge within. There the young Ocular hid from the sun, as did she. Their needs were entirely different, though. In the case of the Ocular, the sun effectively blinded them. The only Ocular whose eye pigmentation had permitted him to function during daylight was Nagel, and he was dead, obliterated by whatever that hideous green glow had been that had transformed their city into a dead zone.

Clarinda, on the other hand, could function in the sun as long as she was covered from head to toe and thus shielded from the damaging effect that the sun's rays had upon her.

So while the Ocular hid within darkened buildings, preserving their ability to see, Clarinda would scout the area as thoroughly as she could to make certain that there was no one lying in wait to attack them during their slumber. Once she had ascertained their safety, she returned to the building they had selected to be their shelter, and she and her small army would get some much needed rest.

When the sun set, they headed off on their way once more.

"How do you know for sure where we're going?" Kerda asked her.

The others were watching her carefully, obviously concerned over the answer. Perhaps they had been talking to each other while she was not around, stirring up concern over their fate under her leadership, instilling doubts. She supposed she couldn't blame them.

"My mother," she said, "was an avid collector of various artifacts relating to Morts. She had, among other things, a map. A chart of the terrain that we're traversing. It marked various cities."

"You can read the Mort language?"

"A little. Not terribly well, and I can't pretend to understand the words. But I can sound out city names, and my mother told me who resided in what cities. She enjoyed educating me just for the sake of doing so."

"And you remember the details of the map? Without looking at it, you know which way we're heading?"

"Yes. I remember the directions. I have it all up here, tucked away in my head. If I close my eyes, I can see them as clearly as if I had the document in my hands. I know which directions north and south, east and west are...initially by the stars . . ."

"Did she have a map of the stars, too?" said Turkin suspiciously, sounding far less credulous than Kerda.

"As a matter of fact, she did," Clarinda said with a certain amount of satisfaction. "A star chart. Groupings of stars in certain patterns can serve as reinforcement for direction. And then there's the rising and the setting of the sun, which may be woefully inconvenient in many respects but at least serves as a firm determination of east and west."

"But how do you know?" demanded Turkin.

"How do I know what?"

"That the maps were correct. That your mother's teachings were correct."

She was about to come up with a dismissive response, telling him he was foolish to voice such concerns. But then she paused, considered it, and shrugged. "I don't. Not really."

"You don't?" Turkin didn't sound especially happy to have won his point. The other Ocular had stopped walking and were looking at each other with uncertainty.

"No. It's entirely possible that everything I was told was a lie. That everything I believed to be true was false. You know," and her voice grew harsh and pointed, "the way it was for all of you when your parents said they would always be there for you. And now they're all lying dead, moldering, and birds are trying to eat their flesh and keeling over dead as well . . ."

The younger Ocular were already starting to sob, and Turkin stepped in close to her, towering over her and said angrily, "Stop it."

"Then stop trying to sow dissent, Turkin," Clarinda said, not backing down. "Stop trying to undermine me. If you have no faith in my ability to lead you, then simply walk away. And any or all of you," she called out, "are welcome to join him. I am not forcing any of you to stay with me, or accompany me to Perriz. You have free will. Go." She paused and then repeated louder and more forcefully, "Go, I said! Go, if you're of a mind to! I will do naught to stop you. I will go ahead on my own, if that is what is required. Or you can come with me, and perhaps find a city where we can take refuge and know some measure of peace amongst the wise and peace loving Firedraques."

The Ocular exchanged uncertain looks, and Clarinda no longer had any patience for it. "Do what you will," she said, and she started walking in the general direction she knew Perriz to be. At that moment she honestly didn't know if they would follow her or not. Within moments, though, she heard their heavy tread, and suddenly she was raised into the air. She looked around in surprise and saw that Turkin, looking annoyed but resigned, was lifting her onto his shoulders. "No point in moving at your speed when we can move at ours," he said.

Every single one of the Ocular moved into formation behind him and they continued to make their way across unknown terrain, guided by the memories of a Piri and the glittering of the North Star.

II.

"WHAT ARE THESE?"

Berola had lost track of how many days and nights had passed since they had embarked upon their journey. They had blurred one into the other, each pretty much the same. They would find shelter for during the daylight hours and during the night would march across the tattered landscape of what had once been a world of humans. They crossed long roads made of hard, black surfaces with white stripes down the middle that seemed to go on forever. They crossed bridges, they passed shattered statues. Berola had never given much thought to humans beyond the notion that they had once been the dominant species on the Damned World and now no longer were. Seeing this staggering array of achievements, brought low by the Third Wave of the Twelve Races, she felt the first tinge of regret, starting to think that perhaps something great had once inhabited these lands and that maybe it wasn't quite fair and just that they had had it all taken away from them. When she had conveyed her thoughts to Turkin, however, he had simply shrugged indifferently. "If they were meant to keep it, they would have managed to overcome the invasion," he said, and Berola couldn't think of a way to argue that.

Now, though, Berola had come across something that was new. It cut across the ground, two sets of metal rails with wood planks between them. They seemed to go a great distance in either direction. The other Ocular gathered around to see what she had discovered. Clarinda crouched next to her, touching the coldness of the rails and letting out a low whistle.

"Clarinda, what is it?" Berola said again.

"It bears a strong resemblance to the tracks crafted by Trulls for their Trullers."

"Their what?"

"Special conveyances that run underground very quickly and take them wherever they wish to go."

"Have you ever seen one?"

Clarinda smiled grimly. "Trulls have no more love for Piri than your sires did."

Berola noticed that Clarinda hadn't exactly answered the

question, but she did not pursue it. Clarinda, meantime, rose and took a few steps along the track. "Perhaps they had conveyances similar to Trullers," she said thoughtfully.

"If we can find one, we can move more quickly," Kerda said.

"I doubt that will happen. But this track is heading in the general direction that we wish to go. I say we follow it, see where it leads us."

"Which way?" said Turkin.

Clarinda glanced heavenward once more to make certain that she was properly aligned with the stars and then said, "That way." Turkin then lifted her onto his back and they set out.

They moved for a good long time without complaint. Berola was rather relieved by this. She had gotten frankly sick of the younger ones mewling about their lost parents. The fact that she had yet to do so was something Turkin picked up on, and he asked her about it. She had just fixed him with a steady gaze and said, "My parents are no great loss."

"What do you mean by that?" Turkin had asked.

"What I mean by that is that I am not interested in discussing it," she had said, and that had more or less ended the conversation.

Then one of them, a female, began singing. It was some sort of Ocular marching song, one that they had been taught when they were very young. Another female joined in, and then one of the males, and soon the lot of them were singing in unison.

Clarinda was looking at them nervously, and Berola asked her what the problem was. "I am just worried that someone who would be better off not knowing where we are could overhear and . . ."

"Shall I tell them to cease?"

Clarinda thought about it for a time, and then smiled wanly. "No. No, it's all right. This is the first time I've seen them happy as a group since the fall of their home. I'm not about to deprive them of that."

"I think that's wise, mistress," said Berola.

"Don't call me that," Clarinda said sharply.

"I'm sorry. I . . . it was just a term of respect . . ."

"It's all right." Clarinda reined herself in and then assured her,

"You said nothing wrong. Did nothing wrong. I just . . ." She closed her eyes. "Do not worry about it. 'Clarinda' will be just fine."

"As you wish, Clarinda."

So they continued to walk and sing and when the singing ran its course, it was replaced with idle conversation about things having to do with other than their current situation and the loss of their old life. Berola realized that they were actually becoming comfortable with each other.

Every so often they would come upon additional tracks, flaring out to one side before reconnecting with the main one upon which they walked.

With sunrise imminent, they saw a small house a short distance ahead of them. There was what appeared to be a platform raised above the track. The Ocular converged on the small house, and Berola noticed what appeared to be signs posted up on a pole to the left of the tracks, opposite the platform. There were two of them with arrows pointing in opposite directions. "I think those say the directions of cities," said Berola. "Clarinda, do you have any idea what those say?"

Clarinda climbed down from Turkin's shoulders and studied them. "Vuh . . . aye . . . enn . . . ay," she translated of the one pointing in the direction from which they had come.

"Was that on the map your mother showed you?"

"I think so. I think it was. And the other . . . ." The sign was shorter, and this time she sounded it out to herself before a broad smile broke across her face.

"What? What is it?" said Berola.

"Perriz."

This immediately prompted excited murmurs in response from the Ocular. "Are you sure?"

"Yes, Berola, I am sure."

"How far?" said Turkin. "How far does it say it is?"

"I don't know. The distances don't mean anything to me. But that tells us for absolute certain that we are heading in the right direction." She looked defiantly at the Ocular. "Unless there are any of you left doubting me."

Many heads were shaken in response.

"Good," she said, pleased.

They took refuge in the small house opposite the tracks and slept.

III.

CLARINDA . . . WHERE do you think you are going, my love?

Clarinda twists and turns in her sleep, uncertain, frightened, sure that she is beyond her mother's grasp, but fearful that she is wrong.

Sunara is drifting naked in a pool of blood in her sanctum back in Subterror, and now she stands and looks contemptuously toward her daughter, one perfect eyebrow raised in amusement. Slowly she rises so that she is standing, the blood coming to her hips, her hair thick with red, pushed back from her flat chest so that Clarinda can see the gashes where her breasts once were.

Do you truly think you can escape me? Escape my reach? Do you honestly believe that anything you are doing is beyond my control or without my permission? You are exactly and precisely where I need you to be. You believe yourself to be operating on your own, but you have no free will. You will serve me and the needs of the Piri, even when you think that you are doing what you wish to do. You have nothing save what I give you, and you are nothing save what I allow you to be. And all that you will ever be is my daughter.

She throws back her head and laughs, and Clarinda let out a loud and terrified scream.

Clarinda sat up violently awake and realized that all eyes were upon her. The Ocular were sitting up in various states of confusion. Other Ocular who had been sleeping under the platform (since there had been insufficient room for everyone within the house) were shouting, demanding to know what was happening since the sun had not yet set and so they were effectively blind.

"It's nothing!" Clarinda called out, her voice carrying. Her breath was still ragged in her chest. She felt disoriented and not a little frightened. "Everything is fine!"

"How in the name of the gods is everything fine?" said Turkin challengingly, his single great orb affixed upon her.

"It was just a dream. A bad dream."

Berola took both of Clarinda's hands in one of hers, and they seemed to disappear into the Ocular's grasp. "Are you sure it was just a dream?"

No. I'm not sure at all. In fact, I'm almost positive it was anything but.

"Yes," said Clarinda firmly. "That's all it was. And dreams can't hurt you."

UPPER REACHES OF SUISLAN

THE LODGE WAS ALIVE WITH laughter and music and celebration. The only member of the Serabim who was not feeling especially merry was Pavan. Unfortunately, he was the one for whom the festivities were being held.

Serabim musicians were sitting in the rafters of the vast wooden structure which hugged one of the lower peaks in the Upper Reaches. One of them was steadily banging away on a drum, while two more on either side were blowing into curved rams horns of varying sizes. The result was more cacophony than symphony, and the general belief was that Serabim music was capable of sending even Mandraques running. But the Serabim liked it, and of course that was all that mattered.

The dancing that ensued through the lodge mostly consisted of the Serabim thudding against each other chest to chest. Every so often one of them would shout, "Pavan!" and the rest would bellow, "Pavan!" in response. Pavan would wave to them, and be handed another flask of yond to drink. He would obediently toss back the yond, and it would dribble around his mouth and down his fur because he wasn't really much of a yond drinker. But it didn't make any difference because the Serabim would cheer just as loudly as ever.

Eventually Pavan drifted away from the main body of the partying and found himself staring out one of the large windows which opened out onto the magnificent view of the Upper Reaches. It was dark out and he could see the wind blowing drifts of snow off the mountain tops. Thanks to their thick coats of fur, the Serabim were generally immune from the ravages of the Upper Reaches even when the winds and chill were at their most devastating.

A hand rested gently upon his shoulder. He did not even have to look up to know who it was. "Shouldn't you be at the party before your father notices your absence?" he said.

Demali dropped down next to him and pressed her body against him. Her soft, golden fur smelled the way it always did, and Pavan found it as intoxicating as it ever was. "My father," she said, and yond wafted from her breath, "my father knows nothing about nothing."

"Your father is our chief and I don't think he'd appreciate your describing him that way."

She grinned widely, displaying her teeth. She was extremely proud of them, particularly their healthy yellow sheen. "I think I will describe him in any way I wish. He doesn't much like Akasha, you know."

"Nobody likes Akasha," said Pavan, but he was starting to get rather uncomfortable. "He is an independent thinker. Like you," he added teasingly.

"I have no idea what you mean."

"Oh, come now, Demali. Do you think I don't know about your wanting to be a rider?"

She shushed him hurriedly, looking around as if concerned that her father was eavesdropping. "A meaningless fantasy. I have never shown any aptitude for being able to control a Zeffer."

"When have you even tried?"

"Only the biggest and strongest of us can control them. You know that."

"So maybe you could control a smaller Zeffer."

"Stop speaking of such things. It's a waste of time. To be daughter of the chief is sufficient responsibility for one lifetime. I'll leave more important concerns to you and to Akasha. He is the Keeper, after all. He knows what he means to our people. My father doesn't like that he can't control Akasha. That is why," and she encircled her arm around his, "he is very much looking forward to the day when you become Keeper."

"That's very kind of you to . . . wait, what?"

Instead of replying with anything that he was expecting, Demali pressed her face forward against his and nuzzled the base of his neck. Pavan's concerns over what she had said quickly vanished in a wave of warmth from the touch of her lips and the delightful sensation of her teeth nipping at him. In the past, his relationship with Demali had always been more of mutual teasing than anything. Now, though, there was nothing teasing in what she was doing. Instead she was moving her hands with very clear intent, far more deliberately than anything she had ever done in the past.

Pavan pushed her away, as surprised at his own actions as she clearly was. "What's the matter? Aren't I doing it right?" she said.

"That's not the problem. The problem is—"

"And what goes on here?"

Pavan nearly jumped high into the air as a result of the very loud and unexpected interruption. The boisterous voice, and Pavan's reaction to it, was sufficient to generate loud and raucous laughter from the onlooking Serabim.

The chieftain of the Serabim was standing over him, and he gripped Pavan firmly by the elbow and hauled him to his feet. He took his official title of "Sera" from the first part of their race's name, and his surname was affixed to it. Thus was he Seramali, and he was laughing loudly as a disoriented Pavan was brought to standing next to him. Seramali was nearly a head shorter than Pavan, and yet he seemed much larger somehow, his boisterousness capable of filling the largest of rooms. "Just how well," he said with mock sternness, "are you getting to know my daughter?" Then he gestured for the others to howl their amusement, which the Serabim obediently did.

"We were just talking," said Pavan defensively.

"It seemed to these old eyes that you were just talking and she was interested in far more."

"Father!" said Demali in horror, although it might well have been faking her being appalled. Pavan was not well schooled in the ways of females and found it hard to be sure.

Pavan wanted to confront Seramali right there, right in front of everyone. He wanted to shout in his face, *What are you up to? To what end are you manipulating your daughter? Would you try to use my interest in her to seize control of the Zeffers?*

On the other hand, what if he were imagining it? How would that come across to the rest of the Serabim, showing such disrespect for, and anger with, their leader?

Besides, it was impossible for Seramali to take over the Zeffers from the Keeper in any event. That was just the way it was, and always would be. Having influence over the Keeper didn't even necessarily translate to having influence over the Zeffers. The Riders had the Zeffers, but the Zeffers had the Keepers, and such was the way in which balance was maintained.

Seramali was laughing loudly at his daughter's expression of mortification. The other Serabim were joining in. There were not that many Serabim in this particular tribe, less than a hundred. There had been enough cold, mountainous regions for the Serabim to spread out, and the different tribes preferred it that way. The white furred males disliked the prospect of mixing with the brown furred males, and the browns with the blacks, and so on. Akasha tended to rant about it at length, claiming that it was a dangerous position for the Serabim to take because it left them vulnerable. Seramali and the other Serabim routinely laughed off such concerns. Pavan likewise didn't think they had much foundation, but out of respect to his mentor, he tended to keep his doubts on that score to himself.

"I believe I have embarrassed my daughter enough," said Seramali. He stretched out a clawed hand and automatically someone thrust a mug of yond into it. "Today we celebrate the nineteenth cycle around the sun of Pavan, our great Keeper in waiting. Akasha speaks very highly of you, Pavan."

"Well," and Pavan gave a half smile, "he tries to keep it to himself."

This prompted yet more spirited laughter from the collected Serabim. One had had so much yond that he toppled off the upper railing he was sitting on and hit the floor hard. His mug of yond spattered everywhere.

"In two more cycles," Seramali went on when the laughter subsided, "Pavan will be ready to undertake the responsibilities of the Keeper. On Pavan will rest the needs of the Zeffers, and personally I do not think their needs could be in better hands."

"With all respect, Seramali, they are already in firm and capable hands, and I am not ready to—"

"Do not," Seramali ordered him, "attempt any false modesty, Pavan. You are a valued part of the great circle."

"Oh, here he goes again," muttered Demali, except her voice carried more than she expected and so everyone heard. She clapped her hands over her mouth in mortification even as her stray comment prompted laughter from everyone within the lodge.

Fortunately her father was laughing loudest of all. "My daughter knows me all too well. She knows that I will say that you, Pavan, are part of the vast circle in which all life exists. Those residing in the heights will be brought down to the depths, and those dwelling in the depths will be raised on high. That is simply the way of things, and you should not try to dismiss or diminish your place in that vast cycle."

"I was not attempting to do either one. I was just—"

Seramali cut him off with a swift gesture. "You're about to defend Akasha again, aren't you."

"I do not think for a moment the Keeper requires defending. I just—"

The main door to the lodge banged open and a dark figure entered in a burst of swirling snow. "I believe I heard the name 'Keeper' mentioned just now. I would meet this Keeper. I suggest you tell me where he is and give him no more thought."

All eyes turned to the speaker, who had a deep, gravelly voice that was not remotely akin to the more sonorous tones common to the Serabim.

It was a Mandraque.

Pavan had no idea how in gods' name a Mandraque had managed

to gain access to the Lodge. Mandraques' hides were typically durable, and yet this Mandraque was wrapped in furs from head to toe. It made sense; Mandraques were warm-blooded and didn't do especially well in cold weather, which made the presence of one in the Lodge remarkable.

Even more remarkable was that he was wielding a sword. Vastly outnumbered, he looked as if he was actually intending to pose some manner of threat. The main door to the Lodge was hanging half open, the stiff wind trying to push it open further. With a snap of his broad tail he slammed the door shut.

Seramali stepped forward, moving protectively so that he was between Demali and the intruder. He carried no weapon because this was a time of celebration and therefore no combat had been anticipated. Not that Serabim necessarily needed weapons, although they were known to carry them if the situation warranted it. Still, they were massively built, incredibly strong, with thick layers of fur that protected them from attacks ranging from harsh gusts to fearsome blows, not to mention fingers and toes that ended in curved black claws. Serabim were living arsenals of combat. So much so, in fact, that between their physical prowess and their choice of habitat, they were never in positions where they had to battle foes or defend themselves.

For the most part, Pavan was sure that this was not going to be one of those times. Still, mental warning bells chimed within his head. Mandraques did nothing in half measures, and if a Mandraque had shown up in the Lodge acting as if he had nothing to fear from the inhabitants, then the chances were that he really did have nothing to fear. That fact alone should have been sufficient to cause concern for all the Serabim in the Lodge.

Unfortunately Pavan seemed to be the only one who was worried about it.

Several of the Serabim were swaggering toward the Mandraque, who never lowered his sword or acted in any way as if he were in the slightest amount of trouble. Seramali approached as well, although he remained toward the outer edge of the advancing circle.

"Who are you and what do you think you're doing here?" said Seramali, raising his voice so that the whole of the Lodge could hear him. Some of the Serabim were not in the main lobby but instead had retired to other rooms further away to engage in individualized entertainment. Seramali's voice would doubtless carry and alert them to return because a potential threat had presented itself and all Serabim should be around to deal with it.

The Mandraque bowed slightly. It was obvious from his smirk that he was doing so out of a sense of irony rather than any genuine respect for those whom he was facing. "I am Thulsa Odomo. Leader of the Odomo Clan, foremost of the Five Clans."

"I do not know that there is such a thing as a foremost clan when it comes to Mandraques," Seramali said drily. "To those on the outside, all you Mandraques are identical in your belligerence and bellicosity. What matter to us which clan you belong to? All that matters is that you do not belong here. However," and he returned the bow in as ironic a manner as Thulsa had initiated it, "you are a guest in our Lodge, however uninvited you may be. As long as you abide by the rules of hospitality, no harm shall come to you."

"No harm?"

"Shall come to you, yes."

Pavan would have expected Thulsa Odomo to be pleased upon learning that. A guarantee of safety from the head of their Serabim tribe? What could be more desirable?

Instead the Mandraque tossed back his head and bellowed laughter. This drew angry glares from the Serabim, who were unaccustomed to company of any sort, much less company that displayed such open disdain for their chieftain.

"What," said Seramali with a dangerous edge to his voice, "do you believe to be so amusing? Especially considering the gratitude with which you should be—"

Before Seramali could complete the sentence, Thulsa Odomo's free hand move with such speed that it was little more than a blur.

One moment it was right there, easily visible, and the next it was extracting a blade from behind his back and then the blade was whistling through the air. Thrown with incredible accuracy, it sped across the Lodge and embedded itself deep in Seramali's leg. Seramali went down, howling, grabbing at the still quivering blade.

A collective roar of fury went up from the Serabim. They started to converge on Thulsa, who swept his blade around in a vicious arc, keeping them at bay. He had positioned himself so that his back was against the wall, ensuring that none of them could come up behind him. On the other hand, there was no means of retreat available. And there was only so long that he was going to be able to stave off a concerted attack by the enraged Serabim.

Demali was crouched over her father, her hand fluttering above the embedded knife, shouting for a healer. Seramali was clutching the leg, shoving Demali away, seemingly more concerned about his daughter seeing him in a wounded state than the actual injury. "You Mandraque bastard!" he shouted. "You'll die by inches for this!"

"And if your death was my goal, then you would be a large furry rug right now," the Mandraque taunted him. "I know that with your thick hides, the placement of my blade will provide, at most, a minor pain. I could have targeted your eye if I were of a mind to kill you."

"Then what do you want?" Demali cried out.

"Shut up, Demali!" said Seramali sharply. "This is not your concern!"

"My father was attacked! How is this not my concern?"

"I shall tell you what I want," said Thulsa, and he pointed his sword directly at Pavan. "I want him. Your Keeper."

"Me?" Pavan's legs trembled and he prayed no one noticed.

"Your crest betrays you." Thulsa gave him a curious look. "I thought you were older."

He doesn't know. He doesn't know me from Akasha. To him, one Serabim looks more or less like another, save for the fur that distinguishes me. Pavan drew himself up, willing his legs not to betray him. "I am older than I look," he said defiantly. "And if you think I am simply going to surrender myself to you, cooperate with—"

"I do not seek either your surrender or your cooperation. You will come with me because it is strategically important that you do. Only by having you in our possession can we attain our true goal."

"And that would be?"

"Time enough to discuss that after you are in our hands."

Seramali clenched his teeth and spoke with deliberate effort. "He will never be in your hands. You will never leave this Lodge. You will die where you stand."

"You could not be more wrong."

Thulsa raised his free hand over his head and clenched his fist. Pavan couldn't help but think that it looked very much like a signal of some sort.

Every window in the Lodge shattered.

A barrage of arrows hurtled in, and the heads of the arrows were blazing. They thudded into various parts of the Lodge and, as the harsh winds blasted in through the newly created openings, the fires were immediately fanned into a full blown inferno. Within seconds the entirety of the Lodge was ablaze. It was filled with smoke and screams of Serabim who suddenly found themselves unable to see or even breathe.

Pavan tried to get to Demali, but he couldn't find her. He could scarcely see his own hands in front of himself. He drew his arm across his mouth and nose, trying to find a way out. He had lived in the Lodge his entire life and would have sworn that he could navigate the place blindfolded. Instead Pavan was now discovering that he was dead wrong. He tried to shout Demali's name but started coughing violently and quickly closed his mouth. He stumbled, fell, tried to stand and instead fell again. Then something grabbed him by the scruff of his neck and pulled him to his feet.

"Thank you!" he started to say, and then he looked up and saw the face of the Mandraque sneering down at him.

Pavan lashed out, but he was never much of a fighter, and Thulsa brushed the desperate blow aside. Then the Mandraque slammed Pavan in the face. Pavan heard something crack, a bone. Immediately his face began to swell and his blood was pouring down over his lower jaw.

Before he could make another move—not that it would have done him much good even if he'd managed it—a canvas bag was yanked over his head and his arms were pulled behind him and lashed at the wrists. But he'd been looking directly at Thulsa when it happened, which meant that someone else had done it. "Let's go," said another gravelly Mandraque voice from behind him.

The next thing he knew his feet were lifted clear of the ground and he was being hustled forward. Thulsa was chortling softly in his ear, "Smoke and fire don't bother us, Keeper. We were born for it. We thrive on it. We are equally dangerous no matter where we are, and that's why Mandraques will always triumph!"

"Oh? Tell that to the Sirene!" Pavan said defiantly, and was rewarded with a sharp punch to the gut. His feet had been tied together as well, so aside from trying to twist his body away from his captors—a useless proposition—he was effectively helpless. The only thing he could take any consolation in was the fact that he had managed to annoy one of the Mandraques enough to warrant being struck. His only hope was that he might somehow be able to exploit that, although his aching side didn't seem to readily suggest any way in which he might do so.

Then he was out, out in the cold night air, and the wind howled around him in a way that usually brought him comfort. Now, though, all it did was seem to be howling mournfully for him, as if regretting what was happening to him and asking him why, why had this transpired. He had no answer for that. He had no clue why in the gods' name the Mandraques would be interested in him. What could they possibly hope to accomplish? What did he have that they could want?

That was when he realized. It was so obvious. Obvious and terrifying, for Akasha had taught him many things about the world, and particularly about the Mandraques and their hopes and dreams and desires for conquest.

For the first time in his life, Pavan truly felt cold.

THE VASTLY WATERS

I.

IT WAS BECOMING MORE AND more obvious to Jepp that the Travelers were doing their best to keep their distance from her.

That one Traveler who had come down to her cabin and awakened her continued to hover, but he was obviously trying not to get too close to her. This gave her a strange feeling of empowerment that only added to her growing confidence.

She would walk around on the deck of the ship and watch her personal Traveler (as she had come to think of him) drift within range of her. At one point, just to see what would happen, she placed one foot on the bow as if she were preparing to throw herself in, making good on her earlier threats.

The Traveler simply stood there a distance away, making not the slightest effort to stop her.

She lowered her foot back to the deck and said nothing. He said nothing in return.

Jepp endeavored to engage him in conversation. It didn't work. He would constantly turn away from her, reinforcing to her the notion that for whatever reason, the Travelers were actually afraid of her. She didn't know why, though, and the fact that she didn't know was extremely frustrating to her.

She would have loved to talk it over with someone, but unfortunately the only ones around with whom she could converse were the very ones who were frustrating her.

"You feel vulnerable around me, don't you," said Jepp. "If Karsen and the others could see this now. The way they trembled at the mere mention of your names, and here I am, talking to you, being openly defiant, and you just hide in your cloaks and make vague threats and yet here I am, still talking. You need me for something, and sooner or later, I'm going to find out what it is. And I have this funny feeling that you're not sure whether my finding out would be a good thing or a bad thing." She paused and then approached him. "Does it have something to do with my dreams? Is that it?"

He turned away from her and to her own surprise as much as his, Jepp grabbed at his cloak. "Stop!" she ordered. "I said—"

His gloved hand lashed out and grabbed her around the throat. He lifted her off her feet with no effort at all, and for the first time in days, Jepp truly did know fear once again as it occurred to her that maybe she had pushed the Traveler further than would have been wise.

She had as much as challenged the Traveler to kill her, and now he seemed more than prepared to do so. Her air was closing off, and the world was becoming a hazes of dots floating before her eyes.

"I'm sorry," she managed to whisper, "I'm sorry . . ."

And then another Traveler was at the first one's side, putting a hand firmly on his friend's arm, slowly shaking his head. Again came that same eerie whispering that she had heard before. The Traveler who was holding her aloft was actually trembling with suppressed rage, and suddenly Jepp was falling. She thudded to the deck and slumped over, clutching at her throat, coughing and fighting to get air back into her lungs. She looked up at the Traveler who loomed over her, and then she managed to gasp out, "Okay . . . I was afraid of you. Is that better? Does that make your world just . . . just all right somehow?"

He did not respond. She did not expect him to, and then as he turned away, she shouted, "I feel sorry for you!" Slowly she got to her feet and continued, "That's right. Me. The lowly human. I feel sorry for you, for whatever you are. You're the most pathetic creature since . . . since . . ." Her mind raced for comparison and she found it. "Gant. The most pathetic creature since—"

One moment he was across the deck from her, and the next he

was right there, in her face, speaking with a sense of urgency.

"Gant?"

"Yes," she said uncertainly. "One of the Bottom Feeders. The clan I was with for a time when you . . . when your brethren . . . carried me away. Gant."

"Describe him," came the whispery voice.

"I don't—"

"Describe him."

She jumped back, frightened by the Traveler's intensity. Her bouts of bravado suddenly seemed very far away and long forgotten. "He's hard to describe!" she said defensively. "He's just . . . he's sort of this . . . this blob. He doesn't really have much of a shape at all."

"A blob." His voice was flat. She couldn't tell if he believed her or was echoing her or mocking her. "A blob, you say."

"Yes. And I know, there's no race like that. At least not that I know of. But you would know. Is there a race? Of blobs?"

There was just the smallest shaking of his hood. The other Traveler, the one who had prevented him from snapping Jepp's neck, had drifted back and now appeared to be watching the two of them. He appeared uncertain as to what to do next. Jepp could sympathize.

"I didn't think so. He claimed . . . that is to say, I was told . . . that he used to be a Phey. But I've never seen a Phey, so I don't know if they look like blobs at all . . ."

"They . . . do not," said the Traveler.

"Karsen told me that he was transformed. That he was romancing first one Phey sister and then another, each without the other knowing. And once they discovered it, they exacted a terrible vengeance upon him, turning him into . . . into whatever he was."

"He told you that."

"Yes."

"What else?"

It was the closest thing to a conversation Jepp had had since setting foot aboard the ship. It didn't involve threats nor the concern that the next word could be her last. "Not much else. That Karsen's clan came upon him and made him one of them. They are Bottom Feeders, after all, and so not especially strict when it comes to matters of race. Well . . . except where I was involved. That seemed to make a huge difference. But they probably didn't think of me as a race, anyway. I'm a human, which makes me little more than an animal in their eyes."

"No."

"No?"

"Animals have uses," the Traveler said with an edge to his voice.

She felt a stinging in her cheeks. She would have thought, after all this time and all that she had endured, that it was no longer possible for her to feel embarrassed. She was dismayed to discover that she was wrong. This time when he turned away from her, she made no effort to stop him, but instead shouted after him, "Go to hell!"

"Already there," the Traveler whispered back at her.

II.

IT WAS SEVERAL TURNS OF the Damned World later that Jepp saw the storm rolling toward them.

She had witnessed foul weather countless times before, but she had never in her life seen anything quite like this. One minute she was gazing out at the same, unchanging vista that she had grown accustomed to over all this time. She was beginning to wonder if this was what the rest of her life was going to be like. After all, Jepp didn't know of a certainty that the Travelers had any particular destination in mind. It might have been that their intention was to just sail around with her until she died and then pitch her overboard. It didn't make any sense, of course. If they wanted her dead, they could have simply killed her when they first took her. *We're talking about Travelers. It doesn't have to make sense.* That was what she told herself, but even as she did, she didn't quite believe it. Nobody did things for no reason. Even the insane had reasons for their actions; they were just insane reasons that made sense only to them. Whatever else they were, though, the Travelers were not insane.

Jepp started paying closer attention when the Travelers were talking to each other. She discovered that if she listened closely enough, she could pick up isolated words here and there. One of the words that she was certain she had heard was "Gant," and that was of great curiosity to her. Why were they so interested in Gant? What was it about a lone Bottom Feeder that would so intrigue the mighty Travelers?

A possible solution suggested herself, but she found it hard to believe. Still, it was a notion worth pursuing. Subtlety was not Jepp's strong suit. Her belief was that if someone wanted to learn something, there was no better way to go about it than directly. So she had gone straight over to the Traveler that had spoken to her of Gant the other day. When she had first boarded the ship she had not been able to distinguish one Traveler from the other, but by now she had learned to discern who was who simply through observing small tics in their body language.

"Are you a Phey?"

If she was looking for him to give something away in his reaction, she was destined to be disappointed. He didn't react in the slightest.

"I said," she began again, "are you a—?"

"I heard you."

"Well?"

He approached her and she involuntarily took a step back. He seemed to loom over her, occupying the entirety of her world.

"To look upon the Phey is to die," he said. "If I am of the Phey, and you look upon me, then you will take that knowledge to the next world." He lifted his hands to either side of his hood. "Are you prepared for that?"

She wanted to stand up to him with as much gusto as she had days ago, but this time she hesitated. She felt as if there was so much more for her to learn, things that were just beyond her comprehension that could be greatly important for everyone and everything. If she died, she would never be able to understand any of it, much less make things better.

And she could make things better. She wasn't sure quite how yet, but she was beginning to get a sense that she had a role in the grand scheme of things. She wanted to find out what that role was.

But she also wanted to find out if she was right about the Travelers. That was going to be important as well.

She was reminded of an artifact left over from the days when humans actually were in charge of the Damned World. She had seen it when she was much younger, little more than a child, being played with by a young Mandraque who seemed to be having some difficulty with it. He had noticed that Jepp was watching and, rather than hissing at her in anger, had brought it over to the slave pen, placed it just outside, and gestured for her to try her hand at it.

The toy had consisted of small pieces of wood that interlocked and seemed to come together to form a picture of several whores. The young Mandraque was unable to figure out exactly how the pieces interlocked, however. Slowly at first but then with increasing speed and confidence, Jepp assembled the puzzle. She displayed it proudly, at which point an adult Mandraque had come by, seen what she had done, grabbed the puzzle away and smashed it into so many small pieces that an army of Jepps wouldn't have been able to reassemble it.

She had always remembered that moment, though, and how easily she had been able to see how the pieces fit together.

Jepp felt as if the world had transformed into a vast puzzle. There were pieces out there, pieces that she needed to find. Once she did so, she would see how all of them came together, and she would hold the entire picture in her hands.

My dreams are a piece. The Travelers are a piece. Apparently Gant is a piece, and the Phey might also be as well. I need to get all the pieces in order to see the picture, and I have to say or do the correct thing at any given moment if I'm going to accomplish that.

"No," she said softly to the Traveler. "I am not prepared for that."

Slowly the Traveler lowered his hands from his hood. He did not commend her or tell her that she had made a wise decision. Instead he was about to turn away from her.

But then he looked off toward the horizon line and stopped, something having caught his interest. Jepp's back was to where he was looking, and so she turned to see just what was so interesting.

The storm was rolling right toward them.

It was dead ahead of them and inescapable. The sky directly above them was still blue and pleasant, but ahead of them it was absolutely black, with thick gray clouds and lightning dancing within them. She could see a solid sheet of rain barreling toward them as if some great unseen being were gripping it by either edge and drawing it across the skies. The waves were surging fiercely, and the waters beneath their own craft was starting to buck in response to the oncoming churning.

"Go below," said the Traveler with a rasp. The second Traveler was already at the sails, preparing them for the violent weather that was bearing down on them. The third was lashing the wheel in order to keep the ship on course. "Now," he added forcefully when Jepp didn't move fast enough.

Jepp did as she was bid, fleeing to the lower depths of the ship. By the time she got down there, the ship was already tilting violently. Jepp had never been more glad that she had been eating lightly. She had developed a stronger constitution than when she'd first boarded, but had anything been in her stomach at that moment, it likely would have been decorating the inside of her room before long.

Within minutes the wind was howling outside. She tried to find something to grab onto, and when she couldn't, contented herself with sitting on the floor, putting her hands to either side. She forced herself to breathe slowly and regularly, determined to remain calm. And as she did so, the storm continued to grow in intensity, howling like a thing alive.

The more she listened to it, the more fascinated she became by it. *I want to see it*, she thought, and the thought surprised even her.

I have never seen a storm like this. Maybe there's never been a storm like this. And yet here I cower. I should see it, witness it. I should pay obeisance to it. I think . . .

I think it is coming for me. And it would only be respectful to look it in the eye.

She clambered up the ladder, up onto the deck. The wind immediately hit her with the force of an anvil, knocking her backwards onto the rain-slicked deck. She drew her cloak more tightly around her and fought her way to her feet. The rocking of the boat was even more severe topside. If this had happened during her first days on the ship, she would have been tossed around as helplessly as a pebble skipped across the surface of a pond. As it was, even with the amount of sea craft she had developed over the past weeks of travel, it was still all she could do to resist being thrown about.

She got to her feet, staggered, and then skidded yet again. She hit the deck hard, banging her elbows, and she cried out in pain. Suddenly she was yanked to her feet by a Traveler—her Traveler, as she had come to think of him—who bellowed practically into her face, "What are you doing here!? Go below!"

"No! I want to see it!" she shouted and she pulled away from him. Ordinarily she never would have been able to do so, but his gloved hands were wet from the rain, and so was she. She staggered across the deck.

He came right after her, his cloak billowing around him. "You're being an idiot!"

"I'm being a human!"

"Same thing!"

He grabbed for her and she eluded his grasp. "Are you a Phey?!"

"Not that again!"

"I need to know!"

"Why?"

"I don't know!"

She suspected that if she could see his eyes, he would have been rolling them at that point. Truthfully, she wouldn't have blamed him.

Jepp backed up, stumbled again, and this time fell solidly on her rump. The Traveler advanced, swaying with the motion of the ship but otherwise not appearing discommoded by the movement. He grabbed at her but she rolled out of his reach, grabbed some rigging and pulled herself to her feet once more.

"Thunderation, human, if you have a death wish, then just indulge yourself and save us some time!" He grabbed at her and she eluded him as much by the pitching of the ship as from any effort on her own part.

"I want to know what's happening! I want to know what this is all about!"

"No!"

"I have the right—!"

"You are human! You have no rights!"

"You're wrong!" she shouted, gripping the edge of the rail. "We had a right to live! To laugh! To love! We had a right to exist!"

"Yes, and we took it away! Rather easily! So it couldn't have been that important to you to begin with!"

"You didn't take it away!" Jepp said defiantly. "It's still there! You may be keeping us from it, but it's there just the same, waiting for us to take it back! That's what you're really afraid of, isn't it!"

Thunder blasted overhead at the exact same time that lightning crackled. When the light flashed, Jepp saw a glint of silver beneath the hood. "I am not afraid! We are not afraid! We are masters of this world!"

"How dare you! How dare you make such a ridiculous claim to be masters of this world when you stand in the face of this!" and she gestured overhead. "This world can brush you off like insects if it so chooses! Who are you to think you are anything other than interlopers, fearful that sooner or later, this world will notice your presence and cast you aside!"

"We are *not afraid*!"

"Then answer my question! Are you of the Phey?"

Having had more than enough, the Traveler advanced upon her, his dark form almost disappearing against the backdrop of blackness that surrounded them. "Come here! Right now!"

III.

GRAVES HAD HAD MORE THAN his fill of humans in general and certainly this one in particular.

It was all he could do not to say, "To hell with you!" and leave her to the elements. But that wasn't an option. He knew that and, worse still, she was obviously figuring it out as well. He never would have imagined her capable of that. Morts should have had no capacity for reason, and yet this one was constantly finding ways to frustrate him, second guess him, and in general annoy the hell out of him.

Jepp backed up, and suddenly a massive wave of water cascaded over the edge of the ship as the vessel rocked violently. It slammed into Jepp and lifted her up and over the far side.

IV.

FOR A MOMENT, GRAVES WAS tempted to let nature take its course.

There was no question that the human female was getting on his nerves with her incessant questions and her inability to respect the natural boundaries that should have come with his being a Traveler. He was accustomed to the strongest races of the Twelve recoiling from him whenever he was remotely in the vicinity. This human, this Mort, this "Jepp" should have been no different. Indeed, when his brethren had kidnapped her and presented her to him at the dock for transport, they had assured him that she would present no problems. That she was as easily malleable and weak-willed as any of her nearly extinct race, if not moreso.

Something had happened. Something had gone horribly, horribly wrong. He would have suspected a Changeling was involved somehow, if it weren't for the fact that the Changeling race was still happily and contentedly in the Elserealms, looking down at the travails of the Banished and doubtless laughing their shapeshifting asses off. For some reason, the young woman who had stepped aboard the ship had become, in doing so, a very different creature than the one who had initially been carried off.

Graves was beginning to think that the reason for it had to do with the kidnapping itself. By giving her that sort of attention they had elevated her opinion of herself. The very action of focusing on her served to give her a sense of importance in her own eyes. If they had just left her alone, then the chances were that nothing she would have gone on to say or do in her life would have mattered in the least.

But no. No, they had been compelled to seek her out, to take her away from her natural habitat of being a nobody. They had allowed her to get far too close, closer than any resident of the Damned World aside from the Overseer himself had gotten.

And now it had come to this.

Graves watched in horror as Jepp was knocked over the edge of the ship and vanished into the darkness. Despite the fact that every instinct was screaming at him, *Let the bitch just drown already,* he moved quickly to the side of the ship and looked down. Despite the hellacious situation that was surrounding him, he nevertheless sighed in relief.

Jepp was clinging to the anchor. It had not been lowered during the storm; to have done so would have risked the ship being torn asunder. Better to ride out whatever buffeting the waves had in mind. There was the anchor on the side of the boat, and there was Jepp, her arms and legs wrapped around it. She looked like a drenched bat as she held on, the waves continuing to slam into her.

Damn, but the girl is strong, thought Graves, impressed in spite of himself. He had grabbed a length of rope, tied it off to the mast, and had now lashed it around himself. The last thing he needed was to be washed overboard himself. If he'd had more rope, he would have lowered it down to her, but it was all he had on hand and he was more interested in securing himself than Jepp. Besides, she was still within arm's length. He leaned over the side of the boat and stretched out his hand to her. "Come here, girl!" he shouted.

"No!"

"Don't be afraid!"

"I'm not afraid! The worst I can do is die, and I've been ready for that from the moment you took me away from Karsen!" She clutched the anchor with even greater ferocity. "Answer my question!"

"I'm going to kill her," he muttered. "I'm going to kill her, I'm going to kill the Overseer, watch my entire race die out, and then find a way to annihilate every living thing on this world before capping it off with a knife through my own skull. Nothing is worth this."

"Answer my quest—"

"Yes! All right? Yes! I'm one of the Phey! All the Travelers are!" He yanked back his hood and his silver metal face glittered in the reflection of lightning that tore across the sky. "Are you happy? Are you satisfied, you stupid bitch! Now take my hand and get up here or—"

She didn't wait for the alternative to be presented. Instead she grabbed his outstretched hand and he started to pull her to safety.

As if the Vastly Waters had taken on a spiteful life of its own, a massive wave chose that moment to slam up at Jepp like a fist. It literally tore her out of Graves' grasp and Jepp was thrown down into the water. The water folded down and over her and Jepp vanished beneath the surface. The last thing that Graves saw of her was her hand reaching up in supplication, and then she was gone.

Graves screamed her name, which he realized distantly was odd because he had never spoken her name before. He didn't even remember trying to clamber over the side, and the only thing that prevented him from doing so was Trott. Trott, who had appeared at his side as if from nowhere, yanking him back from oblivion. "You'll sink, you fool!" he shouted at him. "Sink like a damned stone!"

"Gods damn it, Trott, she was fated! You know it! She was a Fated One, and we had to—"

Trott was shouting into his face. "This was her fate! We did not seek it for her nor wish it upon her, but it was hers, and neither you nor I can gainsay it! It is what it is, Graves! You of all people know that!"

"She knew Gant! She knew my brother! She—"

Trott's hand flew as if it were doing so on its own, cracking across Graves's face and making a hollow ringing sound when it did so. "He is as dead to us as she is! Forget her, Graves! And forget him! We need never think upon either of them again!"

Graves looked at the churning waters beneath which Jepp had disappeared and said grimly, as much to himself as to Trott, "Would that it were that easy."

PERRIZ

I.

CLARINDA HAD NEVER ACTED AS if reaching Perriz was anything other than a foregone conclusion. Her concerns about the eerie dreams that were pervading her sleeping mind more and more, her worries that they were somehow being played and that the Piri were going to pounce upon them at any moment . . . all of those she kept entirely to herself.

It was a heavy responsibility. She desperately wanted to talk to someone about it, but she didn't feel as if there was anyone in her ragtag army and core of defenders to whom she could confide.

Perversely, the only one she could really talk to was her mother who kept taunting her whenever she sought to bury herself in slumber. She managed not to wake up screaming every time, but it wasn't easy. The dreams were become so forceful that the last time she had awakened, she had bitten deeply into her lower lip and blood was trickling down her chin. She still had the puncture wounds in her mouth. One of the Ocular had inquired about it but she had brushed it off.

The closer they drew to Perriz, the more concerned she became. She started to convince herself that a devastating Piri attack would befall them once they drew within sight of the city. That Sunara Redeye was just sadistic enough a creature to take her and her defenders down with sanctuary within reach. There was always the possibility that the Piri would wait until they were settled in Perriz and then send in warriors to destroy them, but she didn't really think that was going to happen. Would the Piri really be so precipitous as to attack the Firedraques? Would they cross that line?

Then again, why not? Sunara Redeye had made it clear that as far as the Piri were concerned, there were no such things as lines.

So it was that, the closer they drew to their goal, the greater was Clarinda's anxiety.

As they continued to walk the tracks, Clarinda found herself wishing that Eutok was at her side. Yes, she had been disappointed in him that he had been unwilling to stand up to his mother and bring Clarinda down into the world of the Trulls for safekeeping. But she couldn't claim that his concerns weren't valid. There was little likelihood that the queen would have been willing to issue any sort of decree that Clarinda's life was sacrosanct. And even if she had . . . what of it? Sooner or later—most likely sooner—someone would have stolen in upon a sleeping Clarinda and killed her rather than allow her to continue congress with Eutok. There was no guarantee that the queen would seek vengeance; she might actually be relieved to have Clarinda disposed of. Even if she did track down and destroy Clarinda's murderer or murderers, so what? Clarinda and the child who was growing within her belly would still be just as dead.

Ultimately, despite his character weakness, she drew strength from him. And right now she needed more strength than ever before. Strength, she was starting to think that she would never be able to develop for herself.

By contrast to her growing concerns, the young Ocular were positively bubbly in their attitudes. The more they had walked, the greater distance they had put between themselves and their poisoned homeland, the more their spirits appeared to rise. So Clarinda was faced with a situation where the closer they got to achieving their goal, the more depressed she became about it, and the harder she had to work at keeping a positive face about all the concerns that were raging through her head.

They had once again taken refuge in a building that was riddled with holes and seemed as if it was going to collapse at some point in the near future, but at least not this night. As the sun set and the Ocular prepared to set out again, Turkin sidled over to Clarinda and said in a low voice, "I just wanted to say . . ."

She looked at him expectantly. "Say what?"

"That I am sorry I mistrusted you initially."

"Did you? I had not noticed."

He appeared confused at first, and then a wry smile spread across his face. "You are being ironic."

"Somewhat."

"It is just that . . . you are what you are, and we are what we are. So it is natural there would be distrust and division."

"It is the fact that such distrust and division is considered natural that we have many of the problems we, as the Twelve Races, have. For that matter," continued Clarinda, "according to my mother, it was part of the problem that humans had. Their inability to pull together, to decide on what the best mutual course of action should be about . . . well, about everything, really . . . that contributed to their downfall as a race. Do you have any desire to wind up like the Morts?"

Other Ocular had heard her, making no effort to hide their eavesdropping, and now they were all shaking their heads.

"Well, that is what's going to happen," she said. "As long as the Twelve Races continue to be in conflict with each other, sooner or later we're going to go the way of the Morts."

"And then what?" Kerda said. Of all the youngsters, she had developed the closest bond with Clarinda, oftentimes hanging on her every word. "If we go away, who then takes over the world?"

"I don't know," Clarinda said with a shrug. "Perhaps the humans will rise again. Perhaps something else that we haven't seen or discovered yet. The Damned World will continue, although there's no assurance that we will."

"But," said Turkin slowly, "if only one of the Twelve Races could dominate...could be the last one left standing . . . wouldn't you want it to be the Piri? Wouldn't you want it to be your own race?"

"Of what advantage would that be to me? If the Piri were all that existed, there would be nowhere for me to go. Right?"

Turkin lowered his gaze. "I suppose not."

"You suppose correctly. Come," and she gathered her things. "Nothing is to be gained by standing around here and talking. We have places to go, and we may as well go there."

There were nods from all around, and soon they had set out again, walking the tracks.

As they walked, Clarinda heard Kerda singing something, and overheard her name. "Kerda," she said, "what was that song?"

"Just an old Ocular tune. But I'm putting in new words. Words about you."

This drew amused glances from the others. Berola moved closer to her and said with interest, "Let's hear it."

"It's not ready," said Kerda.

"Well, let's hear what you have."

"No."

"Do you think," Turkin said, "it's so bad that we'll all keel over and die if you sing it?" He laughed at the notion and only stopped when Berola sharply elbowed him in the ribs.

Speaking with exaggerated patience as if she were talking to an imbecile, Kerda said, "I don't think it's bad. I just think it's not finished. I don't want to start singing something that I don't have the end to."

"When will it be finished, then?" He was rubbing the place where Berola had elbowed him and, even though he was speaking to Kerda, he was giving Berola an annoyed glare.

"When we're finished, obviously," said Kerda. "How am I supposed to sing a song about a great adventure when I don't know how the adventure is going to end? That would be stupid."

Clarinda, who had been walking for a time because she was growing weary of being carried around like a sack of potatoes, stopped where she was, She did it so abruptly that Turkin almost stepped right on her, which would have been catastrophic. Fortunately he managed to rein himself in just in time.

"If that is what's concerning you, Kerda," said Clarinda slowly, "then it would appear that we may be able to attend to that once and for all." She pointed and all eyes turned to see where she was indicating.

They had just come around the remains of a building and so they had an unobscured view of miles ahead of them. There, in the growing darkness, was the unmistakable outline of a city. Unlike the many small villages that they had passed, this one was vast and spread across their view with such majesty that it literally took their breath away.

There were even lights scattered about the city, no doubt glowing courtesy of hotstars. What drew their attention the most was a tower, generally triangular in shape, giving off a golden glow in the rapidly spreading night.

"It's beautiful," whispered Berola, and there were concurring murmurs from the others.

"Is that really it?" said Turkin. "Is that Perriz?"

"I think so. I truly think so," said Clarinda. "I'm fairly certain I recognize the tower from a painting my mother had. She even said it had a name."

"What is it?"

"Eyeful. The Eyeful Tower."

"I can see why," Berola said with reverence. "It truly is an eyeful."

Then, to their surprise, the lights on the tower flickered. Moments later, it had gone dark. The Ocular looked at each other in confusion and then Clarinda shrugged and said, "We do not need to see the light to be able to find it. Come, children. Let us see what we shall see."

Perriz was much further than it initially appeared, and for the longest time they felt that they were drawing no closer to it. It almost started to seem as if it was not truly a city, but rather a mirage that would tempt them with the promise of their journey's end yet never really deliver upon that promise. The moon crawled across the sky, and the trip was becoming all the more frustrating with its conclusion in sight, but still so far off.

At some point during their journey, though, when the night had reached the midpoint, Perriz suddenly seemed a lot closer. Several of the Ocular began to move to a slow jog, and then the nearer they drew, the more they began to pick up speed. Soon they were moving so quickly that it became impossible for Clarinda to keep up. Turkin noticed and put out a hand to her. She grabbed it and he swung her up and onto his back.

"Once, I wouldn't have trusted you there," he said. "I'd have expected you were going to sink your teeth into me."

Clarinda's stomach grumbled and she tried to ignore it. "Never even occurred to me," she lied. "Now move. We're falling behind."

With a grin, Turkin picked up the pace. He kept to the back of the group, bringing up the rear so as not to jostle Clarinda too thoroughly. Even with him moving at half the speed he possessed, the ground still sped past beneath Clarinda's gaze.

She laughed.

The noise startled her, particularly since it was coming from her own throat. She was not one for laughing even on her better days, and it wasn't as if she had had terribly many of those. Yet here she was, laughing with almost childish delight as their potential sanctuary drew just within reach.

The area that the tracks were taking them through seemed mostly agricultural, or at least it had been at one time. Much of the area had been burned out in the wars, and only now were the first hints of green beginning to return. Clarinda couldn't help but reflect on the foolishness that was involved in destroying the natural resources of a world upon which you were trying to establish residence. Destroy some humans, hell, destroy all of them if you must. But leave their means of food production alone because you're going to need it. That was just common sense.

A metal bridge stretched over a waterway in front of them with the tracks running right down the middle. Because of their size and the relative narrowness of the bridge, the Ocular were required to go single file or, at most, two by two for some of the smaller ones. That minor inconvenience did not slow them, though, as they quickly started to run across the bridge. The structure shook beneath their pounding feet.

It was at that moment that Clarinda suddenly sensed danger.

Since they were bringing up the rear, she did not realize it until almost all of the Ocular were already on the bridge. None of them had yet reached the opposite shore.

"Wait! Stop!" Clarinda shouted. "Something is wrong!"

They didn't hear her at first. They were too busy shouting and cheering and Kerda was composing new lyrics that were going to write an end to their successful journey. But since she was on Turkin's back, naturally he heard her. He skidded to a halt, almost causing Clarinda to lose her grip on him and take a spill. She held on, but not without effort. Turkin bellowed, "Everyone! Wait! Clarinda says to wait!"

This had the desired effect, with the Ocular stopping wherever they were and turning to learn what the problem was.

That was when there was a splashing of water and then, in the darkness, there were bodies overrunning the bridge. Bodies moving with such eerie silence that they were almost like shadows come to life.

We're dead, thought Clarinda, and then the shadows were upon them.

II.

GORSHAM OF THE HOUSE OF Chen had been bored.

Before he had risen to the head of the House of Chen, he had been in command of his own time, doing what he wished and going wherever he wanted to. The one downside of his particular situation was the fact that his father, Gorsh, was officious and annoying and physically abusive and tended to complain incessantly about every other family head including, most particularly, Arren Kinklash. Consequently when Kinklash had approached Gorsham about a plan that would remove Gorsh from the grand equation of the

Mandraques in exchange for Gorsham attempting no retaliation, Gorsham had eagerly availed himself of the opportunity. He had very much looked forward to being in charge of his own destiny for a change.

He had been dismayed to discover upon his father's passing— said passing involving being crushed by a gigantic bell that had fallen with suspiciously convenient timing upon him—that as soon as Gorsh was dead, Gorsham's time was very much not his own. Suddenly everyone in the House of Chen was approaching him to approve, oversee or overlook this, that and the other thing. It was incessant and it was annoying and Gorsham was starting to think that if he could go back in time and tell his father to get out of the way of the damned bell, he would do so without hesitation. Unfortunately that opportunity was not available to him and now he was stuck trying to accommodate as many individuals as he could lest someone take umbrage and arrange for a bell to fall on him, too.

At this particular point, it involved patrolling the borders of Perriz, something that was his least favorite way to pass the time because, really, who would be insane enough to try and attack the home of the Firedraques, the wisest and most benevolent of races on the Damned World? A race whose attempts to hold others to peace treaties were widely known to be approved by no less a figure than the Overseer?

There were squad captains in the House of Chen—which shared such duties equally with other houses—who were perfectly capable of leading and did so at all times. But it was customary for the heads of the Houses to accompany their captains every so often to make certain that the borders and crossings were well watched. Naturally it was impossible to cover every square mile of the borders, but they did what they could. If anything, it was for convenience sake, because if intruders did manage to make their way into Perriz, they would quickly be dispatched by either the patrolling Mandraques or the resident Firedraques. It wasn't as if Firedraques were incapable of defending themselves. They might well embrace pomp and pomposity and enjoy their self-proclaimed roles of peacemakers. But Gorsham had had occasion to witness a Firedraque in full fury, and it had not been something that he was anxious to see ever again.

After a lengthy and frankly boring trek across Perriz territory, Gorsham and his squad of a dozen Mandraques had taken up residence under a bridge. It seemed as good a place as any to set up a watch post. There was plenty of room on the banks under the bridge, and the steady stream of water guaranteed that they wouldn't be going thirsty anytime soon.

There they had remained, chatting idly about the foolishness of patrols and, generally speaking, how boring life was when various members of the Twelve Races weren't trying to kill each other.

The Mandraques wouldn't have minded taking off after that Zeffer that had made off with Nicrominus. That certainly seemed a challenging endeavor, and there wasn't a Mandraque alive who didn't relish the possibility of taking on those walking hairbags known as the Serabim with their renowned high-and-mighty attitudes. But Evanna, the daughter of Nicrominus the Preceptor, had informed them that the Zeffer was acting on behalf of, and presumably the direct orders of, the Travelers and the Overseer. That had put an end to discussion of counterattacks. "What's one less Firedraque anyway?" had been the general opinion, and that had been more or less that.

As for border patrol, the only moment of interest that had occurred in patrol anytime recently had been the squadron of Mandraques who had come upon none other than Arren Kinklash endeavoring to leave the city. Normally it was of little interest to Mandraques if one of their own came or went, but Arren was leader of the Five Clans and was expected to be available at all times to oversee disputes, of which there were typically many. Gorsham didn't know why Arren was endeavoring to sneak away, although there were rumors that it had something to do with that brainless sister of his. Gorsham wasn't really all that interested, but the law was the law and responsibilities could not be ignored. Especially when, as Arren had, one had connived and maneuvered oneself into that position of authority. So Arren had been returned to Perriz and, from Gorsham's understanding, had received a rather thorough tongue lashing from Evanna. Because of that, the entirety of the population of Perriz had been keeping a wary eye on Arren and he hadn't been going anywhere. Apparently he had resigned himself to his situation and made no further attempts to depart.

They had been on station for several hours and the only thing that was stopping Gorsham from falling asleep in the warm night air was the buzz of conversation. Even that was beginning to lull him, and suddenly there was the sound of a distant pounding that was rapidly getting louder.

The Mandraques looked at each other in confusion. "A stampede of whores?" guessed one.

"Draquons," whispered another, and this prompted fearful exchanges. If a squad of Travelers was galloping in, ready to carry out the Overseer's bidding, then there was no way in hell that any of the Mandraques were going to get in their way.

"Someone should take a look," whispered a third, and all eyes turned toward Gorsham. As a house head, he was senior among them and it was expected that he was to take point on such things. The prospect of seeing Travelers bearing down on them was terrifying to Gorsham, but he didn't see how he had any choice. The only available option seemed to be clambering up the side of the bank, verify what was bearing down on them, and then scampering back down, inform his fellows that it was indeed Travelers, and then hiding and hoping that the Travelers passed them by. When Travelers were heading somewhere, that was really all you could reasonably do.

Taking a deep breath and praying it wouldn't be among his last, Gorsham climbed up the side, digging his fingers and toes into the dirt as he went. He got to the top and peered over, trying to reveal as little of his head as possible.

The oncoming noise was being generated by something in the distance that was mostly shadows. What he discerned immediately, though, was that there was a complete absence of mounts.

"There's no draquons," he whispered.

"No draquons? Are you sure?"

"Positive. Whoever it is, they're on foot."

"On foot?" There were mutters of incredulity. "How the hell are they making that much noise on foot?"

"They would have to be huge. They'd . . ." Gorsham's eyes widened. "Gods, they are! It's Ocular!"

"Are you sure?"

Gorsham dropped back to the banks and said, "Do you think I wouldn't recognize one-eyed giants when they're stampeding right toward me?"

"What do we do?"

Glancing at the bridge over their head, Gorsham said grimly, "We stop them. That's what we do. They'll have to cross over there. We lay in wait and we take them down."

"How many of them are there?"

"Hard to say. Around thirty or forty, I think."

This garnered some apprehensive looks from the Mandraques. Gorsham couldn't believe it. As spoiled and occasionally indolent as he was, he was still fired with racial pride. "We are Mandraques! We have war in our blood, chaos in our hearts! Do you seriously think we cannot handle some Ocular?"

"Of course we can!" said one of his lieutenants. "But to what end? To defend the city of the Firedraques? Who cares if some Ocular overrun them? They are more hindrance than help. We would be well rid of them."

Gorsham yanked out his sword. The lieutenant took a step back, apparently concerned that Gorsham was going to run him through. "There are Mandraques aplenty living within Perriz as well. Plus, for better or worse, we have already pledged troops to serve on behalf of the Firedraques, to protect the common interest. Mandraques do nothing in half measures. If we give our pledge," and he had to raise his voice to be heard above the oncoming thundering, "then we see it through!" Without waiting for a response, he leaped straight up and clutched the underside of the bridge, pulling himself up to a ready position. He prayed that the others followed him, because otherwise he was going to wind up as nothing save a green/brown spot on the bottom of some gigantic feet. He breathed a sigh of relief when he heard his fellow Mandraques climbing up behind him, getting ready to leap upon the interlopers. For the first time in a long time, he truly felt like a leader of Mandraques.

"Come in low!" Gorsham called to the others. "Go for the tendons behind their ankles, or at their knees. Sever those, and their size won't do them a damned bit of good!"

The Ocular drew closer, and then they hit the bridge. The Mandraques wanted to start scrambling up immediately, but Gorsham made a whipcrack gesture with his tail, indicating they should stay where they were. Gorsham had positioned himself at the far end of the bridge, ready to head off the point of the charge, with his lieutenant right behind him. He was both tense and yet oddly relaxed. It had been far too long since he had been able to thrust himself into direct battle. His body practically craved it.

He was about to move, to tell them all to move, and suddenly the Ocular stopped running. He couldn't understand it. Yes, Ocular had particularly acute vision during the night. Perhaps it was the gods' way of making up for the giants being almost blind during the day. Even so, there was no way that the Ocular could possibly have spotted them in hiding below the bridge.

Then he heard one of them say, from toward the back, "Everybody wait! Clarinda says to wait!"

"They know!" whispered Gorsham's lieutenant, and Gorsham had to agree. But there was no time to wait around and see what happened next. He made another decisive gesture with his tail, one that was unmistakable, and immediately he and the other Mandraques were climbing over the bridge and coming at the Ocular.

Everything was instantly chaotic.

Gorsham came at the lead Ocular, swinging his sword quickly, trying to get at the giant's legs. To both his annoyance and chagrin, the Ocular—a female, by the looks of her—was extremely deft. She practically danced out of his way, and she shouted, "Up! Go up! Get the high ground!"

The Ocular instantly did as they were instructed, moving with such uniformity of purpose that it was obvious to Gorsham that this was not simply a random grouping of Ocular. This was an army.

Within seconds the Ocular had grabbed the upper sections of the bridge and taken refuge there. They shouted defiance and contempt at the Mandraques, and the female that Gorsham had tried to attack was the loudest. She had a club in her hand that had been dangling from her belt. It was the size of a small tree. It probably had been one before she had transformed it into a weapon. "Come here, little lizard!" she called down to him. "Is it true that if I tear your tail off you, it will grow back?"

With a furious snarl, Gorsham tried to leap toward her. She swung the club and caught him in mid leap. It slammed him to one side, sending him crashing back down to the bridge. He managed to cushion some of the impact with his tail but was still jarred from the hit and a bit rattled. It jolted the sword from his hand and it clattered to the bridge. His lieutenant was there and handed it to him, looking a bit chagrined on Gorsham's behalf. Gorsham grabbed it out of his hand. His mood was not helped by the delighted laughter of the Ocular . . .

Laughter? Delighted?

He looked up at the Ocular, looked at them carefully, really seeing them clearly for the first time. Gorsham was hardly an expert on Ocular, but as he studied their demeanor, their attitude, their general appearance, the truth began to dawn upon him.

"Children," he muttered.

His lieutenant looked at him. "What?"

Gorsham spoke louder and with greater irritation. "They're gods damned children!"

"Children or not," said the taunting female, "we're still more than enough to dispatch the lot of you!"

He wasn't entirely sure she was wrong. Nevertheless the situation required that he keep up a bellicose attitude. Keeping his sword at the ready, he called up to her, "Go home, children! Go home to your parents and stop wasting our time!"

"We have no home." It was another who had spoken, another female, smaller than the first one and with a mournful sound in her voice. "We have no parents."

"That is none of our concern!" Then Gorsham paused a moment and, his voice a bit softer, he said, "What do you mean, you have no parents? If you have no parents, who do you have?"

Every single one of the Ocular pointed toward the far end of the bridge.

For a moment Gorsham thought, *Don't look! It's a trick!* But just as quickly he dismissed the idea as ludicrous and looked where the female was pointing.

At first he didn't quite understand what it was that he was seeing. Then he stared at it some more and he still didn't comprehend it.

There was a male Ocular standing at the far end of the bridge, and he appeared to have someone riding on his back. The one-eyed giant stared unblinkingly at him, and then whoever it was upon him slid off and dropped lightly onto the ground. It was impossible to determine whether it was male or female. The figure, though, was definitely not an Ocular. The proportions were completely wrong. It was cloaked and hooded, and as it approached the Mandraques it didn't see to walk so much as glide. There were nervous glances among Gorsham and his fellows as the same thought occurred to all of them: Traveler? But that didn't seem to make much sense. What would a Traveler be doing with a small army of young Ocular? Then again, what were they doing so far away from normal Ocular territory in the first place?

Gorsham's nostrils flared as he tried to pick up a scent from the oncoming figure. He didn't quite understand what he was perceiving.

It smelled like . . . dirt. And blood. And death.

The figure came within a few feet of him and then stopped. It pulled the hood back and Gorsham couldn't believe what he was staring at. "Are you . . . ?"

"A Piri. Yes."

"And these are what?" he said disdainfully. "Your meals on legs?"

"They are my..." She seemed to be seeking a proper word and then shrugged. "My charges, I suppose."

"You," and his face twisted in disgust as he stepped closer to her, "are a Piri. You are little more than an animal. Speak truly: What are you doing with these children, and what is your business here?"

"My business here," she said, "is that we seek sanctuary."

Gorsham looked at the others for a moment and then, almost as one, they burst out laughing.

The female who had so cavalierly dispatched Gorsham said angrily, "Stop laughing! Stop laughing at us!"

Managing with effort to gain control of himself, Gorsham finally said, "You cannot be serious, child."

"We are deathly serious, and my name is not 'child.' I am Berola and on behalf of myself, Clarinda, and these, the last of the Ocular, we demand sanctuary as guaranteed by the Firedraques for those in need of the protection of Perriz."

"Last of the Ocular?" the lieutenant said, looking with astonishment at Gorsham.

Gorsham was no less flabbergasted. "The last? What the hell happened?"

"We will tell you once we have been granted sanctuary."

All eyes were upon Gorsham. His mind was racing. The fact was that the Ocular bitch was right. It was known far and wide that the Firedraques, in an attempt to bring life and vitality to Perriz, had made the city available for any seeking sanctuary, ranging from the politically estranged to victims of wars. Thus far no one had taken advantage of it, because that was simply not the way the Twelve Races operated. Aside from the mixing of Firedraques and

Mandraques—not unusual since they were basically two branches of the same tribe—the various races stayed to themselves. As for victims of war, most of them tended to be extremely dead and thus not much in need of sanctuary. So although there was indeed precedent for the request, the action itself was unprecedented. The Mandraques patrolled the borders to keep invaders out; not those seeking help.

Gorsham's instinct was to prevent them from entering Perriz, feeling it to be some sort of ruse under the guise of a sanctuary request. But he didn't have the authority to make that decision, to fly in the face of stated Firedraque policy. Besides, the Ocular weren't typically that interested in conquest these days. Not with that simpering fool Nagel in charge. Except Nagel was mostly interested in finding ways to battle the Piri, and yet here was a Piri leading them.

"Are you saying Nagel is dead?"

There were sullen nods from the Ocular.

Gorsham scratched his throat thoughtfully while his tail twitched. Finally he said, "Very well. Sanctuary is granted for the Ocular . . . but not," he continued, pointing at Clarinda, "for you."

"What?" said Berola. There were angry murmurs from the rest of the Ocular. The only one who did not react was the Piri, except to cock one pale eyebrow and smile as if she were not the least surprised.

"Sanctuary is intended for true beings. Not parasites."

"She is not a parasite," said Berola heatedly. "She is our friend."

"She is an animal. She will turn on you sooner or later." He pointed at her with his sword. "She cannot help it. It is her nature. Whatever you think her motives are . . . however you may think she is trying to help you . . . I assure you, she has her own agenda. She may well be a scout for a possible invasion force."

"My understanding is that scouts generally try to obscure their presence," said Berola, her voice dripping with sarcasm. "They do not generally walk right in and make their presence known."

"A spy then. She's likely a spy."

"Is that not a determination for the Firedraques to make? It is, after all, their policy. Their city. Not your city. But I forgot: Mandraques don't have a central city. You're all nomads because anyplace you settle tends to get destroyed in your endless wars. Some of you serve as bondsmen to the Firedraques, but the rest of you are doubtless out on the plains trying to kill each other yet again."

"You," he said to Berola, "know a great deal for someone who knows nothing at all."

And then the Piri, the one named Clarinda—a revelation surprising in and of itself since Gorsham had never given thought to whether the Piri even had names—said softly, "Berola, it's all right. I'll leave."

"What?" Berola looked stunned, and protests began to well up from the other Ocular.

She put up her hands and they were instantly silenced by the gesture. "Listen to me," she said. "He is right." She spoke over the immediate tumult. "He is right. When first I encountered you, my concern was solely for my well-being. Not for yours. For mine. It is my nature to take without any thought of giving. I saw you purely as bodies to shield me against others of my kind."

"And we did," spoke up one of the males, the one who had been carrying her. "And it felt good to do so. It felt as if we were accomplishing something." He thudded his fist into his open palm. "Whatever your motivations, you helped us."

"Merely as a byproduct. I did not truly care about you. Only about how you could best serve me." She let out an unsteady sigh. "But you are children. For all your strength, for all your size, for all your bravery . . . you are children. And children . . ." She hesitated and then her voice dropped even more, so soft that the Mandraques could scarcely hear her. "Children should be protected."

Gorsham was paying less attention to her words, though, than he was to her right hand. Without even thinking about it—without even being aware of it, apparently—her hand had drifted to her stomach and rested there for just a second. Her fingertips momentarily brushed against her belly, and then her hand dropped away.

And Gorsham knew. He knew the gesture all too well.

"Children," Clarinda said, "should not have to live . . . the way I'm going to have to live. I should not have made you a part of it. It was wrong of me. I did not realize that at the time, or if I did, I managed to rationalize it in my own mind. Now, though, faced with the prospect of you having genuine security, as opposed to the illusion of it that I offered you . . . there really is no choice to be made. This, my children, is where we part company."

She drew up her hood, obscuring her face, and turned away from them. Some of them began to protest, particularly the younger ones, but she again raised her hand preemptively and they lapsed into silence once more. Clarinda reached the far end of the bridge and kept walking without looking back.

Berola cast a defiant glare at Gorsham and then with no hesitation, followed her. Clarinda stopped, turned to face her and said, "What do you think you're doing?"

"Going with you."

"The hell you are. You're staying here."

She drew herself up, emphasizing the size disparity. "Make me."

Clarinda looked as if she were about to argue, and then moaned and shook her head. "Do as you will." She continued to walk and Berola followed her.

Then the male who she had been riding fell into step behind the two of them. Then another Ocular, and another, and within moments the entirety of the group was walking away.

The Mandraques stared at each other with undisguised amusement and a measure of relief. "Well," said the lieutenant, "that takes care of that. The last thing we needed is—"

"Wait!" Gorsham bellowed.

The Ocular stopped and looked back to him. And as his fellow Mandraques regarded him in total shock, he said, "The Firedraques have established no parameters as to who may seek sanctuary, and it is not for me to gainsay them, however much my own opinions may be at variance with their policies. All of you, follow me." He paused and then added, for the benefit of the other Mandraques more than anything else, "Feel free to bring your pet with you."

His lieutenant whispered to him, "Are you insane? Have you lost your mind?"

"One more word and I rip your throat out with my teeth. If you don't believe me, speak. I dare you. I beg you."

His lieutenant said nothing.

"Very wise," said Gorsham.

THE SPIRES

I.

THE FIRST THING THAT NORDA Kinklash felt she needed to do was properly dispose of the body of New Daddy. She had not lost sight of the fact that she was going to exact revenge on the metal man. He would pay for New Daddy's death. But there had to be an order to these sorts of things. And before the dead could be avenged, they had to be laid to rest properly.

It had taken her a great deal of time to get down the Scary Tower (as she had come to think of it) to the street level. She had encountered large ornate doors and had pressed her earhole against them, hearing "whooshing" from the other side as if there was a vast tunnel of air on the other side. Norda wasn't entirely sure what it was or what it looked like, but she knew she didn't want any part of it.

After many false starts, she had discovered a stairwell that appeared to lead down to the bowels of the Scary Tower. She started taking it. At first she had been extremely stealthy, taking care to make as little noise as possible. Eventually, though, she had grown bored and started bounding between the stairs and the banister in order to pass the time. She even started singing and humming songs to keep her mind occupied, and by the time she finally made it to the bottom of the stairs, she had completely forgotten the mission that she had been so determined to follow up on top.

She reached a dead end in the stairs, and there was a door to the right. It had large red writing over it and some sort of bar in the middle. Norda went over to the writing and, extending one finger, traced the curve of each letter. What she traced was, "EMERGENCY EXIT. ALARM WILL SOUND." None of it meant anything to her.

Finally, once she had meticulously brought her finger around the bottom of the "D," she pushed on the bar. The door popped open and fresh air wafted in.

A klaxon began to wail.

With a startled shriek, Norda bounded out through the door and slammed it shut. She blinked against the sunlight and then ran from the disturbing blaring, eager to leave it far behind her.

Norda looked up, shielding her eyes against the sun. She tried to see the top of the Scary Tower but couldn't make it out. It made her aware of just how high up she had been. Anyone else might have been intimidated or shaken by the notion of dangling from such altitude. Norda, however, was not anyone else.

"Look what I did, my brother," she whispered. "I was above the Damned World. It was all spread out below me, and I was above it all. Nothing could touch me, nothing could hurt me. How I wish you could have seen it."

Winds whispered to her then, and she was certain that they were saying, *I saw you, Norda. I saw you, and you were ever so much more clever than the rest of them. I have never been more proud.* She could not tell if it was really Arren's voice or her imagination at work. Fantasy and reality had always been such abstract concepts to her that she had trouble staying focused on the line of demarcation.

Her mind wandered back to her home at Firedraque Hall, or at least her unofficial home, bounding around in the bell tower. And she remembered how New Daddy would come to talk to her about . . .

She gasped. "New Daddy!" Norda had completely forgotten.

Quickly she circled the perimeter of the Scary Tower, having lost her sense of direction and not at all sure where Nicrominus had come down. Part of her was hoping against hope that somehow he had managed to survive the plummet. New Daddy was a magical, wonderful individual, and if anyone could avoid death despite such a catastrophic fall, surely it was he.

Then she heard some sort of snarling. She didn't know what it was, but when she turned the corner, she found out quickly enough.

Five hairy beasts were grouped around New Daddy's body.

She knew instantly what they were: dugs. She had seen dugs occasionally in the streets of Perriz, but they had been fairly peaceful and restrained in their conduct. The Firedraques regularly fed them sweet meats and such, and the dugs responded with devotion and affection.

Not these dugs. These dugs were bristling with fur and there was drool trickling down from their jaws. They were various shades of brown and black, and they were busily fighting over the remains of New Daddy that were splattered on the street. Much of his body was still intact, but there was blood everywhere. Two of the dugs were wrestling over some organs that had oozed from his corpse. A third was lapping up some blood that had pooled to one side. Two more of them were squaring off over New Daddy's body, their tails stiff, each trying to warn off the other and neither interested in giving way.

Upon seeing the tableau spread before her, Norda let out a screech like the damned that brought all the dugs to a halt.

As one, the pack came together, ready to converge upon her.

Norda did not wait.

With a roar of fury, she came right at them, her claws out. As one of the largest of the dugs came at her, something that tasted like extremely bitter saliva welled up in her mouth. She spat it directly at the lead dug. Thick and viscous, it splattered all over the dug's face. The creature flipped backwards, howling, thrashing about on the ground. A sizzling noise arose and the smell of burning meat pervaded the air.

Norda was taken aback. *I can do that? I didn't know I could do that. I don't think Arren knows either. I wonder if he can. Will he be proud of me or jealous?*

She became so lost in thought that she nearly forgot, yet again, the circumstances of her surroundings. But then more dugs came at her. She sprang out of the way and whipped her tail around, wrapping her tail around the throat of one of them. Norda tightened her tail and then yanked, and there was a satisfying snapping of bone accompanied by a startled and very final "yip" from the dug. She tossed it aside with a casual flick of her tail and bared her fangs at the remaining three.

One backed off, but two more came at her from either direction. She dodged to the right, then the left, and then vaulted over them. She landed and as one tried to pivot to face her, it reared up on its hind legs, perhaps thinking it could bear her to the ground with its forepaws. That proved to be a mistake as she swept her outstretched claws across the dug's momentarily exposed underbelly. Blood jetted from it and entrails spilled out, and the dug flipped over and died before it even realized what had happened.

The fourth dug got lucky. The largest of the pack, it leaped through the air while Norda was still distracted by the one she had just disemboweled. It landed squarely on her, and she was slammed to the ground under the dug's weight. It howled in triumph atop her, its fetid breath washing over her, and Norda reached up and grabbed its upper and lower jaws with either hand. Realizing its danger, the dug tried to pull away, but it had no chance. Norda gritted her teeth and applied pressure in opposite directions to the dug's muzzle. The dug struggled in her grasp as its jaws widened, widened, and seconds later Norda was rewarded with a satisfying tearing and snapping as the dug's mouth was torn apart. The dug made a few halfhearted attempts to claw at her, but they were as much automatic reflex as anything else, and then the creature's corpse slumped against her. Norda shoved it off herself and stood.

The fifth dug was standing a few feet away, its tail between its legs. It was a patchwork of brown and black, and the smallest of the pack. She recognized it as the one that had been lapping up the blood, keeping clear of the others. It simply stood there with its tongue hanging out, staring at her pathetically.

"What?" Norda demanded to know.

It backed up and lowered its head, looking utterly submissive.

Her eyes narrowing, she continued to watch the dug warily as she sidled over to New Daddy's body.

"I am so sorry, New Daddy," she said mournfully. "I so wanted to know you better. There was so many things that I was sure you were going to be able to tell me. And now . . . now you can't. Not anymore. You seemed ever so clever, and I will make the metal man pay. I will make him hurt as he hurt you, and hurt me. And I will make sure that you are with me the entire time."

She lifted his right hand to her mouth and kissed it gently. Then, one by one, ever so delicately, she bit off each of his fingers, crunched the bones thoroughly, and swallowed each one.

One she was done with the fingers, she turned her attention to his hand, and then the rest of the arm. Most of his bones had been shattered by the impact of the fall, so it was not quite as crunchy as it would ordinarily have been.

Then she started on the rest of his body, or at least what was left of it.

It took quite a few hours, although it helped that she was hungry anyway. The birds that she had managed to catch had only gone so far in stilling the grumbling in her stomach. She was relieved to find that his heart was still there, if somewhat pulpy. She set it aside to save for last, as was the custom.

She stripped away the meat from his head but only nibbled at it because she was not particularly fond of head meat. With his skull exposed, she carefully removed his lower jaw. Despite his age, he had kept his teeth nicely sharp, and she admired it briefly before tucking it into her belt.

Norda devoured enough of him to fill up her first stomach and most of her second. Finally she picked up the heart.

"I am sorry that you have died so far from home. May the . . ." She stopped, searching her recollection. "May the gods guide you in your course. May they bless you and keep you. May the answers that you find be worthy of the questions that we posed. Go in grace."

It was hard, which was surprising to her, because he had seemed so soft hearted in life.

Finally, when the heart was done, she looked at the remains of the body and wondered if she should bring some of it along for further possible meals. But that seemed wrong to her. Typically there was always more than one Mandraque around to do the honors, so leftovers were not an issue. To eat the deceased as part of the customary rites of passing was part of tradition. To do so over a period of days as hunger demanded . . . that just seemed undignified. But to just leave him there was wasteful, and she had been taught to abhor waste.

She heard a whimpering and looked toward the remaining dug. He was still sitting there with his tongue hanging out and was looking hopefully toward the remains of Nicrominus.

Norda sighed. "Fine," she said, and she stepped back and gestured for the dug to approach.

The dug did so tentatively at first, as if suspecting that there might be some sort of trick involved. But when Norda made no move to intercept it, it went for Nicrominus's remains eagerly. It seemed to Norda as if the creature hadn't eaten in days. For all she knew, it hadn't.

"I suppose," she said softly, "that we all try to pay respects in our own way."

She remained where she was and watched until the dug ate its fill. There was almost nothing left of Nicrominus by that point except a few stray bones that had somehow managed to remain intact despite the force of the impact. She picked up one and used it to pick her teeth while she watched the dug lap clean as much as it could.

Finally, feeling that everything that needed to be said and done had been accomplished, she turned and walked away with absolutely no clue of where she was going to go or what she was going to do. She wanted to find the metal man, of course, but didn't know where to look. Furthermore, exhaustion was beginning to weigh heavily upon her. She wanted someplace to rest, but it was a strange and alien city that she was in and she couldn't imagine where she might feel safe enough to close her eyes.

She heard a clicking of nails and looked down. The dug was next to her, looking up at her with big brown eyes.

"You live here," Norda said. "Where should I go?"

The dug stared at her for a few more moments and then started down the street. She watched it go, shaking her head. But when she began to turn away and head in the opposite direction, the dug barked at her in a very deliberate manner. It waited for her, its tail wagging.

Curious, Norda set off after it.

Apparently satisfied that Norda was coming along, the dug headed off down the street at a slow trot. Norda followed, marveling at the size of all the buildings. None of them were as tall as the Scary Tower, but even the smallest of them seemed larger than the buildings of Perriz (save, of course, for the Eyeful Tower.) Confident that Norda could keep up, the dug picked up speed and she did so as well. Soon both of them were at a full-out run, and when the dug barked yet again Norda responded with as close an approximation as she could come up with to the dug's vocalizations. *It's teaching me its language. How clever. I wonder if it's one of the Twelve Races that I haven't met before.* She was starting to regret that she had dispatched the others, although perhaps that was a wise thing since they had behaved in ever-so-impolite a manner to her and probably deserved a good disemboweling.

She crossed a number of intersections, and then a statue caught her eye. It appeared to be a statue of a Mort, and he was crouched with a large sphere balanced atop his shoulders. But her passing interest in that quickly gave way when she saw the building opposite it, the building that the dug had stopped in front of. Apparently it was the dug's home, and the dug was inviting her to share it.

Norda put a hand to her chest and could scarcely breathe. She would not have thought it possible, but there it was: a building that reminded her so much of Firedraque Hall that she felt as if she had returned home. It wasn't quite as big or majestic, but it was nevertheless formidable. Twin spires straddled the vast front door, and the entire thing seemed carved out of marble. Huge crosses were mounted on the front, and she could make out stained glass windows, further evoking Firedraque Hall back in Perriz.

She wished that New Daddy could have seen it, and then realized that—through her eyes—he was.

The dug paused on the stairs, waiting for her, and Norda scampered up behind it, laughing delightedly as she went.

Norda ran down the vast main hall. There were large scraps of cloth, presumably flags, hanging from either side. It was filled with a musty odor and she ran up to the podium on the front, looking around eagerly. The dug bounced around, barking excitedly, apparently seeking approval from Norda for its bringing her there. Norda absently patted the dug on the head and then turned her attention to finding some stairs.

She did so in short order and soon was sprinting upward as fast as her legs would take her. The dug lost interest in following her halfway up and came to a rest on a landing, panting and then settling down to wait for her return.

The closer she drew, the more she felt fresh air blowing through, the more excited she became. Finally she burst through a trap door and entered the open air. Above her was a gigantic array of bells. She threw wide her arms and sobbed in joy. "Yes, yes, yesssss!" she cried out and she bounded around the bells, swinging from the ropes, dangling on the clappers. She could not recall the last time she had been so happy.

When she finally tired of ricocheting around the bell tower, she climbed up on the edge and looked out. Lining the ledge were stone statues that looked vaguely like Mandraques, crouched and looking out across the city. Without hesitation she clambered out next to them. She ran her fingers over one of the statues, studying it carefully and curious as to whether it might spring to life somehow. Then she found a space for herself next to it, crouched beside it, and shared the statue's view of the city.

"It's quite nice," she said.

The statue did not reply at first. That made sense. It was made of stone, and stone was ponderous and cold and thoughtful. Finally the statue replied, "Yes."

A small gray and white bird flew down and settled on the statue's head. She was not hungry, but she couldn't help but think such an action was disrespectful. So she snatched the bird off the statue's head, crushed it, and tossed it away.

"Thank you," said the statue.

"Happy to do it," said Norda, and then she settled in next to the statue, closed her eyes, and drifted happily to sleep.

II.

THAT WAS THE DAMNEDEST THING.

The Colonel was certain that he had heard the bells of Saint Patrick's Cathedral ringing. But that should have been impossible.

He had been some blocks away, relaxing in Bryant Park behind the Public Library, thinking about all that had transpired recently. He had removed his helmet and was allowing the sun to shine down upon his face. He used to enjoy that sensation. Now, like all sensations, it was simply something that he experienced without feeling strongly about it one way or the other.

Now if he could have removed the rest of his armor, well . . . that would have been a different story. But that wasn't going to be happening anytime soon. He was too thoroughly locked into it, with all his bodily needs and requirements being attended to. He would not have lasted ten minutes outside of the armor.

But what if it was a worthwhile ten minutes?

And so the Colonel sat and tried to contemplate just what that ten minutes would have to consist of to be worth certain death, and that was when he heard the bells ringing. At first he had accepted them as a matter of course, but then realized that the sounds shouldn't be possible. The bells hadn't chimed in years. There had been a mechanism that caused them to ring at particular times. He had always considered that to be a grim and yet amusing irony, the bells of God's house summoning the long gone faithful. It was as if God was calling out, begging, pleading, wheedling, saying, "Remember me? Your creator? The one you used to worship all the time? I've really gotten to miss that. Won't someone, somewhere please come to my house and praise me in the highest? Please? Pretty please?"

Eventually the mechanism had run down or broken or whatever happened to mechanisms when there was no one around to attend to them, and the bells had gone silent. God had lost his voice. That was fine by the Colonel. There wasn't a damned thing that arrogant, useless prig on high could have to say that would be of the slightest interest to him.

But when the bells began chiming for no reason, the Colonel considered that to be a bit disconcerting.

He left the back of the library straight away and strode down 42nd over to 5th. Once he hit 5th, he started to run. The armor was extremely useful in that score, allowing him to do pretty much anything that occurred to him physically, short of flying. He considered that to be a damned inconvenient oversight, but one that he was willing to live with.

The armor wasn't clanking. It never did when he ran. He didn't know why that was, because it could make a hell of a racket when he walked. When running, though, it was as if the ground absorbed all the noise. Years ago he had found it odd. Now he didn't notice it.

The strangest thing about the sounding of the bells was that it was not happening in any sort of pattern. Back in the days when the bell sounded, they did so in a particular order that he had come to recognize. This wasn't in any order. It was as if something was just banging around in there.

Even at the speed with which he was moving, the bells ceased ringing by the time he was halfway there. So when he arrived in front of Saint Patrick's, he stood there and looked upward toward the bell towers without actually knowing what he was looking for. The last of the bells' echoes had vanished into the air, leaving him staring up at gargoyles.

He frowned. Was there something off about one of the gargoyles?

He looked down. There was a dead pigeon on the sidewalk. He picked it up and studied it. It looked as if it had been crushed. That could, of course, be due to the fact that it had hit the ground. It could have had some manner of pigeon heart attack, plummeted from on high, and the damage he was seeing was a result of the impact. Still, it seemed . . .

At that moment, a dog started barking furiously from the doors. The Colonel glanced toward it and the dog, as if anticipating an attack, continue to bark as if warning the Colonel not to even think about coming in.

"Dogs," he muttered.

"What about them?"

A Traveler was at his elbow. The Colonel had not heard him coming. In the old days, he'd been disconcerted by their random appearances. At this point he was used to it. Nothing fazed him.

"Had a dog as a child," said the Colonel. "When I was a child, I mean. It was the only creature on earth that I could ever count on, and that included both my parents and my younger brother. When the animal—Mickey, is what I named him—ran out in front of a truck and got himself struck and killed, I cried for a week. On some level, though, I admired him for the death he chose. I didn't see it, but according to the people who did, he didn't just get clipped while trying to cross a street. No, Mickey darted in front of an oncoming truck, turned to face it, and barked defiantly like he was challenging the truck to take its best shot. Which, of course, it did, and that was the end of Mickey. Point is: Once I dried my tears, I decided that when I went, I wanted to go like that. Lot to be said for that."

"Is that not what you did?"

He glanced at the Traveler. "What do you mean?" But then he paused and frowned and said, "Yeah. Yeah, I guess you're right at that. Facing off against the thundering hoards, telling them to get off my world, leaping to the attack . . . I thought I was going to die that day. And I was going to die on my own terms."

"Yet you did not."

"No. I didn't. Maybe I should have. Because if I had, I wouldn't be going so crazy with loneliness and boredom that I'd be contemplating statuary and dead pigeons." With a grunt of disgust, he threw the deceased bird toward the barking dog. The dog snapped it up on the fly and darted back to the recesses of the cathedral.

There was probably a pack of them in there. And they'd gotten up into the bell tower, and pulled on some of the ropes, and that's where the ringing came from.

That's what it has come down to, has it? God with his voice gone, depending upon stray dogs to speak on his behalf. Then again, that's the way it's always been, hasn't it. God on high, the pitiless, uncaring, master. And humanity serving as nothing but his whipped dogs, to bark and scrape and beg for some measure of His mercy when there was none to give. Children dying of disease before they had a chance to live, and people congregating to worship in churches that are destroyed by earthquakes, and that wasn't enough for us to realize that He doesn't give a damn about us. And so we were invaded and damned near wiped out. And how much you want to bet that somewhere out there, there are still humans bowing down and worshipping and waiting for Him to rescue us, as if all this is just some sort of huge test of mankind's resilience.

He was disgusted with his race. He was disgusted with himself.

He looked up once more. "Does something look off with the gargoyles to you?"

"Off?" the Traveler faintly echoed.

The Colonel was about to pursue it and then thought better of it. "Never mind. It's stupid. Don't worry about it." He turned away and began walking. The Traveler fell into step alongside him. "What do you want?"

"What do *you* want?" said the Traveler.

"Oh, it's one of these deals, is it?" said the Colonel with a groan. "Where one of you types simply shows up because you feel a summoning . . ."

"Calling," the Traveler corrected him. He continued to make no noise at all as he moved.

"Right, right. A 'calling' that somehow something is going to be required of you. That you have to be at a specific place at a specific time although you don't always know why or what purpose your involvement is going to serve. That about right?"

"Yes."

"Terrific."

The Traveler stopped walking so abruptly and so silently that it was several steps before the Colonel realized that the Traveler was no longer at his side. He turned back to the Traveler, who bowed slightly and said, "If I am wrong and you have no need of me, then I will depart."

"I didn't say that." The Colonel scratched the underside of his chin and then, for some reason, felt self-conscious. He raised his helmet up over his head and then lowered it. It clicked into place and automatically snapped shut tightly. When he spoke, his voice boomed. He wished there were some manner of volume control, but if there was, he had yet to discover it.

The fact was that there was something on his mind. He had been considering what Nicrominus had told him, and his own feelings on the subject. He was ancient by this point, older than any human had a right to be, but that didn't mean he was too old to develop some manner of payback that would work on more than one level. Perhaps there was something to be said for this entire business of Travelers and their receiving the Calling after all. "But since you've brought it up . . . there is something that I have been giving thought to of late."

"Yes, Overseer?"

"Humanity. What there is left of it, I mean."

"Yes, Overseer?"

"I believe it is time to attend to it. Matters should not be left where they are."

"They should not? Your people are all but extinct, Overseer."

"I do not think of them as my people. They have not been for a very long time. Truthfully, I felt very little attachment even before . . . this," and he rapped on the armor, causing a faint echo.

"Understood, Overseer. But it is still unclear what you are saying."

"Is it? I am saying that something needs to be done about the situation."

"Are you saying that breeding needs to be encouraged—perhaps even organized—for the purpose of growing the population?"

"Good lord, no. I was thinking about having the remainder of them rounded up and executed. Do you think you and your fellows could arrange that?"

The Traveler did not hesitate. "Easily, Overseer."

"Good. Keep me apprised of how that goes, would you?"

Without waiting for an answer, the Overseer walked away with a gentle clanking of his metal booted feet. He did not glance again over his shoulder, and so did not notice that the Traveler was instead looking behind him. Behind him and up toward the row of gargoyles atop the cathedral.

"Yes, Overseer," said the Traveler almost as an afterthought, even though the Overseer was already walking away. "I will indeed keep you apprised of everything that transpires. Just as I always have." Then he turned away from the gargoyles with no further comment.

OFF THE COAST OF THE CITY/STATE OF VENETS

I.

KARSEN FOUX RODE HIS WHORES slowly along the coast, with Eutok directly behind him. The waters were lapping against the shores, and he stared out upon the seas without the slightest hope of seeing anything useful.

The whores was gasping tiredly, as was Eutok's. It wasn't surprising since they had been riding their whores rather hard and there was only so much riding even the sturdiest of whores could withstand. Finally deciding to take pity on the poor thing, Karsen dismounted and strode over to the shoreline. Eutok did likewise.

He moved to the edge of the water and stared out onto the horizon. Some distance away the coastline of Venets was visible. Karsen knew a bit about Venets and its residents, but had never had the opportunity to visit there since it had not been the source of any major wars. Bottom Feeders tended to stay in the areas of land wars since those tended to provide the most opportunity for enrichments. On the other hand the Sirene, the denizens of Venets, held unquestioned superiority over the waters and thus were generally left alone since the various races were not exactly equipped to fight a water battle.

There was a long silence, and finally Karsen said, "Now what?"

"This was the direction they came. This was as far as they went. At least as far as I can track them that they went."

"And that's it?" He spun to face Eutok, towering over him, fist cocked as if he desperately wanted to slam it into Eutok's face and needed but the slightest excuse to do so. "This is as far as you can track them?"

"What would you have of me?" demanded Eutok. "I told you

I'd lead you in the direction that I saw them transporting her. We've managed to find enough traces of their subsequent tracks to verify that I was right. So what now?"

"That's what I'm asking you! What now?"

"I don't know what now!" Eutok said with exasperation. "It's not as if I have a grand scheme for all of this! I was simply trying to get myself healed, and you were the only one who seemed capable of attending to it! And I did everything I promised I would do! More!"

"You're right."

"So if you think that—"

"I said," Karsen said, putting up his hands in a calming manner, "that you're right. You did what you said you would do. And you're healed. At least as much as what arts I possess can manage." He took a deep breath and let it out slowly. "This isn't your fault. You brought me as far as you could go. We're done, you and I."

He took a few steps away from the Trull, trying to determine which direction to go or what his next move would be. He wound up dropping down to the ground and sitting on the shoreline, with the water lapping up to just around his hooves. He wondered if the best thing to do at that point wasn't to just let the water wash over him and carry him away.

There was a noise from nearby and he realized that Eutok was standing near him. "What do you want?" he said.

"I was just wondering what you were going to do now?"

"I have no further information on that," he said drily, "than the last time we discussed that. Why do you care? What are you still doing here? You're healed. You've fulfilled your rather self-serving obligations to me. Why are you still here? Why don't you go—?"

"Go where? Where would you suggest I go? Back to the Hub? So I can stand trial and be executed, presuming it even gets that far? Wander the lands until my feet bleed? What do you envision me doing with my life?"

"How the hell would I know, Eutok? I don't know what I'm going to be doing with my life, so I certainly haven't given the particulars of your situation any thought."

Eutok grunted acknowledgment.

Karsen ran his fingers through his wiry hair as he tried to determine what his next move would be. Nothing was coming to mind. Instead all he could do was chide himself over having charged headlong into this mess so precipitously, and not leaving himself any options beyond—

"You know . . ."

"What?" said Karsen, his frustration boiling over. He was seriously considering unslinging the hammer and trying to use it to stave in Eutok's skull.

Karsen's tone did not seem to bother Eutok in the slightest. "Perhaps someone else saw where they went."

"Someone else?"

"Yes."

Karsen simply shook his head in slow disbelief. "Are you serious?"

Eutok shrugged. "Why not?"

"Because there's no reason for it to happen! No reason for anyone to pay attention and take notice of Jepp being taken to . . . to wherever it was they took her!"

"No reason for them not to have either."

"That's ridiculous. That makes no sense."

"What does make sense to you?" said Eutok, pointing a meaty finger at him. "Sitting here like a pathetic sop, helpless in the face of events? Admitting defeat? Doing nothing?"

"Why do you care?"

"Well . . ." Eutok looked frustrated. "Because everybody's got to care about something."

"And this is it for you? I'm it? I'm what you've chosen to care about? Do you have any idea how ridiculous that sounds? Have you never cared about anything else?"

"Only that which can destroy me."

There was something in the way he said it that caught Karsen's attention. "What are you talking about?"

The Trull stared at him, various emotions playing across his face, and then he said gruffly, "Never mind. Do as you will."

He started to walk away with that typical Trull side-to-side swagger, but for some reason it struck Karsen less like a biological necessity of the way the Trull was built and instead a show of empty bravado.

There was no reason for him to have Eutok there. No reason at all.

"Wait," he called out.

Eutok stopped and faced him.

Karsen looked out toward the water, and then back to Eutok. "Find someone, you say?"

"Someone. Anyone. You never know."

"No. No, I don't suppose that you do."

He got to his hooves, went back to the whores, took his by the rope that was hanging around its neck and held out the other to Eutok. The Trull took it in his thick hand and they started walking.

For a time they said nothing. Finally:

"Tell me about her."

Eutok looked at him. "Her? What do you—?" Then he understood and scowled as fiercely as only a Trull could. "Oh. Her."

"You said I knew nothing about her. Tell me, then. I mean, who am I to judge? I'm in love with a human." He considered the words that he had just spoken. "Still sounds odd for me to say that aloud. Anyway, my mother treated me with nothing but contempt for feeling anything for Jepp. So I don't quite see where I have the moral authority to condemn you for choices that others might deem . . ." He paused. " . . . questionable."

"That's very open minded of you," said Eutok, his voice dripping with sarcasm. At the same time, though, there was something in his tone that conveyed he was pleased to hear Karsen say that.

"How did you meet her?"

"I was hunting her in order to kill her and present her head as a trophy to my mother."

"Oh. How . . . sweet," said Karsen, the last word just sort of falling out of his mouth and lying on the ground.

"I wasn't looking for it to happen!" Eutok said defensively. "And even when it was happening, I didn't want it to happen!"

"Well . . . these things happen."

"Yes. They do."

"Where is she now?"

"With her people."

"Well, then . . ." His voice trailed off.

Eutok stopped walking and looked at him with irritation. "What? Well then what?"

"Why don't you go to her? You obviously have no place with your people any more. Perhaps her people will accept you . . ."

"No. They won't. If I know anything of a certainty, it's that. I can't see her again."

"Why not?"

"Because I can't."

"That's not a reason—"

"Shut up!"

Karsen rolled his eyes but said nothing further.

They trudged along for a while longer and then out of nowhere, Eutok said, "I made a promise to her and I can't keep it."

"You can't?"

"No. I mean, I could . . . but I cannot bring myself to."

"Can I ask...?"

"It's complicated."

"Perhaps you can explain it to me using small words."

At first Eutok glared at him, but then his expression softened ever so slightly and he even allowed for a gruff chuckle. Then he grew serious, as if embarrassed that he had permitted himself to be amused by anything. "The Piri have a sort of queen. They call her the Mistress. It is the job of the Mistress to represent all of the Piri."

"All right," said Karsen, not quite understanding the significance.

"Her name is Sunara. The Piri I am involved with—was involved with—is her daughter, Clarinda."

"And you are likewise the son of a queen, even if you did want to kill her."

"And Clarinda would eagerly see Sunara destroyed as well."

"So despite your differences, you have much in common."

"Except Clarinda would never do it. Ever. She is too afraid of her mother even to seriously contemplate such an action. And eventually Clarinda is to become Mistress herself."

"And she is daunted by the responsibilities of the office?"

"It is not a matter of the responsibilities. It is what they . . ." He took a deep breath and said, "Upon becoming Mistress, Clarinda will be forced to have her breasts removed and her feminine parts will be burned into nothingness. Thus as a sexless being, she can equally represent both genders."

Karsen stopped where he was. Eutok followed suit. "That's . . . that's hideous," he said. "This promise you made . . . is it related to—?"

"She made me promise that, were that to transpire, I would kill her, because she had no desire to live like that."

"Gods." Karsen's head was reeling from trying to take it all in. "And . . . they're going to do this to her soon?"

"After she is mated and produces an heir."

"Wait . . ." Karsen was back to being confused again. "That's going to take some time, yes? I mean, I don't know the gestation cycle for Piri, but I assume it doesn't happen overnight."

"That's unlikely."

"Then you could return to her! Take her out of there!"

"One Trull against Piri hordes? How long do you think I would last?"

"Not long," Karsen admitted. "But—"

"But what?"

He thought for a long moment and then squared his shoulders. "She has not been mated yet with a Piri. She is not with child." When the Trull shook his head, Karsen continued, "Then we have some time. Time to find Jepp, or at least do our damnedest to find her. And however that quest ends then, for good or ill, I in turn will assist you in going to the territory of the Piri and getting Clarinda out of there."

"Why? Why would you do that?"

"Because you are aiding me."

"I did so out of self-interest."

"And now?"

Eutok considered it and then said, "I have naught better to do."

"Yes, you do. Helping Clarinda. And I will do that in return."

"You say that now," said Eutok dourly. "But when you have your lady love in your arms, you may well feel differently."

"If I have her in my arms, I will be grateful to you, and my gratitude will be appropriately displayed."

"We'll see," said Eutok, but he sounded doubtful.

II.

IT WAS TWO FULL SUNS later, when Karsen was beginning to feel growing frustration and Eutok was beginning to wonder if maybe it wouldn't be a better idea for him to just go after the Piri singlehandedly and get ripped to shreds rather than deal with this frustration and guilt, that they encountered the oddest Merk either of them had ever seen. Not that either of them had ever seen a Merk, since they—along with their brethren, the Markene—stayed to the waters. Still, it was rather obvious that this curious creature was most definitely a Merk, and probably unusual even for one of them.

They had been astride the whores, going at a slow trot, when they first spotted the Merk and reined up. His scaled skin was dark brown, and his green hair dangled from his head as if someone had taken a plate of seaweed and dumped it upon him. He was in some sort of odd floating device, which was a strange thing for him to have considering that the Merk were aquatic. He wasn't moving his arms or his legs, but instead simply allowing himself to drift aimlessly. The

Merk didn't appear to spot them; it was almost as if he were staring inward. He was so quiet that Eutok didn't notice him at first, and it was Karsen who drew the Trull's attention to him. Once Eutok spotted him, he turned to Karsen questioningly. "Do you think . . . ?"

"Worth a try," said Karsen, and then he raised his voice. "Excuse me!"

The Merk regarded him with half-lidded eyes. "Which of the four of you spoke?"

"The four of—?" Karsen wanted to laugh but he had no desire to seem impolite. "These are just whores. Animals."

"Ah. I did not assume, having never seen them before. Actually, I wasn't eliminating the possibility that you were a sort of combined creature. One never knows what one will see on the Damned World."

Eutok and Karsen exchanged glances that said, *That's for sure* with regards to the individual floating in front of them. Then Karsen, clearing his throat, said, "Yes, well . . . we were just wondering about something that may have been seen. By you, I mean."

"Any particular something?" The Merk looked mildly amused. He still wasn't moving any part of his body. "There has been a good deal of things to see as I drift."

"Why are you just drifting?" said Eutok. Karsen glared at him because he was wandering off topic, but Eutok persisted, "Can't you swim?"

"Most of my body is broken," said the Merk. "An accident. Well . . . not exactly an accident. I caused it. Or at least was instrumental in it. Nothing you need to worry about. I would have raised my hand in a sort of dismissive manner while saying that, but, well, you can see why that wasn't an option."

"Certainly," said Eutok, who was already sorry he'd asked.

"This something that we're looking for," said Karsen, "would be a female. A Mort female."

"In the company of Travelers?"

Karsen felt jolted, as if someone had just slammed a spear into his backside.

Meanwhile the Merk continued, "Black haired? Lovely, if you believe that human females are capable of loveliness?"

"Yes! Yes, that's her! I can't believe it!"

"Nor can I," said Eutok dubiously. "You realize it might easily be some other human female . . ."

"Who matches Jepp's description and is in the company of Travelers? Impossible! Or at least insanely unlikely." He hesitated, almost afraid to ask. "Do you know which way they went, Merk? Or remember?"

"They were heading to the Spires."

"The Spires! Are you sure?"

"One of the Travelers said as much to another." He smiled wryly. "Mentioned it in conversation. They have a very curious language, the Travelers do, when speaking to each other. You'd probably hear nothing but whispers. But Markene have far sharper hearing."

"You're a Merk," Karsen said uncertainly. If he had to remind this creature of his own race, he was starting to wonder just how dependable anything he was saying was.

"I'm aware of that," said the Merk, sounding not a little amused. "But a Markene was with me, and followed the vessel for a bit. He returned to me and told me what they had said. Markene are accustomed to being able to hear under the waters, you see. Very little that can be said in their presence that—"

"Wait . . . their vessel? They were on a ship?"

"Of course," the Merk said reasonably. "Walking to the Spires isn't exactly practical."

Karsen felt a sense of helplessness welling up. "How the hell are we supposed to follow them to the Spires?" With fading hope, he said to the Markene, "Do you have a boat we can borrow? Or keep?"

"We're Sirene. What would we need with boats? Besides, has either of you sailed?" When they shook their heads, he said, "So you don't know where you're going, and you have no experience with the means to get there. If I did have a boat to give you, I would be condemning you to a slow death."

"Better that," said Karsen morosely, "then living with the knowledge that Jepp is in their hands and we remain helpless to do anything about it."

"Oh, please!" Eutok shook his head in disgust. "She's a Mort, Karsen. When all is said and done, she remains a Mort. How much melodrama do you require?"

Karsen glared at him. "I'm not like you, Trull. I'm not so cold hearted that I can just shut my mind off to the needs of a female I love. Do you even understand the concept of love?"

"I understand more than you think. Don't presume to know my mind."

Rage began to surge in him, but just as quickly it subsided, overwhelmed by a sense of despair. "Forget it. Forget it, Eutok. You've exceeded your obligation to me, real or imagined. I have no way of reaching the Spires, and Jepp is going to be in the hands of the Travelers, and I can't get her back, and there's nothing you can do about it. If you want me to come with you to try and rescue Clarinda, I will do so. If you don't, then you'll receive no judgment from me. I'm really in no position to sit in judgment on anyone."

They sat there upon their whores, no words passing between them. Eutok seemed as if he wanted to say something, but was hesitant to do so.

"There is, of course, the Crossing."

It had been the strange, floating Merk who had spoken. Karsen looked at him in confusion. "The what?"

"The Crossing." He said it so matter-of-factly that Karsen unaccountably felt stupid for not knowing what he was referring to.

"And what would that be?"

"I shouldn't have to tell you that. He can." He nodded toward Eutok, causing his boat to bob slightly.

Eutok looked stunned. "How do you know about the Crossing? You're not a Trull. Only Trulls know of the Crossing."

"What's the Crossing?" said Karsen.

"It goes under the water," said the Merk.

"So?" said a clearly irritated Eutok.

"What's the Crossing?" Karsen repeated.

"So anything that goes under the water is going to be known to the Sirene," said the Merk.

What's the Crossing!?

Eutok shifted uncomfortably on the back of his whores. "It's a tunnel. A Trull tunnel that runs under the Vast Waters. There's even a Truller track, although I have no idea whether it's functioning or not."

"Why did the Trulls build an underground tunnel from here to the Spires?"

"We didn't."

"But you just said—"

"We built it from the Spires to here."

Understanding began to dawn. "When we first arrived here, you wound up in the Spires."

"Not me personally," said Eutok. "It was long before my time."

"As it was before mine."

"When the Spires was made the home of the Overseer, our then-leaders decided that the wisest course would be to put as much distance between the Trulls and the Overseer as possible. My understanding is that the Spires is situated on a vast continent, but our ancestors felt that it was better to leave it to the Overseer and his minions."

"They felt the Overseer needed an entire continent?" Karsen shook his head in astonishment. "How much power does this one individual have, anyway?"

"It is said his power is limitless. He can destroy you with but a look. With a wave of his hand, he can command the elements. Annihilate you with lightning, blow you away with a vast wind. He can turn back the hands of time, and emit blasts of force from his eyes."

"I accept that it's all said. But has anyone ever purported to see it himself?"

"None have survived," Eutok said gravely.

"Really. None."

"None."

"Then how," said Karsen, "would anyone possibly be able to report the specifics of what the Overseer can or cannot do? And whie we're at it, why did you say there were no Trull tunnels to other lands?"

Eutok started to reply but fell silent.

The odd Sirene was continuing to float there as if he were enjoying watching a show of some sort. When both of them fell silent, he prompted them. "So what are you going to do? I'm just interested, mind you."

Karsen hesitated and then said, "The Crossing isn't guarded, you say?"

"I didn't say that. I said it wasn't maintained."

"Why?"

"Why would it be?" he said with a shrug. "It's not as if my people would have the slightest interest in heading back to the Spires. We focus our resources where they will do the most good. It seemed ridiculous to have maintenance crews involved in a section of tunnel that we never intend to travel."

Karsen had to admit that it made sense. "So we should be able to take this tunnel, this Crossing, to the Spires."

"If the Trullers are functional, yes."

"And if they're not? Can you repair them?"

"I have absolutely no idea."

Karsen considered that and then said, "All right. Fine. That's enough for now. Do you know which direction this Crossing is?"

"Yes. The entrance is in a city called Porto, in the country of Espan."

"Minosaurs run rampant through Espan, and they can be notoriously territorial."

"I know. One of several reasons I lied earlier. So let's not go."

"But we have to!"

"Make up your mind!"

"All right!" He put his hand to his head. "If you're willing to guide me, then I'm willing to follow you. And you," he turned to the Merk who was continuing to float there. "I am in your debt."

The Merk did not seem particularly concerned. "You owe me nothing. The truth is that I have been floating around for quite some time with not much to occupy me. I have to depend on passing Markene to feed me. It is not much of a life, really. But we can only make so many choices in our lives, and the rest is left to blind chance. It is what it is."

"At least tell me your name so that I can offer prayers of thanks to the gods on your behalf."

"Ruark."

"Ruark." Karsen rolled the name around in his head. "I seem to recall the Sirene have a ruler by that name."

"Yes. Yes, we do. And he brought destruction and damnation down upon his people, and will likely be paying for that for the remainder of his life." He smiled lopsidedly. "Poor bastard."

The currents seemed to shift on their own, and the bobbing Merk drifted away from them. "Best of fortune to you," he said. "May you receive the destiny that you desire, if not the one you deserve."

They sat atop the whores and watched him float away.

"What is that supposed to mean?" said Eutok. "And do I even want to know?"

"I strongly suspect you do not. I know I don't." With that he wheeled his whores around and the two of them galloped off on the path to Porto.

UPPER AND LOWER REACHES OF SUISLAN

I.

PAVAN'S THOUGHTS FLEW BACK TO those times when Akasha had warned him against the dangers of wishing too hard for things. *The gods have a way of giving us that for which we've wished in such a way that we wished we'd never brought it up in the first place.*

In that regard, he thought about the times when he had looked down, down from the upper reaches of Suislan and gazed in fascination at the magnificently structured castles far down in the lower reaches. There weren't a lot of them, at least not from where he could see. But they were certainly majestic things, and he would wonder what it would be like to reside in such a structure. The Lodge was perfectly serviceable and had been a decent home to him, but it certainly wasn't a castle. The Ocular were said to live in a castle. Why not the Serabim?

Well, the answers to that were fairly obvious, actually. The Serabim were hardy enough to survive anywhere; indeed, some preferred the lowlands, especially forests. But for the most part, and certainly in the case of Pavan's tribe, they were more comfortable in a chillier climate. And so the magnificent castles remained something that were nothing but a distant, unfulfilled longing for Pavan.

Until now. Apparently Akasha had been right yet again, and the gods had provided Pavan's wish in such a way that his newest wish was never to have wished for the previous wish.

Now he was gazing out the small window of his small room, looking longingly toward the Upper Reaches that now seemed so astoundingly far away. He thought about the unfettered freedom he had there, and of Demali's soft caresses, and even Seramali's boisterousness that he considered so annoying at the time and for which he was now incredibly nostalgic.

The room in which he was being kept was five stories high. Normally that would not have presented a problem for him. He could easily climb down the side of the castle, his claws either seeking out nooks and crannies in the wall or even sinking their own grips when necessary. Unfortunately, there were half a dozen Mandraques on the ground standing guard to make sure he didn't do exactly that. And there were several more outside his door. He didn't know how many, but he heard exchanges of conversations, and knew there were several.

The door suddenly burst open and Pavan whirled to face whatever threat it was that was coming through the door. A Mandraque sauntered in, and Pavan growled low in his throat when he recognized him. There was another Mandraque visible standing guard.

"I trust you are enjoying your stay with us?" said Thulsa. He gestured toward the Mandraque outside. "Belosh has been tasked with attending to you. If you have any needs, you have but to inquire." The one he called Belosh made an irritated expression.

Pavan said nothing; he just glowered at him.

"Ah. You are annoyed with our actions. I understand." Thulsa was walking back and forth with his arms draped behind him, looking like the king of all he surveyed. Were Pavan of a bellicose nature, he would have taken the opportunity to launch himself at Thulsa and try to tear his head off. It likely would not have gone well, though, because not only was Thulsa clearly a warrior-born, but several more Mandraques were visible through the open door, glaring in in a manner that was doubtlessly intended to be threatening. Since Pavan felt threatened, it was obviously working. "This must be daunting for one such as you. It is my understanding that Keepers, by nature, are pacifistic. Not for you are the ways of war. Such emotions would make you useless to the Zeffers. Am I right?"

Pavan considered continuing his silence, but was starting to get bored with it. Thulsa was far too in love with the sound of his own voice and wouldn't stop talking whether Pavan responded or not. "You know you're right," he said. "Then again, I am of no use to the Zeffers when I'm down here in your clutches."

The Mandraque took a step toward him and there seemed to be genuine curiosity on his face. "What is it like?"

"I'm sorry?"

"What is it like when the Zeffers feed on you?"

I have no idea from personal experience. I know what Akasha has told me. The sense of communion. The fact that yes, they are taking something from you, but they are giving something back to you as well. You are providing sustenance for them, without which they would wither and die. In turn, you become part of something greater than yourself. Something primal. But I have no first-hand awareness or means of describing it because I have never done it. Which you don't know, you moron, because you thought you were stealing the Keeper and instead you simply took an apprentice. And I'll be damned if I tell you that, lest you return to the Upper Reaches and try to find and take Akasha.

Pavan made a face of disgust. "They don't 'feed' on you. It's not like that."

"Then what is it like?"

"Why do you care?"

"I don't care. I am simply curious. Are Mandraques not allowed to display curiosity?"

"You're not exactly renowned for it, no. Not as much as you are for your displays of cruelty and wanton destruction."

"We do not destroy," said Thulsa without the slightest trace of anger. If anything, he sounded proud. "We take what should be ours. By force of our personalities when possible; by force of arms when necessary."

"And who decides what should be yours?"

"We do."

Pavan chuckled softly. "And here I had heard it was the Firedraques who kept you on their leash. Who decided what was yours, and what was not, and endeavored to keep the lot of you from tearing each other to pieces like the monsters that you are."

Thulsa lurched toward him for a moment and then caught himself. He forced a smile, which looked all the more appalling because of its blatant insincerity. He waggled a finger scoldingly and said, "You are trying to provoke me. Perhaps you think you can get me so angry that I will kill you. That, my friend, is not going to happen. Your cooling corpse will be of no use to us."

"I am not quite certain how my living, breathing body is of use to you."

"Yes. You are. Because whatever else you may be, you are not stupid."

"Thank you," said Pavan, and thought, *Which is more than I can say for you, you idiot.*

"You have already figured out that you are being used as a hostage. Sooner or later, the Zeffers will indeed wither and die without their Keeper. That is obviously not a situation that the Serabim wish to experience. And so they will do whatever they need to do to make certain that doesn't happen. They will use the Zeffers to accomplish what we want to accomplish."

"And what would that be?"

"Again, you are not stupid. You have already intuited what it is. You need merely put the pieces together."

It took Pavan only moments to realize. "The Firedraques."

Thulsa nodded. "We wish to break our leashes."

"You would not dare. The authority of the Firedraques to keep the peace stems directly from the Overseer. You would not dare his wrath."

"Would we not? We, with our reputation for cruelty and wanton destruction?"

"Listen to me—"

"*We are not children!*"

The outburst of fury was unexpected, but Pavan fought the impulse to back away. "I did not say that—"

"Yes, you did. " He was restraining his anger, but barely. "With your gestures, with your tone, with your expression. You think my kind to be nothing but petulant children, fighting for toys in a box of sand, and the Firedraques are benevolent adults who are trying to keep us in hand. You are going to discover that you are wrong. The Firedraques will discover they are wrong."

"And the Overseer?"

He bared his teeth. "Bring him on."

II.

"AKASHA? ARE YOU WITHIN?"

Seramali, walking with a pronounced limp and a tentative air, stuck his head into the mouth of Akasha's cave. "Akasha? I have no interest in your games of making yourself unseen, or springing out and surprising visitors." He paused and then said more loudly, "Akasha!"

There was a stirring of shadows from within and then Akasha emerged. He seemed older than he had before. His gaze flickered to a leather strap with a short sword dangling from Seramali's shoulders. "Armed? How very unlike you. Or us."

"Regrettably, it has come to that. I have grim tidings, Akasha . . ."

"We were attacked by Mandraques, much of the Lodge has been destroyed, and Pavan has been kidnapped. Did I leave anything out?"

Seramali was unable to keep the astonishment from his face. "How did you know?"

"Your daughter."

"Demali?"

"Have you another of which you are unaware?"

"No! I just . . . I mean, I had no idea that she had come to you."

"Poor thing was distraught. She felt I should know what transpired with Pavan. I was, after all, his mentor, so naturally I have some interest in his fate. Besides, she had many things to say on the subject."

"She could have said them to me."

"Indeed. But there was much going on to which you needed to attend, and I imagine she didn't want to be a further burden to you. Besides, do you feel that this is the best time to worry about being territorial in regards to your daughter? Certainly there are matters of greater moment to worry about."

"Yes. Yes, there are."

"Which is why you have come here." His voice was grave.

Seramali hesitated, concerned over what Akasha might be thinking. "It is."

Akasha nodded and then spoke thoughtfully, as if he were addressing himself rather than the chief. "She spoke to me woefully of things."

"Woefully?"

"Yes. She was saddened that I was not present at the gathering. As I recall, you repeatedly asked me to attend. Indeed, you were expecting me to, were you not?"

"You had left me with the impression that you would be attending."

"Of course I did. You would not leave me in peace until I intimated that I would come. It was more a matter of self defense than anything else."

"Well!" Seramali blustered. "I . . . I do not think it appropriate that you lied to me over such a—"

"Had I been there, I would have been the one taken instead of Pavan. They grabbed the wrong individual. Am I correct, Seramali?"

"They took who they thought was the Keeper—"

"For obvious reasons," Akasha said mildly. "Our crest marks us. Had they seen Pavan and me together, they naturally would have taken me since I am obviously the elder. But they saw Pavan by himself and just assumed. Mandraques are notorious for that . . . for assuming. It tends to get them into trouble and yet they go ahead and do it repeatedly. And now . . . what? They are demanding our cooperation?"

"Yes."

"They want to use the Zeffers for war."

"That's correct."

"Against who? The Firedraques? The Ocular? Minosaurs, maybe? Or just other Mandraques?" Seramali was about to answer, but Akasha waved it off. "It matters not. War is war. The Zeffers should not be used for war. It will destroy them."

"Zeffers cannot be destroyed. No missiles can harm them, no—"

"Zeffers are living creatures, my chief, and anything living can be made unliving. There is more than one way to destroy something. It can happen at the spiritual core. The stain will spread within the Zeffers and bring them down far more effectively than any missile ever could. It matters not who you would bring them into war against. It will garner you results you neither expect nor desire."

"You may well be right, Keeper—"

"I may well be right?" Akasha seemed amused. "How generous of you to make that allowance. And how generous of you to allow us this time to converse. To put matters of importance off long enough."

"I have no idea what you're talking about . . ."

Akasha was no longer amused. "Yes. You know exactly what I am talking about. Do not waste my time and do not pretend, because you may be able to fool the others, and even your own daughter. I was supposed to be at the gathering because I was supposed to be taken by the Mandraques. No one ever has a proper estimation of the Mandraques, it seems. Those who count on them to properly execute even the simplest plans overestimate them, and those who expect them to be allies tend to underestimate them. You have already experienced the former, and I suspect an eventual betrayal by them will underscore the latter."

"They are not my allies, Keeper."

At that declaration, Akasha gave him a faint look of contempt. "Oh. Of course not. They are merely your tools, to be used to suit your own ends."

"My own ends. And what might those be, Akasha?" He was

dripping with sarcasm. "What nefarious deeds have you attributed to me?"

"Aside from culpability for Pavan's kidnapping and the destruction done to the lodge?"

"Keeper, with all respect . . . a respect that you apparently feel no need to accord me . . ."

"You want war."

"How dare you—?"

Akasha waved off the protests. "Save your indignation for those who might be impressed by it. I am not among them."

Seramali made an impatient grunt, but then said, "Speak your mind, then, Keeper. You have earned that right with your many years of service."

"Gracious of you, my chief. The fact is, Seramali, that your smiling face has always served as a mask behind which a would-be warlord has hidden. I have watched you bridling against the more ethereal nature of our people." He slowly approached Seramali as he spoke. "Oh, you hide it well. Most could not perceive it. But I know what to look for. Little tones of voice, certain postures, that way you force your patience since it does not come naturally. You do not wish to be above it all. You want to be down at the ground level, with the taste of battle in your mouth. You are a Mandraque born into the body of a Serabim. I have always sensed that about you, but I have kept my own council over that because it has never interfered with your abilities to carry out the duties of your office.

"The Mandraques intended to kidnap the Keeper to force our hand. But they do not have the Keeper. They have my student. Which means their leverage is severely lessened. I still have a good many years left to me; plenty of time for a new heir to surface . . . as heirs have reliably tended to do in anticipation of their need. They could, of course, return to try and kidnap me as well. But they would have to mount a return, and you would likely have to lead them here because they could not find their way with both hands and a torch. And besides, why go to all that effort when there is a much simpler means of solving the problem?"

Seramali said nothing. He no longer looked angry; just a bit saddened.

Akasha was almost nose-to-nose with Seramali. "I see where all this is going, Seramali. I see what you are doing to our people, and what you are going to do. And here's the hell of it: You're going to succeed."

"Am I?"

Slowly he nodded. "Yes. You are. I have seen it. The Zeffers helped me to see it. You are going to succeed, and there is nothing that can be done about it. And I have no desire to see my people put through it. But if I am around, then I will see it. Which would seem to leave us at an impasse. Except you have a solution to that, do you not? The same solution that you had to the problem of Pavan's parents when they were reluctant to give him over for training. Or did you think I did not know about th—?"

Akasha suddenly jolted, and then he grinned, blood seeping through his lips. He did not even deign to look down at the blade that Seramali had drawn from his belt and driven deep into his chest. A blade capable of penetrating even the formidable hide of the Serabim.

The Keeper chuckled as he began to lose strength in his legs. "You did the only thing . . . you could . . . my chief. Very wise . . ."

"Does nothing stop you from talking?" said Seramali with impatience. "Yes, I did the only thing I could. Are you happy? You should not have spoken of Pavan's parents, Keeper. You made my decision that much easier."

Akasha fell backwards onto the cave floor. Lying flat, he still managed to say, "Feel that strongly . . . about it . . . do you . . . ?"

Seramali went to the fallen Akasha and placed the dagger in Akasha's hand. "Grief stricken over the fate of your student, you will have committed suicide. Everyone knows Keepers are high strung. They will accept it."

". . . your . . . your daughter."

"She will accept it, too." He turned to walk away.

"No . . . your daughter . . . I told her about Pavan's parents . . ."

That turned Seramali right around. "You did what?"

"Are you . . . to kill her next . . . ? Bit of a problem . . . isn't it . . . how far . . . are you willing to go, Seramali? How . . . far . . . ?"

Akasha's head slumped. He stopped talking, his eyes staring off into a future that only he could see and that everyone else would have to experience. And Seramali was left with the prospect of a conversation with his daughter that he was not looking forward to . . . and an action he prayed he would not have to take.

CHE VASCLY WACERS

I.

IC'S A BLUR CO HER, a series of images that skitter across her consciousness, which seem to have happened to someone else.

She is watching herself sink into watery depths, blackness closing in upon her. She is afraid of it but also welcomes it, for in that blackness is a surcease of problems and the beginning of peace. Then something grabs her, holds her, and a mouth that smells raw and foul clamps over hers, breathing in air that is so rank that she nearly vomits into it. Then she is on the surface, but the waters are still insane and furious, and then she does vomit, her spew fountaining from her and landing in the water where it will be of no consequence to anyone. She is knocked around and she feels consciousness slipping from her, and a voice that she does not know shouts into her ear, "I have you! Don't worry!" And she reflects on the absurdity of not worrying considering the situation in which she finds herself, and then blackness reaches out for her again. This time she does not chase it away, allowing it to envelope her and surrendering to its cool and calming touch.

II.

JEPP BECAME AWARE OF CWO things almost simultaneously.

The first was the gentle rays of the sun upon her face. When one is being hammered by a storm the way she had been, it's easy to believe that calm skies and sunlight are two things that you will never see again. That was how she had felt when the vessel that she had been on was being buffeted by the vicious weather that had rolled in.

The second was that she was on a very large rock in the middle of nowhere.

She felt its hardness beneath her head and slowly rolled herself over to get a better look at it. It was large and brownish black and incredibly smooth. She rapped on it and it seemed to echo slightly. Not knowing what to make of that, she slowly got to her feet so she could have a better view of where she was.

Her clothes were damp but drying out in the warmth of the air. The sensation gave her a chill, but hopefully nothing that would wind up taking up residence in her lungs and making her ill. She shielded her eyes against the brightness of the day. It was hard to believe that weather could be so vicious one moment and so welcoming the next. The sky was azure, with not a hint of clouds. The Vastly Seas were no longer threatening and vicious, but instead gently lapping against the huge rock that had provided her haven. As for the rock, or the rocky surface, it appeared to comprise the entirety of the island upon which she had found herself. It was quite large, perhaps a mile or so across. It was flat and featureless, crusted with vegetation so slimy that the very thought of eating it was enough to make her considering vomiting again . . . presuming that she had had anything in her stomach left to evict.

Obviously she had washed up on this island and had crawled to safety without even being aware of it. What she was going to do next, however, was anyone's guess. There was no fresh water for her to drink, and the plant life, such as it was, was inedible. Nor did there appear to be anywhere in sight for her to swim to that might provide her more sustenance. Plus there was the little matter of her being unable to swim in the first place.

"So what am I supposed to do?" she wondered aloud.

"That is up . . . to you."

She let out a startled shriek and jumped and spun all at the same time. As a result, when her feet came down, they went right out from under her and she fell on her ass. She sat there for a moment, feeling confused and not a little ridiculous.

There was a strange being lying perched on the nearby shoreline of the island. His body was large and blubbery, and his thick arms ended with hands that had large folds of skin between the fingers. He seemed to have no neck, his head set down practically atop his shoulders. When he spoke, it was slowly and with what seemed pronounced effort.

"Who are you?! What are you?!"

"I am a Markene. My name is Gorkon. And you are . . . a Mort. I know that much. Who are you?"

"I am . . ." She was still confused and flustered, but there was no reason that she could not be polite. "I am Jepp. I am . . . I am pleased to meet you."

"We met a bit earlier, actually. You nearly . . ." he paused and then said with what seemed a bit of chagrin, "vomited into my mouth . . ."

Her eyes widened and she pointed at him with a quavering finger. "It was you! You were there! Underwater!"

"Yes."

"You saved me!"

"Yes. I did that."

"But why?"

"You were in need of saving."

She certainly couldn't deny that. Still: "But I don't understand. You're one of the Twelve Races. You don't . . . your kind doesn't typically care what happens to my kind."

"That is true. Although I hear your kind makes excellent pets."

"I suppose we do. But I—"

"But you what?" He leaned forward, crisscrossing his arms and placing his chin on his fins, looking at her with overlarge eyes.

"I would like my race to have more than that. I would like to be more than that."

Understanding seemed to dawn in the Markene's eyes. "I can appreciate that, believe it or not."

"What do you mean?"

"My people, the Markene . . . were little more than servants to the Merk. Drug addled servants. Pawns to be used . . . in pathetic and pointless games of power."

"I'm sorry to hear that."

"It is all right. We . . . attended to it."

She drew her knees up and wrapped her arms around them. "Really. How did you attend to it?"

"We staged a revolution and brought a gigantic wave of water crashing through Venets, annihilating it."

"Oh. Well . . . that would do it."

"Yes." His voice sounded vacant. "It would. It did."

"And then . . ." Jepp was confused. It was becoming a familiar feeling for her. "You . . . came out here? Why are you here? I mean, the Vastly Waters are . . ." She tried to come up with a better word and none sprang readily to mind. " . . . vast. And you just happened to show up here?"

"Not exactly."

"Then what exactly?"

"I saw you. Ruark and I, we saw the ship taking you away. I had never seen a human before, much less one who was in the company of Travelers. And I was just going to watch you sail away. But I—"

"But you what?"

For a long moment he said nothing. Jepp didn't press him; he spoke in a manner that was slow and methodical, and she had a feeling that it matched the way he thought as well. There was no reason to rush him. It wasn't as if she was going anywhere.

III.

{"SHE IS A HUMAN," SAYS a voice from next to him.}

{Gorkon glances over to see Ruark Sydonis floating next to him. Floating is about all Ruark Sydonis can do these days, with his arms and legs having been shattered. Gorkon has fashioned a floation device for him and Ruark seems convinced that his limbs will eventually heal. Gorkon is dubious, but he defers to Ruark's wisdom on these matters.}

{"A human," says Gorkon. "I have never seen one."}

{"You haven't missed much," replies Ruark.}

{Gorkon considers the situation. "Do you think," he says slowly, "that the Travelers will notice that much of Venets is destroyed?"}

{"As they pass it? Perhaps."}

{"Will they care?"}

{"I very much doubt it," says Ruark. "Travelers only care about things that you and I cannot begin to understand."}

{"Such as humans? Why would they care about humans?"}

{Ruark Sydonis considers it for a time, and then says helpfully, "I hear they make excellent pets."}

{"And is that to be her fate? To be a pet?"}

{"I do not know her fate, Gorkon. Fates are not for such as I to perceive. Only to determine."}

{"I heard them say something about the Spires. They whispered to each other of the Spires."}

{"You heard them?"}

{"Yes. They sound like the sighing of currents. It is almost beautiful to listen to. It is also a bit frightening. I am not sure why."}

{"It could be that the fact that you do not know why is what makes it a bit frightening. Do you know of the Spires?"}

{"Not much of them, no."}

{"A vast city, far greater than Venets ever was or could hope to be, situated upon a far off island. Buildings so tall you cannot see the top of them. It is said to be where the Overseer dwells."}

{"The Overseer." He feels a chill in his spine. "If that is their destination, then I fear it will not go well for the female."}

{Ruark studies him for a moment. "Of what consequence is it to you what happens to her?"}

{"It is just that . . . she seems out of place. And distantly sad."}

{"You have never seen a human being before. You have no idea how one of them appears when they are sad."}

{"Ruark . . . do you remember what I was doing when we first met?"}

{"Of course. You were trying to kill yourself. Beach yourself so that eventually you would not be able to breathe. And you were doing so because you felt so disconnected from your own people, so lonely, that you could not see any reason for continuing to live."}

{"Yes. That is right."}

{"And your point is?"}

{"My point, Ruark, is that I know sadness when I see it. The race matters not. It is the emotion with which I am the most familiar, because I have lived with it for so long. I lived with it until I could live with it no more, and the only thing that stopped me from destroying myself was you."}

{"And you believe she is going to try to destroy herself?"}

{"I do not know."}

{"And once that vessel sails from sight, you will never know."}

{"That is true."}

{He continues to watch the vessel as it recedes. Ruark allows more time to pass before he finally says, "That disturbs you. The not knowing. Ever."}

{"Slightly."}

{"Perhaps more than slightly. Tell me, Gorkon . . . how do your people regard you these days. As their liberator? After all, they are no longer dependant upon Klaa. They are no longer under the domination of my kind."}

{"They are . . . appreciative."}

{"Are they?"}

{Gorkon looks down. He is unable to look Ruark in the eyes and lie to him. "No. They hate me. They despise me. Now that the initial fury of the revolt is over . . ."}

{"They need somewhere to put their hate."}

{"Yes."}

{"Because they are growing nostalgic for the time not long ago at all where they were able to float in a blissful haze of stupefaction."}

{"Yes. And . . ."}

{"And . . . ?"}

{"My mother finally noticed that my father is gone. She asked me what happened to him. I told her he was dead. And now she and my entire family hate me."}

{"Why would they hate you?"}

{"Because I told them it was my fault."}

{"Ah. Well . . . that would do it."}

{"It certainly did in this case."}

{"And so now they hate you?"}

{"Well," Gorkon says, "perhaps 'hate' is too mild a word."}

{"Really? What word would you think better summarizes it?"}

{"They have made it clear that they intend to kill me at some point soon."}

{Ruark looks at him sadly. "Oh, my dear Gorkon. The situation that I have placed you in . . . I am so sorry. Perhaps I should never have interfered. Perhaps I should have allowed you to perish at the time and place of your choosing. Look what I have done to you."}

{But Gorkon shakes his head firmly. "What I have done, Ruark, I have done to myself. There was a great wrong, and thanks to you, I have righted it. Whether my people realize that or not at the moment, eventually they will. Even if I am not alive to see it. And besides . . . it was a grand adventure."}

{"And now the only adventure left for you is to be murdered? It hardly seems fair."}

{"I have learned that very little in life involves fairness, no matter where you look."}

{"That is true," Ruark agrees. "But what if where you look leads you to more adventure?"}

{"I do not know what . . ." Then he realizes what Ruark is saying. "The human. The girl."}

{"She interests you. She calls to you."}

{"I would not say that she does. She is, overall, a rather ugly thing."}

{"True. Rather say that her fate does."}

{"I suppose it does. But what am I to do about it?"}

{"You could follow her. See where her fate brings her. See if you are a part of it, or at the very least can influence it. She may well be someone in need of help, just as your own people were."}

{"But she is not one of my people."}

{"Yes. However, are you still one of your people?"}

{Gorkon gave a soft grunt. "That is a valid point. But then there is the matter of you."}

{"Me?"}

{"I owe you my life, Ruark. And now you are . . . broken. I cannot simply abandon you to this . . . condition."}

{"You owe me nothing, Gorkon. All I did was point out possibilities. You are not eternally beholden to me for that. You are still young. You have much to accomplish, and I will not be a burden to the possibilities that remain to you. Besides, you said yourself that your life is threatened by your own people. Of what use will you be to me, or to anyone, if you are dead?"}

{"Still . . . I am not sure . . ."}

{"You do not have to be sure. That is the advantage of your position right now. If you allow the ship to depart from view, then you will never be sure. You will always wonder, 'What if I had followed the vessel?' But if you follow it, and you decide that the aim is misbegotten, or a waste of your time, then you can always turn away and come back here."}

{Gorkon looks out at the receding ship, seeming so lonely upon the waters. "I could just return here."}

{"Yes, you could. You would be committed to nothing."}

{"Still . . . I have never done anything like this. Gone any true distance from home. Been alone . . ."}

{"You will not be alone. You understand that, do you not? You are not alone. For good or ill, you never will be again. And you know why."}

{And Gorkon does. He understands precisely to what Ruark is referring. He does not like to think about it, because the connection that he had now has with . . . the Other . . . is daunting, intimidating. He has learned to live with it, even though he is certain that the Other will bring about his destruction one day.}

{"Very well. That is what I will do. Just for a little while. Just to satisfy myself that the endeavor is pointless. Then I will return to you."}

{"Of course you will," says Ruark.}

{And so Gorkon turns away from Ruark and swims away without even looking back.}

{He catches up quickly with the ship, but keeps a safe distance. He does so because he does not want to draw attention to himself. He is as daunted by the Travelers as anyone else. He has had no direct interaction with the Travelers, but he knows the stories. He knows what they are capable of doing. That is why no one dares to stand up to them. Had Ruark's demented queen had her way, the Markene would have gone up against the Travelers and unquestionably been destroyed en masse as a result. }

{From his vantage point he continues to listen to the discussions aboard the ship, to eavesdrop on their daily interaction. Every day that he pursues them, he tells himself that this is the day that he is going to have sated his curiosity about the girl. This is the day that he is going to turn back. Yet he does not do so. Because every day he finds the human girl more and more intriguing. He is not romantically interested her in the least. They are, in every way imaginable, from two different worlds. He simply finds her personality interesting, and maybe even kindred to his own, because in the way she comports herself, she challenges many old assumptions. He has never had a kindred spirit before. Ruark was something of a mentor to him, but also had his own agenda. Gorkon is not a fool. He knows that to some degree Ruark was using him to his own ends from the very beginning. He initially bristled at the idea, but he has since come to accept the reality that everyone uses everyone else. Sometimes for good, sometimes for ill, but in the end, no one engages anyone else unless there is something of value in it for they themselves, and

Ruark is no different.}

{But of what value can this human girl be to him? None that he can think of. Certainly none that is readily apparent. He is certain that his future lies back in Venets, even if it is only to die at the hands of his own people in order to sate their need for vengeance. By any reasonable measure, there is no reason at all for him to have any interest in this Mort.}

{Yet he continues to follow her. Several times he actually endeavors to turn and swim off in the other direction, but each time he finds himself continuing his pursuit of her.}

{As night begins to approach, he becomes concerned over the prospect of losing the ship because fatigue is overtaking him. He dives, looking for something that can be of benefit. It takes repeated excursions, but he finally finds a length of cable in a vessel already sunken to the floor of the Vastly Waters. Taking his newly discovered treasure, he overtakes the vessel once more and, as the sun sets, uses it to secure himself to the hull. Thus is he able to sleep while the ship pulls him along.}

{And while he sleeps . . . he dreams of a better world. One in which the Twelve Races do not live in a perpetual state of strife. One in which his own people celebrate him as a hero instead of loathe him as the one who upended their life of bliss. One in which he has a place. Yes. A better world.}

{He just wonders if it can ever be this one.}

IV.

"I SAW YOU. RUARK AND I, we saw the ship taking you away. I had never seen a human before, much less one who was in the company of Travelers. And I was just going to watch you sail away. But I—"

"But you what?"

For a long moment he said nothing. Jepp didn't press him; he spoke in a manner that was slow and methodical, and she had a feeling that it matched the way he thought as well. There was no reason to rush him. It wasn't as if she was going anywhere.

"I changed my mind," he said finally.

Jepp felt slightly let down by that. "That's it?"

"Is more required?"

"I suppose not. Except . . . why did you change your mind?"

"You interested me."

"Really?" She cocked her head. "How so?"

"The way you speak to the Travelers. The way you stand up to them. No one else does that that I know of. No one else would dare. Everyone fears the Travelers."

"People fear what they don't understand. They don't understand the Travelers, that's all."

"And you do?"

"No," she admitted. Then she brightened. "But I know that there's something there worth understanding. And that's enough of a start, I suppose."

"Why were they taking you to the Spires?"

The question surprised her and she made no effort to hide it. Then again, Jepp wasn't particularly skilled at hiding any response she ever had to anything. "They were taking me to the Spires?"

"Yes."

She did not bother to ask how he knew. It wasn't her way. He seemed fairly positive about it and that was sufficient for her. "I do not know. The Spires is the residence of the Overseer, yes?"

"That is correct."

"Then I suppose that the Overseer has some interest in me. I have no idea what possible interest one such as he could have in one such as me. And I suppose now I will never find out."

"I suppose not." He continued to study her for a time longer. "So . . . what do you wish to do now? Where would you like to go?"

"It is odd," she said thoughtfully. "Ever since the Travelers took me, all I wished to do was return to Karsen."

"Who is Karsen?"

She told him all about Karsen then. All about the circumstances that had brought them together and resulted in her being with a group of Bottom Feeders for a time and entering into an intense relationship with Karsen Foux of the Laocoon, until being kidnapped by the Travelers. "And all during the time I was with the Travelers, I kept insisting that they should return me to him."

"Where is he?"

"I don't know," she admitted. "That is the problem. Because the Travelers are—well—who they are, I had assumed they had the ability to bring me straight back to Karsen with little effort. They could find him, if anyone could. Now, though, they are gone, and my chance of being reunited with Karsen may well have gone with them."

"I could return you to the land you left behind if you wish. That way you at least have an opportunity to try and track him down."

"That is a possibility. Unfortunately, far more likely is that I will be captured by someone—a Mandraque, something like that—and forced back into a life of slavery. I am a Mort, after all," she said, allowing traces of bitterness to creep into her voice. "My kind are nothing but slaves. I have a one in a million chance of locating Karsen once more. And even if I do . . . then what? His mother will have nothing to do with me, so we will have to be on our own. I mean, honestly . . . what sort of existence is he then supposed to lead? An aimless life of wandering around with nothing but me for company?"

"You should not think so little of yourself."

"I don't," she said firmly. "I used to, but I don't. That's not the point, though."

"Then what is?"

"The point is that I think Karsen can have a better life if I'm not a part of it. Not a . . . a burden to him. He would be able to have congress with his family and with his own kind. As long as I am with him, our feelings for each other are going to be..." She sighed. "Inconvenient."

"Then what do you wish?"

"I wish . . ."

She stopped. For reasons she still could not quite fathom, those two words seemed extremely loaded to her, as if they were not to be uttered lightly, nor without some acknowledgment of their power and potential.

"I wish things could be different."

"What things?"

"That my people could be free, to begin with. Presuming," she added ruefully, "there are any of my people left. That is something else I would like to see different. More of my people. Many more. I . . ." Her mind wandered. "I had a dream of that. I dreamt of a city with tall buildings, buildings so tall they seemed to touch clouds. And there were so many of my people there. Tens of hundreds, thousands. They were just . . . they were everywhere. And a Mandraque . . . a female. I'm not sure how she fit into it all. And I could not for the life of me tell if I was seeing something that was long in the past, or in the future, or would never be anything other than in my imaginings."

"Buildings that touched the clouds? You may well be speaking of the Spires."

"Really?"

Gorkon nodded. "Ruark described them as such. You may well be dreaming of your destination."

"What does that mean, do you think?"

"I do not know."

She stared off toward the distant horizon. "It would be . . . interesting . . . to find out, I suppose. To see the Spires for myself. Perhaps to speak to the Overseer."

"You cannot speak to the Overseer. He would destroy you with a glance."

"I have heard much the same about the Travelers. Yet I did so, and I am still here to tell of it."

"Because of me."

"Yes," and she smiled. "Because of you. I was an orphan of the storm and you saved me, and I do not believe I can ever thank you adequately for it. But thank you I do. Now if only you could get me to the Spires . . ."

"I have never been there myself," said Gorkon. "But the vessel upon which you sailed was traveling a fairly straightforward path. The storm did not disorient me. I can continue to follow the trajectory of the ship and reach its destination, presuming the ship was not intending to change its course."

"You're saying you can take me to the Spires?" Excitement was starting to rise within her.

"Yes. Yes, I believe I can."

She looked behind her, in what she fancied was the direction from which she had come. "I hope . . . I pray . . . that the path of my life will lead me back to Karsen," she said slowly. "But if there is to be any chance of living in a world in which Karsen and I could be together and be happy—genuinely happy—then I have to think my path lies forward rather than back. You have already done me a tremendous service, Gorkon, for no real reason I can discern other than that you . . . well . . ."

"Were not otherwise occupied?"

"I wasn't going to put it that way, but yes. That's what I was thinking. Anyway . . . if you can indeed bring me to the Spires, then you would have even more of that relatively worthless thing called my gratitude."

"Believe it or not," said Gorkon, "gratitude would be a most welcome commodity for me at this point in my life."

"Then you will have all of mine there is to give and more besides." With that said, Jepp got to her feet and then strode toward Gorkon.

Gorkon gave her a very puzzled look. "Where are you going?"

"I am . . . I thought I was going to the Spires. That you were going to take me."

"Yes. And?"

"Well . . . I figured that I would come back into the water and that you would swim there with me."

"The water is quite cold. I do not think such prolonged exposure would be advisable for you."

"You're not going to swim me there?"

"No. I am not. I will accompany you to see you safely there . . . but the bulk of the travel will be by another means."

That declaration intrigued her. She could not imagine to what he might be referring. "Another means?"

"Yes. The Other will bring you there. The Old One. The oldest one, in fact."

"Oh," said Jepp uncertainly. "Uhm . . . all right." She pushed her hair out of her face. "Is he a friend of yours, this . . . other?"

"A friend? Not exactly. We are . . . bonded, in a way."

"I am likewise bonded with Karsen," she said, feeling a bit better, as if this was something she could more readily comprehend. "Is he going to come here to the island?"

"What island?"

"This one."

"Ah," said Gorkon, suddenly understanding. "All right. I have been foolish, Jepp. My apologies. I have forgotten that that which is obvious to me is far less so to you. The Other is not going to be coming to this island because there is no island. The Other is already here."

Jepp was starting to get an uneasy feeling, concerned that Gorkon might actually have lost his mind somewhere along the way. "What do you mean, already here?" She glanced around, trying to humor him. "Is he invisible?"

That was when the island shook beneath her feet.

She let out a startled scream and fell over, nearly rolling off before she found purchase upon it. "What's happening!? It's a quake!"

"It's not a quake." Gorkon sounded amused. "It's the Other."

"The Other is moving the island?"

"Not exactly."

The island began to move, not just forward, but also—as Jepp began to be aware—up and down. Very slowly and very rhythmically, and she realized that it was just like a living creature breathing.

"Oh my God," she whispered. "He . . . it . . . is the island?"

"That's right."

"What kind of creature could . . . what is it?"

Gorkon paddled next to her and then softly, almost reverently, he said, "He was the first."

"The first what?"

"The first. Before there were the Magisters . . . before there was anything . . . there was the Other. All life in the Elserealms rose up, and everything changed except him. He was there, he was always, he was eternal . . ."

"You make him sound like a god."

"He is, in his way. And the Magisters were sore afraid. He was the one being over whom they had no influence. He does what he will. And because of that, he was one of the very first who was sent here. The Magisters put him at the forefront of the First Wave. They got to him while he was slumbering, and he awoke here, surrounded by a handful of the other races and various primitive beasts that once roamed this world before the First Wave hunted them into extinction. His rage was mighty, and his image was so terrifying that the sight of him burned itself into the deepest recesses of your race's memory. Your kind did not yet exist, but your ancestors' ancestor beheld his rage and thus do you all fear the very concept of him."

"I don't fear him," said Jepp. She had had a lifetime of experience of adjusting readily to shifting circumstances, and this was no exception. "I don't know him. How can I fear something I don't know?"

"Not knowing is typically what causes it, actually."

"Does he have a name?"

"If he has a name that he calls himself, none know it. There is a name that others have for him. He is called . . ." He hesitated as if concerned that simply speaking the name could prompt some manner of disaster. " . . . Liwyathan."

"Liwyathan." She rolled the name around in her mouth. "It is an impressive name. It is filled with majesty and fear and . . . and . . ." She paused. " . . . sounds."

"It is said that it is an approximation of the squawks of terror made by the very first creatures that beheld him. He is old beyond old. On this sphere alone, he has resided for over a million cycles around the sun."

"Over a million?" She could scarcely conceive of the number, much less the actual amount of time it represented. "That's impossible. Isn't that impossible?"

"Obviously not, considering that you are riding on him."

"I can't argue with that," said Jepp, who actually could have but felt it wasn't exactly appropriate considering her present circumstances. "How did you come to . . . ? I mean, is he your . . . your friend?"

"I have a connection to him," said Gorkon. "I cannot explain it in anything approaching definitive terms. There are some who claim that Liwyathan is the wellspring from which all Markene are descended. That he is our common ancestor, and thus we have the closest relation to him. It could be that he was waiting for us to rediscover him, and that I was the one who happened to reconnect with him. There is no way to say for certain, though. Liwyathan keeps his own council."

"Well . . . I think he's sweet."

"Sweet?" Gorkon was incredulous. "Of all the terms used to describe the Liwyathan over all the countless generations of our kind who have known him, I feel safe in saying that 'sweet' was never one of them."

"I'll take my victories, however small, wherever I can get them." She patted the surface beneath her. "Thank you, Liwyathan." She looked to Gorkon. "Does he know I did that? Does he understand?"

"Hard to say. As I said, he keeps his own council. He has a very slow thought process, and it is not always easy to get his attention or—more significantly—hold it."

"What do you mean?"

"Well...I'm just hoping that the Liwyathan remembers not to submerge."

"Submer—?" Jepp was suddenly nervous. "You mean he could

forget that I'm up here and just . . . you know . . . go underwater?"

"There is that possibility. But worry not. I will be right here with you." He paused and then added, almost as an afterthought, "unless I forget to breathe. For my kind, breathing is not something that happens automatically. We have to remind ourselves to do it. So if I were accidentally to die or some such mishap, then you would be on your own and the Liwyathan could forget and, well . . ." He smiled. "But the chances of that happening are incredibly small."

"But not impossible."

"Jepp . . . consider where you are and what you're doing. I think you have to admit that nothing is impossible."

She pictured her salvation sinking beneath the waves while a dead Gorkon floated nearby. "I guess I do," she said, even as she wondered if she might not have been better off just taking her chances with drowning.

FIREDRAQUE HALL, PERRIZ

I.

EVERY DAY WHEN EVANNA AWOKE, she approached it with unstinting optimism. She prayed that this would be the day her father would be returned to her safely. I will expect nothing save for the unexpected, was her mantra. She said it in the morning of the day that lay before her, and she repeated it in the evening in regards to the next day.

Yet for all her lack of expectation, certainly the sight that stood before her was beyond the furthest edge of the unanticipated.

A group of weary Ocular and a single, rather imperious-looking Piri, all of them covered with the dirt of the road, were standing in front of her. They looked exhausted, even numb. They were ringed by a Mandraque patrol with Gorsham standing at the forefront. It was purely cosmetic; if the Ocular had been of a mind to bring Firedraque Hall down around their ears, they would have been able to do so and the Mandraques would not have been able to prevent it. Fortunately for all concerned, they didn't look as if they were in the mood for a fight.

"Sanctuary?" she said, fighting to keep the astonishment from her voice. Evanna glanced toward Xeri, who was standing a short distance away and looked no less amazed. When he noticed she was looking to him, he shrugged as if to say that he had no more idea of what to make of this than she did. She walked in a slow circle around them, as if she might have a better understanding of them from behind or perhaps to the side. "You want sanctuary here in Perriz?"

"That was our hope," said the Piri, who had been introduced as Clarinda. She sounded bone-weary but she maintained her poise. This alone was surprising to Evanna because she was accustomed to thinking of the Piri as no different than the small vermin she routinely saw skittering around the hall and occasionally feasted upon when she was in the mood.

"Are you—?" She paused, unable to believe the questions she was asking. "Are you in charge of this assemblage?"

The Piri smiled mirthlessly. "I have taken them under my wing. Our association has been one of mutual protection."

"They are Ocular, far larger and stronger than you. Larger and stronger than nearly anyone else. I am not exactly sure what you bring to this association."

"You may find it difficult to believe, but these Ocular are considerably young for their race. And I am somewhat older for mine. We Piri tend to have rather brief life spans."

"I was unaware of that," Xeri spoke up. "Is that a happenstance of your biology?"

"No. When others are not killing us, we tend to kill each other."

"Cutting short your lives is certainly something to which the Mandraques can relate," said Evanna drily. Gorsham made an annoyed face but she ignored it. "Although providing sanctuary to the Ocular is not a problem, your presence certainly poses something of a difficulty. My people are no more trusting of Piri than is any other race on the Damned World."

"I am not asking for your trust," said Clarinda. "Merely your tolerance. I assure you I am not here to cause any trouble. I am simply looking for a home since I am no longer welcome in mine."

"Why is that?"

"I had a disagreement with my mother, the Mistress of our kind."

"What manner of disagreement?"

"She wanted to make me into something I am not."

"And what would that be?"

"Her," she said.

Evanna's eyes narrowed as she stopped circling the group and walked slowly toward Clarinda. "There is something else. Something you are hiding. And before you deny it," she continued quickly, cutting off Clarinda before she could offer protest, "consider that hiding the truth from someone whose trust you are requesting is not the best way to go about gaining that trust."

Clarinda seemed to be thinking long and hard about what Evanna was saying. She met Evanna's eyes for a time and then cast her gaze downward, at which point Evanna was certain that the next words she was going to hear would be the truth.

"I am with child," she said so quietly that it was difficult to hear her, "and the father is not of my race."

There were startled mutterings, some whispered and some less so, from everyone surrounding them. Only the Ocular did not appear startled. Either she had already told them, or else there was simply nothing she could say that would diminish their loyalty to her. That alone spoke volumes to Evanna. One of the Ocular, a smallish (by their standards) female, put an arm around Clarinda protectively.

Xeri drew near Evanna and said under his breath, "Damnedest thing I've ever seen." Evanna nodded in agreement. "What do you think?"

"I am not even close to being able to answer that question." Returning to her normal conversational tone, she said, "Of what race is the father?"

"I am not going to tell you that," said Clarinda. "There are some matters I should be able to keep close to my heart. And if privacy is the price for residing in Perriz, then I will urge my good friends here to remain for safety's sake but I will take my leave."

"As will we," said the female Ocular, and others echoed her sentiments.

"Threatening to leave," Evanna observed, "when no one asked you to come here in the first place is hardly what one would call a potent threat."

Xeri stepped forward and spoke in a stentorian manner, as if he were addressing people residing in another country. "Evanna will give full consideration to your request," he said. "And once she has pondered the many aspects and ramifications of this particular situation, she will render her decision."

"They can stay."

Looking caught off guard, Xeri gaped at her. Then, with the same tone of voice, seemingly trying to sound as if he were delivering news that they were unaware of, he announced, "She has decided you can stay."

"All of us?" said the female Ocular pointedly.

"Yes. All of you."

Several of the Ocular visibly sighed in relief, and a couple of them sagged against each other as if they needed the support. It underscored for Evanna just how utterly exhausted the lot of them were, and how they had been fighting desperately to keep body and soul together. She suspected that if she had informed them they had to depart, they might well have tried to do so but collapsed before they reached the city limits. Despite the oddity of what she was faced with, she felt a deep sense of empathy for them that she couldn't help but feel was misplaced. The majority of them were Ocular, a race that certainly was not without sin when it came to matters of war. And the Piri were notorious parasites, bloodsuckers who posed a threat to all races including, apparently their own. Yet here they had come together for whatever reason—necessity, desperation. And they had managed to work together for their mutual survival. They had even formed bonds of friendship. Was that not the very sort of philosophy that the Firedraques had been preaching? It had been the bellicose nature of the Twelve Races that had gotten them banished from the Elserealms in the first place. Who was she, Evanna, to second guess or reject beings who were fulfilling the fundamental tenets of Firedraque philosophy? On what basis could she do such a thing? Because she was respulsed by the Piri? Then she would be allowing herself to succumb to the same sort of bias and hostility that created so much strife in the world.

All of that went through her mind in moments, serving to reinforce the decision that she had made instinctively. "For the time being," she said, "you will stay here. Xeri," and she indicated him with a sweep of her arm, "will find space for you. Most of the rooms are not exactly constructed to accommodate someone of your . . . proportions . . . but we will do our best to provide for you. Certainly if nothing else, you can take your ease and converse and even sleep in the main hall. The ceiling is so high that even such as you cannot scrape your heads upon it."

Clarinda bowed in a stately manner and said, "You have my eternal thanks." The other Ocular made similar noises of gratitude, a number of them imitating Clarinda's bow. Evanna bobbed her head in response and Xeri, after giving her a final, slightly incredulous look, led them away.

Gorsham moved toward Evanna and waited until the others had been led away before speaking. "I honestly do not know how the Five Clans are going to react to this."

"React to what? Giving sanctuary to those who ask for it?"

"Allowing such creatures as a Piri to take up residence in Perriz. What if she cannot control her bloodlust? What if one of my people is found drained of blood with puncture wounds in his or her neck?"

"Then," Evanna said patiently, "it will be patently obvious who the perpetrator of the crime is, since we are dealing with precisely one Piri. At which point she will then be killed for her crime."

"But one of my people will still be dead!"

"Which means you would be minus one Mandraque who was so inept that he couldn't defend himself against a single Piri."

Gorsham considered that and then shrugged. "There is something to be said for that, I suppose. Still, I am naturally going to inform Arren of this development."

"That is as it should be," Evanna said approvingly. "And for what it is worth, Gorsham, should the Piri turn on us, I will personally hold her still while you take her head off with a sword. Will that satisfy you?"

He bowed deeply. "You are too kind."

"Yes. I know."

II.

CLARINDA LAY DOWN UPON THE mattress that had been arranged for her on the floor of the chambers assigned her. The chamber itself was filled with all manner of iconography that meant nothing to her. There were illustrations of a long-haired, bearded Mort who appeared to be suffering greatly, splayed upon a cross. Obviously he was some sort of vicious criminal and the Morts simply could not get enough illustrations of watching him die. There were also a couple of statues of a female Mort smiling down at an infant in the universal imagery of mother and child. Clarinda supposed that perhaps the man on the cross had murdered the mother and child and that was the crime for which he was being punished. It made sense. "If that is the case, bastard had it coming," she said to herself.

"I've often thought much the same."

She was startled by the voice, and that in and of itself was surprising to her. She was generally more attuned to the world around her and was not easily startled. Clarinda immediately bounded to her feet into a protective stance, her teeth bared against a possible attack.

A Mandraque whom she had not seen before was leaning in the door, his arms folded. He was not particularly big, but his chest was a bit puffed up, seemingly filled with confidence. He was the type of individual who swaggered even when he was standing still.

"Presuming," he continued, "he is a bastard, that is. I still have not ruled out the possibility that his job was to keep birds out of the crops. You can relax, by the way. I am not here to attack you."

"How can I be certain?"

"Because if I were here to attack you, I would wait until daytime when you were asleep and dispatch you."

"Is that how the mighty Mandraques slay their enemies? In their sleep?"

"It could be argued that you are not an enemy, but simply an invading vermin, to be accorded the exact same level of respect."

She tilted her head slightly. "Your phrasing is careful. You say, 'It could be argued' without giving any indication of your own allegiance."

"My allegiance is to the Five Clans," he said, "and the matters that are of interest to them. Frankly, I do not see how a single Piri and a platoon of Ocular are going to fall into that category."

Clarinda regarded him thoughtfully. "But we may be of interest to you?"

"You may be." He bowed slightly. "I am Arren Kinklash, son of Arjon, and leader of the Five Clans."

"Clarinda Redeye, daughter of . . ." She paused and then shrugged. "None."

"You must be someone's daughter."

"Not anymore."

He chose not to pursue the comment.

In the brief, ensuing silence, Clarinda stepped in. "You have not answered me. You have something in mind. You want to make use of them. Or of us."

"I am curious as to why you would say that."

"Because one parasite can always recognize another."

Arren laughed at that. His laugh came out as a sort of soft, repeated hiss. "Is that what you think? That I am so very much like you?"

"I do not know about 'so very much,' but I perceive general similarities." She folded her arms and stood there, waiting with as much patience as she could muster. "Do you wish to waste more of my time, or yours for that matter? Although admittedly I'm less concerned about the latter."

"I have no desire to waste anyone's time."

"Then what—?"

"Actually, I am somewhat interested in finding use for someone else's time. Specifically, your young associates."

"The Ocular?" She frowned. "Of what possible interest could they be to you?"

"They might be of use to me."

"In what regard?"

"A . . ." He paused and then smiled. It was an expression that Clarinda considered to be disconcerting; the look of a predator who was smiling because he has just seen prey and is anticipating the devouring of it. She knew the look all too well. She had seen it any number of times on the face of the Piri. It could well be that Arren and she were more alike than even she had originally thought they were. "A small quest, as it were."

"A quest?"

"A journey seeking an answer or some manner of goal."

"Yes, I know what a quest is," she said impatiently. "I am not a fool."

"I did not say you were."

"No, but you may well have thought it if you believe that I would simply turn the Ocular over to you."

His tail twitched slightly, which was the only outward display of his irritation at her tone. "You are not their mother, milady, no matter how this—bizarre—relationship you have with them may have developed. You are what you are, and they are what they are."

"And what are they, pray tell?"

Arren closed the distance between them with several quick steps. When he spoke she was reasonably sure she could smell the odor of some recently dead rodent on his breath. "They are warriors, milady. They have the fire of war in their veins."

"If that is the case, they certainly did not get it from their parents. The Ocular had no stomach for battling my kind when they had the opportunity. Fortunate for us, really. Had they truly endeavored to apply themselves, they might well have been able to wipe us out."

"Whatever their parents were, they are dead now, yes?" She nodded in confirmation. "Lesson learned, then. Their parents became too soft by living a life not steeped in the warfare that fired their ancestors."

Clarinda hesitated and then, in spite of herself, found herself nodding in agreement. "That does, in fact, agree with what they themselves told me. They told me of a demonstration that their king performed. He commanded one of the adult Ocular to strike one of his fellows. The adult hesitated, confused. He asked the king what the purpose of doing such a thing was. He pled for the reasoning, desirous not to inflict unwarranted pain and damage upon another of his kind. Rather than pressing the point, the king turned to a youngster and placed the same command upon him. The youngster's sole question was whether he would get into trouble as a result. When the king assured him that there would be no negative consequences from his actions, the youngster turned and, with no further hesitation, struck another child. The king's point was that the young Ocular were possessed of a spirit for war that the parents had not drained from them."

"Much as parasites would?" said Arren drily.

"Much like." She stroked her chin thoughtfully. She hated to admit it, but there was something about this Arren Kinklash that she found intriguing. Not the same sort of intriguing that she had felt when she first encountered Eutok, gods knew, but nevertheless something within him that was appealing. That was how it was when kindred spirits met each other. There was a sort of familiar ease that made conversations such as this one come naturally. "What did you have in mind?"

"For the Ocular?" She nodded. Arren continued, "A trip would be all. There may well be very little danger involved. I need to embark upon a bit of sojourn."

"To where?"

"The upper reaches of Suislan."

"Suislan?" she said in surprise. She hadn't been sure of what he had in mind, but that certainly had not occurred to her. "Why Suislan, of all places? Do you have some manner of business with the Serabim?"

"That is, in fact, exactly what I have."

"What possible interest could you have in those cloud dwellers?"

"That is my concern."

"If you desire to make the Ocular a part of this business, then you would do well to be more forthcoming."

He hesitated, and then shrugged. Apparently being secretive was his automatic response to any situation and he had to work a bit to overcome it. "Very well. The bastards took my sister."

"Your sister?"

"One of their damned Zeffers came sweeping into Perriz and made off with my sister. With Norda."

"And what possible interest could your sister have held for the Zeffers?"

"In point of fact, none. They came for Nicrominus, one of the Firedraque elders."

"You are providing me this story in bits and pieces, and it is becoming tiresome, Kinklash. Why did they want Nicrominus, and how did your sister become involved?"

"Gods as my witness, I have no idea why they wanted him. I presume that they did so at the command of someone else, but I cannot fathom who or why. I do not know what Nicrominus represents to them. As for Norda, it was simply a matter of being in the wrong place at the wrong time. Norda is a very impulsive creature; I believe that she saw Nicrominus being taken and the impulse was to accompany him. Do not," he put up a hand, warding off her next question, "ask me why she would do such a thing. I have long ago learned that it is a waste of time to try and fathom the innermost workings of my sister's mind. All I know is that, as a result of her actions, I am left with no sister and a host of questions."

"And you think the Serabim would be able to address them?"

"They are, after all, the Zeffers' Keepers. If not they, then who else?"

"I suppose. Still . . . you are not considering several aspects. You have no proof that the Zeffer returned her to Suislan. For that matter, you have no proof that the Zeffer was connected to the Serabim who dwell in Suislan. There are several tribes of them, you know, scattered about the Damned World. You have no way of knowing of a certainty that she is there, or that those who dwell there would be able to tell you where she is. Nor would the Serabim necessarily be willing to provide you whatever information they may, in fact, have."

"All of that is true, but—"

"But what?"

He shrugged like one lost. "What other choice have I?"

She hated to admit it, but there was something noble about the sentiment. She wondered what it would be like to have a sibling—or for that matter anyone in her life—who was so dedicated to her welfare that he would throw in his lot with strangers solely for the purpose of trying to find her. Still, something about this didn't seem entirely right to her.

"So your thought is that the Ocular will serve as your army? Is that your plan?"

"It would be my hope that the Serabim would not force matters to come to a war. I have no desire to fight; merely to determine what the infernal Zeffer did with my sister."

"But you suppose that if you have the Ocular accompanying you, then the Serabim will be somewhat more cooperative when you approach them with your questions."

He nodded slightly.

"It is not a theory entirely without merit," she admitted. "Still . . . I strongly suspect there is something else you are not telling me. Some other matter to be addressed."

"I have no idea what you are talking about."

"I think you do, actually. If you are so concerned about your sister's welfare, why are you still here at all? I take it that this theft by the Zeffer did not happen extremely recently. Some time must have passed, yes?"

"Some."

"Yet here you are, still standing before me. You remain in Perriz while your sister is gods know where. You had no idea that we were going to be showing up, so you had no reason to remain here waiting for us. Why, then, are you still here? Why have you not already embarked upon your great adventure by yourself? What has stopped you thus far?"

For the first time, Arren Kinklash seemed truly annoyed. She quickly determined, however, that she was not the source or reason for it. "I attempted to do exactly as you suggest. I wanted to go after my sister immediately. Instead I was met with . . . impediments."

"What manner of impediments?"

"The Firedraques," he said sourly, "desired the pleasure of my company, and thus made certain that I was not permitted to depart the city. As head of the Five Clans, it was felt that my presence here was of greater import than my presence elsewhere."

"Ahhhh. Now it becomes clear. You want the Ocular to fight their way through your own troops on your behalf."

"That," said Arren, "is exactly right."

"And what, may I ask," she said skeptically, "is in it for them?"

"They will be true to their nature. They will be—"

She waved it off before he could continue. "You will need more than that, Arren. A chance to fight? Aye, some of them might welcome that. But they're also bone weary and soul sick. You speak of concerns over your sister? They have lost parents, cousins, uncles . . . damned near their entire race. And they have not yet had the opportunity to mourn that properly."

"Mourning will accomplish them nothing. They need to channel their frustration into a cause. But," he said as she was about to respond, "I can promise them something that will be of use to them. For as long as they dwelt in the land of Feend with its insanely long nights, the daylight presented little problem to them. Now, though, they are constrained by their blindness. And around here, depending upon the season of the turn, the daylight hours are extended and night is quite short. How frustrating for them to have to sit around, accomplishing nothing, hampered by their inability to see."

"Frustrating, yes, but certainly they are accustomed to that by now."

"True. How joyous, though, for them to become unaccustomed."

She stared at him, confused. "What are you talking about?"

For response, he reached into a pouch that was dangling from his belt and removed what appeared to be a round piece of glass. It was extremely dark, much more so than Clarinda had ever seen. Then again, living most of her life underground, she had not had all that much opportunity to see glass before. He held it out to her. "Go ahead. Take it. Hold it up to your eyes."

She did as he bade and was surprised to see the entire room appear to darken around them.

"Many of the windows throughout Perriz have similar glass in them," Arren said without giving her an opportunity to pose any questions. "It would be possible to fashion coverings for the Ocular to place over their eyes. With such coverings, the Ocular would be able to see even in the broadest of daylight. They would no longer be prisoners to their biology."

"You would be able to accomplish this?"

"I would. In exchange for your aid."

"Why go to me? Why not just speak to the youngsters themselves?"

"Because if it comes from you, it would carry more weight."

She knew it was true. As formidable, as powerful as the Ocular were, they would still hold what she said in such high regard that they could not help but attend to it, even if their common sense said otherwise.

You do not want to do this. There is something here that you are missing. There is nothing in this for you. Keep your head down. Do not cooperate. There is naught to be gained. Naught. This is setting you upon a collision course for disaster.

"I will . . . take the proposition to them," she said.

He smiled. "You know it will be the best for them. So sure am I that they will embrace the idea, that I will begin immediately upon the production of the coverings for their eyes." He bowed nearly in half, gesturing from the heart and waving a small circle in the air that she imagined was supposed to be some sort of sign of deference.

"Still . . . there is one thing I do not quite understand. You want to have the Ocular aid you in fighting your way past your brethren?"

"That is correct."

"Why not just simply go underground? Avoid them entirely?"

Arren stared at her uncomprehendingly. "What are you talking about? Do you suggest that I build tunnels in some way?"

"You do not have to build them. They already exist. There is an elaborate sewer system beneath the streets of Perriz."

He took a step toward her, an array of emotions playing across his face. "A sewer system?"

"Yes. A sew-er-sys-tem," she said very slowly, as if addressing a child or perhaps a moron. "A series of conduits constructed by the Morts to process their waste materials. They didn't simply leave it in small heaps buried under dirt like your ilk do."

"Are you serious?"

"Why would I jest about such a thing? To begin with, it isn't remotely funny."

"I know that, I . . . it is simply surprising to learn. How does one access these tunnels? And how do you know about them?"

"My mother told me of them. She is quite the scholar when it comes to such Mort-related trivia. But she simply knew of them. She did not know how to reach them, or where they come in or out. It was not as if she had some concerted plan in regards to them; it was simply something she knew about. Interesting that in her far off realm, she knew they existed, while you were oblivious to that which was beneath your feet."

"It certainly is." His voice sounded distant as if his thoughts had wandered far away.

"Will you still desire the aid of the Ocular, now that you know of these subterranean passages?"

"Yes. Yes, of course. Because who knows what manner of challenges may remain? Again, presuming that they have an interest in accompanying me. Now if you'll excuse me, I must attend to arranging for their eye coverings." He exited quickly, his tail whipping around behind him in agitation.

Clarinda watched him go. *You will live to regret this, Clarinda. And—quite possibly—not for very long.*

III.

XERI LOOKED UP FROM HIS worktable as Arren practically exploded into the chambers. The entrance was so violent that a delicate piece of jewelry he had been restoring into its mounting flew out of his hands and hit the floor. "Do you mind?" Xeri demanded, making no attempt to hide his irritation. "I was in the middle of—"

"Why the hell didn't you tell me?"

"Tell you wh—?"

Arren didn't let him complete the sentence. Instead he grabbed Xeri by the front of his gown, yanked him to his feet and slammed him up against the wall. The impact knocked Xeri's breath out of him.

"Why the hell didn't you tell me?"

"About *what*?"

"The sewers!"

"What sew—?" Then he stopped and said softly, "Oh. The sewers. The ones that run beneath the city."

"Yes! Those sewers!" He released Xeri in disgust and stepped back.

Xeri smoothed the folds of his gown where Arren had grabbed him. "It's not as if I was keeping that from you. You never asked."

"And you didn't think to volunteer that information?"

"I had no reason to assume you didn't know about it."

"Here's a reason: Had I known about it, I would have made use of it!"

"And how precisely would you have done that?" said Xeri patiently. "I have never been down there, but from my understanding, there are hundreds of miles of tunnels down there. You could wander around down there for dozens of turns and wind up right back where you started. So why do you think that the sewers would have been of the slightest use to you?"

"I don't . . . I just . . ."

At which point, seized with an unaccustomed uncertainty of what to say, Arren backed off. Hesitant and unsure, he said, "So are you saying that they would in fact be completely useless to me? That they are a means of avoiding my enemies and yet I cannot utilize them?"

"You cannot. Others can."

"Others?"

"Well . . . as luck would have it, Piri are reportedly gifted with an exceptional sense of direction. Piri and Trulls. Perhaps it has something to do with the fact that they live underground and cannot depend upon the same manner of landmarks that we do. If they did not possess some sort of internal guidance system, they would probably be in a perpetual state of confusion."

"And as luck would have it, we happen to have a Piri right among us." Arren smiled. It did not look pleasant. "Can you tell me how to get to the sewers?"

"I know of several entrances, yes. And the Piri—?"

I'll have to get her to cooperate as well."

"What about the rest of the Ocular?"

"They're going to do it."

Xeri was taken aback. "Seriously? They have agreed to it? They have barely gotten here . . ."

"Not yet. But they're going to agree to it. The Piri woman will see to it."

"How do you know?"

"I know her type," Arren said with conviction. "Her type is never satisfied with where she is. She has lusts. Lusts for anyplace that is not where she is at any given moment. And I will do my best to satisfy them. And you, Xeri, are going to help me."

"Yes, yes, of course," Xeri said, excitement beginning to rise within him. "Do you truly believe they will be able to do it? Get you to the Serabim?"

"I do not see why they should be unable to do so."

"And the Serabim will lead you to the Preceptor?"

"To Nicrominus, you mean?" Arren shrugged. "I do not see why they should be unable to lead us to Norda. And Norda is with Nicrominus. So it should not be all that much of a chore. How long will it take you to fashion the coverings for them?"

"Lenses," said Xeri. "They are called 'lenses,' and not all that much time at all. A day. Two at the most. I already have a general idea of how large to make them, so I needn't worry about taking measurements and such." He looked as if he could scarcely believe it. "When I think of the possibility of the Preceptor being rescued—"

"Yes, well," said Arren in uncontained disgust, "it is nothing short of astounding to me that you damned Firedraques are sitting around waiting for someone like me to initiate some manner of rescue. Where is Evanna in all of this? She's his damned daughter. Why are we all still sitting around talking about this when she should be leading the charge?"

"She has her reasons," said Xeri. He sounded uncertain, though. He added half-heartedly, "And I'm sure they are good ones."

"Are you? I am not so sure," said Arren.

"She loves her father."

"Yes, I can see by the way she boldly attempts to go to his rescue."

"It is not as simple as that."

Arren leaned forward, his knuckles on the table. "If you truly love someone, then yes, it really is as simple as that."

"She has no desire to fly in the face of the Travelers."

"My sister has been taken, and because she is my sister and I love her, I would fly in the face of the Overseer and all his minions and track her straight into the bowels of hell if that was what was required. Because that, Xeri, is what it means to love someone. Tell me: If they had taken Evanna, whom you profess to love, and it was Nicrominus advising caution . . . would you be listening to him? Would you be sitting here? Or would you be going out of your mind, mad with worry, and doing whatever it took and to whomever you needed to do it in order to get her back?"

"I would accept the decisions of the Preceptor because we trust him to be in charge and know what is best for all concerned. Not just for me; for all concerned. That would be showing respect for those above me."

"Well then, Xeri my friend, that is ultimately the difference between us. Because, to me, that would not be showing respect. That would be showing cowardice."

"Are you calling me a coward?"

"I suppose I am. Why? Do you wish to challenge me on it?"

No. I wish you to leave Perriz because Evanna continues to speak of you incessantly, and because when compared to you I am pathetic and undesireable. So I want you out of my city and out of my life. If you return with Nicrominus, fine. If on the other hand you die in the attempt, even better.

"No," said Xeri after a moment's hesitation. "No, I have no wish to challenge you. Why should I care what your opinion is of me? At the moment we share the same goal, and getting into some sort of battle with you will do nothing to achieve that goal. Now if you'll excuse me, I have lenses to fashion."

"Yes, of course you do," said Arren. He placed a hand on Xeri's shoulder. "I suppose I should apologize for my rather rough treatment of you earlier."

"Forget it," said Xeri dismissively. "Think nothing of it. We are all endeavoring to cope with the stress of the current situation. And we express that stress in different ways." *In my case, I endeavor to find a way to arrange for a potential rival to send himself off on a suicidal mission.*

"You are right, of course. And I expressed it through brute force. It was unworthy of me. Thank you for understanding, Xeri."

"'Twas not a problem." He made a sweeping gesture that was supposed to come across as magnanimous but instead appeared as if he were swatting insects. Arren stared at it in confusion for a moment, then shrugged. As he started out, he paused and said, "Imagine. A series of tunnels. That is exactly the sort of thing Norda would have loved. Let us pray that I can find her and bring her back here so that she can enjoy exploring it."

"I am certainly hoping with all my heart that my prayers will be answered," said Xeri solemnly.

THE SPIRES

NORDA KINKLASH HEARD SOMETHING.

She had been draped over her friend, the statue, deeply involved in conversation with it. She could not recall when she had last had such engaging discussions. Back home, back at Firedraque Hall, she had endeavored from time to time to chat with the statues that lined the upper walls, but it had been difficult. They had spoken to her in a language she could not understand. A lot of "voos" and "weees" and "see vooplay" that made no sense to her. On the other hand, the statues in her new home at the Spires were far more approachable and easy to comprehend.

She had just been in the process of reminiscing about New Daddy. She knew he was gone, and was saddened over that. She could not quite recall what had happened to him, though. "Do you know where he is?" she had asked the statue.

"I seem to recall you saying something about eating him, actually."

"Did I?" She tried to remember. Her memory was ever so frustrating a thing. It was not unlike a thousand little insects, buzzing about in countless directions, and she was always trying to gather them in and collect them into one place so that she could nail down her recollections.

Then it came back to her. The mess of her New Daddy lying all over the street, and her devouring him piece by piece, finishing with his heart. And the dugs running around trying to get at him, and the dug that had then led her to this place. All of it came back to her in a rush and she made a soft choking sound. "Oh, yes. I did do that," she said sadly, wistfully. "I wish that had not happened. In fact . . . I think my wishing it hadn't happened is why I wasn't remembering it."

"That could very well be," agreed the statue. "It's always easy to forget things when you want it to be so."

Matters were complicated even more by the fact that she couldn't recall exactly how New Daddy had met his demise. She knew that he had fallen, but the sight of it had been so upsetting to her that she couldn't gather up the little flitting creatures that held the memory of how he had died. Had he leaped? Had he been thrown? She was leaning slightly toward the latter, but still couldn't pull it all together.

That was when she had heard the sound.

It was a voice. A voice that she had not heard before, or at least she thought she hadn't heard it. As always, it was difficult for Norda to be absolutely sure about such things.

She tilted her head slightly and listened more carefully. Her tongue flicked the air; the holes in the side of her head gave her some degree of aural sensation, but her tongue aided her further in sensing vibrations.

"There is definitely someone down there," the statue said. It didn't move its mouth or head or any part of itself; it never did. But it spoke with a voice that was firm and even strident. "A male, I think. Young, by the sound of him."

"Who is it?"

"I haven't the faintest idea. How would I know? If you want to find out, then you are just going to have to determine it for yourself."

"Yes. Yes, I will do that. Ooo! Do you think," she said, taken by the idea, "that it will be someone that I have to kill?"

"Impossible to say without checking first."

"Because I could do it, you know. I could kill someone. I have before. I could again. Arren was very proud of me the last time I killed someone. It helped him get what he wanted."

"Yes, yes, yes," said the statue impatiently. "So you've said and nattered on about, far too frequently and for far too long. Are you going to stay here and continue to blather about it, or are you going to take some active initiative?"

"I'm going to do the second thing," Norda said with determination.

She swung herself off the ledge and skittered up and over the tower. Her clawed fingers sought and found purchase within the bell tower. She glanced up at the large array of bells hanging over her and fought the impulse to grab onto the long ropes hanging within. They would have provided the fastest way down, but she did not want to alert anyone below to the fact that she was approaching.

Instead, the moment she was within the tower, she leaped to the far side. When she struck it, she bounced to the other side. Like a fast moving ball, she rebounded from one side to the other, dropping down the tower with dizzying speed. Had one been listening carefully one would have heard the faint but steady "whump" "whump" of Norda as she made her way down. Fortunately whoever it was that was down at the bottom was much too involved in saying whatever it was that they were saying to take any notice of her.

Just before she hit bottom, Norda wound her tail like a spring. When she dropped lightly to the ground, she landed on it and it cushioned her fall. She sprang forward off it and landed on all fours. Her head snapped back and forth and her tongue flicked out once more, tasting the air, sensing the intruder.

Yes, it was definitely a male. His voice was rising and falling in a cadence that suggested he was singing. She didn't know what he was singing about and didn't recognize the words.

What she did recognize, though, was the concept of intruders. This male, whoever he was, had entered her place, her adopted home. How dare he? How dare he do such a thing? It was monumentally rude to come in without knocking or requesting a right of entrance. It was just . . . just bad manners. And in such an instance, the only thing she could do in response—absolutely the only acceptable thing—would be to kill him. Only thing for it, really. Anyone who was that utterly bereft of manners couldn't be taught. He just had to be disposed of before he spawned and produced more creatures like himself who were similarly unburdened by any concept of how one conducted oneself in a polite society.

Hugging the shadows, she made her way toward the sound. Staying low, remaining on all fours, she entered the huge hallway that constituted the majority of the bottom floor of the building. The vast chamber that reminded her in so many ways of Firedraque Hall, which had a similar chamber replete with much of the same meaningless iconography.

She spotted the intruder. He was kneeling directly in front of the raised stand at the far end, and he was continuing his singing. Every so often he would stop, pause, apparently trying to remember some of the words, and then he would continue.

As much as she did not recognize the language he was speaking, she likewise didn't quite comprehend what she was looking at.

It certainly wasn't a Firedraque. Nor was it a Mandraque. Those were the two races that Norda knew best, and definitely, most definitely, it was neither one. Instead of red or dark green, its skin was quite dark. Brown and smooth. Fur seemed to be covering the top of its head but was confined to that area; it didn't appear to have fur anyplace else. It had two arms and two legs, but no claws on either that she could make out. It was wearing simple clothing, little more than rags, really. On the whole it seemed small and weak and utterly incapable of defending itself in any manner.

Which would make the entire business of killing him that much easier. Because whatever it was, it had intruded upon her. That wasn't up for debate.

So then the question wasn't whether she would kill it or not; the only thing left up for discussion was the how of it. Would it be quick or slow? Quick would certainly be the more merciful way to do it. And she was, after all, a merciful individual. With that decision made, Norda crept forward, stealthily, silently. She was prepared to duck under the long benches at any point in order to keep herself out of sight, but it didn't seem necessary. The creature continued to have no idea that she was there. How pathetic its senses must have been for it to be oblivious to her presence.

Yes. A quick death, definitely. Something as pathetic as this didn't warrant her expending any energy upon him.

On the other hand, a slow death would drive home the notion of punishment.

What good punishment, though, if one wasn't going to live to learn from it?

The notion froze Norda in her tracks, still a good thirty feet from her prey. This was certainly a poser. Should she perhaps almost kill it so that it would then be able to realize the wrongness of its actions? Could it realize? Whatever creature it was, whatever species unknown to her, was it high enough on the evolutionary ladder to be able to learn? What if she was wasting her time?

Well . . . she certainly had an abundance of that. What else was there for her to do, after all? Simply wait around for Arren to come find her and take her home. And . . . something else. There was something else she wanted to do, and she thought it was in connection to New Daddy, but again her memory and mind betrayed her. Frustrated with herself, Norda thumped herself soundly in the head in hopes of jogging her memory, but nothing presented itself.

And still the boy sang.

Suddenly an angry barking filled the chamber.

It was the dug. The dug, who had apparently been out foraging, had now returned, and he was apparently no more thrilled about an intruder into their home than was Norda.

The brown skinned creature's head snapped around as it heard the dug's barking. It looked startled at the sound, but then its gaze fell upon Norda, who was remaining in precisely the ready-to-strike pose that she had adopted upon her approach. The dug growled and the creature let out a high-pitched and startled shriek, and at that point Norda charged.

Its hand a blur, the creature reached into the folds of its pathetic garment and yanked out something else that Norda didn't recognize. It appeared to be some sort of curved club with a hole at the end. It wasn't particularly intimidating and she wasn't the least concerned that a club could do her any harm, especially when wielded by something as small and pathetic as that.

Then the club exploded.

It echoed throughout the vast chamber as if a thunderstorm had formed right there in the building. The force of it was so great that it knocked the boy off its feet. As for Norda, something struck her in the left shoulder with such impact that it slammed her backwards with the force of a boulder. One moment she was airborne, and the next she was flat on her back, staring up in confusion at the ceiling.

She was only caught that way for a moment. Pulling herself together, Norda scampered to the side and took refuge under one of the long rows of benches. Her right hand trembling, she reached up and touched her shoulder. There was blood seeping from a hole in it. Norda whimpered in confusion, craning her neck, and saw that there was another hole directly on the other side. Something had gone through and come out, like an invisible spear. Something had actually drilled a hole right through her body, and it was at that point that she realized it could just as easily have gone through her chest or her head.

Every scrap of common sense told her that the smartest thing she could do was to hide.

The dug began to bark furiously and snarl, and she heard the "clack clack" of his paws running across the floor. Then the thunder erupted again, repeatedly, and the dug yipped and howled and then stopped. There was the sound of fleeing footsteps, and a door banging in the distance, and then silence.

The pain, which had been slow to come initially, began to spread through Norda's upper body. She whimpered even more loudly and then slowly climbed out from under the bench.

The dug was lying a few feet away. His body was twitching, and Norda went to him quickly and poked him and begged him not to go, but he did just the same. In fact, he was likely already dead by the time she touched him; it was just some after-the-fact spasming.

Norda realized what had happened. The dug had been protecting her. He had seen that she was injured, and heedless of any danger to himself, he had attacked the creature that had thrown the invisible spear at her . . .

. . . and he had died for his efforts.

The pain began to subside as it gave way to a swell of anger, and that swell quickly escalated into a virtual maelstrom. The dug had sacrificed himself defending her, and the thing that had killed him was running away on the assumption that it was going to get away free and clear and that nothing could stop it.

The creature was going to discover that it was wrong.

With a roar that would have sounded at home in the throat of a monster roaming a primeval forest, Norda Kinklash sprinted down the aisle as fast as her legs would carry her. *It should have been quickly. I should not have hesitated for even half a moment. I should have just killed it quickly and not even paused to wonder whether it should live or die. I made a mistake. It will not be a mistake I make a second time.*

There was a door at the far end of the chamber. Assuming that that was the door through which the creature had passed, she burst through it without slowing. It opened out onto a garden, and for half a heartbeat she was almost distracted by the attractive scents wafting her way. Then she remembered where she was and what her goal was, and with that recollection came the scent of the creature that she was trailing. He had run across the yard and kept going, and there was no way that he was going to get away from her. She paused only a moment for her nostrils to flare and his spoor to be brought solidly into her consciousness, and then she took off after him. (She had started thinking of "it" as a him, not realizing it was the beginning of the end of her ability to kill him.)

He had been moving quickly, she would give him that much. Under ordinary circumstances, she would have overtaken him in no time. As it was, she was slightly slowed from blood loss. Her instinct was to climb under a rock somewhere and allow herself time to heal. But that was not an option; she could not allow the creature to get away, and there was no telling how long his spoor would remain on this surface. Instead she gave herself over to her rage, allowing it to push away any impulse to pass out or give up. It drove her forward and she hurtled down the sidewalk after her target.

Down and around a corner, she heard another sound of a door shutting. This one was even heavier than the one back at her home. She rounded the corner and found the door immediately. The creature's scent brought her right to it.

There was a broad, flat upright handle on the door. Norda pulled on it and the door didn't open. Clearly it was locked.

Norda let out a howl of fury. Her left shoulder was starting to go numb but she shook it off. She grabbed the handle with both hands this time and pulled. The door seemed no more interested in giving way to her than it had when she first pulled on it. Norda, however, was not as easily deterred as that. Instead she leaped up onto the wall, sank her clawed toes into the brick face for additional purchase, and pulled again with all her strength. The pain in her shoulder was searing by this point, and again she shook it off, determined to let nothing distract her.

The door continued to remain unmoving, resisting her every effort, and Norda bit down on her lower lip so tightly that she drove her fangs into them and caused a small trickle of blood to run from it. Just at the moment when her brain was screaming at her that this was getting her absolutely nowhere and if she had the slightest bit of intelligence she would just give up already, the door suddenly flew open with the sound of metal shattering. Even though it had been the result that Norda was fighting for, it still caught her off guard with the result being that she fell right off the wall, chipping the brickface as she went. Her legs hit the ground and the only thing that prevented her from lying flat on the sidewalk was the fact that she was still clutching on to the door.

She lay there for a moment, pulling herself together, and then she scrambled to her feet and ran through the door.

She would have been well advised to do so with far less velocity.

Darkness swallowed her and before her eyes had the opportunity to adjust, her feet went out from under her. It was at that point that Norda realized there was a flight of stairs running off a small landing at the door, and Norda had charged right off the landing and hit the stairs without slowing. As a result she went headlong off the platform and down the stairs, tumbling end over end, losing any hope of stealth as she made a hellacious racket. She tried to reach out and grab something, anything, to slow her descent, but she was too busy being flipped around as she practically somersaulted down the stairs, which seemed to go on forever even though it actually only occupied a few seconds.

She hit another landing and nearly skidded right off it before sinking her claws into it and halting her downward flight. Between the tumble down the stairs and the blood loss, the world was spinning around her. She paused for breath, pulling herself together, determined not to move until she had managed to sort out her own head. She didn't know how long she remained that way, but finally she got to her feet. Her head was aching terribly, and for a moment she forgot why she was there or what was so important that she was throwing herself headlong into the exact sort of trouble that Arren would have been ever so cross with her for getting into.

Then the pain in her shoulder stabbed her into recollection of how she had gotten there and precisely why. She remembered the noble dug that had tried to avenge her and been slain for its trouble, and that the creature that had slain her had fled here like a rat. The recollection galvanized her and focused her once more.

By that point her eyes had adjusted quickly to the darkness. She saw a series of stairways and gratings around her, and was also aware of a distant heat from below. She found it soothing, even comforting. She liked heat. It made her want to stretch out and enjoy it, but she knew now was not the time. Furthermore she needed to proceed with caution lest she run headlong into some manner of trap. These creatures were unquestionably tricky, and possessed weapons—or at least a weapon—that was outside her familiarity and beyond her understanding.

The metal of the stairs rattled under her as she made her way down them. This caused Norda to come to a halt. She was concerned that the noise she was making would easily alert the creature that she was on her way down. He might be lying in wait there, prepared to throw more invisible spears at her. Instead she leaped onto one of the railings and clambered down it, wrapping her hands and feet around it and keeping a sure and steady grasp upon it. At one point she nearly slipped and she steadied herself using her tail for an additional grip.

She reached the bottom of the stairs and there was another, and still another after that. There were also other gantries and catwalks, leading off in a myriad of directions, accompanied by what she took to be signs that indicated which way was which. But she had no means of reading the signs, nor did she especially care about any possible detours because she was busy following the scent of the creature she was hunting: the creature who had killed the dug.

The stairway came to an end and there was still no sign of her prey. She looked around and then up and then dropped to all fours again, sniffing the ground. Momentarily woozy, Norda forced her attention back to the situation at hand and then scuttled forward, back on the scent. She found a metal grating inset into the floor and it was dislodged, indicating to her that someone had just passed through it and hadn't taken the time to restore it properly to its place. It wasn't as if she required the visual cue, but it was still a reassurance that she was on the right track. She yanked clear the grating, sending it clattering away, and dropped through.

She landed on yet another surface and looked around, trying to get her bearings. The walls around her were flat and tiled and had lettering that read "GRAND CENTRAL TERMINAL" across them. Unable to read them, the words meant nothing to Norda. The ground beneath her feet had some manner of tracks running down it going in either direction. There were fixtures overhead where lights had once gone, but they were dark. Everything was dark. Fortunately the night vision of Mandraques was extraordinary and Norda was able to see everything quite clearly.

There was high-pitched squealing and scuttling around her feet. Rats. She snatched one up in either hand, bit the heads off so they would stop squirming, and shoved them down her throat. She hoped that the sustenance would counter the increasing sensation of lightheadedness that she was battling.

Then she heard something down the tunnel and, more importantly, saw it as well. There was a small spot of light that was bouncing up and down. She had never seen anything like it, but Norda was able to intuit almost instantly that it was some manner of torch. Smaller than she had ever seen, but nevertheless effective.

And the creature was doubtless holding it.

Yes. Yes, she could hear him. She could hear him running, and huffing and puffing, and he was obviously scared.

She realized she was pleased about that.

She sprinted after him, and he must have realized that she was behind him because he let out a startled yelp. Then something flashed up ahead of her, something other than the torch, and she had barely enough time to realize that it was that same black club that he had been waving at her earlier. Norda threw herself down upon the tracks and heard the invisible spear whiz over her head. The thunder came again, and repeated itself several more times. But there was no more pain inflicted upon her. The invisible spears were coming nowhere near her, and that was when Norda realized that the creature had to see her clearly in order to hurl the spear accurately. It would not find her of its own accord; its dissimilarity from standard weaponry ended with the fact that it could not be seen.

Then she heard a brand new noise. It was a faint empty "click" sound, followed by the boy shouting something that she thought might be a profanity.

Not spears. Not spears at all. Arrows. It throws invisible arrows, and the quiver is empty.

With a roar designed to freeze the creature where he stood, Norda leaped to her feet and sprinted in the darkness. She could see the creature, but he could not see her. He knew she was coming, though, and he ran desperately, frantically, as Norda closed the gap with distance-eating leaps.

The creature yanked open a door inset into the wall and ran through it. He tried to slam it behind him, but Norda had gotten there too quickly. She caught the door and her mouth opened wide as she roared her fury, and the creature screamed. Suddenly there was a knife in his hand, and Norda may not have understood everything that the invisible arrows entailed, but she comprehended knives readily enough. She slapped it out of his hand, sending it flying into the darkness, and leaped upon him. He went down under her, falling backwards, and there was another flight of stairs. This time Norda leaped clear, though, and the creature tried to grab at a support but missed. He fell down the stairs, much as Norda had, but whereas she had fallen silently, the creature yelped and howled and cried out every single bump and thud of the way.

How easily these creatures are hurt, thought Norda, even as she gripped the railings and slid down them with confidence.

The creature was lying there at the bottom of the metal stairs. The air was thick with heat and steam, which Norda was enjoying more and more with each passing moment. The creature, however, didn't appear to be enjoying it at all. His face was covered with beaded water and his mouth was twisted in what seemed a grimace of pain. She noticed that his right leg was bent at an odd shape; then again, she couldn't be certain just how flexible this species was. Perhaps it wasn't so odd after all.

Then she saw him looking in horror at the leg and crying out, and she realized that, no, that wasn't a proper direction for it.

It was as if he didn't know where to look first: at the leg or at her.

New wetness began to appear on his face, dribbling down from his eyes. His lower lip was trembling and from the darkness he glowered at her. His torch, a single beam of light, was lying several feet away. He must have dropped it when he had tumbled down the stairs.

He seemed so young. Lying there helpless, distressed, without his unseen arrows to inflict destruction and death, he appeared to her as nothing more than a terrified child.

Then she remembered that she was going to kill him.

"I'm going to kill you," she said, except it didn't sound particularly vengeful or threatening when she said it aloud. Instead she sounded almost apologetic about it, as if she felt badly that she was going to ruin his day.

His chin seemed to stiffen and he tilted it back as if daring her to strike it. "If you're gonna do it, monster . . . then do it." His voice was quavering as he spoke but he was clearly trying to muster reserves of bravery.

Still, Norda was taken aback by his word choice. "I'm not a monster," she said, sounding more defensive than she had intended. "You're the monster. You killed dug."

He wiped the wetness away from his eyes. "Who's Doug?"

"The dug. The one in my home."

"The . . . dog? The one who was attacking me?"

"Yes! You killed him!"

"Because he was attacking me! I didn't want him to tear my throat out!"

"And you tried to kill me!"

"Because you were attacking me! And how the hell are you speaking English?"

"I don't know what 'English' is. You're speaking Firedraque. And I was attacking you," she said angrily, "because you were in my home!"

"That wasn't a home! That was a church! And if we're going to get into people being in other people's home, then let's remember that this was our damned planet before you freak shows got here!"

"It's called the Damned World," said Norda archly, "which shows how much you know."

"It's called Earth, which is how much you know."

Her eyes narrowed in anger. She could not say that she appreciated the way he was talking to her, not one bit. The problem would easily be solved if she simply ripped his vocal cords from his throat. She drew back her claws and prepared to do just that. Sensing what she was about to do, the boy closed his eyes tightly and braced himself.

The clawed hand froze in midair as she fully processed what he had just said.

"Your world?"

"Yeah! My world! Which you and the other monsters took over!"

"I didn't take anything over," said Norda. "I was hatched here."

"I was born here, too," he said defiantly. "Except your kind runs around up there, and me and my family and the others, we're—"

Suddenly he seemed to realize that he was saying things he shouldn't have said. He clamped his mouth shut for a moment to regroup and then said firmly, "So kill me, already, bitch. Just do it."

"Are you a Mort?"

"A what?"

"A Mort."

"My name's not Mort! I'm a human being! A goddamned human being! The people that you and yours tried to hunt into extinction!"

"I've never hunted any . . ." She paused and tried to handle the unfamiliar words. "Hooman beans. I've never hunted any of your kind. Or any kind."

"Yeah? Then what are you doing down here?"

"I was hunting you. Oh." She shrugged. "Well . . . you are my first." She smiled brightly. "Aren't you excited for me?"

He stared at her uncomprehendingly for a moment. "Are you stupid?"

"I am Norda."

"I don't care! I don't care what you are or who you are! Stop screwing around and just do it! Just goddamn kill me already!" He tried to sit up as if he were about to lunge at her and then he

screamed so loudly that she had to cover her ear holes to ward it
off. He fell back, clutching at his leg and sobbing openly this time.
"Dammit! Goddamnit!"

"You have a god?"

"Why do you care?"

"I don't know. I just . . . wonder if you do. And if your god is the
same as mine. And if it is, then maybe we should not be killing each
other."

He stared at her, bleary eyed. "You are so weird . . ." he said with
a tone of wonderment. He looked as if he wanted to say something
else. His voice suddenly trailed off, and then his head slumped back
as his eyes rolled up into the top of his head.

"Hooman?"

He said nothing.

"Hooman Bean?"

This time when he did not reply, she poked at him experimentally
to see if it generated any response. None was forthcoming. "Hooman
Bean!" she said more insistently, this time poking him so hard that
she might well have left a bruise. When she wasn't able to prompt
any further movement from him, her fractured mind raced, trying
to determine what she should do. She ran through the options in her
head.

She could kill him.

She could eat him.

She could kill him, then eat him. Or she could kill him and bring
him back home to be supplies.

Or she could just leave him lying there and hope that others like
him found him.

Or she could bring him to others like him.

Of all the possibilities that filtered through her mind, that last
was the one that she considered the most intriguing.

She had not forgotten that, until very recently, she had been
driven by an overwhelming desire to slay this creature, this Hooman
Bean. But Norda's nature made her unable to cling to such ideas for

terribly long. She remembered the "why" of what she had wanted to do, but minutes had passed—minutes that, for Norda, were like unto an eternity—and the fury that had driven her had already dissipated. She was a being entirely of the moment, and for the moment, she saw only a poor, injured creature, and she felt some degree of pity for him for reasons she could not fathom.

The problem was that she had no idea where others of his kind might be. The only thing she knew for sure was that they weren't behind her, or above her, or right there alongside her. So instead they must be below her.

Norda crouched and picked up Hooman Bean. She was astonished how light he was. Perhaps, she reasoned, his bones were hollow. She wondered if he was so light that he could fly, and briefly considered taking him above and throwing him off a roof to determine if that was so, but quickly decided against it. Instead Norda started down.

She had no idea where she was going, but hoped that wherever it might be, she would arrive there soon, because she was starting to feel woozy and lightheaded.

The longer she went down the stairs, the hotter the atmosphere became around her and the heavier that Hooman Bean seemed to get. She wondered why it was that he was picking up weight with each passing minute. It never occurred to her that she was becoming weaker because, aside from the occasional dull throb from the area of her shoulder, she was having trouble remembering that she had been injured. At one point she stopped, shifted his weight, and drew an arm across her head to wipe away moisture dripping in her eyes. When she did she discovered that there was blood running down her arm, and further realized that it was her own. "That's unfortunate," she said.

Soon her left arm went completely numb. Norda compensated by moving Hooman Bean over to her right shoulder and slinging him over it like a sack. His leg continued to dangle at a strange angle and he was muttering something in his unconscious state, but she couldn't make out what it was.

From below her, she heard what sounded like rushing water. She looked around for the source and eventually found yet another door. Clearly whoever had built this wherever-she-was had certainly been obsessed with doors. She found herself wishing that Arren were there. He knew how much she liked tunnels and secret passages and would no doubt have been pleased to see the way she was enjoying herself.

This door pulled open far more easily than the others. She stepped through and found herself standing on the edge of a long platform. Below her was some sort of huge metal pipe. The sound of the rushing water was coming from within there. She licked her lips because she had grown very thirsty and the sound of the water reminded her of that.

With that realization came even more dizziness, and suddenly Norda could no longer stand. She didn't know why this was, nor did she realize that she was in trouble. All she knew was that one moment, she was on her feet, and the next, she wasn't. She sat there, pondering the oddity of being in a seated position when she should, by all rights, be standing.

That was when she heard something moving in the shadows.

"Hello?" she called softly. "Hello? Are you friends of Hooman Bean's?"

"What did you do to him?" It was a female voice speaking with great urgency. She emerged from the shadows as someone else, a male, yanked at her arm, trying to stop her.

"Wait! Lenore! Don't get near it!"

"Shut up!" She pulled free and ran toward Norda. Norda looked up at her, her eyes bleary. "What did you do to him? What did you do?"

"He fell down stairs," said Norda. "His leg looks funny. Oh," she added as she remembered, and her voice became stern, "and he killed the dug. He should not have done that. Are you his mother?" When the woman nodded, Norda told her firmly, "Well then, it's your responsibility. You should punish him. Perhaps a sound thrashing. Or you could kill him and eat him. But you might consider that a little extreme. Where are you going?"

"Going—?" the woman said helplessly.

"Yes. You're fading away. That's amazing. How are you doing . . . that . . . ?"

Norda's suddenly discovered that she had forgotten how to speak. She couldn't put words together. They were floating around in her head but she could not for the life of her recall what the proper order for them was. Every word she knew was drifting behind her eyes, and she picked one at random.

"Home," she said and then Norda slumped over and hit the floor next to Hooman Bean. The world around her was blacking out, and she heard a rough voice say, "Let's kill it while we can," and she thought, *Well, that is certainly rude,* and then the world went dark around her and she heard nothing further.

THE STREETS OF PORTO

EUTOK AND KARSEN HAD JOURNEYED all the way from Venets to Porto and, as absolutely nothing of consequence occurred, Eutok kept saying the same type of thing over and over: "It cannot keep being this easy."

When they would make camp, Eutok would lie there staring in the darkness and mutter, just before falling asleep, "We will likely wake up dead; something is going to go wrong."

When they would awaken and recommence their travels, Eutok would say, "Just watch; today is when it goes awry." Karsen would roll his eyes and try to ignore the Trull's eternal pessimism. It wasn't as if Karsen was relentlessly upbeat—truthfully, his thoughts were running along the same lines as Eutok's—but if nothing else he had the good grace to keep it to himself.

So they rode, mile after mile, knowing that at any moment they could find themselves in the middle of some insurmountable danger, perfectly aware that their quest could come to an abrupt and terminal end. Every turn, when the worst failed to materialize, it seemed nothing but a cruel precursor to the inevitable.

At first Karsen's pronouncements were enough to fill Eutok with a growing sense of dread. By this point, it was just annoying the hell out of him.

They had ridden through or past any number of cities on their way, and it was much the same as most cities in the Damned World. They were deserted, all signs of the species that had constructed them wiped away courtesy of the incursion of the Twelve Races.

When they had initially begun their sojourn, Eutok had been taken aback by what he had witnessed. Having spent his entire life underground, his knowledge of the Morts and the destruction inflicted upon them by the Third Wave had been entirely in the abstract. He had learned about it, heard about it. Seeing it, though, was a very different matter.

They passed shattered city after shattered city. Buildings had tumbled down upon themselves or been destroyed through the incursions of the Twelve Races. It wasn't as if the Twelve Races had needed all these cities in which to live. The Races were spread out through the Damned World and since they were far fewer in number than the Morts had been, they did not need remotely as much space within which to live.

Why did this happen? He kept coming back to the question, but no reason suggested itself.

Karsen, for his part, kept glancing back at Eutok as they made their way toward Porto. He seemed to realize that something was on Eutok's mind, but since the Trull chose not to say anything about it, Karsen didn't pursue it.

Day after day they rode, the paths and the devastated cities flying past them. Karsen kept thinking that this might well be a waste of time, but there was no reason not to pursue it. There only remained two questions: Had that strange creature, Ruark, been correct about Jepp's destination, and was the Crossing functioning? Only time would answer the former, and as to the latter, it would then come down to whether Eutok was capable of repairing it. He claimed that he was, but there would be no way to know for sure until they were faced with the situation.

Upon their arrival in Porto, they slowed their mounts and made their way through the city. The whores seemed to be moving more reluctantly than before. Karsen was wondering if there was something in the city that was bothering them. He brought his mount to a halt, and that caused Eutok to rein up and look at him questioningly.

"I think it's time to part company," he said.

"Where are you going?"

"Not the two of us," said Karsen impatiently as he dismounted. "Unless you're going to tell me there's some way to get these creatures into the Truller cars."

"No. No way whatsoever." Eutok got off the whores as well, and he patted the creature affectionately on the side of the neck. "Believe it or not, I'm going to miss the thing. It has served us well. They both have."

"I agree. And they deserve their freedom." Karsen removed the ropes that he had used to devise the guidance system around his whores' head. Eutok did likewise. "All right, creature," said Karsen. "You are free to go."

The whores stood there, staring at him. It made a snuffling sound.

"Go, I said!"

"You, too!" Eutok told his whores. He clapped his hands. "You're done! On your way!"

The whores looked at each other as if trying to determine mutually what it was that the Trull and Laocoon were demanding of them.

Eutok yanked the stone sword from his belt and bellowed as loudly as he could. The whores reared up, crying out in fright, and together they turned and ran. Karsen and Eutok watched them go until they passed from sight. "That," said Karsen, "was more trouble than expected."

"Mayhap they believed we were making a mistake in sending them on their way."

"Who knows? They might have been right. But there's nothing to be done for it now. So . . ." He turned to Eutok. "Do you know which way to the Crossing?"

Eutok frowned, considering, and then he got to one knee and spread his thick fingers upon the ground. The road was badly broken. "I wonder what the hell came through here."

"Minosaurs."

Eutok glanced toward him, eyebrow raised. "Are you sure?"

"Oh yes. I know the marks all too well."

"You traveled with a Minosaur, as I recall."

"Yes. And we cleaned up after any number of skirmishes in which the Minosaurs were participants. They tended not to leave much in their wake. Not surprising, really, considering their preferred method of combat was the stampede."

"We've heard them from time to time," said Eutok. "Every so often they would charge above us in great waves, and the ground would shake, and debris would fall from overhead. My mother would unleash the most formidable string of curses you would ever hear pass from the lips of any living creature. It was the only time that I found her remotely entertaining." He paused and smiled. "Amazing how it is possible to find pleasant memories in even the most unlikely of circumstances."

"Yes, tremendously amazing," said Karsen, who was far less amazed than he was impatient. He was looking around at the city. As was the case with many other cities that they had passed through, a number of them had already collapsed. The city had been built along a fairly mountainous region, and large sections of the rises were exposed when the buildings had come down. Up in the distance there was some sort of wall with large chunks of it gone. Karsen could not determine whether it was a section of castle, or else some sort of defensive wall that had been constructed to keep enemies at bay. If the latter had been the case, it hadn't done much of a job.

"Why did they do it?"

Eutok had spoken, and his voice sounded softer, more bewildered than it ever had before. Karsen looked at him in confusion. "What they? The Minosaurs, you mean?"

"Not just them. All of them. The Twelve Races."

"Is that what has been on your mind?" When he saw Eutok's look, he added, "You seem to have been preoccupied during much of our ride. Particularly when we are passing through cities. I had not wanted to say anything . . ."

"You noticed."

"I tend to notice...well, everything, truth to tell."

"It just makes increasingly less sense to me. This world was so vast, and the Twelve Races only need a relatively small portion to survive. I had always been told of the great battles that the other races fought—"

"Not your race, of course."

"Of course. It is not the Trull way to take sides."

"Just provide weapons and aid to all concerned and benefit from all sides."

"That's correct. Anyway, I am beginning to wonder if there was any point to it. Were the Morts truly that worthless, that they deserved to have their entire world taken from them?"

"That's rather advanced thinking for a Trull."

"Lying on your back for an extended period of time while you're convinced you're dying from internal injuries sends your thoughts to unexpected places. I am just starting to wonder if the Morts could not have been more use to the Twelve Races alive than dead."

"It may well be," said Karsen, "that our peoples' collective inability to consider that may be one of the many reasons that we were banished to this godsforsaken world to begin with."

"Aye."

"So . . . anyway . . . the Crossing . . . ?"

"Yes, of course." He went from one knee to both and then laid the side of his head against the ground. He rapped on the ground several times with his knuckles. He did this for a time, and then moved to another section of road and once more rapped on it. He kept that up for a while, and then moved to another section, and then another. Karsen stood behind him patiently, his arms folded, until he could no longer take it and said in exasperation, "What are you doing?"

Eutok raised his head and said, "Do you want me to find it or not?"

"This is going to lead us to it?"

"The few times I've been to it, it was from below, not above. And it was many years ago. But if you don't like the way I'm going about it . . ."

Karsen impatiently indicated that Eutok should continue as he was doing. Eutok nodded once and went back to the painstaking and frankly irritating method of checking the street for . . . well, Karsen really didn't know what the hell he was checking for, and that was irritating him most of all.

"So where are they?" Eutok said after two hours of tapping around on the ground. His patience seemed astonishing considering the Trull reputation for being short tempered.

"Where are who?"

"The Minosaurs. Presumably they went to the trouble of killing all the humans. Why leave the city after that?"

"They left because the entire purpose of coming into the city was to kill the humans. Once they were dead, why stay?"

"It doesn't make sense."

"It does not have to make sense. We are talking about the actions of races that make war for no other purpose than to make war. You're hardly new to this world, Eutok. I don't see why this should come as a tremendous surprise to you."

"You," Eutok said, "have had a lifetime to become accustomed to seeing the stupidity and pointlessness of these actions first hand. So if is taking me more time to adjust to the mindset that you so easily grasp, then—"

His voice trailed off.

"What?" said Karsen, who had frankly gotten sick of following Eutok around aimlessly. When Eutok did not immediately reply, Karsen said again, "What? What is it? For the love of—"

"For the love of the one you love, shut up," said Eutok brusquely. He had gone from rapping on the ground to banging on it with a clenched fist. "Yes. Here. It's here."

"Are you certain?"

"Yes."

"All right. So . . . how do we get down there? Where is the entrance?"

"There is no entrance that I know of. Not directly from here to there."

"Well, then," said Karsen, unable to contain his frustration, "what are we supposed to do?"

"We are not going to do anything. Stand back."

"What?"

Without waiting for Karsen to obey him, Eutok started pounding on the ground. It took him only seconds to break through the shattered remains of the street. He tossed huge chunks of thick black rock to either side and then started to paw away at the ground. He started slowly but then picked up speed. Dirt was flying toward Karsen, who shielded his face and backed up in order to give the Trull some room.

Trulls excavated using various tools, but that did not mean that they were incapable of doing so using nothing more than their huge hands, their formidable strength, and their determination. Eutok employed all three of those now as he tore at the ground with what Karsen could only think of as pure glee. If Karsen had not been certain earlier that Eutok was fully recovered from the injuries he had sustained, he was definitely sure now.

In less than ten minutes, Eutok had already excavated a hole of sufficient depth that he was no longer visible from the surface of the street. Karsen circled the area, watching in amazement as Eutok continued to dig without the slightest hint of slowing up. There was no doubt that Eutok was in his element. He was a two-handed, two-armed excavating machine that was being employed for precisely the purpose of its creation. Several times Karsen called out tentatively, suggesting that he would be perfectly happy to pitch in. Eutok either ignored him or simply grunted something that sounded vaguely negative, never slowing in his endeavors.

Karsen took up a seat and ate carefully from their food stocks. He was judicious with his consumption. Presuming that the Truller car was up and running for the Crossing, there was still no telling just how long the journey was going to take. They couldn't exactly go hunting while riding on a high-speed vehicle; they would have to subsist on whatever they happened to have with them.

As Eutok continued to work, and as Karsen kept feeling increasingly lazy in the presence of Eutok's energy, he found this thoughts wandering to Eutok's question. What had happened to the invading Minosaurs? It wasn't so much that they had destroyed the inhabitants of the city and then abandoned it. Despite Eutok's bewilderment, it really was not atypical for the Twelve Races to behave in a wasteful manner. It was their nature to care less for the spoils of war than the action of war. The Bottom Feeders were held in such universal contempt because their interests lay with what was left behind after battles. This ran counter to the typical mindset of the more belligerent races which dictated that one fought, killed or was killed and, presuming one was still able to do so, then moved on to look for the next battle. That was why the Banished had done such a superb job reducing their own number, a feat that the humans had been less than successful in accomplishing.

Still, the path that the onslaught of the Minosaurs had obviously taken would have brought them to this waterside town. There was nowhere else for them to go had they continued to proceed in the direction that the sun moved.

So where were they?

Their congregating here in Porto would have explained why Eutok and Karsen had not encountered anyone in their travels to this point. But their absence from Porto was still bewildering to him. It was always possible that they had gone off in yet another direction, but it was odd that at least some of them had not taken up residence in Porto. Minosaurs tended to overwhelm a town, then leave some of their females to breed (with one of their studs to attend to the impregnating of same.) They would stay there until all the resources in the village or town or city were used up, at which point they would move on.

"I'm going to look around," Karsen informed Eutok. Eutok simply grunted and kept at his work. This was the happiest that Karsen had seen Eutok since they had first embarked on this insane escapade. That was not saying much since Eutok had never been happy to any degree since their association began. Apparently the only thing that Eutok enjoyed was mindless digging. No wonder Trulls were so good at it. Karsen wondered if it might not be a substitute for sexual frustration, and decided that it would probably be best not to ask that. Ever.

He looked around the city, not wandering too far from the dig site. It wasn't necessary to go far afield; he found supplies in abundance. He was able to find plenty of food stored in those peculiar but terribly effective metal cylinders that humans appeared to adore. (He still remembered that breakthrough moment in his youth when he had actually connected the odd tool that the Bottom Feeders had unearthed during a surveying expedition with the metal cylinders and realized that the tool was the key to opening the cylinders. They had had no clue that there was food inside until he had managed, through much trial and error, to open one. It was the first time in his life that he could recall that his mother had embraced him and sung praises of him. It was also the last. Zerena Foux was many things, but demonstrative of her affection was not one of them.)

To this day he kept that tool with him at all times, so he would continue to be able to open the cylinders and feast on the contents. He found plenty of those cylinders now, which should not have been a surprise. The cylinders tended to be remarkably strong, defying any conventional means of opening them. Indeed, some members of the Twelve Races would use them as throwing weapons since they could do a considerable amount of damage if hurled with sufficient force. They could be dented and even opened if battered sufficiently, but in those instances the contents were generally mashed beyond use. To the best of his knowledge, only Karsen had discovered the secret to opening the cylinders and leaving the food inside edible.

He shoved as many cylinders as he could reasonably carry into his bag, but that was not what concerned him. What concerned him was that there was much food still lying around that had remained unconsumed. Meat, in particular, or at least the remains of the meat, was hanging in windows of various shops. There wasn't much left there; bones for the most part. The rest had either rotted away or been picked clean by animals.

The question was, why were the bones of animals still hanging there? Minosaurs ate damned near anything, including bones. Karsen had been startled the first time he'd seen Mingo cheerfully chowing down on a skeleton, crunching the bones. He'd seemed to consider it quite tasty. If that was the case, why had the Minosaurs left the bones in the windows untouched?

Karsen had seen far too many sites of devastation and war not to know what was normal and what was not.

This was not normal.

As much as he wanted to get to Jepp—as much as he was convinced that this Crossing he'd been told about was the means by which to go about it—he was becoming increasingly convinced that there was something here that he was overlooking. Something that could have catastrophic consequences if he did not figure it out soon enough.

Shouldering the bag with the cylinders in them, he hurried back to the dig site. There he found a massive mountain of dirt and debris. "Eutok?" he called cautiously. "Eutok?"

"Down here!" came the Trull's voice from deep in the hole.

Karsen cautiously made his way to the edge of the dig site and looked down. He couldn't see a damned thing except a very dim glow. "Are you all right?"

"I'm perfectly fine."

"Can you see down there?"

"There are still glow torches left here from the excavation. They appear to be functioning."

"Powered by hotstars?"

"Of course. How else?"

"Considering how inconsistent they have been as of late, I wasn't assuming."

"Yes, yes, it's hotstars," Eutok said with growing irritation. "Are you coming down here or not? I'm weary of shouting up to you."

Karsen hesitated and then said, "I'll be right down." He reached into his bag, pulled out his rope, looked around and found an upright metal projection of some sort in the walk nearby that he could use for an anchor. He affixed the rope to it and then pulled on it as hard as he could to assess how good a job he'd done securing it. It appeared to be holding solidly. He carried the rest of the rope over to the hole and dropped it down.

"What was that?" called Eutok from below.

"A way up in the event that things don't work out for us."

"You have no confidence."

"Just trying to anticipate all possibilities." Having no idea exactly how far down it was, and not wanting to risk breaking his leg, Karsen gripped the rope and eased himself into the hole. He could not believe how deep the Trull had managed to dig in such a relatively short period. He knew they were formidable excavators, but this was simply absurd.

He climbed down, his hooves skidding off the walls whenever he sought purchase. No point in trying to establish toeholds when one doesn't have toes. He lowered himself hand over hand, depending entirely on his considerable upper body strength. The hammer weighed heavily on his back since he had no ground to support him.

He made his way down as quickly as he could. He didn't bother to look down; doing so wouldn't get him there any faster. Besides, he knew that it wasn't any further than the length of his rope since Eutok had seen it.

Moments later he dropped into the tunnel. Eutok was standing right there and put out a hand cautiously lest Karsen hit the ground and fell over. "You all right?"

"Your concern is appreciated."

Eutok grunted. "It has nothing to do with concern."

"What, then?"

The Trull shrugged. "You are tolerable company. When one has lived his life for as long as I have without such, one tends to . . . appreciate it. Anyway," he continued brusquely, as if talk of such things was annoying to him, "it's this way."

Karsen followed Eutok along the tunnels. It wasn't as if rock or dirt was a particularly vital organism, but these seemed dead even for underground. When Karsen and the other Bottom Feeders had ventured into the subterranean lair of the Trulls, even though it was underground, there was a sense of life there. It was clearly somewhere where the Trulls were residing. It was abundant with purpose and vitality.

Where they were walking now felt as if they were striding through a grave.

Even though there was some lighting, it was minimal, and Karsen made his way slowly. Eutok moved with more confidence, probably because he was in an environment that was much more to his liking. Soon it was all that Karsen could do to keep up with him.

The corridor widened out and they got to an intersection. Eutok moved with confidence to the right. Karsen didn't know if Eutok genuinely knew where he was going or just wanted it to appear that way since he would be loathe to admit that he was just guessing.

Before Karsen could round the corner to keep up with him, he heard Eutok's voice utter a clear and frustrated, "Damn it!" He came around the corner and found Eutok standing next to an overturned Truller car. It was lying on its side, covered with cobwebs. It was extremely large, much bigger than the one that Karsen and his family had leaped into when they'd gone to the Underground.

There were twin grooved tracks set into the rock that led down a darkened tunnel. "Is that it?" he said in a low voice.

"That's it. That's the Crossing." Eutok was barely affording it a glance. "But this Truller has certainly seen better days."

"How is it going to function, anyway? From what I understood, the Trullers back at the Hub operated via some sort of central command station."

"Not this one. There's no intersection of the Crossing with any other vehicles. It's a straight shot, there and back. Once we get it moving . . . assuming we can get it moving . . . it will just keep going until we reach the other end."

Eutok gripped the Truller firmly and, with a grunt, shoved it up and over until the bottom engaged with the twin grooves. He pushed on it tentatively. It didn't seem interested in moving. "Hold on," he said and pulled it back over so that it lay on its side again. Then he tugged open a hatch beneath it and began muttering to himself.

"What's wrong?"

"The hotstars that are supposed to be powering the damned thing seem dead. We were having this same problem in a scattered fashion around the Hub," he said. He pulled out three hotstars and glowered at them as if they had failed in order to cause him personal aggravation. "I do not understand why this keeps happening. The things aren't supposed to become depleted."

"We were having the same problem with the hotstar that powered our vehicle. Sometimes it would work, and sometimes it wouldn't."

"We can't afford to have hotstars that are unpredictable. The last thing we need is for the Truller to run out of energy halfway across. Walking the rest of the way would not be pleasant." He glanced around thoughtfully. "The ones powering the lanterns seem to be functioning."

"Can you adapt them to use in the Truller?"

"Easily."

He walked past Karsen and started looking over the lanterns. Karsen followed him, not feeling as if he had much to offer in the way of advice or observation and so decided to remain silent.

Then Karsen noticed something lying off to the side. At first he thought it was a rock of some sort, but it did not appear shaped like any others that he had seen. Leaving Eutok to his inspection of hotstars, he crouched next to the rocks and sifted through them.

It took him almost no time to realize that they were not rocks.

They were bones.

Slowly he held one up, studied it closely. It was long and tapered and came to a point. The point was stained with what Karsen was reasonably sure was long-dried blood.

It was a horn. The exact sort of horn that projected from the heads of Minosaurs.

"Oh, hell," he muttered.

He heard a noise behind him and jumped to his hooves, but it was only Eutok holding up three hotstars in triumph. "I found us—"

"We have to leave. Now."

"Now?" Eutok frowned. "Well, give me a few minutes to attend to—"

"We may not have a few minutes. We need to get out of here immedi . . ."

Suddenly Eutok put up a hand. "Did you hear that? Some sort of scraping noises. Like . . ."

"Something approaching, perhaps?"

The severity of their situation registered on Eutok. "Yes. Yes, you're right. Let's get out of—"

Then Karsen's nostrils flared as he picked up a new aroma. It was a smell with which he was unfamiliar, but it chilled him to the bone nevertheless. It was like rotting meat. Moving, rotting meat.

The clicking and scraping noises were becoming more pronounced. Something was heading their way and showing less and less interest in trying to mask its presence.

Eutok and Karsen began to head for the hole that had been their means of entrance, but dark forms were blocking the way. They seemed to be emerging from the walls, as if the very darkness around them had come to life.

"We have a problem," Karsen said under his breath.

Eutok pulled out his battle axe and backed up, as did Karsen. He didn't reach around for his war hammer. The tunnels were narrow and he didn't think there would be sufficient space to swing it. Instead he kept the Minosaur horn up in a ready stabbing position. "Yes. I was noticing."

"The Truller. Back to the Truller."

Karsen didn't bother to point out the obvious flaw with the plan: The Truller wasn't functioning. Eutok was going to need at least a few minutes to fix it, and it seemed unlikely that whatever was converging on them was going to provide him that opportunity.

But there was no choice. They were cut off from the way they'd come. Besides, the Crossing was the only means at their disposal of getting to the Spires. If they were going to find Jepp, then retreat was not an option.

They backed up as quickly as they could, and then from around the corner, from the direction that the Truller car was waiting for them, there were more sounds, more scraping, and this was accompanied by the unmistakable sounds of derisive laughter. It was high-pitched and nervous and yet not really nervous because whatever was stalking them unquestionably had the upper hand.

By that point there was no question in Karsen's mind what was approaching them from either side. "Piri," he whispered.

Eutok nodded. "Aye. Piri."

Hearing the name of their race spoken aloud, the Piri gave up any pretense of caution. They emerged from the shadows, their fingertips rubbing together in anticipation, their lips drawn back to reveal their fangs. They were deathly pale, and there were dozens upon dozens of them, far more than Eutok and Karsen could possibly handle. Above ground, perhaps, but not here, not in their lair.

They killed the Minosaurs. The Minosaurs came here and wiped out all the humans, and endeavored to settle here, and a colony of Piri made it here through tunnels that the Trulls had constructed, and they emerged during the night and killed and drank the Minosaurs. Poor bastards probably never knew what hit them.

But we're going to know.

"Stay back!" Eutok shouted, and then he waved his axe threateningly and bellowed, "Stay back! Or let he who would be the first to die come at me!"

They attacked en masse.

THE UPPER REACHES OF SUISLAN

DEMALI, DAUGHTER OF THE CHIEF of the Serabim, fled down the mountain as quickly as her furry legs would allow her to.

The wind and the snow whipped fiercely around her, and the passages through which she was moving were treacherous, at times narrow, at other times slippery, and all too often a combination of the two. Occasionally she would stop to catch her breath, and at those times she would flatten herself against the mountain's walls in hopes that her blondish-white fur would enable her to blend in.

It isn't true . . . it cannot be true . . . The same words kept floating through her head, telling her that the things Akasha said had to be mistakes or misunderstanding or in some other way not related to reality. But the things he said had made so much sense, and he had seemed so sure. Why would he lie? Why would he make up such things?

The answer was obvious: To divide her from her father. That brought her back, though, to the whys of the situation. Why would he be interested in trying to drive a wedge between her and her father? What would he have to gain from that?

Nothing. He had nothing to gain. It made no sense for him to take such actions, which for Demali underscored the likelihood that everything he had told her was the absolute truth. All the more reason, then, for her to get as far from her father as she possibly could. At the very least, it would give her time to think.

The wind blew even more fiercely. Darkness painted the skies above her, and Demali whimpered, afraid. She had never been off on her own like this before. The mountains of her homeland, always so familiar to her, now seemed foreign and alien. Every step was fraught with peril, and she knew it was all in her own mind, but she couldn't help herself.

Something blocked out the moonlight.

She looked up and gasped.

A Zeffer was hovering above her, its surface rippling in the wind. A rider was astride it, but she couldn't make out who it was. Someone else was being held by one of the Zeffer's long tentacles and being lowered down to the narrow path upon which she stood. She was able to discern who that individual was all too easily.

"Get away!" she howled above the wind. "Get away!"

Her warnings were not heeded, and moments later her father, Seramali, had been deposited on the narrow path in front of her. The Zeffer, guided by its Rider, floated up and away, leaving the two of them alone.

"Where," he said, "do you think you're going?"

"I need to get away! I need to think!"

"Think about what?" He was clearly trying to sound reasonable, but there was clear irritation in his voice. "What did Akasha tell you?"

"What makes you think he told me anything!"

"An educated guess." His fur was rippling in the wind. He tried to smooth it out, which simply looked ridiculous. "Demali . . ."

"He told me you killed Pavan's parents! That you had them killed! That they had no desire to see their son become a Keeper and did not want to turn him over to you, and you killed them because of it!"

"Demali!"

"And then you let Pavan believe all these years that his parents had abandoned him! Is it true?"

"Demali, you have to understan—"

"Is it true?!"

He hesitated, emotions warring with each other on his face, and then he shrugged and said, "Yes."

"Oh my gods—"

"They left me no choice!" he shouted above the winds. "They were going to take him away! They were going to leave with him and find another tribe to live with! Is that what you would have wanted for us? For Akasha's heir to depart? I know how you feel about him. If his parents had their way, he would not have been here for you to be with!"

"But that doesn't excuse . . ."

"Yes, it does," he said forcefully. "I am the chief of this tribe of Serabim. Anything I do to benefit this tribe is excused! I have to make the decisions that no one else can make! Pavan's parents refused to acknowledge that! I had to do it!"

"You're a monster! That is what you are. Nothing but a monster!"

"Am I?" Seramali's face twisted into a sneer. "Akasha knew of it! He knew all this time. Pavan's mentor knew what I had done, and he allowed Pavan to believe it. What of that, eh? Why did Akasha not tell him?"

"Because he said he was waiting for Pavan to reach his twenty-first cycle! To reach his first communion with the Zeffers. Once he accomplished that, he was going to trust Pavan with the knowledge. He didn't know that you were going to betray us!"

"I've betrayed nothing and no one!" Becoming impatient with Demali and the entire situation, he grabbed at her arm. "Come here!"

She yanked her arm clear of him, shouting, "No! Get away!"

"Demali, I have had more than enough of this . . ."

"You turned Pavan over to them! To the Mandraques! This whole thing is your fault! I've heard you through the years! Do you think I haven't? Your mutterings about how our people have exiled themselves here! How we could do so much more with the right alliances! How you did not believe that the Overseer was as all powerful as others say!"

"You are distorting my . . ."

"The Mandraques, father? You allied with the Mandraques? Are you insane?"

"The Mandraques have a vision for the Damned World!" he said. "And it is a vision that does not include the Firedraques, with their endless treaties and attempts to deprive us of our true nature. So we are going to do something about them, and about every Mandraque who is spineless enough to be in their service! And everything is in motion, and there's nothing you can do to stop it because it's already happening, and we are going to lead the Serabim to greatness, with you or without you!"

"It's definitely going to be 'without'!"

"You are right about that!"

He lunged for her then, and this time when he grabbed her, Demali did not simply try to pull away. Instead she pushed back, shoving hard, and she let out a challenging roar. Seramali howled back, his voice carrying, and he slammed her up against the snow covered surface of the mountain. He pinned her there with one hand and she saw that in his other hand was a knife.

He drove the blade forward and Demali twisted her body. It grazed her torso but not deeply enough to cause any damage. He tried to pull it back, to assault her again. Demali shifted her weight, bracing her feet, and the next thing she knew she had his arm immobilized, trapped between her own arm and her body. Seramali shouted her name in fury and now he was the one who was trying to pull away.

She drew back a fist and hesitated only a moment before, with a roar, she drove it into Seramali's jaw. Seramali reeled, his eyes wide in pain. He looked stunned for a moment, and then before she could strike him again, he recovered his wits and head butted her, slamming his forehead into her face. She cried out, staggered, and he tried to slip out of her grasp so that he could bring the knife around again. But even though he was the stronger of the two, she was quicker of hand and nimbler of mind. She managed to position herself so that she caught his wrist and bent it back and around. Her leverage advantage more than compensated for his superior strength. The knife clattered to the path and Demali, for good measure, sank her teeth into her father's arm.

Seramali howled like the damned, and that, as it turned out, was the last straw.

There was a rumbling from overhead, a noise that the Serabim knew all too well. Demali was momentarily startled by it, fear striking her in a way that even her father's attempts to murder her had not, and Seramali chose that moment to pull loose from her. He drove his foot forward and caught her in the pit of the stomach, knocking her backwards. As his daughter hit the ground, the ground shook furiously under Seramali's feet. He turned and saw an avalanche of ice and snow, hurtling not just from down the path, but from overhead.

There was an overhang about ten feet above him that was projecting outward. Seramali leaped upward, sinking the claws of his hands and feet into the icy wall. He crushed his body against the mountainside as a sheet of white descended past him.

It was only at that moment, with his daughter's death imminent, that the immensity of what he was doing apparently truly began to sink in on Seramali. "No! Wait! I was just trying to scare you! I . . . I never truly wanted to . . ." With a frightened and alarmed cry, he reached out toward her. It was too late. In a cascade of snow and ice, Demali was knocked off the narrow path and sent plummeting off the mountain. Her white, furred body blended in with all the snow around her and within seconds she had disappeared from view.

Seramali turned away, hugging the wall for long moments until the last of the snow and ice fell past him and left him clinging there, sad and pathetic alone.

He sobbed then for as long as his grief as a father would permit him to.

He sobbed for about ten seconds.

Then he stepped down, brushed himself off, and worked to make his way back up the side of the mountain, already determining exactly what he was going to say to explain to his people that Demali had, as near as he could tell, slain Akasha out of some rage-induced haze and then thrown herself to her death when reason had returned to her.

THE SEWERS OF PERRIZ

I.

TURKIN AND BEROLA WERE THE only two who agreed to go and, as it turned out, Clarinda could not have been happier. This outcome surprised Arren, who had thought he would have far more Ocular backing him up than was going to be the case, and it also surprised Clarinda, who was amazed to discover that she had come to care about the fate of the gigantic creatures as much as she had.

She had gathered all of them in her quarters and walked them through Arren's offer. They listened closely, without interruption, until she was done. She made certain not to take any sides or try to direct them in any particular way. This ran contrary to her original determination to urge them to accompany Arren Kinklash.

They trust you. Look at them, gazing up at you. They have faith in you because you brought them to this haven of safety and now they will attend to your words and do whatever you tell them to. This is a responsibility you cannot take lightly.

She did not know why that was the case. Why in the world should she care what happened to them? The fact that it was so was disconcerting to Clarinda because she had spent so much of her life knowing exactly what her mind was at all times. That was likely because she had spent so much of her existence hating and despising both her mother and her people that she had become accustomed to feeling a particular way.

Even her involvement with Eutok was an outgrowth of that. It was a rebellion against the expectations put upon her by her mother and her people. Did she love Eutok, truly love him? So much had happened to her that by this point even she was unsure.

After she had told the Ocular precisely what would be expected from them—the benefits (the ability to function during the day; the chance to engage in battle which was the birthright of their people) and the drawbacks (hitting the road yet again, plus the fact that since they didn't know what they might encounter, there was always the possibility of death)—the Ocular sat there and considered her words.

Then Kerda asked the one and only question that the Ocular were going to ask. It happened to be the exact question that Clarinda not only feared, but knew would be forthcoming:

"What do you want us to do?"

Fortunately enough, she was ready for it. Her answer was simple and facile. "I want you to do whatever will make you happy."

"What will make me happy," said Kerda without hesitation, "is to remain here with you." Most of the other Ocular nodded.

Clarinda felt the unfamiliar sensation of a smile tweaking at her mouth. She quickly smothered it. "I think you are being ridiculous," she said crisply. "I am not your mother. I am not your anything except the individual who got you here."

"That is more than enough," said Kerda.

"I'll go."

The words caught Clarinda off guard and she looked to the speaker. It was Berola. Next to her, Turkin glanced at her for a moment and then said, "Me, too."

Clarinda wondered if this was going to set off a round of "me-too'ism" from the rest of the Ocular, but it did not. Instead they just stared at the elder Ocular as if the pair of them had spoken out of turn.

Clarinda knew she should have accepted their volunteering without hesitation, but to her surprise, hesitate she did. "Very well," she said and then went on uncertainly, "May I ask—?"

"I have . . ." Berola paused, trying to find a way to put it into words. "I don't . . . I have this need . . . I just . . ."

"I want to hit something," said Turkin. "Kill something."

"That's it," said Berola, looking relieved that Turkin had articulated it. "That is exactly it."

"Kill something . . ." Clarinda wasn't entirely sure that she understood.

Berola had been seated on the floor since there was no furniture that readily accommodated her. Now she stood, towering over Clarinda. "We have lost our people . . . our family. The lives that we knew. I would like nothing better than to be able to simply settle into this great city and enjoy peace. That was what I thought I wanted until I got here. And now I sit here, and all I can think of is all that I have lost. It fills me with such rage . . . such overwhelming rage that I want to strike out at the entire Damned World. I tremble with fury and there is nothing I can do, nothing, for as long as I remain here. There is nothing for me to lash out against, and if I do not find a means of releasing all that anger, all that frustration, all that fury, then it is going to consume me, Clarinda. It will devour me whole, and whatever of me is left will not be recognizable as Berola or an Ocular."

"She is right," said Turkin. "The gods have visited death and destruction upon us. We cannot strike back at the gods, for they are above the fray save when it suits them to make our lives miserable. If this sojourn with the Mandraque will give me the opportunity to vent some of the wrath that I cannot unleash upon the gods, then I am all for it. I'm anxious for it."

"As am I."

"And," and she looked at the others, "the rest of you would rather stay here?"

They nodded almost as one. Apparently they were bereft of the burning fury that seemed to be driving the elders. Perhaps younger Ocular were simply more malleable than older ones, and had an easier time adapting to circumstances. That could well have been the truth that prompted Nagel to press the youngsters into service.

For a moment she considered trying to talk them out of. What, really, were they staying there for? To be near her? She had nothing to offer them . . . except, obviously, they felt differently.

"All right," she said. "All right. I will convey your decision to

Arren. Be prepared to depart within the next turn or so."

She got to her feet and headed for the door. And then Kerda said softly, "Thank you, Clarinda." Before Clarinda could reply, another of the Ocular said, "Thank you, Clarinda," and then a third and fourth and all of them, murmuring either individually or together, "Thank you, Clarinda."

Her breath caught for a moment and then she said "You're welcome" so softly that even she could barely hear it.

She had no trouble hearing Arren Kinklash, however.

"Two?" he practically bellowed when she went to his sanctum to inform him of the outcome of her meeting. "I am going to have an army of two?"

"Three."

"You said—"

"I was counting you."

"I thought you would be able to influence them. Persuade them."

"I might well have been able to," she said with a shrug. "I chose instead to lay out the options for them and allow them to make their own decisions. Berola and Turkin decided to accompany you. The rest desired to stay here."

"With you."

"With me."

Arren stalked the room, his tongue flicking in and out in agitation and annoyance. "Xeri has already designed a score of the lenses."

"If he wishes to give them as gifts to the Ocular, I am quite certain they will be most grateful. Beyond that . . ." and she shrugged again.

He looked as if he wanted to say a great deal, but then he reined himself in, albeit with effort. "All right. All right, this can still be made to work."

"Can it?" It wasn't a question; she only sounded mildly interested.

"Yes, and you are the key to it. We can bypass the patrols and those who would endeavor to bring me back here if we make use of the sewer system that you were kind enough to alert me to. All you need to do is lead us through it using your reputed extremely keen sense of direction."

"And why would I volunteer my services in such an endeavor?"

"Because," said Arren, "I will generously instruct Xeri to provide the remaining lenses to the Ocular, even though they have decided to forego the adventure. Plus it means that your beloved Ocular will not wind up having to fight their way past Mandraques, especially considering that—courtesy of your reluctance to convince the others to join me—the Ocular would be severely outnumbered. You do want them to be as safe as possible for as long as possible, do you not? And besides, you get to run around underground. It will be like going home again."

She pursed her lips. "The notion of reliving my home experience is not the best way to entice me to do your bidding." Clarinda pondered it a moment or two longer and then slowly nodded. "Very well. You have your guide. But I only take you as far as the exit of the sewers, wherever that may lead. Beyond that, you are on your own."

"So that you can return to your children?"

He was smirking. She desperately wanted to wipe the smirk off his face. "They are not my children. But whatever they are to me . . . they are important. And I would ask you," she added stiffly, "to respect that."

He stopped all movement and then slowly, mockingly, bowed with a great sweep of his arm. "As you wish, oh mistress of the Ocular."

"Call me 'mistress' again and I swear that, once in the darkness of the sewers, I will rip your throat out and drain you dry, and neither of the Ocular accompanying you will lift a finger to stop me."

His smirk faded. "Understood," he said, and this time any aspect of mockery had vanished from his bearing.

"Good."

II.

WITH TORCHES IN HAND, CLARINDA, Arren, Berola and Turkin made their way under the streets of Perriz.

The entrance had been through an old, unremarkable building to which Arren had led them, courtesy of directions from Xeri. Xeri himself had not accompanied them, supposedly because he did not want to take any chance of being linked in any way with the endeavor, since it was not expected to sit well with Evanna once she found out.

Arren alone carried a torch, a hotstar that glowed softly in the darkness. He was the only one who required it. Clarinda was fully at home in the darkness, as were the Ocular. They had with them the lenses that Xeri had fashioned for them. They had been secured via cords to their heads, and the Ocular were wearing them slid up onto their foreheads until such time that they required them to shield them from the sun.

Clarinda was dazzled by the tunnels. These tunnels were nothing less than extraordinary. She had never had the opportunity to encounter the Morts, but seeing what she was now of what they had been capable of accomplishing—simply to dispose of waste!—she was beginning to have a new respect for the nearly extinct creatures.

Even though there was no longer any waste running through the sewers, there was still a steady stream of water. When they had first descended into the tunnels, Clarinda had simply stood there, her eyes closed. Minutes dragged on, and Arren became gradually impatient. But when he tried to hurry her, Turkin had said sharply, "Do you want to get where you're going? Or do you simply want to get lost?" This had prompted Arren to withhold whatever impatience he might have been feeling.

The water continued to run beneath their feet, coming to about her ankles, but that was nothing. That was deceptive. Instead she endeavored to drink in the direction of the air. That was what she needed. The air currents were going to guide her.

Finally she was satisfied.

She did not bother to raise a hand and point or declare loudly,

"This way!" Instead she simply started walking, splashing through the water around her feet. The two Ocular promptly followed her, as did a slightly uncertain but most definitely determined Arren.

They walked and kept walking, almost entirely in silence. Every so often Arren would try to ask a question, but it was always intercepted by a curt "hush" from either Clarinda or one of the Ocular. Arren had a sack of supplies strapped to his back and a sword dangling from his hip, which gently slapped against his thigh as he walked.

Finally, deciding that something should be said of substance, he dropped back so that he was walking alongside the Ocular. Despite the size of the tunnels, they were still bending so as not to bump their heads against the tops. They didn't seem to mind. It was likely that such huge beings were accustomed to having to live in a world that wasn't exactly designed to accommodate their height. "Thank you for accompanying me," he said stiffly.

Turkin looked about to silence him again, but Berola simply said, "You're welcome."

"My sister is very important to me."

"As was mine," said Berola.

Arren was surprised. "You had a sister?"

She nodded. "Her name was Kaita. She was an infant. Obviously far too young to fight in the army, and thus of no interest to the king or the captain. Her body no doubt lies rotting in the arms of our mother. Flying carrion eaters are probably picking at it right now. I hope they choke on her. I hope they die."

"As do I," said Arren with unfeigned fervency. He turned his attention to Turkin. "And you?"

Turkin shook his head. "No one. A mother. My father died before I was born, so I never had the chance to know him."

"What happened?"

He hesitated only a moment before saying, "Piri attack. He died defending my mother."

That brought Clarinda to a halt, the first indication that she was paying attention to anything other than their way out of the sewers.

She turned and looked at him, and her face carefully maintained its neutral look. "That is why you were suspicious of me at first."

"I was suspicious of you because you are a Piri. I didn't really require any more reason than that."

"I understand. I just want you to know, though, that I was no part of that attack."

"If you had been," he said, "would you admit it?"

She wanted to lie to him. She knew that if she did so with confidence, he would likely believe her. Curiously, she could not bring herself to do so.

"No. No, I likely would not." Clarinda paused and then added, "But I didn't."

He nodded. There didn't seem to be any point in pursuing it.

They walked the rest of the way in silence, save for the water lapping at their feet. They had gone under cover of darkness, Arren hoping to put as much distance between himself and Perriz as possible before it was realized that he was gone.

Although Clarinda maintained her sureness of direction, in her journey from Feend and the land of Subterror to Perriz she had passed through so many time zones and differences in day and night shifts that she had lost all track of time. So she had no real clue how long they wandered through the tunnels. She felt as if the prolonged silence made it longer than it actually was.

Her people had killed Turkin's father. Taking that into consideration, it was nothing short of astounding that he had been willing to trust her at all. What did it say about Turkin that he had eventually accepted her as their leader when the Piri were responsible for his father's death? It made her feel . . .

She didn't know how she felt.

Yes. Yes, she did. She felt pride. She was unaccountably proud of him.

Why? Why did she—?

And suddenly she felt movement.

She stopped dead in her tracks. Something was moving in her

belly. It was nothing more than a stirring, almost a gentle tickling.

The fact that she stopped walking naturally caught the attention of her companions. "What is it?" said Berola. "Is something wrong?"

Clarinda wanted to put her hand on her belly. She wanted to rub the little resident therein gently.

My gods, is that what's going it? Am I unaccountably maternal towards all of them because of the creature growing within me? Maybe. Maybe the pregnancy is causing me to affect others around me. Maybe I'm generating something . . . some scent, something like that . . . and it's causing them to respond to me in a certain way. Which means . . .

. . . which means . . .

. . . that when the baby is born, they may stop feeling any sort of affection toward me, and I likewise might feel nothing but disdain for them.

I believe . . . I would hate that.

"This way," she said abruptly, the air wafting toward her, calling to her. She moved quickly, so much so that Arren and even the Ocular had to hustle to keep up with her.

There was shift in the light as well. It was still nighttime outside, but even so it was still lighter outside than in. That was enough for the others to realize that they were almost out.

For just a moment, Clarinda felt a burst of concern. What if she had miscalculated? What if they had gone in a tremendous circle and were about to emerge in the middle of the city?

The moment that they got to the exit, she knew that she had nothing to concern herself about.

The water from the sewer was spilling out into a lazily rolling river. Vast countryside spread out before them. It was still cloaked in night. Clarinda sniffed the air several times, as did Arren. "Nothing," she said. "No scent of any Mandraques."

"I'm not perceiving anything either," said Arren. "Still . . . are you sure?"

"Reasonably."

Slowly he nodded. "Yes. Yes, I am sure as well. My friends," she said to the Ocular, "it appears that we will not have to contend with my brethren after all. I hope that you will not be too bitterly disappointed by that news."

"It is fortunate for them," was all Turkin said. Berola nodded in silent affirmation.

Berola then shifted her attention to Clarinda. "Are you going to be able to find your way back?"

"I found here, didn't I?"

"Very true."

Clarinda took Berola's hand in hers. It required both of Clarinda's hands to hold one of Berola's. "Good luck to you. Come back safely."

"You know that we will, if the gods wish it so."

"Yes, well," and she fired an angry glance heavenward, "that seems to be the issue, doesn't it."

Then Clarinda gasped as Berola pulled her toward herself. For a moment she felt as if the Ocular was about to break her in half. Instead Berola embraced her, as carefully as she could lest she wind up shattering the Piri's light bones. "We will come back to you," Berola assured her.

"I am counting on that."

Berola released her, then stepped back and bowed slightly. Turkin did the same, although he obviously felt no need to hug Clarinda. She was grateful for that. For all she knew, he might suddenly lose control and, in a paroxysm of fury, rip her apart.

Then she was left facing Arren. "I was not planning on embracing you," he said stiffly.

"That is probably fortunate." She paused and then said, "Make certain that no harm comes to them."

"I suspect they are big enough to take care of themselves."

I suspect you may be wrong about that, she thought.

"So," Arren continued briskly, consulting his map. "We have a long way to walk."

"Walk?" said Turkin disdainfully. "Who said anything about

walking?" He grabbed the startled Mandraque and swung him up and around. Arren landed on Turkin's back and was clearly about to climb down, having no idea what Turkin was up to, when Turkin started to run. Berola kept up with him easily as the two Ocular proceeded to sprint in the direction that Arren urged them to go.

Clarinda stood there at the mouth of the sewers and wondered, as the dawn remained hours away, whether she was ever going to see them again. She strongly suspected she would not.

And with that realization, to her shock and frustration, crimson tears began to run down her face. She wiped them away with an annoyed sweep of her arm and retreated to the sewers.

THE SPIRES

I.

THE SKIES WERE GRAY AND overcast when Graves's ship made port in the Spires.

Graves had remained at the prow for most of the rest of the trip, simply staring off into the horizon and mentally picturing Jepp's bloated body sunk to the bottom of the Vastly Waters.

She had been, without a doubt, the single most infuriating female that he had ever encountered. And that included Tania, the harridan who had transformed his brother into . . .

What? What the hell had she changed him into?

Tania had refused to tell him. He had raged at her and shouted at her, but she had simply stood there with her arms folded and that damned smile on her face, saying, "He had it coming, Graves. If I had it to do again, I would do so in a heartbeat. And were the situations reversed, you would have done the same—"

"If they were reversed? How so? Gant ill-used your sister and so you punished him. You ill-used my brother! How should I not then punish you?"

Tania had tilted that pointed chin of hers challengingly. Her skin had not yet acquired the silver tint that all Phey were slowly developing since they had first arrived on this godsforsaken sphere. "Go ahead and try," she had said.

He had not done so, and had subsequently cursed himself for his cowardice. He had thus been left wondering about his brother's fate.

And now he had to continue to do so.

"You look depressed," said Trott.

He hadn't heard Trott come up behind him, but that was fairly standard. Nothing moved more silently than a Phey; even they couldn't perceive each other. Graves finished tying off the ship at the dock as Trott stood behind him. "We had her, Trott. She was a Fated One."

"We don't know that."

"We do know that. We were drawn to her. We would not have been drawn to her had she not been a Fated One."

"That's circular reasoning."

"The circle is nature's most useful shape. Why not employ it for logic as well?" He shook his head. "Perhaps her purpose was to somehow lead me to Gant. To reunite me with my brother. I literally had Gant's salvation in my hands and it slipped through."

"That is a great deal of responsibility to ascribe to one female Mort. A dead female Mort."

"Dead because of me."

"Dead because of the storm," Trott gently corrected him. "How much responsibility are you planning to place upon your shoulders? You didn't cause the storm to come upon us."

"Didn't I?"

"Oh, you cannot be serious."

"She was getting on my nerves. Despite the possible connection she represented to Gant, her attitude was infuriating."

"You're not a climate sensitive."

"Who knows what the hell we are anymore, Trott? I mean, look at us!" He tapped his glistening metal skin. It made a hollow, ringing sound. "Our ability to adapt has always been our greatest strength! Now it's a liability! This world is poisoning us, Trott. We're dying by inches, and we remain fortune's fools."

"We are not dying. Don't be so overdramatic. As for the Mort, I don't disagree that she was a Fated One. But perhaps her fate was to die at sea."

"And she needed us to enable that to happen?"

"Apparently so. We are but the playthings of the gods, my friend."

"I don't mind being the playthings of the gods. I mind being like unto excrement on the feet of the gods."

"It is what it is, Graves."

Graves looked at him disdainfully. "You are one of the great thinkers of our race, Trott. Do you know that? Just incredibly deep."

"I need to speak with you."

The voice sounded in both their heads, accompanied by the chiming of bells. It hit with such force that Trott and Graves staggered slightly as if from an assault.

"Damnation, Spense!" shouted Graves, which was not necessary since Spense was nowhere within hearing distance. "What are you going on about?"

"The old man has lost his mind."

"What else is new?"

"I think we may have to kill him."

Trott and Graves exchanged looks. Trott shrugged, indicating that he had no idea how to respond to that.

They began walking toward the vast hall that was the home of the Travelers as the rest of the world knew them, and the Phey as they knew themselves. "Spense," Graves said with forced calm, "we cannot kill him."

"We can find a way."

"Yes, there is a way. We kill him and our entire race dies. That is the way."

"We do not know that."

"We do know that."

"No. We believe that. We do not know that."

"Trott," Graves said in frustration. "Talk to him."

"What would you have me say?"

"That what he's suggesting is madness. He would risk the existence of our people."

"You call this existence? Living in thrall to a demented, armored creature who gets madder with every passing turn? Should we not be taking the quality of our lives into account?"

"I am not going to keep discussing this until we are face to face."

"As you wish."

Spense's rantings faded from his head. He looked at Trott in annoyance. "Well, you were of no help at all. 'What would you have me say?'"

"'I'll admit my support for you was a bit tepid . . .'"

"You would have to leave it out in a blazing sun for many turns in order to get it warm enough to qualify as tepid."

"You know Spense. He lives in extremes. He rants one day and is calm the next. As much as he may be making declarations about the Overseer today, by tomorrow it will likely be forgotten."

"And if it is not? If he winds up mounting some manner of attack against the Overseer? If he does somehow, against all odds, manage to kill him, what then?"

"Then I guess we'll have to see."

"Have to see?" Graves could not believe what he was hearing. "And if we see our people shrivel and die?"

"Except . . ."

"Except what?"

"Well . . . Spense is right. How do we know? We do not really. We 'know' because the belief has been placed within us by the Magisters. We believe it because they have forced us to believe it. But what if it is a lie? What if we could seize control of our destinies instead of being bound to the Overseer? Would that not be something worth pursuing?"

"And would it be worth the lives of all Phey living throughout the Damned World if it turns out that what we believe to be true is, in fact, true?"

"I don't know," said Trott. "But what I do know is that nothing worthwhile is attained without some degree of risk."

"Well, if it is all the same to you, I do not feel inclined to risk the collective life of our race."

"There is a difference," Trott said, "between 'life' and 'existence.' What we have right now, at this moment in time, is an existence. Whether you could truly call it a life, I could not say."

"Now you're starting to sound like Spense."

"Well, if I'm right, and Spense is right, then that would explain the similarities."

Graves rolled his eyes, having had more than enough of a conversation he felt to be nonsensical.

They approached the great hall of the Phey, the enormous building in which the Travelers dwelled. It was one of the largest meeting halls in the Spires, and the Phey had adopted it for their home because of its considerable spaciousness. There were, after all, not all that many Phey left in existence. They were long lived, but more and more of their females turned out to be barren. It was not a phenomenon that was new to this world; their numbers had been steadily diminishing back when they were still in residence in the Elserealms. Matters had simply become aggravated since the transition.

"At least Spense stopped his complaining," said Graves as they approached the bank of glass doors that were the main entranceway to the great hall. "Although when we're face to face, I imagine he's going to start in immediately with his incessant . . ."

His voice trailed off and he stopped walking. Trott, who was just behind him, nearly bumped into him. Considering the typical grace with which the Phey moved, this was unusual.

The Overseer was standing just outside the doors. He was holding Spense's head in his hands. The rest of Spense's body was nowhere to be seen.

"Greetings. How fares it with you gentlemen this fine day?"

"It . . ." Graves was doing everything he could to hold himself together. Spense's vacant eyes nevertheless seemed to be gazing at him accusingly. "It fares well, Overseer."

"You two are newly arrived in town, correct?"

"That is correct, Overseer. We have been in your service from the beginning, but recently our presence was required . . . elsewhere."

"Where? And I suggest you tell me truthfully, because if you don't, I'll know, and you'll end up like your friend here. He wanted to kill me. Can you believe that?"

"It is hard to fathom, Overseer."

"Could scarcely credit it myself. Yet it was, tragically, true. He thought I wouldn't find out. He was wrong. I always find out, as you boys can readily see. Am I right?"

"Yes, Overseer."

The Overseer seemed to be considering them. Trott was paralyzed, unable to say anything or even contemplate saying anything, for fear that a stray thought could result in their immediate annihilation.

"I was speaking to your associates about a plan of mine, and this individual seemed reluctant to implement it. Instead he was going to his brethren and trying to convince them that they should consider rising up against me. You don't feel that way, do you?"

"It is our function in life to satisfy the needs, wants and desires of the Overseer."

"Needs, wants, and desires. Well, you gentlemen certainly have all the bases covered"

"If I may ask, Overseer, what is the nature of the plan?"

"Quite simply, I want the remainder of the human race to be wiped out from the face of the planet. Just put an end to them. After all, if they wound up losing this world to your kind, they've already proven ourselves too stupid to live. Don't see any reason why the job can't be finished once and for all. Am I right?"

"Of course you are right, Overseer. You are the epitome of rightness."

"Excellent." The Overseer turned and glanced back at the building behind him. He seemed to find it amusing. "It totally breaks me up that you guys took up residence in the Javits Center. Of all the damned places. Hundreds of four-star hotels in this goddamned city, and you live in a convention center. You people crack me up, you know that? You really do. So . . . get on that other thing with the remaining humans, would you? And don't let me down. It doesn't go well for people who let me down."

He casually tossed Spense's head to Trott, who caught it more out of reflex than anything else. "You . . . make your point quite well, Overseer," said Trott.

"I almost forgot. You still haven't told me where you two were off to?"

Graves did not even consider for a moment the possibility of lying. "We were drawn to a Mort woman. Her name was Jepp. We were in the process of bringing her here because we believed she would be of some importance."

"I see. And where is she? Show her to me so that I can kill her."

"Actually, she is already dead. She fell off the boat on the trip over and drowned at sea."

"Good job. Saved me the trouble."

The Overseer turned away from him and headed off down the street, the clanking of his armor diminishing until he was out of sight.

Trott looked down at Spense's head. "Graves," he said softly, "I think it would behoove us to find every remaining human and kill them. Because if it is them or us, then I vote for us."

"I am sure that, were Spense in a position to, he would agree," said Graves.

II.

THE COLONEL STRODE DOWN BROADWAY, feeling better about the world than he had for a very long time.

After all these years accomplishing nothing . . . of being an all powerful figurehead on a world that was once his and was now unrecognizable . . .

Except that isn't entirely true, is it. Year after year, the world became less and less recognizable even before they showed up. Less and less the place that you wanted it to be and knew it should be.

What matter the standards of a man of honor when he lives in a world where honor is nothing but a joke? Where the dishonorable win? This was once a world filled with potential for greatness, and it became nothing that any rational person would believe was worth a damn. If the Third Wave was the first step in ending it all, then who am I to stand in the way of the inevitable? Better to hasten the end of everything than drag things out.

The Colonel was certainly aware that eradicating the rest of humanity might have no impact whatsoever. That Nicrominus's theories may have been the ravings of a crackpot and nothing more. Still . . .

Why not give it a shot?

Suddenly the Colonel stopped walking. He turned quickly, his senses convinced that he was being watched. He had long ago learned to trust them.

There was nothing there.

He surveyed the entire area and still there was nothing.

From on high he heard a distant rumbling, which was odd because it had been a sunny day until just now. He looked up and saw thick black storm clouds rolling past. They seemed to have come out of nowhere, nor were they unleashing rain upon him. Instead they kept moving as if they were late for an appointment, moving with insane speed out to sea.

He tried to recall if he had ever seen anything like that before, and could only come up with one parallel instance: watching timelapse photography. One of those films where, in order to artfully convey the passing of time, clouds go rolling past at insanely high speeds.

But he had never seen anything like it in real life.

He looked behind himself once more. There was still nothing there. Nothing watching him. Nothing standing there.

He was alone. Except he wasn't. And he did not know how that was possible.

Hidden within his armor, impervious to attack, the Colonel—for the first time in a long time—felt vulnerable.

III.

"ARE YOU INSANE? ARE YOU insane?"

Those were the words that brought Norda to consciousness. The odd thing was that she hadn't even realized she had been unconscious. As far as she knew, she had simply fallen asleep because, well, because that's what one did on a fairly regular basis. It didn't occur to her that weakness had caused her to lose her hold on wakefulness.

"I think I may be," she said softly. "I've certainly heard it mentioned."

She had not yet opened her eyes, so whoever was near her was unaware that she was awake. This much quickly became evident to Norda when whoever it was said, "Oh my God, it's awake. And . . . it talks!"

"Of course it talks!" came an annoyed response. "What did you think?"

"I don't know! I figured they just hissed or something!"

"I can if you'd like," said Norda, and she offered up a half-hearted hiss. It was at that point that, slowly, she opened her eyes and tried to sit up.

Her environment was still steamy and moist, and she heard the steady drip-dripping of water from somewhere in the distance.

Before she could fully sit, a hand gently rested on her right shoulder and said, "Stay still. I'm not done."

She looked over and saw that a Mort was busy dressing her wound. It was a female Mort, she was reasonably sure of that. She had dark skin similar to the boy that she had encountered earlier, and fur on her head that seemed to go in all directions at once. She was using a damp cloth to clear away the last of the blood that had dried. "You're lucky. The bullet went clean through. Since the bleeding has stopped, it's obvious that it didn't hit anything vital."

"That's good," said Norda dreamily.

The Mort went on about her business with brisk efficiency. As she began to apply bandages, she said, "You sound very young. How old are you?"

"I don't know."

"How can you not know? When were you born?"

"You mean hatched?"

"Right. When were you hatched?"

Norda shrugged. "I have no idea. I was very young at the time and so my memories of it aren't really dependable."

"This is ridiculous!" It had been the Mort who had spoken moments before. Norda turned and saw him standing nearby, with various other Morts as well. They had varying skin colors and amounts of fur, both on their heads and bodies. She wasn't able to distinguish much in terms of their facial features since they all looked pretty much alike to her. "You're his mother! You're his goddamn mother! How can you be treating the . . . the thing," and he gestured toward Norda, "that damn near killed him!"

"From the way Anton tells it," she said, "the only reason she 'near' killed him was because she chose not to totally kill him. She could have, and she didn't."

"And that's where we're at now? We make nice to them because they did us the favor of not killing us?" He looked challengingly at Norda and said, "Why didn't you kill Anton?"

"Who is Anton?"

"The kid! The kid you brought down here!"

"Oh." She paused, considering the question. "I was always of the opinion that you needed a reason to kill someone, not to not kill someone."

"I agree," said the woman firmly who was busy bandaging her shoulder. "You risked your life to bring my son down here into enemy territory even though you yourself were already injured."

"I did?" Norda's eyes widened in surprise. "Why in the world did I do that? Maybe I am insane."

The male Mort, who reeked of leadership, looked in astonishment at the woman. "Come on—!"

"Calm down, Darryl. The poor thing's obviously not right in the head."

"You're feeling sorry for it?" There were grumblings from the other Morts behind him. "Look at where we are! Look at what we've come to, and you're actually feeling sorry for that . . . that thing! Why aren't you feeling sorry for us, considering what we've got!"

"You have your lives," said Norda. "That's something, isn't it? Most Morts don't have their lives, so that puts you ahead of just about all of them."

"Stop calling us that," said the one called Darryl, stabbing a finger at her. "We're not 'Morts.' We're human beings!"

"Oh, right!" Norda said, her memory suddenly jogged. "Hooman Bean! He said his name was Hooman Bean!" Then she frowned. "You're all named Hooman Bean? That sounds very confusing. Don't you get confused from that? I know I would. Then again, I may well be insane, so . . ."

The male Mort looked as if he had lost all capacity for speech. The female was doing something with her face that looked very much like it could be a smile. "Human beings are what we are. It's the name of our race, just like you're a Mandraque. My name is—"

"Don't tell her your name!"

She snorted. "What, do you think she'll use it as part of some magic spell to gain control over me?"

"It's possible," he said, but sounded a little less certain.

"My name," she said, "is Caralee. That," and she pointed to the scowling male, "is my husband, Darryl."

"Husband? Oh. Your mate."

"Yes. And Anton's father. Anton is the boy you brought down here."

"And his name is not Hooman Bean?"

"No," and Caralee laughed gently. "It's really not. I've never met anyone named that. Now . . . who are you?"

"I am Norda Kinklash," she said. "My brother is Arren Kinklash, leader of the Five Clans. I dropped a bell on someone else who wanted to be leader," she added proudly, "and that's why Arren is leader."

"Okay," said Caralee, clearly not understanding but trying to look as if she did. "And where is this brother of yours?"

"He is going to come and take me away from here."

"Oh my God," said Darryl, and now there were concerned mutterings from the other human beings. "They're going to be mounting a rescue mission. They're going to come flooding in here. An entire swarm of Mandraques. You heard her, Cara. Her brother is a goddamn leader!"

"We hold her hostage," said another of the humans. "We have her prisoner, after all. Shouldn't be hard."

"I'm a prisoner?" This was news to Norda. "When did that happen?"

"I'm sorry, I couldn't stop them. They were afraid," said Caralee, and she nodded toward Norda's foot.

Norda looked to see where she was indicating and was surprised to discover that there was a manacle attached to her right foot. A length of chain ran from the manacle to a metal loop that was bolted into the floor. Norda pulled on the chain experimentally. It made an interesting sound. She liked it.

"Where is this brother of yours?" said Darryl. He had drawn closer to Norda, and was glaring at her in what he no doubt thought was an intimidating manner.

"I don't know."

"Is he in the city?"

"Which one?"

"This one! This city!"

She looked around, surprised. "This is a city? It's very odd for a city."

"Not this! This isn't a city! Not down here. I know he's not down here."

"Okay," said Norda cheerfully. "So that's one less place Arren is. That narrows it down a little, doesn't it?"

Darryl stood there for a moment, looking overwhelmed by the haphazard direction of the conversation. Finally he turned to Caralee and said, "You talk to her."

"Norda," said Caralee patiently, as if addressing a child, "when you are not down here with us . . . where do you and Arren live?"

"Together?"

"Yes. Where do you live together?"

Norda thought about it. "Perriz. We both live in Perriz."

"Perez?" She looked to Darryl, who shrugged. "Where is Perez?"

"It's very far away, I think."

"What else is there?" said Caralee, fishing for something to help her get a handle on Norda. "In Perez, I mean."

"Well, there's Firedraque Hall. It's very beautiful. It's where the bells are. Were. And there's the Eyeful Tower . . ."

"Paris!" Caralee clapped her hands and started to laugh. "Paris! She's from Paris! Eiffel Tower. She's from Paris."

"Yeah, we get it, she's from Paris," said Darryl sourly. It seemed to Norda that he said everything sourly. She wondered if he ever smiled. Caralee did it nicely. "Except how the hell did she get from Paris to here?"

Norda tried to remember. As always, the past was ever fluid to her. She tried to recall the specifics, and could only recollect that the ground had been very far below her and she had drifted like a cloud, in and out of clouds, faster than clouds, then slower, and then she was in the Spires, and now she was here.

"I flew," she said.

"She flew." He shook her head. "We're not going to get any straight answers out of her."

"My answer was crooked?" It was strange to Norda; they seemed to feel that she was insane, and yet much of the time she had no idea what they were talking about. "You say such strange things."

"Anton said that she was the only one he saw up there," said Caralee. "That she was in St. Patricks and there wasn't another Mandraque around anywhere."

"They could have been hiding."

"Hiding? They were hiding while the sister of one of their leaders got shot? What were they hiding for?"

"Maybe they were afraid of getting shot as well."

Caralee looked skeptical. "One scared boy with a gun against a bunch of Mandraques? They breathe fire, Darryl. If they wanted to take Anton down, I have to think that the odds favored them. Instead of thinking that she's hiding something from us, maybe we should be thanking God that she really is out here on her own, no matter how she wound up getting here."

"Mandraques don't breathe fire," said Norda. "Firedraques do. Now Mandraques, we—"

"Whatever," said Darryl. "The point is—"

"The point is that they're going to come for you."

"See? She's threatening us with her Mandraque pals!"

"No," said Norda, and she sounded distant. "No. They won't. They don't know you. They don't know about you. If they did know about you, they would not care enough to come all the way over here to try and get to you. The others are going to come for you."

"Others? What others?"

"I don't know. But they're going to come. They're going to come for you." Images, recollections of things that had not happened, began to bang around in her head. "They're going to come for you, and it's going to be terrible, because the metal man said to do it. You should not be here. You should be far from here."

"No one's ever come down here. We've always been safe here. It's just about the only city we know of that's mostly in one piece. They stay up there, and we stay down here, except when we're on foraging runs. Or," Darryl said with annoyance clearly directed at Caralee, "when someone fills their son's head with nice fairy tales about a caring God and he winds up going to God's house to address Him personally. During daytime, no less. What the hell was he thinking?"

"He was thinking that God would watch out for him," said Caralee drily.

"Right, right, because He's been done such a bang-up job on behalf of humanity so far."

"Maybe He's trying to help us now."

"How?"

"By sending her," she said, pointing at Norda.

"Her?"

"Didn't you hear what she said, Darryl? She was trying to warn us of something. Perhaps the reason she's so . . . odd . . . is because she's seeing the world in a way that the rest of us don't, and it's affected her. Maybe she's seeing the world, you know . . . backwards. The past is a blur to her but the future is clearer. Couldn't that be?"

"That is absolutely ridiculous."

"More ridiculous than ignoring warnings?"

"The rantings of a brain-scrambled Mandraque!" said Darryl in frustration. "I'm supposed to take that seriously?"

"Excuse me," Norda said. She was busy playing with the chain, banging the links on the floor. "I like the shiny thing on my ankle, and the little metal loopy things make a delightful noise. But I can't move from where I am, which is no fun."

"Yeah?" said Darryl. "Well you're going to stay right there, because there is no way that we're going to—"

Norda wasn't listening. Instead she was gripping the chain with both hands, and even though one of her shoulders was sore, it diminished her strength only slightly. She drew the chain taut and then wadded up her spit and let fly. It landed midway down the chain, and one of the links immediately began to sizzle. There were gasps from the human beings. She ignored them. Instead she pulled hard on the chain and the damaged link yielded immediately, snapping clean. As if it was the most natural thing in the world—which, to her, it was—Norda stood and shook out her leg, which had been getting stiff.

Then she turned to the still gaping humans.

"Do you have more of the invisible bows and arrows?"

"The—what?" said Darryl.

"The thing that did this," and she pointed at her bandaged shoulder.

"The gun. She means the gun," said Caralee.

The humans glanced at each other and then all looked to Darryl, apparently uncertain as to how forthcoming they should be with her. Darryl hesitated, and then shrugged, apparently resigning himself. "Yeah. Yeah, we have some others. A lot others that we collected over the years. But . . . we didn't think they worked. They didn't when you lot first overran us. Soldiers tried to shoot and nothing happened. Scientists tried to come up with all kinds of reasons why, but what it came down to was magic. One of you creatures used some kind of hoodoo and made it so that none of our weaponry was of any use. Otherwise we could have slaughtered the lot of you. As it was . . ."

"Then why did Hooman Bean have one, if he thought it wouldn't work?"

"He wasn't supposed to have it," said Caralee. "He just took it. He said he wanted it 'just in case.' He was surprised as anyone that it worked."

"Well then," and Norda's tongue flicked out, "imagine how surprised other people would be?"

There was an acknowledging chuckle from one of the human beings, and murmurs of agreement. Caralee looked with smug satisfaction at Norda and then to Darryl.

"I hate to admit it . . . but I like the way she thinks," said Darryl.

"I think?" said Norda. "Truly? That's amazing. I didn't know I was able to think. Thinking is good . . . I think."

Norda was now in a crouch, and she was fiddling absently with the end of her tail. Caralee kneeled near her. "Norda . . . is there anything else? Anything else bopping around in that head of yours?"

Norda shook her head from side to side experimentally. "My brain, I think."

"I mean is there anything else you see?"

"You really think she's seeing anything?" Darryl said. "I mean,

I know you're into all that stuff, Cara, but still . . . her? Kind of a stretch, don't you think?"

"There's the other Hooman Bean."

That caught their attention. They both looked at Norda. "What other Hoo . . . what other person?" said Caralee.

"The female. I think she's a female. She had the bumpy things. And she was here. Not here here. Up there here. And she was looking at me, and I was looking at her."

"And then what?"

"And then she was gone," said Norda. "It's very strange. I had not been thinking of her at all until just now. It was as if she was in the past and in the future, all at the same time. You'd think that would make her easy to remember instead of harder. I wish she would come back. Or arrive in the first place. I guess she'll have to sleep on it first."

"What do you mean?"

She tilted her head and said dreamily, "I have no idea."

THE VASTLY WATERS

I.

{GORKON HAS BEEN UNHAPPY FOR so long, he had almost decided that such emotions as joy were not intended for such as he. But that is not the case. Jepp makes him happy.}

{He feels nothing for her romantically. In fact, he has come to believe that when it comes to matters of love, he is largely asexual. He cannot recall a time when he felt passion for any individual. For ideas, for concepts, for freedoms, yes. But not on any sort of spiritual or even physical level.}

{He does, however, enjoy spending time with Jepp. She sees the Damned World through an intriguing perspective that is a combination of naïve and worldly wise. She speaks with confidence about such matters as freedom and independent thought, and she does so with the fervor of someone who is newly introduced to the concepts. She has seen far more in the world than he, and Gorkon considers himself a student of the world.}

{By the same token, she seems to enjoy listening to, and learning from, him. She finds fascinating Gorkon's detailed description of how he liberated his people. She applauds his determination. She mourns the loss of his father to death and of the rest of his family to unreasoning anger.}

{And she talks of Karsen. Oh, does she talk of Karsen. She speaks of him with such adoration that Gorkon finds himself envying him and even despising him. Not because of Karsen's clear attachment to Jepp, but because Karsen felt love and Gorkon never had, and probably never would.}

{Furthermore, Gorkon knows that once he delivers Jepp to her destination, he will never see her again as well. She would be walking around on land, doing whatever she needed to do, seeking out her fortune, perhaps even—who knew?—changing the world. And Gorkon would be left behind. It is not as if Liwyathan can even get into proximity of the Spires. He is too mammoth. If he draws near to the Spires, it will be flooded. Uninhabitable by anyone currently living there. What it comes down to is that once they draw to within distant sight of the Spires, Gorkon will have to remove Jepp from the Liwyathan's back and swim with her to the shores. And then she will leave. And he will be forgotten.}

{Gorkon knows that the parting is inevitable. But that does not mean that it has to be soon.}

{And so he tells the Liwyathan not to hurry, because Jepp needs additional time to gain her strength. And he tells the Liwyathan that if he senses any incoming storm—because the Liwyathan can always sense incoming storms, the churning waters gives him plenty of warning—then the Liwyathan should feel free to change his course and make certain that he gives the storm a wide berth. Meanwhile Gorkon easily finds fish and plant life and whatever else Jepp needs to survive.}

{Yet she seems to be getting weaker, and the problem, oddly enough, is water.}

{At first it would not have seemed to be a problem. They are, after all, surrounded by water. Jepp endeavors to drink it, but all it appears to do is make her increasingly thirsty. She does not know why that would be, nor does Gorkon. He asks her if, while on the ship with the Travelers, they brought her water from the sea to drink, but she assures him they did not. They had water already in skins on the boat, and carefully maintained it as if it were a precious thing. This leads Gorkon to conclude that, for whatever bizarre reason, the water that surrounds them will be of no use to Jepp in surviving.}

{When the next morning comes, Jepp is looking worse than ever. Her skin is blanched, her eyes look yellowish, and her lips are swollen. Her clothes are thick with morning dew. She takes the cloth and sucks on it ferociously in order to extract whatever moisture she can from it. She sighs gratefully for the small amount of liquid she is able to draw from it. She then slumps back on the Liwyathan, muttering softly to herself. Her lips look slightly less swollen, although she is clearly still in distress.}

{Rain water. Water from the sky is potable for her. Water from the sky, but not water down here. Why would that be? It makes no sense to him. Water is water. It is clear, it is wet. Why should one be drinkable and the other not? Whatever the reason, though, that is clearly the case.}

{Gorkon dives. He searches the sea bottom to see if there are sunken vessels down there that might contain water she could consume. He finds some, because there are always sunken ships to be found. So many, in fact, that sometimes it is hard to believe that humans ever kept the damned things on the surface. In one such vessel, he finds bottles that are unbroken and still sealed. He also finds several pots that could easily be used to catch falling rain. He grabs them up and hurtles toward the surface, but en route the bottles shatter in his grasp. He howls in fury, uncomprehending and frustrated.}

{It is at that point that Gorkon suddenly realizes he may well have killed Jepp. In his selfish desire to prolong their time together, he has clearly thrust her into an untenable position. He has urged the great beast to take its time, and steered it away from the exact sorts of inclement weather that might well provide her the liquid sustenance she requires. He has done great evil to this woman who had done nothing to him.}

{He urges the Liwyathan to hurry. Now he is faced with a race against time, as Jepp lies upon the back of the Liwyathan and drifts in and out of consciousness, and the cursed blue skies above show absolutely no sign of rain.}

{I am evil.}

II.

"YOU ARE SO GOOD."

She spoke slowly, her voice thick. Gorkon appeared startled that she had addressed him. She lay still, feeling too tired to move her arms or legs. The sun shone down upon her, and the cloudless skies seemed to beckon to her.

"What? What did you say?" said Gorkon. He looked confused, and she realized that her words had been uncomprehensible.

She swallowed deeply, trying to find some few drips of saliva to wet her lips. She drew her swollen tongue across her lips. Unable to find any more moisture, she spoke even more slowly and over-enunciated every syllable. "I said . . . you are . . . so good."

"Me? No . . ."

"Yes." She wanted to reach out and touch him, pat him affectionately. "You saved me from downing, and you've stuck with me all this time, and you care so much about me even though you really didn't have any reason to. You—"

Her head slumped back. Saying all that had taken so much energy. Even her eyes were feeling dry. She closed them.

"But I'm not good," Gorkon said, shame filling him. "I'm not. I have done you a great evil."

He kept speaking, telling her what he had done, how he had delayed things, how he had very likely destroyed her with his pathetic attempts to prolong their time together. He told her all of it.

She heard none of it.

III.

SHE STANDS AMONG THE SPIRES *yet again, naked once more, and she looks to the building with the tall spike where the female Mandraque had been. The Mandraque is no longer there, and Jepp begins to wonder if she ever was.*

Then she sees another.

It is a huge armored being. She cannot discern just what he is, or what race he might be a part of. But he is definitely there, and he is clearly formidable. She just wished she knew what she was looking at . . .

The Overseer.

The name springs to her mind unbidden.

The moment that it does, the Overseer turns and looks at her. She trembles but stands her ground. The confrontation between them will have to come sooner or later; let it be sooner, then.

Even though he is covered head to toe in armor, he seems confused. His body tilts to the right and left. He appears to be searching for her even though she is standing directly in front of him.

Jepp begins to realize that her standing up to the Travelers had given her a false sense of security. She was convinced that, because the Travelers were not necessarily as devastating and horrific as many believed them to be, that the Overseer's reputation was likewise overblown. She had been certain that she would be able to confront him and convince him to make the world . . . well . . . a better place somehow. Now, however, she is beginning to sense that such is not the case. She will face him and she will die and that will be the end of it.

She cannot do it alone.

I need Karsen, she thinks desperately. Karsen . . . and his family. His clan. The Bottom Feeders. All of them together, there is nothing they cannot accomplish. He needs them. They must be with him. They must come to this place together. They must. They must . . .

I must . . .

Drink . . . I need . . . water . . . desperately . . . now . . .

Her throat is closing up. The reality of her situation is beginning to intrude on the fantasy of her dreams, and they are becoming inextricably linked. It is harder for her to retain her dream state, and the urgency of her being able to do so is being driven home to her.

And there, in the Spires, she throws her arms wide and howls to the skies that she needs water right now, and she needs Karsen and his family to be on their way to the Spires right now, and there is no time to delay because she is not going to be alive to see any of it transpire unless it all happens right now . . .

And water drips into her mouth. She flinches, expecting it to be unpleasant and salty, as was the clear stuff from the Vastly Waters when she had tried it earlier. But it is not. Instead it tastes like the water that she had sucked from the edges of her clothes. Then there is more of it, and more, and she cannot believe it. It is dribbling out of her mouth, there is so much of it, and she feels reborn, she feels . . .

"Jepp!"

Jepp shuddered, and blinked, and tried to shield her eyes against the pouring rain . . .

"Rain?"

"Yes!" Gorkon was laughing delightedly, which was a rather odd sound for him to be making. It sounded like a loud barking. "Yes, it's rain! Rain!"

The skies above her were dark, almost pitch black, and there was the distant rumbling of thunder. Fortunately enough, though, it was having none of the vicious impact on the waters around her that the previous storm had had.

Gorkon was ready. He placed the pots out upon the surface of the Liwyathan and quickly they began to catch the water from on high. Jepp lay on her back, her mouth wide open, and the water continued to pour into her.

Jepp began to laugh as well. It was scratchy and hollow because she did not have her voice recovered yet, but even after just a few minutes of rain, she was already displaying more energy than she had been in the previous days.

The water continued to collect in the pots. Jepp became more and more drenched. She did not care. Revitalized, she shrugged off her cloak and the shift she was wearing and stood naked in the rain, letting it absorb into every pore of her body.

At no point before had she been naked in front of Gorkon. He stared at her body, fascinated, and decided that it was without question the ugliest damned thing he had ever seen. If the longevity of the human race depended upon human males being attracted to such an odd agglomeration of randomly placed bumps and fur, then there was little doubt that humanity would have died out on its own without any help from the Twelve Races.

THE UPPER AND LOWER REACHES OF SUISLAN

I.

IF ANYONE HAD EVER ASKED Demali about the chances that she would be utterly silent while falling to her death, she would have considered that to be very unlikely indeed.

This, then, was a curious example of the turns that unexpected life—and imminent death—could take. Demali fell, and as much as she wanted to scream in terror over her imminent and inevitable demise, she kept her mouth clamped firmly shut. She had no idea if her screams would carry to her father's hearing, but she kept her desire to cry out to herself because she did not want to give him the satisfaction of hearing her.

This is it . . . this is how I die . . . oh, Pavan, I'm so sorry, there are so many things I wanted to do with you and to you . . . I'm so, so—

She hit something. Her body tensed, automatically expecting it to be the ground, knowing that she had perhaps a fraction of a second to experience that sensation before feeling nothing more.

The ground bent deeply under her, cushioning her fall. It felt thick and viscous., and also warm and pulsing with life, a stark contrast to the cold that normally suffused every moment of her existence . . .

Oh my gods . . .

She slowly rose to the top and found herself situated on something that she had seen any number of times, but never from this particular angle.

"A Zeffer," she whispered. "I'm on a Zeffer."

It was the smallest Zeffer she had ever seen. The ground was still at least a hundred feet below her. She could see it down there and imagined it being frustrated that she had not wound up smeared all over it. Then she realized that attributing that much power of thought to inanimate ground was ridiculous, bordering on stupid.

She was accustomed to the huge, billowing creatures that could contain many riders at once. Creatures so huge that even a dozen riders astride it at once would barely take up half the available surface space. This one was a fraction of that size. Her first thought was that it was a young Zeffer, but then realized that probably wasn't the case. Young Zeffers lived within the bodies of their sires even after birth, and remained there until they were nearly the size of their parents. The Zeffer that Demali was riding, if it had been a young Zeffer, would have been with its sire. The fact that it was by itself, drifting far closer to the ground than Zeffers typically floated...

"You're a runt," she said. "An outcast from the rest of your herd! I can sympathize with that. I can totally . . ."

Her head suddenly jolted back.

Something was entering her mind.

She had heard it described countless times before by riders: That first contact with a Zeffer. It was said that the physical aspect of the tentacles hanging below the vast floating creatures was akin to the way their minds worked as well. What first contact felt like . . . what it really felt like...was having invisible tentacles insinuate themselves into your mind, wrapping around in such a way that it would never, ever let go. She felt that sensation now.

Only Riders can be entwined. Only those trained to be Riders. Only those destined to be Riders. No females, ever. That had been drilled into her so thoroughly and for so long that it had become one of those things she simply "knew." So what she was feeling now seemed illicit and wrong, because it flew in the face of all that she had been taught. Yet it was that very illicitness of the entwining that made it feel so wonderful.

The Zeffers did not communicate in words. They were empathic beings, and the one that was entwining itself with her now was no exception. A wave of feelings washed over her, as if giving her emotional buoyancy. It was as if every single thing the creature had ever felt in its entire life was being dumped en masse into her psyche.

And what the creature was feeling right now was hunger. Overwhelming hunger. It was starving to death all around her.

Instantly she understood. Pushed away from the rest of the herd, segregated and left to fend for itself, it had not communed with its Keeper, with Akasha, the last time that he had fed the herd. The other Zeffers were sated and would remain so for quite some time, but this poor thing was withering away. It had some time yet, but she sensed that it was not much.

"We need to find Pavan," she whispered. She knew that accomplished Riders were able to convey their thoughts to their mounts without having to speak a word. But she was only just now entwining for the first time with a Zeffer, and so she felt more comfortable talking aloud. "We need to find him and bring you to him. He can help you. He's young and untested, but I know he can help you. I don't know where he is, but it's certainly not up here. It's somewhere else, down at the base of the mountains. I'm sure I can find him. We can find him. And . . ."

She sensed something else, then. It almost felt like a sort of resigned longing. The Zeffer was seeing, or at least sensing, something, and was mourning its passing like the outsider that it was.

Demali flipped over onto her back and looked up, seeing with her own eyes what the Zeffer was sensing and trying to convey to her.

High, high above, the sky was thick with Zeffers. A dozen of them, clustered together. Their tentacles were coiling and uncoiling. Their bodies undulated, drawing air in through their fronts and expelling it behind them, propelling them forward with remarkable speed. They began to pick up velocity as they moved, and from where she was she could see the individuals riding them high above.

Each of the Zeffers had a Serabim riding it, but was packed with Mandraques as well. She could not hear them, but she saw the Mandraques waving their weapons, no doubt shouting chants and war cries.

They were off to war. It had happened just that quickly. Of course it had. It was what her father had wanted, and her father historically managed to achieve that which he wanted. Nor was there any doubt in Demali's mind that this was not an overnight development. She could see it now: Seramali approaching those of his Riders whom he most felt that he could trust, convincing them through a combination of wistfulness and wheedling that the Serabim were wasting their lives in the upper reaches. That there was a vast, wide world out there that their unchallenged, indisputable command of the skies would enable them to conquer. If harnessed for such a task, the Zeffers possessed formidable strength and irresistible power.

She fancied that she could pick out her father's voice among the war cries that were being shouted. She had no way of knowing for sure; she might well have been imagining it. There was no doubt in her mind, though, that her father was there amongst the other warriors. He was, after all, a leader, and what else does a leader do if not lead his people, even if it's on a direct path to damnation? A leader who had killed Pavan's parents, and Akasha, and arranged for Pavan's kidnapping. In the grand scheme of things, the fact that he was ready to dispatch his own daughter seemed the most minor of his crimes. Pavan, his parents, Akasha, they had all been minding their own business, trying to live their lives as best they could before Seramali had disrupted them or deprived them of those same lives. Demali had deliberately thrust herself into Seramali's plans and brought his wrath upon her.

Knowing that somehow didn't make her feel any better.

She remained crouched upon her Zeffer. Her Zeffer. She had been upon the thing only for a few minutes and she was already thinking of it in possessive terms. How perverse was fate, that her father had done her the greatest service of her life in endeavoring to dispatch her. Had he not done so, she would not have literally fallen into this incredible good fortune. Still, he had always taught her that vast good and vast evil go hand in hand; one would lead invariably to the other, like a mighty circle. "Those from great heights will be cast into great depths, while those below will be lifted on high." That was what he had said countless times, or words to that effect.

In his attempt to hurl her to the depths, he had raised her on high. It seemed only right that she return the favor. And however inadvertently, he had provided her the means to do so.

The last of the Zeffers had passed overhead. They were alone now. Except she knew that as long as her Zeffer—*her* Zeffer—was alive, she would never again have to worry about being alone. Which was yet another reason for her to take immediate steps to make sure that the Zeffer remained alive.

That meant finding Pavan immediately.

"Down," she urged the Zeffer. "Down to the low lands. Let us make our presence known. Let us draw close enough so that Pavan will be able to see us, and so that we can hear him. And I suspect that he will do the rest."

II.

ARREN KINKLASH HAD HAD GREAT hopes for the Ocular as potential allies when it came to both defensive and offensive capabilities. What had not occurred to him was that they would be magnificent means of transport.

The youth and vigor of Berola and Turkin were simply beyond all reasonable measure. They ran steadily and with no apparent indication of tiring, each huge stride of their legs consuming such distance that miles would hurtle by at incomprehensible speeds. From time to time they would need to rest, of course. And they were going through the food that he had brought along alarmingly quickly. "I'm so hungry," Turkin had said at one point, "that I could eat a whores." Then, by great good fortune, they came across a couple of whores who were wandering around, apparently separated from their herd. The Ocular ate them, and seemed—at least for a time—satisfied with that.

During the brief times that they rested, Arren would speak to them of their lives before their lives had fallen apart. They were resilient, these young Ocular, but the cold fury that still burned within them was always there, just below the surface. Arren was relieved that the Ocular had no particular grievance against the Mandraques; he would not have liked his chances in pitched battle with the giants. "Should an opportunity for combat arise," he said, "I very much suspect that you will enjoy it."

"Should that indeed occur," said Turkin, "I will imagine that I am faced with the gods themselves—the ones who chose the fates for our loved ones—and take joy as I smash all of them beneath my feet and crush them in my mighty hands."

"I admire your spirit," said Arren. He glanced at the female. "And you—?"

"I will take no joy in destroying anyone," said Berola. "There is no joy left to us anymore. There is only the hope that vengeance can be exacted on behalf of those we have lost."

"I share your hope."

She looked at him disdainfully. He found it somewhat unsettling, having a single large eye looking at him with that much scorn. "Do not think for a moment that you are fooling either of us. You do not share our hope. You have your goals that you wish to accomplish, and we are simply a means to an end. By the same token, we see you as an outlet for our anger. We serve each other's needs, and are nothing more than that. So let us not pretend that we are going to become friends or appreciative of each other's innermost feelings. We are allies until it serves our respective needs not to be. Do we understand each other?"

"Perfectly," said Arren.

Much of the rest of their trip passed in silence, until that silence was eventually broken by an exclamation of shock.

Arren had actually been dozing while astride Turkin's back when he was jerked awake by Turkin's skidding to a halt and a gasp of, "Oh my gods!" The abrupt action was enough to cause Arren to drop off his perch and hit the ground. He had his sword half-drawn before he fully registered that there was no one attacking them.

He saw that the Ocular were looking skyward. The lenses over their eyes were functioning exactly as they were intended to do, shielding them against the intensity of the sun. At first Arren could not understand what it was that had so captivated their interest. There was nothing but clouds in the—

"Oh my gods," he said, echoing the sentiments.

They were not clouds. They were alive. They were Zeffers.

Arren had seen them from time to time throughout his life, drifting along lazily. And the last time, of course, was the most significant: the Zeffer that had departed with his sister.

These were far more than he had ever seen together; perhaps more than anyone had. And seeing them up there, drifting along, uncaring of anything Arren might think or say or do, underscored for Arren the difficulty of his situation. How was he supposed to impose his will on such creatures when they were so far above him, in every way, that to them he was of no greater significance than an insect?

The same thoughts were clearly occurring to the Ocular. "How are we possibly supposed to assert our will over creatures like that?" said Berola, making no attempt to keep the awe from her voice. "How could we even get to them?"

"Jump," said Arren. "Jump quickly. Jump as high as you possibly can, and perhaps you can grab hold of their tentacles and climb up."

They stared at him.

"I was making a jest," he said.

Berola looked confused. Turkin just looked relieved.

"They are going in the direction whence we came," said Berola. "Now what? We retrace our steps? Try to—?"

"The plan hasn't changed," Arren said firmly. He pointed at the mountains that loomed in the near distance ahead of them. "We are almost to our goal. It doesn't matter where the Zeffers are going. Our business is with the Serabim. They, not the Zeffers, can tell us where my sister has gone."

"But if the Zeffers took her there—wherever 'there' is—then

we'll need one to get us there, won't we?"

"One thing at a time," said Arren. "First we need to—"

"Look!" Berola cried out, pointing.

Another Zeffer had floated into view. But it was smaller than the ones they had seen earlier, and was flying much lower. Not remotely low enough for them to get to it, but not as high as the clouds. It was heading in a totally different direction from the others. There was a single rider visible upon it, looking puny in comparison, but nevertheless firmly in control.

"Change of plan," said Arren. "We follow that."

"You realize we still can't jump up to it, right?" said Berola sarcastically.

"Of course. But it has to come down sometime. And when it does, we are going to be there waiting."

PORCO

"STAY BACK!" EUTOK SHOUTED. AND then he waved his axe threateningly and bellowed, "Stay back! Or let he who would be the first to die come at me!"

They attacked en masse.

Eutok struck first, his axe cleaving the skull of the nearest Piri, truncating its scream. He yanked the axe clear and swung it at another, and still another. Karsen deftly wielded the Minosaur horn as effectively as if it were a short sword, slicing and gouging and driving the Piri back. One came up behind him and he lashed out with his powerful hooves, crushing the Piri's head against the wall. The tunnel reverberated with the sounds of smashing and screeching and still there seemed to be no end to them. For every one that they managed to kill, another three seemed to appear to take their place.

Karsen cried out. One of the Piri had gotten near enough to sink its teeth into his leg. He grabbed it and yanked it clear, slamming it against the nearest wall, causing blood from the Piri to splatter all over it.

Then Eutok let out a howl of fury. A Piri had ducked under the sweep of his axe and leaped upon him. He tried to grab at it and then another Piri jumped upon him from behind and another and still another. He staggered, trying to tear them away from him, but they were holding on too tightly.

"Eutok!" Karsen shouted, and he tried to get to the Trull, and suddenly he tripped over a Piri who had thrown himself directly under Karsen's hooves. Karsen went down and before he could fight his way back to standing, a Piri landed upon his back. He tried to reach back and grab his assailant, but then another was grabbing his arm, trying to sink its teeth into him. Karsen twisted his arm around and grabbed it by the throat, squeezing as hard as he could. The Piri's throat crunched beneath his fingers and he tossed it aside, but then two more were grabbing his arm, immobilizing it.

That was when a high pitched voice cried out, "Wait!"

It was one of the Piri who had clambered atop Eutok. He had frozen exactly where he was, and he was sniffing at Eutok like an animal inspecting its prey. The other Piri had likewise stopped their assault. For a long moment everyone was paralyzed, and then the Piri whose shout had brought everything to a halt pointed at Eutok and said, "He has been with a Piri."

The other Piri exchanged confused looks. "What do you mean—?" said one.

"He has been. With. A Piri. A highborn, from the smell of it. Her scent is all over him. He reeks of her. He has not been with her for some time, but her scent lingers."

Not sure if he was perceiving a possible out or was just incredibly desperate, Karsen called out, "Yes! He was with Clarinda. Clarinda of the Piri."

Instantly the Piri backed away from him, staring at him in shock and amazement. They remained upon Karsen, pinning him to the ground, but he did not attempt to struggle. "He was her lover!" Karsen said.

"Shut up, Karsen!"

"He told me all about her. He told me of his love for her. And . . ." His mind raced. "She was taken! Taken away! Kidnapped from the arms of her loving mother!"

This prompted alarmed murmurs. "We had not heard of this!" "Did you hear?" "Who would dare?" "They must die! Whoever did this—"

"They will die," Karsen said, grabbing back their attention. "I can assure you of that. Eutok there is going to take the Truller car further back in the tunnels, and he is going to use it to get to her and bring her back!"

"Is this true?" said one of the Piri.

The answer, of course, was that it was not. Eutok glared fixedly at Karsen for a long moment, and then said with a growl, "Aye. It's true." He did not sound terribly convincing, but apparently it was sufficient to fool the Piri.

The Piri who had identified Eutok as being Clarinda's lover—and who apparently was the one in charge—spread wide his arms and declared, "Very well. I, Wojim of the Porto tribe of the Piri, declare that you are free to go. Go and rescue Clarinda, the daughter of our mistress. Let her know that the Porto tribe of Piri have drank many a feast in her name, and she is revered by all."

Even though he knew he was asking for trouble, Eutok could not help but say, "I had the impression that the Piri would be appalled by my being with one of your own."

"We are," said Wojim, and there were nods from the others. "But I do not feel it is our place to question the choices of a highborn such as Clarinda. And if she is in distress and you can rescue her, then who are we to destroy you simply because we may find your involvement with her to be repulsive?"

"Well . . . thank you," said Eutok, clearly unsure how he was supposed to react to that.

"We are grateful to you," said Karsen. "To all of you. And I can promise you that Clarinda will be reunited with her mother, and we will make certain to let her know that you were instrumental in—"

Wojim looked in amusement at Karsen. "What do you mean, 'we?' The Trull is to be set free. You, we're going to eat."

"No!" shouted Eutok, and he tried to get to Karsen, but there was far too much of a mass of Piri between him and the Laocoon. And suddenly his arms were pinned by Piri who had come up from behind him and immobilized him. He struggled furiously. Any one of them, even any five of them, would have been unable to do anything against him. But the crowd of them upon him, with more piling on every moment, made it as hopeless as trying to fight against an incoming tide.

Karsen saw the faces leering down at him, the burning red eyes all the more terrifying as they contrasted against the pale skin, and the lips drawn back exposing those horrific fangs. *This is how it ends, then. This is how it finally ends. What a stupid way to die, and I never do find Jepp. My mother was right. Maybe that's the most horrific thing of all. That my mother was right. She warned me that my feelings for Jepp would bring me to nothing but disaster, and now here she was proven right. I can practically hear her voice now, saying . . .*

"Get off my son, you bastards!"

One of the Piri who had been atop him twisted around to see who had spoken, and the next thing he knew, his head had been crushed, driven straight down and into his shoulders.

He slumped over and visible directly behind him was Zerena Foux. She was wielding a club that had a huge red splotch on it. The aged Mandraque, Rafe Kestor, was right behind her, waving his sword threateningly, shouting, "Who first? Who desires to be the first to meet with disaster at the hands of my flashing blade?"

Mingo Minkopolis was right behind him. "I don't think blades can have hands, Rafe," he said in his typically imperious tone, but then he glanced around and saw the stray bones of Minosaurs scattered around the caves. When he realized what they were, a frightening growl issued from his throat. "I told you, Zerena. I told you Porto was heavily populated with Minosaurs."

"The operative word being 'was,'" said Zerena.

"You . . . monsters," snarled Mingo. "You dared kill my people? *You dared?*"

"And we'll dare far more than that!" said Wojim. "We'll feast for many cycles, my people! Take them! Take them a—!"

Something amorphous dropped from overhead and enveloped Wojim. He staggered, clawing at nothing, and he tried to scream. It was a reflex and it was a mistake; the blob seeped in through his mouth.

"Gant!" Karsen could not believe it. It did not seem remotely possible that the Bottom Feeders had simply shown up out of nowhere.

There was a bizarre popping sound like a cork exploding from a bottle, except in reverse. Within seconds, as the other Piri looked on in stunned shock, the blob vanished entirely within Wojim. Wojim shook his head back and forth a few times and then his eyes focused on what was in front of him.

"All of you, back away immediately and let us pass unmolested. If you do not," said Gant, having taken full control of Wojim's body, "then he dies."

The Piri looked at each other, seemed to shrug in unison, and one of them said, "Go ahead. More for us." There were nods of agreement and then, again in unison, the Piri charged.

With a roar of fury, Mingo plowed through the nearest group of Piri, sending them scattering in all directions. Zerena swung her club, batting Piri aside, and Karsen almost got his own head knocked off as he clambered to his hooves. "Mother, how in the hell—?"

"Not now!" she shouted over the howling of the Piri as she and the other Bottom Feeders started wading through the Piri onslaught.

"But—"

"Not now!"

"Fine!" He turned and saw that the Piri was still coming nowhere near Eutok. Instead Eutok, seeing that Karsen and his clan were under assault, was preparing to leap into the fray with his axe. Realizing that would be a waste of resources, he shouted, "Eutok! The hotstars! Get them to the Truller! Hurry!"

Eutok hesitated, then nodded and darted down the tunnel.

The Bottom Feeders converged upon one another. The most berserk of them all was Mingo. Karsen had never seen the Minosaur so crazed. He was not fighting in anything approaching an elegant manner. Instead he was running this way and that, slamming full bore with his head into anyone and anything that got close to him. Piri would jump in front of him and scream defiance, and his response was to gore them with his horns before throwing their lifeless carcasses to either side.

Rafe Kestor, never the most reliable of individuals when it

came to maintaining his concentration, remained focused on his whereabouts this time. He utilized his sword with remarkable dexterity, cutting through the Piri who endeavored to get near him.

But there were more Piri, and still more, and even though the floor was running thick with Piri blood, there seemed to be no diminishment of their forces as they continued to attack.

"Fall back! This way!" shouted Karsen. "This way!"

The others did as he instructed, Mingo clearing the way with another furious charge. The Minosaur alternated between trampling the Piri and continuing to gore them, while the rest of the Bottom Feeders followed closely behind.

They turned the corner with the howling of the Piri right behind them. Eutok had finished jamming the hotstars into place on the cart and was trying to shove it back into place on the tracks. "Keep them back!" Karsen said as he ran to Eutok's side, and together they shoved the Truller onto the grooves in the ground. It dropped in with a "click" and Karsen could hear an abrupt build up of energy.

"Get in! Get in!" he bellowed. Gant, still inside the Piri's body, was the first to scramble into the car, dragging Rafe Kestor behind him. Kestor was still swinging his sword at the air, apparently unaware that he wasn't actually coming into contact with anything. With no time to waste, Eutok grabbed the Mandraque from behind and tossed him headfirst into the Truller.

The car was beginning to tremble with suppressed power. Eutok clamped a hand down on the outside to hold it in place. "Now or never, Karsen!"

Zerena Foux grabbed Mingo by the arm as Mingo gored another of the Piri. Mingo whirled, his eyes wild, and for a moment Zerena's own life was in danger. "Mingo! We are leaving!"

It took her words a moment to penetrate his blind fury, and then he nodded in understanding. His eyes seemed to clear and then he managed to say, his voice thick, "Go." She did and he followed behind her, backing up, glaring at the Piri who tried to follow him. They were right behind, never letting up, waiting for him to let down his guard for even a split instant so that they could overwhelm him.

Karsen had still not entered the Truller car, instead standing there brandishing the Minosaur horn. Zerena backed up until she was by his side. "I can't believe—" he started to say.

"Get in the car," she said.

"You first, Mother."

She looked at him in angry astonishment. "Oh my gods. When are you going to learn that—ahhhh!!" That last came because Karsen had dropped the horn, grabbed his mother bodily, and heaved her in. She landed with a heavy thud, startling Rafe Kestor who was still a bit vague on how he had wound up in the vehicle in the first place. Karsen leaped in right after her and then shouted, "Mingo! Come on!"

The car lurched, and Eutok staggered. "I'm losing my grip on it!" His huge feet skidded once, twice, and suddenly the Truller yanked clear of him. It started to roll, building up speed with every second.

Eutok fell backwards and suddenly he was lifted in the air. Mingo had him, having slung him under his arm, and he was now in full charge. The Truller was speeding up, and so was Mingo, but the car was quicker.

Mingo leaped.

He slammed into the back of the Truller car and Eutok fell head first into the vehicle. Mingo tried to hold on, but his massive hand slipped off, and he started to fall.

Karsen lunged and grabbed the nearest thing he could get a grip on: Mingo's left horn. Then Zerena was beside him and she snared the right one. The car was speeding up and Mingo was being dragged along behind it.

"This . . . isn't . . . helping . . ." Mingo said, his voice strangled, in imminent danger of being decapitated. Behind them, the Piri were charging, screaming in fury, their hands outstretched.

Then Eutok reached over, grabbing Mingo under the right arm and pulling as hard as he could. It was just enough leverage for the

Minosaur to get purchase, and just before the car accelerated to the point of no return, the three of them hauled him into the Truller.

"Were you trying to tear my head off?" he said, still rasping as he touched his throat. He pulled down on his skull as if he needed to shove it back into position.

"At least you're here," said Karsen and suddenly he yelped as a hand cuffed him in the side of the head. "Mother!"

"I warned you," began Zerena. "I warned you that—"

Karsen punched her. He did so with no hesitation and full strength. It caught Zerena completely by surprise. There was a loud crack and blood began to pour from her nose and upper lip as she fell to the floor of the Truller, which was continuing to build up speed. Eutok had scrambled forward and seized control of the vehicle lest its velocity overtake it and the Truller go hurtling clear off its track.

Zerena's eyes were wide as she sat there, her hand over the lower part of her face. She started to speak but instead choked on some of her own blood.

"It's not going to go back to the way it was, Mother," he said heatedly. "You made your opinion on Jepp, on me, on all of it, very clear. And I'm not going to listen to it anymore. I don't know why you're here—"

"Neither do I!" Zerena managed to say.

He shook his head, not understanding. "What do you—?" He looked to Mingo, who still seemed somewhat disgruntled over nearly being decapitated. "What is she talking about?"

"Gods as our witness, Karsen, I am not quite certain how we came to be here," said Mingo.

"How can you not be certain?"

"I . . ." He paused, trying to pull his thoughts together. "I remember that we tried to follow you. I remember that the jumpcar gave out. Then I remember it starting up again, and we tracked you all the way to Porto."

"But how is that possible?"

"It's not," said Gant, speaking with the voice of the Piri. "It is not possible."

"But if you remember—?"

"I did not say we did it," said Mingo. "I said I remember it. I remember it as if from . . ."

"From what?"

"As if from someone's mind other than my own."

"That makes no sense."

"Yes," Zerena now said, sitting up in the Truller. "It makes no sense. But the way he describes it is exactly the way it is in my own head."

"No specifics," said Mingo. "No recollections of details. I don't recall stopping along the way, eating, sleeping, anything. Like a waking dream, we started in one place and wound up in another, and the rest is a blur."

"But that makes—"

"No sense, yes, we've established that," said Mingo.

The Truller car lurched, causing everyone within to tumble to the floor, except for Eutok at the controls and Rafe who was keeping himself upright with his tail. The howls of the infuriated Piri were receding to nothing but faint echoes.

"You don't understand anything," said Zerena. Using a cloth from her bag, she was stanching the bleeding. "We are being used. You. Me. All of us."

"Used?"

"By her. By that . . . Jepp. And try to strike me for saying that when I'm actually on my guard this time, it will turn out very differently, I assure you."

"So!" said Rafe Kestor in his typical stentorian fashion, which was actually necessary in this instance since the roar of Truller car made it difficult for anything else to be heard. "Where are we going?"

"The Spires," said Karsen.

"The Spires." Zerena looked at the others. "Where the Travelers and the Overseer roam, and certain death awaits us? Because that's where the Mort has been taken?"

"That's right."

"Certain death!" Rafe looked positively transcendent in his joy. "It does not get more exciting than that!"

"The way things have been going," said Eutok, "I wouldn't bet on that."

FIREDRAQUE HALL, PERRIZ

"I MISS THEM," SAID KERDA. "Why did you let them go?"

Clarinda was in her quarters, which was where she typically was during daylight hours. Cloaked and hooded, she had learned to adapt to and survive the harsh sun, but she still far preferred to remain indoors while the irritating orb hung in the sky. She had been paging slowly through a Mort book, wishing that there was some way for her to decode the odd little scribbles across the pages. Now she looked up from it as Kerda stood in the doorway, or more accurately bent nearly in half so that she could be visible through it.

"Them?" Clarinda said blankly. Then she realized. "Oh. Of course. Berola and Turkin."

"Why did you let them go?"

"I did not 'let them.' I presented them with an opportunity to follow their hearts, and they made their own choices."

"They could very well be in danger."

"They very well could be. On the other hand, danger can present itself anywhere you go, so—"

Suddenly they heard the pounding of feet coming toward them. Reacting instantly, Kerda practically bent herself in half in order to shove her way completely into Clarinda's chambers. "Get back!" she ordered, and even though she was young, there was unmistakable authority in her voice. Clarinda instantly obeyed her, positioning herself so that the Ocular was between her and whoever was heading their way. She could take an educated guess who it was.

As it turned out, she was correct.

Evanna appeared at the doorway, and there were several Mandraques backing her up. Clarinda recognized one of the

Mandraques as having been there with Arren the night that they had first tried to enter Perriz. "Where is he?" Evanna said without preamble.

"Get out of here," said Kerda. She had her arms spread to either side, blocking any possible avenue of access to Clarinda.

"Where is he!"

"Get out of here!"

"Where is he?!"

"Get out of here!"

"I beg the pardons of all concerned," said Clarinda. "But I think we can all agree that this conversation is getting us nowhere. Perhaps matters can progress if you'd be more specific as to the 'he' you seem to have misplaced."

Evanna pointed at her accusingly. "You," she said, "have abused the laws of hospitality."

"I already apologized for breaking that glass the other day. In my defense, it was already cracked."

"Not that! You know it's not that!"

"If I do, it's certainly no thanks to you," said Clarinda.

"Arren Kinklash."

Clarinda tilted her head. "Are you introducing yourself? Because I could have sworn you had a different name."

"Do not play games with me. Where is Arren Kinklash?"

"How would I know that?"

"Because Xeri told me that you and two other Ocular led him away into the sewers."

"Oh." Clarinda's jaw twitched. "Yes, well . . . that would be one way. Why, may I ask, did he tell you that?"

"Because I'm not stupid," said Evanna. "Because I saw the Ocular walking around with these . . ." She gestured toward her own face. "These visors, which I very much suspect that only Xeri could have fashioned! And suddenly I receive word that Kinklash has vanished, apparently right out from under our very noses! And the two oldest Ocular appear to be missing. So I confronted Xeri about it. He managed to hold up under questioning a whole two minutes before he told me exactly what happened."

"Xeri, if I remember correctly, is your intended mate. I can see the attraction. Easily controlled and pushed around. Someone who is as controlling as you—"

Evanna had heard all she cared to. "How dare you interfere in Firedraque policies and Firedraque internal business!"

"I don't give a damn about your internal business," Clarinda said, allowing a tint of anger to creep into her voice. "The laws of hospitality don't require me to help you keep order in your own house. Kinklash came to me and sought release from someone who was holding him in an oppressive grip. That is something with which I have some familiarity. He came to me with an offer and two of my Ocular decided to take him up on it. I lent him my assistance."

"You had no right—"

"To what? To help a dedicated brother endeavor to aid his sister? You, who haven't the slightest interest in helping your own father, dare to lecture me?"

"Do you think I don't want to help my father? Is that what you truly think?"

"You haven't done a damned thing to prove it."

"I don't have to prove it. Not to you, not to anyone." Evanna took a step toward her and Kerda struck an even more defensive posture, if that was possible. "If there is one thing my father taught me, it's that there is an order to the world. And that order flows from the Overseer, and the Travelers are the symbol of the Overseer's authority! The Zeffer no doubt was acting on the Travelers' behalf, and I have no right to question it."

"You are wrong," Clarinda said. "You have a brain. You have intelligence. The fact that you possess those means that you have not only the right, but the responsibility. If you've decided to abrogate that responsibility, that is none of my concern. You cannot control the world, Evanna."

"I'm not trying to control the world! Just my own little piece of it!"

"Evanna!"

It was Xeri. His voice echoed down the hallway and they could hear the sound of his running feet. *"Evanna!"* he shouted again.

She looked momentarily chagrined and then rallied. "Xeri!" she yelled. "I ordered you to remain in your chambers until I—"

Guided by her voice, Xeri was at the doorway. The Mandraques barred his progress, but he didn't appear to notice them. "Evanna—"

She put up a hand preemptive hand. "There is plenty of time for apologies later, Xeri. Now we must attend to—"

"We are under attack!"

Evanna stood there, stunned. She could scarcely process what he was saying. "What?"

"We are *under attack*! We—"

That was when she heard it. From outside there were sounds that at first could have been mistaken for thunder, but then she realized was a building toppling. The windows in the small chamber rattled. "Who—?"

"Mandraques! Mandraques under the command of Thulsa of the Odomo House! And he has . . . he has . . ."

"He has what? Large weapons? A limited amount of time to live once I get my hands on him?"

Another thunderous noise shook the hall to its very foundations. Barely able to speak above a whisper, Xeri said, "Zeffers."

"Zeffers? Are you sure?"

"Who could possibly mistake Zeffers for anything else?"

"They've taken over Zeffers?"

He shook his head. "The Serabim are fighting alongside them."

Evanna had no idea what to say, no idea what to do. It was only at that moment that she remembered that the three Mandraques who had accompanied her were of the Odomo house. They were looking at each other uncertainly, and then—without having to say a word—they came to a mutual decision. They yanked their swords from their belts and shouted as one, "For Odomo!" One swung his sword straight at Xeri, who avoided the thrust by the simple expedient of falling backwards, startled.

Evanna stood there, paralyzed. She could have spit fire at them, but every muscle in her body had locked up. The Mandraques turned their attention from Xeri to Evanna and came right at her.

They did not get within five feet of her. That was because Kerda's arm reach was six feet.

Without hesitation she drove a fist forward, and it struck with such impact that it caved in the chest of the nearest Mandraque. He went down, gasping, his lungs filling with blood. Realizing their jeopardy, the remaining two Mandraques approached her with greater caution, trying to figure the best way to come at her.

With a roar, Clarinda came straight at the one on the right. His attention distracted, the Mandraque only noticed her at the last moment. He brought his sword around but she ducked under it and an instant later was upon him.

It was a joyous moment. Clarinda had resigned herself to the fact that, for as long as she resided in Perriz—which might well be forever—she would never again be able to know the joy of savoring the blood of anything other than animals. Now, though, she was under attack, and she was quite certain she wouldn't have to worry about Evanna gainsaying her. She didn't just sink her fangs into the Mandraque's throat; instead she clamped down and tore it out. Blood gushed from the gaping wound. The Mandraque tried to shriek but his vocal cords were already gone; Clarinda was spitting them out onto the floor. He tried to bring his sword up, but it was already slipping from his numb fingers. With a cry of undiluted joy, Clarinda drank deeply from the Mandraque as if she were a parched person coming upon a geyser in the middle of the desert.

The entire attack took scant seconds. Usually when Clarinda drank, it was from something small and pathetic, some rodent that she drained slowly because food was not always plentiful and she had to make it last. Here, in the heat of combat, fighting for her own life and caught up in the blood lust, Clarinda drained him in no time. He tumbled to the floor and she rode him all the way down, finishing the last of him while on her knees. Then she looked up, her eyes blazing, her lips drawn back, blood dripping from her lips.

"And you . . . ?" she said to the remaining Mandraque.

He needed no urging. The Mandraque turned and ran.

Slowly she got to her feet, new strength flowing through her veins. Then she saw the appalled look on Evanna's face, on Kerda's face. For a moment the look she was receiving from the latter was enough to make her feel ashamed. But then she drew herself up, squared her shoulders. "This is what I am. This is who I am. If you have a problem with it, then now is the time to say something."

Kerda, with effort, shook her head.

She turned to Evanna. "So . . . controlling your own little piece of the world. How is that working out for you, Evanna?"

For once in her life, Evanna had nothing to say.

CHE LOWER REACHES OF SUISLAN

I.

THE CASTLE IN WHICH PAVAN was being held had been fairly quiet of late. The majority of the Mandraques had departed, including the officious Thulsa Odomo. The Mandraques who had been assigned to guard him were still present: the one outside the door, and those who were outside the window of his imprisonment. There was always the chance that he could leap down upon them, overwhelm them, go running off. But he remained a pacifist at heart. It was the aspect of his personality that made him fit to be a Keeper, and useless in a combat situation.

He suspected he knew the reason for their departure. They were embarking on their mad quest against the Firedraques.

On the one hand, he was appalled by their actions. Their willingness to take such an insane risk against the status quo of the world as they knew it to be.

On the other hand, as much as he was reluctant to admit it to himself . . .

He envied them.

Even though he had been victimized by Thulsa's drive and the relentless ambition of the Mandraques, he envied the fearlessness of their actions. He had lived his life tentatively, always trying to please, never wanting to overreach. And look where it had gotten them, and look where it had gotten him.

Having been forced into isolation, Pavan took a long and hard look at his life and did not especially like where it had brought him.

"I have spent so much time blaming my parents for abandoning me," he said, "that I have wasted—"

"Oh, will you please shut up!"

It was Belosh, the guard outside the door.

"I was just thinking aloud."

"You're always thinking aloud! Do you understand that thinking is typically something that is done in your head rather than outside your head? It's bad enough that I'm missing the slaughter, but to have to stand out here and listen to your drivel, hour after hour after hour! Thulsa Odomo told me I cannot kill you, but if this keeps up much longer, I'm going to kill myself!"

Pavan sighed heavily and went to the window. He had been doing that quite often, looking longingly toward the mountains. He knew that it was geographically impossible, and yet he couldn't help but feel as if they were further away with every passing day.

Then he spotted something in the distance.

He couldn't believe it.

It was a Zeffer.

It was his way out.

II.

THE ZEFFER WAS DEFINITELY SHIFTING direction.

Arren didn't know why, and he didn't care. The way that it veered off indicated that it had a specific destination in mind. That being the case, he had every reason to think that he would be able to catch up with it soon and then . . .

Then what? He wasn't exactly sure. He was undertaking a good deal of this with improvisation. He was not comfortable doing it. It ran contrary to his nature, his nature being to plan and scheme and try to anticipate everything that could possibly go wrong. But he really didn't feel as if he had much choice.

He was still riding astride Turkin's back. "How are you holding up, Turkin?" Turkin inclined his head slightly, but that was all.

"I think it's heading toward that castle over there," said Berola. "The one with the Mandraques standing in front of it."

"Mandraques? Wait, stop." He tapped Turkin on the shoulder

and the Ocular slowed to a halt. Arren squinted, trying to see that far into the distance. "Are you sure?"

"I see them, too," said Turkin. "These visors you've created are amazing. We've gone from being blind during the day to being able to—"

"Are you completely sure?"

"Well, not completely," said Berola in annoyance. "It could be a Phey. I hear they're shapeshifters. Or it could be a Firedraque in a cunning disguise. Or it—"

"All right, all right. They're Mandraques. And you are sure the Zeffer is heading toward them? Right, of course you're sure," he said hurriedly, cutting off Berola before she could come up with a scathing retort. He thought about it. "Can you get us there before the Zeffer?"

For answer, Turkin began to run again, and Arren had to hold on more tightly than ever. He realized with a distant shock that the Ocular hadn't really been going at full speed until now. Turkin had been conserving his energy, keeping a pace that he could maintain. With a destination in sight, though, he was cranking himself up to full speed, and it was all that Arren could do to hang on. Berola was keeping up with him easily. He wondered if she might be even faster than Turkin, but couldn't quite bring himself to embrace the notion of riding a female Ocular.

The guards at the base of the castle didn't seem to know where to look first. They saw the Zeffer coming their way, but didn't appear particularly threatened by it. Arren found that curious, since the typical attitude of a Mandraque was to feel threatened by just about anything and try to destroy it before it destroyed the Mandraque. So the fact that they were just watching it rather than, say, seeking out bows and arrows and attempt to shoot it down struck Arren as curious.

Why would they not feel threatened?

"They're allied," he said.

Turkin, still running at full speed, was huffing slightly, but Berola looked at him and said, "What?"

"Those Mandraques. They're allied with the Serabim."

"How do you know?"

"I pay attention to things," said Arren. "From the colors of their leathers, I think they're of the Odomo house. That makes them Thulsa's. Thulsa rules with an iron claw. There is no way they would be acting on their own initiative, which makes me think that Thulsa is organizing it."

The Mandraques had now noticed the Ocular coming their way. Small wonder since the running Ocular were creating a tremor that a deaf person would have perceived. As opposed to their relaxed reaction to the Zeffer, they immediately responded as if the Ocular presented a threat. They drew their swords.

And did not attack.

The normal Mandraque reaction to a perceived threat would have been to come right at it. The fact that they were staying put told Arren that they were guarding something. That immediately made the castle of even greater interest to Arren.

"Put me down," he said. "I am head of the Five Clans and it is high time they knew who they were dealing with."

Turkin promptly did as he was instructed, slowing to barely more than a trot and allowing Arren to drop off him and hit the ground in a crouch. Arren straightened and the Mandraques, even though they were still a short distance away, recognized him immediately. They were stunned, obviously unable to comprehend what the head of the Five Clans was doing in the company of two Ocular . . . in the daytime, no less, when Ocular were typically helpless.

"On your knees! Show respect!" Arren ordered, and when they hesitated, he bellowed, "I said on your knees! Or I'll cut your legs off just above them and feed them to the Ocular!"

This was sufficient threat to prompt them to genuflect. In a low voice, Berola said, "We don't actually eat other members of the Twelve Races. That's just a story."

"Yes, but they don't know that. I know that you would never—"

"Not never. We used to. We just stopped because their bones kept getting stuck in our gums."

He stared at her. "Are you joking?"

"Maybe."

"Do you hear . . . singing?" said Turkin.

At first he did not. His tongue flicked out several times, getting a sense of the vibrations in the air. "No. I hear nothing. Are you certain . . . ?"

"Yes, I'm certain. It's light and airy that it almost could be mistaken for a passing breeze." Turkin looked down at him. "Can't you Mandraques hear?"

"We hear fine," said Arren, feeling strangely defensive at the question.

"Maybe it's too high for them to hear," said Berola. "Maybe they can't perceive sounds in the upper registers."

"Which means that's likely not a Mandraque who's doing the singing," said Turkin.

They walked up to the Mandraques on guard, who had remained on bended knee the entire time. They looked to the left and the Zeffer was drawing steadily closer. Arren wasted no time. "What are you doing here? Who are you guarding?"

"We were given strict instructions," one of the Mandraques said, "to tell no one of—"

"I am not no one," Arren said heatedly. "I am Arren Kinklash, head of the Five Clans, and I do not care if you are taking your orders directly from the gods themselves. You will answer my questions. Keep in mind that I have already figured out much. Thulsa Odomo, who answers to me I might add, has formed an alliance with the Serabim. He is going to be using the Zeffers for conquest. What I do not know is how he has managed to accomplish that, but I suspect the answer is up there. Now are you going to tell me? Or do I have to go up there and find out myself."

The Mandraques exchanged uncertain glances.

Arren had had enough. His voice was brisk as he said, "Turkin."

Turkin stepped forward, all business. "Yes?"

"Eat one of them."

"Which one?"

He smiled mirthlessly. "Surprise me."

Turkin advanced on the Mandraques, who backed up until their backs were against the wall of the castle. He smiled down at them and then, pointing at each one in succession, spoke an ancient Ocular rhyme that was used by children to make a choice.

"Fee, fie, fo, fum . . ."

II.

BELOSH HAD NO IDEA WHY he had been left behind at the castle on this pointless guard duty.

He knew why the others had been left behind. They were idiots. He suspected that they had been dropped while still eggs, and thus were typically given less important assignments. But Belosh had every confidence in his abilities as a warrior and a dedicated follower of Thulsa Odomo. Why, then, had Thulsa chosen to leave him guarding the fool Serabim Keeper?

Oh, he knew what Thulsa had told him. "Because I need someone I can trust. The very fact that the others are—less than competent— is all the more reason that I require someone of intelligence and vision to make certain that nothing goes wrong." Those had been fine words, but Belosh kept wondering if words were all they were. Was it possible that, for whatever reason, Thulsa saw Belosh as no different than those idiots below?

The more he thought about it, the more he dwelled upon it, the angrier he became. But he had no outlet upon which he could vent that anger.

None save the fool in the chamber he was guarding.

He had warned the Keeper not to speak. If the Keeper continued to do so, that would be more than enough excuse for Belosh to go in there and vent some of his frustration by beating the mewling

Keeper severely around the head and shoulders. The best aspect of that was that since the Serabims' hides were so thick, a sound beating wouldn't inflict any permanent damage.

The problem was that the Keeper appeared to have heeded Belosh's instructions.

Belosh placed his ear hole against the door, straining to hear something. A muttered whisper, an abortive soliloquy. Something.

There. He thought that maybe he just might have heard the Keeper saying something under his breath. That was good enough.

Belosh had a short club dangling from his belt on one side and a sword on the other. The sword wouldn't be needed for this business. Pulling out the bludgeon, he unbolted the door, yanked it open, and stalked in.

He stopped dead. His jaw went slack.

The Keeper was standing at the window, his mouth open, gesturing smoothly. He appeared to be saying something, but Belosh could not determine what it was. A distant whisper, at most, was all he could perceive. But Belosh's eyes made the impending threat clear enough. There was a Zeffer drifting toward the window, and a Serabim was astride it.

It was a rescue mission. A damnable rescue mission.

Belosh had no idea how it was possible. He knew that much of the kidnapping of the Keeper was simply a way to force any reluctant Serabim to go along with the plan that had already been concocted between Thulsa and Seramali. The fact was that, for the most part, the Serabim had embraced the notion of flexing their collective muscle. They had use for the Mandraques, and the Mandraques for them, and that would mutually benefit them until the inevitable moment when one of them decided to betray the other. Ultimately there would only be one left standing, for such was always the way of things on the Damned World.

So who the hell was mounting a rescue attempt?

The Keeper was summoning it somehow. That had to be it.

The bludgeon was obviously not going to be sufficient.

Belosh vaulted across the room and grabbed Pavan from behind before the Keeper even realized he was there. As he moved he yanked out his sword and brought it up and across Pavan's throat. Whatever Pavan had been doing to summon the Zeffer, he stopped doing it now, if the gasp and sharp intake of breath was any indicator.

The Serabim who was astride the Zeffer saw what was happening and shouted angrily, "Leave him alone! You leave him alone!"

It was a female by the sound of her. She roared a challenge and bared her claws, and it was obvious from her look and attitude that she shared none of the pacificistic leanings that made the Keeper so easy to control. If she drew near enough, Belosh was going to have a fight on his hands. Not that he wasn't confident that he could handle a single Serabim, but the Keeper might take the opportunity to try and escape while Belosh was busy battling the female.

Fortunately there was another way.

"Back away!" Belosh shouted. "Back away or his blood will be on his fur . . . and on your hands! Back away, I said! Back away or your precious Keeper dies!"

"If he dies, then you're going to follow him!" Her voice was uncertain, though, which was all that Belosh needed to grow confident. She wasn't going to have the will to challenge him; he was positive of that.

"I'm willing to take a chance with my life!" he called out to her. "Are you willing to gamble with his?"

Suddenly a hand clamped down on Belosh's shoulder. Assuming that it was one of the idiots from the guard squadron below, he started to say, "Not now!" even as he glanced behind him.

It was not one of the guards.

"Kinklash?" he gasped.

"Let him go," said Arren Kinklash. His hands were empty, his sword still hanging from his belt. "Right now."

"This is none of your concern!"

"I'm head of the Five Clans. I have to think that makes it my concern."

Belosh ran his options through his mind as quickly as he could and came to a decision. Even as he did, he threw the Keeper to the ground and in one motion whipped his sword around with the specific intent of sending Arren's head flying from his shoulders.

He could not believe how quickly Arren moved. Arren ducked under the sweep and pulled out his own sword. He brought his sword around and down and Belosh barely managed to deflect it. The blades skidded against each other and locked at the hilts, bringing the two Mandraques face to face.

"You have made a serious mistake," said Belosh with a growl.

"It won't be the first, or the last."

"You're half right."

Belosh slammed his head forward, catching Arren squarely in the face. Arren staggered and Belosh swung his sword. Arren parried, as much by blind luck as anything else. Belosh half turned and whipped his tail around, sweeping Arren's feet out from under him. Arren hit the ground hard and Belosh brought his sword up over his head.

"Some leader!" he howled triumphantly.

And suddenly something was snaking around his throat. At first he didn't know what it was, but then he realized.

It was a tentacle.

He brought his sword back around his head, to hack it free, but the sword glanced off the tentacle without doing the slightest bit of damage. Then there was another tentacle wrapping itself around his legs. He felt a sudden jerk and the last thing he remembered thinking before the blackness claimed him was that his tail was much larger than he thought it was.

III.

ARREN WAS GLAD HE HAD not eaten recently, because there was every chance that whatever he had consumed would have made an abrupt return to daylight.

Belosh was in two halves, having been ripped apart at the waist. The murdered Mandraque was staring with a rather stupid expression at his lower half, although in fairness Arren wasn't sure what his own face would have looked like if he had recently been bisected. Then Belosh's head slumped to one side as his brain apparently finally got around to informing him that he was dead.

Another tentacle snaked into the room at that point, and there was a female Serabim enfolded in it. As opposed to the pure destruction rendered by the other tentacles, this one was as gentle as a passing cloud. The moment the female's feet touched the floor, she ran straight to the fallen Keeper and embraced him. "Pavan, I was so worried!"

He seemed scarcely able to put words together. "Demali, how . . . I . . . where did . . . how . . . ?"

"The gods were watching out for us."

"If so, it's the first time in a long time. Did your father, Seramali, send you—?"

"My father . . ." She hesitated, seeming to lack the resolve to speak further.

Arren instantly intuited why. The female knew. She had to know. Arren seized the opportunity to make his presence known and his allegiances plain, especially considering that the Zeffer's tentacles were still twitching around, perhaps looking for another target. "Her father is involved up to his neck."

Pavan switched his attention to Arren, as if noticing him there for the first time. "Her father—?"

"He engineered your kidnapping."

"That . . . that is impossible." He tried to laugh and looked to Demali to confirm the absurdity of it. When he saw the seriousness of her face and her obvious disinclination to refute it, he was stunned. "How . . . how do you know this—?"

"Your guards below were probably more forthcoming than Thulsa Odomo would have liked."

"I suspect there's more than even they know," said Demali.

She put a large hand upon Pavan's arm. "Pavan . . . my father killed Akasha—"

"He—?"

"And your parents. And he . . ." Her voice caught. "He tried to kill me."

Pavan tried to speak but nothing was forthcoming. "That's . . . no . . . that . . . that can't . . ."

Demali took him firmly by the shoulders and said, "Pavan, listen carefully to me . . ."

"My parents . . . ?"

"Listen! You can't take your time coming to terms with this. Right here, right now, you have to deal with it, because the Zeffer out there is dying."

"Dying . . . ?"

"Stop echoing my words!" She thumped him on the chest. "The Zeffer is starving. That's one of the reasons he was left behind. He doesn't have much longer, I don't think. He needs you to Commune with him."

"I can't. I'm too young to . . ." His voice trailed off.

"Pavan—"

"My parents? Akasha?"

She nodded.

A change appeared to come over him. If Arren could have seen such a thing, he would have said that the room seemed to darken. Demali tried to help him to his feet, but he shoved her hand away with such force that she was clearly taken aback. The tentacles that had threaded their way through the window had released Belosh's body, apparently no longer perceiving him as a threat.

Pavan went to the nearest tentacle and, reaching up, stroked it gently.

"Pavan—?" said Demali.

He put out a hand, indicating that she should be quiet. Obediently she lapsed into silence.

IV.

PAVAN HAD SO MANY EMOTIONS roiling within him that he was having trouble what to focus on first. He felt the smoothness, the gentle warmth of the tentacle beneath his hand. He wanted to sing to the Zeffer, but he could immediately sense that the poor creature was so weak, it would not have the strength to return the song.

Besides, it needed something more than songs at this point. It needed something that only the Keeper could provide.

He knew that, according to all Keeper lore, he was too young. But age was simply an arbitrary demarcation. One was ready when one was ready, and now he had to make himself ready. There was no other option.

He remembered Akasha's words about taking all of his strongest emotions and bringing them together to provide him strength. He had been so fearful that he would not have sufficient emotions to accomplish that. Now, though, he had nothing but emotions. Anger, love, hurt, betrayal, and a cold burning fury that he would never have thought possible to countenance, much less embrace.

Pavan envisioned all of them within him and mentally drew them together into a white-hot ball that he pictured as lodging somewhere deep within his chest.

No songs now. Not this time.

I am yours and you are mine. Take from me what you need. Take me . . .

He had thought that he would have a sense of invisible tendrils wrapping themselves around his mind. That was how Riders had described it.

He was wrong.

The invisible tendrils wrapped themselves around his soul.

V.

PAVAN WAS SCREAMING.

The young Serabim twisted and thrust about in the hold of the tentacles and howled a string of words unfamiliar to Arren, incomprehensible. It chilled him to the bone, as if he were hearing language that was spoken before there was language to speak.

Arren, reacting instinctively, came forward with his sword. He wasn't sure if he'd have any more luck doing damage to the tentacles than Belosh had, but he had to do something.

"Don't move!" Demali shouted. "Don't touch him! Don't come near him!"

Arren yanked his sword away, looking at her in confusion. "Are you sure—?"

"I'm positive. Don't go anywhere near him. Don't interfere." She was moving forward slowly, watching in wonderment.

Pavan had lapsed abruptly into silence. The tentacles were caressing him and, even more insanely, Arren was sure he could see a soft glow emanating from around the Serabim. The tentacles were suspending him above the floor, and now the glow suffused the tentacles as well. Arren shielded his eyes, his sword lowered, unable to grasp what he was watching but equally unable to look away.

The tentacles were holding Pavan in the air, or at least that's what it appeared to Arren at first. But then slowly, gently, the tentacles unwrapped themselves and Pavan continued to float. He was hovering a foot or so off the floor, his arms relaxed and out to either side, his feet crossed at the ankles. His head was tilted back, and now there was a subtle humming, the origin of which Arren could not determine. It might have been coming from Pavan, or from the Zeffer, or some combination of the two.

"How is he doing that? How is he flying?" he whispered.

Demali shook her head, her eyes wide.

Arren lost track of how long they simply stood that way, watching a congress between Keeper and kept that none of them could even begin to understand . . . including, perhaps, the Keeper himself.

And then, very slowly, Pavan drifted downward until his feet lit upon the ground. The tentacles had withdrawn from the window, but the Zeffer wasn't going anywhere. It continued to remain there, but clearly far more vigorous than before. Whereas before most of its tentacles were simply hanging there, limply, they were now moving about with great energy, intertwining with each other or whipping around as if looking for something to wrap themselves around.

"Pavan?" Demali said cautiously. "Are you all right . . . ?"

Pavan nodded. "I am . . . quite well, actually." His voice sounded deeper, rumbling within his chest. He seemed taller. Older. He turned to Arren and said, "You prevented the Mandraque from slaying me. You have my thanks."

"With all respect, I need your thanks less than I need your help," said Arren. "One of your creatures took my sister away. My sister and Nicrominus, the leader of the Firedraques . . ."

"Yes, of course. An aged Firedraque and a young Mandraque who was not supposed to be there, but was." His voice sounded almost dream-like. "At the order of the Travelers, they were taken to the Spires. The Overseer had an interest in them."

"The Spires," whispered Arren. He placed a hand urgently on Pavan's arm. "You need to take me there."

"And what of Perriz?"

"Let it burn. Let it be overrun with Serabim and hostile Mandraques. My sister needs me."

"She is one individual," said Pavan. "There are many Mandraques who have sworn loyalty to you, Kinklash, leader of the Five Clans, and they have need of your service."

"How do you know who I am? Did . . ." He paused. "Did the Zeffer tell you somehow?"

"No. The dismembered Mandraque identified you as such."

"Oh. Right." Arren felt slightly stupid, having forgotten that.

"It's not just them," said Demali, her anger palpable. "My father's machinations have brought us to this point. I would not have any aspect of his plans succeed. None. He must be stopped."

"And if you," said Pavan to Arren, "have any interest in our taking you to find your beloved sister, then you will aid us in our endeavors."

"I just came from Perriz," said Arren in frustration. "You want me to go back there now to stop an invasion?"

"Stop it, do not stop it, that is entirely up to you," said Pavan. "But Demali's father cannot be allowed to see the triumph of his plans."

"Meaning?"

"He needs to die," said Pavan. "Even if he is triumphant, at least he will not live to see it."

"I thought you were a pacifist."

"I am. And Demali is his daughter. It is unthinkable that she would try to take the life of her own father."

"Even though he tried to kill her."

"Even though."

"Meaning," said Pavan, "that you must kill him for us. Do that, and we will take you to your sister in the Spires."

Arren looked from Pavan to Demali and back to Pavan.

"Well," he said finally, "why are we standing here? Talking is not going to get him any deader."

CHE SPIRES

I.

NORDA HAD NEVER SEEN ANYCHING like it in her life. Of course, if she had, she might well have forgotten it. But she was reasonably sure that, no, this was the first time ever.

The room was as clammy and damp as any other room in the underground. Anton was next to her, propping himself up on a crutch, his injured leg heavily bandaged. Norda glanced at it once, wondered how he had come to injure himself, and then stopped worrying about it as she became absorbed with her surroundings.

The walls were lined with weapons. They all looked like the one that Anton had been holding, but they were different shapes, different sizes. Some were longer than others. One was shining blue even in the dimness of the room. "Can I—?" She reached for it tentatively and looked to him, her eyes glittering with curiosity.

"I guess. Sure. Just be careful not to aim it at anything."

"Aim—?"

"Don't point it at anything."

"I have to point it at something," she said reasonably. "I mean, it can't be pointed at nothing."

"Fine. Point it at anything except me. It may be loaded."

"Loaded?"

"With bullets."

"Ohhhh. Bullets," she whispered as she held it carefully. Then she mimed the stance that she had seen Anton take when they had first encountered each other. "What are bullets?"

"They're what the gun shoots. What it fires."

"I thought it fired invisible arrows."

He laughed at that, which hurt her feelings slightly, but then

Norda decided that it was nice that she was able to amuse him. When he recovered sufficiently, he said, "No. No, it shoots bullets. Here. These." He reached into a box and pulled one out, holding it up for her to examine. She did so, staring at it in fascination.

"This little thing is what went through me?"

"Yeah, and I'm, y'know . . . sorry about that."

She shrugged and doing so caused her shoulder to twinge. She reminded herself not to do that again, and then promptly forgot. "And these are in here?" She held up the gun.

"Yeah. We got all kinds of bullets. Big ones, small ones . . . even some Teflon coated ones. You're lucky I didn't hit you with one of those. They'd've torn your arm off. I think that one actually has some loaded in—point it somewhere else!"

Norda had carelessly turned it in his direction. Quickly she aimed it down. Unfortunately it was toward his feet and Anton realized it. Stepping to one side, he took the gun gently from her and said, "Look, maybe we'd better just put it back. Mom would kill me if she knew I brought you here."

"Would she kill you with one of these?"

"It's just an expression."

"I thought this was an expression," she said, and twisted her face into a demented grin.

He placed the gun carefully on the rack. "You are so strange."

"You keep saying that."

"It keeps being true."

Taking care to make sure that no one had spotted them going in, Anton stuck his head out, looked right and left, and then gestured for her to follow him. She did so and he closed the door and secured it. "Why do you have all of those?" she said.

"If we get attacked, we need some way to protect ourselves."

"Will they work?"

"I dunno," he said. "Sure worked on you . . . again, sorry about that."

"It probably wasn't you. It was me. My brother always says that anything can happen when I'm around."

"I don't doubt it," said Anton. "You know, if—"

"Oh!" she said abruptly. "I have to go! I have to go home!"

"Home? You mean to the church?"

"Yes!" and she started running through the underground channels. She bounded up a ladder and called behind her, "I have to take care of my dug! He misses me terribly by now! And show him what I gifted myself!"

"Your dug . . . you mean your dog?" He made it to the bottom of the ladder, but his leg was in such bad shape that he didn't have a prayer of climbing up after it. He knew that this particular ladder led to the street, and that she would likely have no trouble knocking aside a manhole cover and gaining access to the street. "The dog's dead!" His voice echoed after her but she didn't seem to have heard it.

II.

EVEN THOUGH SHE EMERGED ON the streets nowhere near to where she'd entered the underground world, it took Norda almost no time to get her bearings. She then headed for home at a dead run and was thrilled to see the building towering in front of her, just as she left it. She was glad that was the case, because it wasn't always so. Sometimes things changed dramatically in her absence. Sometimes they even changed while she was there.

Norda ran in through the door and skidded to a halt. Her nose wrinkled. She heard a steady buzzing. The dug was lying in the middle of the aisle, blood pooled beneath it, and a host of insects buzzing around it.

"Oh. That's right," she said wistfully.

She wasn't especially hungry, and the dug had been lying there too long to be appetizing in any event. But she didn't like the irritating little insects zipping around it either. She leaned toward the insects and her tongue flicked out a dozen times, expertly snagging a bug with each thrust and even two at the same time in several instances. Once she had disposed of them, she picked up the sticky carcass of the dug and brought it to the nice garden that sat outside. Using her hands, it took her less than half an hour to dig a hole that would be sufficient depth for her former friend. Then she shoved in the carcass, which landed with a hollow thud. It took her far less time to shove the dirt back into place. She smoothed it over with her tail and then patted it a few times affectionately before returning to the inside of the building.

Soon she had clambered back to her thoughtful spot, crouched among the statues. One of them was looking at her oddly, and she realized that it looked a great deal like New Daddy. She wondered why she hadn't noticed that before. Was it that he had always looked like New Daddy and it simply hadn't occurred to her? Or was he looking more and more like New Daddy and had developed enough of a resemblance for her to see it?

"So . . . have new friends, do you?" said Nicrominus.

She reached over and tapped the statue tentatively. "Are you really here, New Daddy? I miss you so much."

"Of course I'm here. I'm in you. You ate me, remember?"

"Oh. That's right. I remember that," she said, even though she did not.

"That's how it works, you see, Norda. When you eat the heart of others, you take what they were into yourself. Their hopes, dreams, aspirations. Their knowledge and innermost thoughts. That is a good deal of responsibility for one young Mandraque girl to deal with. Are you sure you're up to it?"

"No. I'm not sure."

"That is a very honest answer."

"Those are the only kind I know. Should I be sure?"

"No reason to be, I suppose. In fact, your nature would dictate that you would not be sure of anything."

"My nature?" She stared at him quizzically. "I don't understand."

"Don't you know what you are, Norda? Haven't you discerned

your true nature? Figured out why the gun worked when you were around but didn't when you aren't?" She shook her head. Nicrominus sighed, but did not even come close to losing patience with her. "Norda . . . the world is a place of order and chaos. One always has to balance out the other. There are those who are pure order. They dream of the world being a certain way and fight to bring stability—orderliness—to it. But they must always be balanced out by those who embrace chaos. And you, my dear, are pure chaos. Anything can happen, and typically does, when you are around. The rules that apply to the rest of us don't apply to you."

"Why is that? Why would that be?"

"I honestly don't know, my dear. The gods have chosen you, I suppose."

"Is that why I'm . . . ?" Her voice trailed off.

"Why you are . . . the way you are?" She nodded. "I suppose it is, Norda. Historically, those who are the most beloved of the gods are also the most insane. Whether steeped in the fever of creation or the fire of vision, madness rules those whom the gods love."

"Then the gods must love me very much," she said.

"I imagine they do."

"And do you love me, too?"

"Oh yes," he assured her.

With a contented sigh, she wrapped her arms around the statue and, as the sun settled down for the night, drifted into a peaceful sleep. Her slumber was filled with cascades of images, none of which she would remember upon awakening.

III.

BONE WEARY, SOGGY, AND CONVINCED that there would never, ever be a time in her life when she would not feel wet, Jepp hung on to Gorkon as he brought her the rest of the way to the Spires.

It was a large island and she had no idea where she wanted to come to shore. "Pick a place," she said. "It will all work out no matter where you bring me."

"I envy you your confidence," said Gorkon.

"I have to think that if the gods have conspired to bring me this far, it . . . wait! There!"

"Where?"

She pointed. "There! Do you see it? Right there! The ship!"

"The—?" Then she saw where she was indicating. "I'll be damned. The Traveler's vessel. The same one, do you think?"

"No way to be sure, but it certainly looks very much the same."

"Wait . . . and you want to go . . . toward it?"

She looked at him levelly. "I am not afraid of them," she said simply.

"They could destroy you so easily—"

"I keep hearing that. Yet they did not. And whatever reason they have for wanting me alive is going to be an interesting one, and I want to find out what it is." She set her jaw. "They are afraid of me, Gorkon, and I would learn why."

"As you wish."

He swam toward the dock where the boat was tied off. The anchor was lowered and he brought her over to it. She reached up and grabbed the anchor chain firmly. "Are you sure," he said, "you wish to reboard the vessel on which you were a prisoner?"

"You still don't understand, Gorkon. They were far more my prisoner than I was theirs. And even more so now. I know them for what they are. They are not some mysterious, unknowable race, these Travelers. They are Phey, banished to this world just as your kind was. Just as all the Twelve Races were. So what if they're wearing cloaks and hoods and serving the Overseer? They're still going to want the same things that the rest of the Twelve Races wants."

"And what would that be?"

"Why . . . freedom, of course. Isn't that what you'd all want? Freedom to live where you want, under your own terms? Freedom not to be prisoners here?"

"Honestly, Jepp?" he said after a moment of thought. "I don't know what I want anymore. When all I was thinking about was freeing my people from the influence of Klaa, yes, it was very clear. Now? I am . . ." He smiled sadly. "Adrift."

Jepp hesitated, and then she reached over while keeping one hand firmly on the anchor chain and hugged Gorkon as hard as she could. He returned the embrace and wished that he could enjoy the warmth of her. Unfortunately his hide was quite thick in order to enable him to withstand the often freezing temperatures of the water, and so all he was truly aware of was the pressure of her body against his.

It was sufficient.

He boosted her up onto the anchor chain and she began to climb it. Then he drifted back and called up to her, "If you need me, come to this place and call for me. I will come."

"But . . . won't you be wanting to get home?"

"Home for me is an elastic concept for the time being. I will be around here for a time, until it suits me to move on, whenever that may be. And if there is an emergency, I will bring my friend."

"You mean—?"

"Yes."

"But wouldn't his presence ensure the destruction of the Spires?"

"Very likely. On the other hand," he said darkly, "if something should happen to you, then the destruction of the Spires will be the very least that I can do.

Jepp was not entirely sure how to react to that. Finally she said, "Well . . . let us hope it does not come to that."

"Indeed."

And with that, Gorkon allowed himself to slide under the water.

Jepp wasn't entirely sure that Gorkon had actually left. In fact, she had a feeling that he had not. But there was no point in hanging from the anchor chain and staring down into the water. Instead she hauled herself up the chain, hand over hand, bracing her bare feet against the side of the ship. She shivered slightly, remembering that she had briefly clawed at the prow before skidding under the fearsome waves. Then she steadied herself and continued the climb up. Quietly she eased herself over the railing and landed softly on the deck. She froze there, waiting for some sign of life from below decks.

There was nothing. They had left the vessel. No reason for them not to do so. It wasn't their home, after all. Their home was somewhere deep in the city of Spires, and she had absolutely no idea where that might be.

She took a moment to look at the skyline of the Spires. It was not as she had seen in her dreams, but that was because she wasn't standing in exactly the same place. Nevertheless, she knew that it was the same city. For instance, she recognized the same tall spike that she had spotted in one of her dreams. But without the dream convenience of impossible vision, she was unable to spot whether that curious Mandraque female was perched upon it. She didn't think so, yet she could not be sure.

Jepp realized that her eyelids were becoming incredibly heavy. She had not had a decent night's sleep since she had been swept overboard. For that matter, she couldn't remember the last time she had had a single, solid night of uninterrupted slumber. She had either been jolted awake by some sort of catastrophe, or someone making a point of waking her up.

She walked across the deck and descended into the room that had served as her quarters during her stay on the ship. She found it easily enough, and then did some further searching of the vessel. The ship's stores were exactly as she had left them, including the skins filled with water. She grabbed one and drained it so fast that she wound up getting hiccups. It took her a few minutes of holding her breath for as long as she could before she finally managed to shake them. She went to a second skin, but only sipped a bit of it to quench the last dregs of thirst. Then she ate a couple of the oddly filling breadstuffs and breathed a sigh of relief.

For the first time in what seemed ages she was sated. However tired she had been earlier, she was even more so now. Her pathetic little bunk had never looked better. She crawled into it, allowing exhaustion to overwhelm her completely. The last thing she wondered before she fell asleep was what sort of dreams she would have now that she had finally arrived in the city that had been calling to her and haunting her.

She had a dreamless slumber.

PERRIZ

I.

THE ZEFFERS FILLED THE SKIES over Perriz, blocking out the sun. Their strength was beyond anything that anyone could stand up to. And that was just the Zeffers; their Riders were equally as formidable. They had armed themselves with boulders brought from the Upper Reaches of Suislan, and were casually tossing them down upon the hapless residents of Perriz who were trying to run and increasingly were finding nowhere that was safe. They would take refuge in buildings that the Zeffers would casually knock over with their massive snaking tentacles.

High above it all, Thulsa Odomo was taking pleasure in seeing the Firedraques running for their lives, and those lives were rapidly being dispensed with. There were Mandraques running as well, but none of them were of the house of Odomo, and so their fates were of no consequence to Thulsa.

Seramali was crouched next to him upon one of the largest of the Zeffers. He was howling in triumph, pointing and shouting to the Riders where they should next focus their efforts, and those of the Zeffers. "You are enjoying this entirely too much," said Thulsa, amused at his enthusiasm. "The thrill of war can be a heady experience. And experiencing a slaughter, well . . . there's no greater feeling."

"Greater than being in a battle where both sides are evenly matched, so that you can face an opponent who is your equal and might kill you before you can kill him?"

"Oh yes. Much better," Thulsa said. "Equal fights are overrated. Give me a lopsided massacre any day. The more who are able to survive and thus enjoy the fruits of their endeavors, the better. And this," and he gestured below proudly, "is most definitely a massacre.

The pathetic Firedraques and those Mandraques not of our house have no—"

And then something extremely strange happened.

The Zeffer upon which they were perched suddenly jolted. It happened so abruptly that all those who were astride it were staggered, and one or two were nearly thrown off the edge before others grabbed them and prevented their tumbling off.

"What was that?" said Thulsa. "A shift in the wind? Some sort of downdraft?"

Once again the Zeffer tilted, this time to the other side. It swung wildly and now Thulsa was able to look to the ground and see what was happening.

He couldn't believe what he was seeing.

"Ocular? Ocular?"

Sure enough, there were Ocular upon the ground. The Mandraques and Firedraques had been running in confusion, the tentacles resistant to swords, or flame breath, or even spit acid. The Ocular however, were doing nothing to try and damage the snaking tentacles. Instead they were simply grabbing the tentacles and yanking as hard as they could. Every time the Zeffer would lash out with one of its remaining tentacles, trying to get one of the Ocular, to beat at them or yank them off their feet, the Ocular would simply reach out with their massive hands and snag them. With staggering strength and relentless determination, the Ocular were hauling the Zeffer out of the sky.

"Bring another Zeffer around! Get at them!" shouted Thulsa.

"We can't! The streets are too narrow! We can't get down at them!" said Seramali.

The Ocular were pulling the Zeffer down, foot by foot. The Zeffer still had plenty of altitude, but the Ocular were making headway. Their strength was beyond anything that Thulsa had ever experienced, and he could not for the life of him figure out what the hell they were doing in Perriz.

He did know, however, that he couldn't simply stand by and wait for the Ocular to yank his Zeffer down from the skies. He and the other Mandraques and Serabim who were with him upon the Zeffer were going to have to take a more direct hand.

"Down! Go down!" he shouted, and without hesitation he threw himself off the top of the Zeffer and snagged one of the trailing tentacles.

"Go with him!" said Seramali to the Riders. The other Mandraques, and a number of the Serabim, followed suit.

The Mandraques and the Riders slid down the tentacles toward the Ocular, howling shouts of defiance. The Ocular saw them coming, but their hands were occupied and they were helpless to take any defensive actions while grasping the Zeffer's tentacles. So they did the only thing they could: They abruptly released their hold on the tentacles.

As a result the Zeffer, which had already been trying to pull away, abruptly hurtled skyward again with almost violent buoyancy. The Riders managed to hang on, but several of the Mandraques were so jolted that they lost their holds and tumbled downwards. A couple of them landed wrong, landing flat on their backs. It wasn't sufficient to kill them, but it was enough to cause them tremendous pain and anguish as they lay there flopping about with their spines shattered. Their pain was ended quickly enough, though, as the Ocular stepped on their heads.

The rest of the Mandraques, though, and the Riders, landed without incident. Among the survivors was Thulsa Odomo, and he faced the Ocular, brandishing his sword, ready for the attack.

"You should not have—" he started to shout, and then he stopped, fully registering what he was seeing. "Children! They're children! We're fighting children?"

"You're fighting us!" bellowed one of the males and he came straight at Thulsa Odomo.

Thulsa appreciated the lad's fighting spirit and bravery. He appreciated even more the fact that the Ocular had absolutely no fighting technique at all. The Ocular obviously expected that his size and his strength would carry the day.

Thulsa spun, dodging easily between the Ocular's outstretched arms, and came in fast with his sword. He cut it straight across the Ocular's stomach and the giant's entrails spilled out right in front of him. The Ocular gasped once, which was all he had time for, and then fell forward heavily and lay still.

Had he been dealing with full-grown, battle-hardened Ocular, his action would simply have spurred the rest of them to action. Instead the sight was more than enough to quell the desire for combat among the other Ocular. They stumbled back at the sight, their eyes widening behind their oversized lenses, and then as one they broke and ran.

"You! Go after them! Subdue them if possible; kill them if necessary!" bellowed Thulsa Odomo to the Riders, who set off in pursuit of the fleeing Ocular. Thulsa then rallied the half dozen Mandraques around himself. "Since we're down here, we might as well do something constructive. Come: We find Evanna, the daughter of that infernal Nicrominus. She's the only Firedraque that matters. We find her, we kill her, and we put her head on a pike outside," and he smiled, "the newly dubbed Mandraque Hall."

II.

COVERED IN HOOD AND CLOAK, staying to the shadows as much as she could, Clarinda followed Xeri as he led her, Evanna and Kerda through the streets of Perriz toward what they hoped would be at least a modicum of safety.

She glanced up, shielding her eyes against the daylight, as the Zeffers hovered above, wreaking destruction and havoc with their tentacles. Suddenly a hand grabbed her arm and she jumped, startled. It was only Evanna, but there was fury on her face as she growled, "If I find out you had anything to do with this—"

"Me? Are you insane?"

"None of this happened until you showed up! Everything was fine!"

"Obviously everything wasn't fine or you wouldn't be under attack! How did you not think that this was inevitable? You Firedraques, all high and mighty, with your treaties and your proclamations, telling everyone that they should not be at war with each other. What did you think was going to happen? You brought this entirely on yourselves! Acting in a domineering fashion, as if you're so much better than the rest of the Twelve Races, when the only thing the lot of you can truly agree upon is that you're all better than my people. And now look where you are! Side by side with me, running for your miserable life, while the blood of your enemy is trickling into my stomach. I don't hear you complaining about my having saved your ungrateful life!"

"Can we please do this later?" said Xeri, looking with terror toward the skies.

"We don't know that there's going to be a 'later,' so now seems as good a time as any," Clarinda shot back.

The air around them exploded with the sounds of another building shattering from nearby. Debris, thrown far by the impact, rained down around them. Kerda grabbed Clarinda and brought her close to herself, shielding her from the rubble with her own body. The Ocular grunted several times as bricks and mortar ricocheted off her, and yet all she asked was, "Are you all right?"

"I'm fine, I'm fine. Are you all right?"

She looked up and saw that there was blood running down the side of Kerda's face. Something had rebounded off the side of her head and opened a sizable gash. She wiped it away with her palm. "Don't worry about me." She stared at her hand, then back at Clarinda, and held up the bloodied palm. "Are you hungry again? Do you need to . . . to eat? You can lick this if it will help."

This was quite possibly the worst moment to laugh in the entirety of Clarinda's life, and yet she couldn't help but do so. It was such an insanely sweet thing to say. It was Kerda's way of trying to tell Clarinda that she was willing to be as accepting as possible of the bloodthirstiness she had seen her display earlier. "I am . . . not in need. But I appreciate the thought."

"Here! Over here!" Xeri called, standing outside a building that looked so small, it was doubtful whether Kerda would even be able to fit. He pulled open the door and they looked down. Darkness beckoned to them. Xeri headed in.

"You next," Clarinda said to Kerda. Screams from fleeing victims floated to them from nearby. "If you're too large to fit, then we might as well know now so we can find another way."

"But—"

"No arguing. Do it."

Kerda nodded and then stepped into the small building, leaving Evanna and Clarinda behind. Evanna turned to face Clarinda and said in a low voice, "We were not trying to be domineering. We were trying to make the Damned World a better place. It is what the Overseer wanted."

"Is it? Or is it what you were told he wanted? How gullible are the Twelve Races anyway? How much do you really know about anything?"

Despite the seriousness of the situation, Evanna actually chuckled. "Believe it or not, my father would ask that very same question of me all the time. I suspect he would like you. Perhaps you'll have a chance to meet him."

"You truly believe that he is still alive?"

"I do."

"In that case, you are even more stupid than I had credited you."

Before Evanna could reply, Xeri's voice shouted from within, "Evanna! Piri! Get in here, hurry!"

They did as they were bidden, running into the building and shutting the door behind them.

Had they moved just the slightest bit faster, Thulsa Odomo would have come around the corner a second too late and not seen them.

But they didn't.

And he did.

III.

SERAMALI LOOKED UPON THE DEATH and destruction being rained down upon Perriz, and he found it to be good.

He was not stupid. He knew that the next step would be for the Mandraques to turn upon them, and he was not going to give them the opportunity. The Mandraques were useful for ground troops—perhaps even aiding in the reconstruction of Perriz—but that was the limit of their place in his vision. The Mandraques proclivity for parties and celebrations was legendary, while the Serabim were virtually incapable of becoming inebriated. Even their beloved yond could, at most, leave them feeling relaxed. In the coming days, relaxation would not be called for. And so all that would be required to dispose of the Mandraques would be to have one truly great, vast bacchanal, at which point the Serabim would slice the Mandraques' throats with their claws while the Mandraques lay in drunken stupors, and that would be the end of that.

After that, the Serabim could turn their attentions to wider matters. There were other Serabim tribes to bring together, coalitions to form. A world to tame. With their power, their build, their durability, and their command of the air, there was nowhere that the Serabim could not go, no height they could not reach. Even the waters provided no barrier to them. Let the Merk and Markene putter around in the depths of the oceans; the Serabim sailed over it with impunity.

He looked down upon those below who were fleeing the unfettered power of the Serabim, and he thought, *Demali will understand the necessity.* Then he remembered, and for just a moment, mourning clutched at his heart. He pushed it away. There would be time for it later, once more important matters were attended to.

That was when something grabbed him from behind and lifted him off his feet.

IV.

IT ALWAYS COMES BACK TO this, thought Clarinda. *It always comes back to me running around underground. Is this what my fate is to be? Is this what my child has to look forward to? Shunning the light? Hiding in the dark? What the hell kind of existence is this?*

"I've never been down here," said Evanna.

"You haven't missed much," Xeri said.

Despite her reservations, Clarinda considered the darkness of the sewers oddly comforting.

Every so often they heard a crashing or thudding from far overhead. Evanna winced with every impact. Clarinda ignored it. She had other things on her mind.

"Is this the way that you led the others?" said Kerda. "When you led them out?"

"Yes, this was it," said Clarinda.

"Do you think they're all right?"

"I'm more concerned about whether we're all right." Then she froze so thoroughly that Kerda walked past her and Xeri nearly ran her over.

"What—?" Xeri began.

She shushed him, putting a hand up, listening. There was the steady dripping of water, the squealing of rats, and something else, something coming behind them quickly and noisily.

"Pursuers. They're right behind us."

"Who is it?"

"I'm not entirely sure that it matters. Come on."

They started to run, moving as quickly as she could. They moved right, right, left again, Clarinda leading the way, trusting her instincts.

They turned a corner and skidded to a halt.

There was a massive pile of rubble directly in their path.

"No," she whispered. "No!"

She wouldn't have thought it possible. Structural weaknesses must have developed in the sewer, and it wouldn't have been a problem except for the steady pounding that the surface was sustaining. It must have caused the collapse.

There was no way forward.

"What do we do?" said Xeri, never sounding more helpless.

Clarinda looked up. There was a hole above them with a ladder running its length. But all that was going to do was head them back to the surface, which was being overrun by Mandraques and Serabim. On the other hand, they might well have no choice but to take their chances.

"Quickly," Evanna said, and she threw herself at the fallen rubble blocking their path. She started grabbing chunks of debris and tossing them to either side.

Kerda immediately followed her lead, tearing at the rubble as quickly as she could.

If they had been given enough time, Clarinda thought, they might actually have managed to accomplish it. Time, however, was not their friend, as they heard gravelly voices shouting from the far end, "Hurry! Hurry, damn it! Don't let them get away!"

Clarinda's head whipped back and forth, assessing their options, trying to determine the best way to go. Then she turned to Kerda and said, "Go. Up."

"What?"

"Go up! Don't you understand? It's Mandraques, and they don't give a damn about me. They're not even really going to care about you."

"I'm not leaving you."

"Yes, you are."

"But—"

"I am not going to be responsible for the death of another young, gullible female Ocular who made the fatal mistake of trusting me! I am not!"

"I don't understand . . ."

"It's not for you to understand. It's for you to obey. Xeri will lead you to another entrance to the sewers. I'll catch up."

"After you . . . what? Take on the Mandraques singlehandedly?"

"You saw what I'm capable of. I'll be fine. Now stop talking and get the hell out of here! Evanna's going to need you to protect her!"

Kerda looked up doubtfully. "I'm not even sure I'll fit up there."

"Then you'd best get started squeezing. Now go. I'll catch up, I swear." She squeezed her hand. "We will be reunited."

She was reasonably certain it wasn't true, but knew that it was the only way she was going to get Kerda going.

Kerda nodded once and then went to the passageway above them. She leaped straight up, and grunted. "It's tight, but I think I can make it."

"Good. Evanna, go."

The sounds of the Mandraques were drawing closer. The echoing made it hard to determine exactly where they were, but she knew it wasn't going to be long.

Yet Evanna wasn't moving. "Why are you doing this? Sending me ahead? Why do you care about me?"

"I don't give a damn about you. You're just something to keep Kerda occupied."

Evanna considered that for a heartbeat. "I find that acceptable."

She turned away and headed up the hole after Kerda. Xeri was right after her.

Seconds later, the Mandraques descended.

With a roar, Clarinda leaped straight at the foremost Mandraque. She expected that he would go down as easily as the one she had killed back in Firedraque Hall.

She was wrong.

Instead he seemed to anticipate precisely the speed and direction from which her attack came. He sidestepped her, twisting out of her way, and he brought his fist down on the back of her head. Clarinda hit the ground hard, and she tried to scramble to her feet but more of the Mandraques had fallen upon her. She struggled furiously against them but they pinned her down as the lead Mandraque shouted, "Hold her! We may need her for questioning!" He glanced around and then up. Seeing the hole above them, he shouted, "Arrows!"

Two Mandraques carrying bows with arrows already nocked took position under the hole and opened fire. The arrows zipped up the hole, making ugly sounds as they sped through the air.

There was a scream from above, and then another. Seconds later, something fell from above and hit the ground heavily.

It was Xeri. One arrow was protruding from his lower back, the other angled downward from his chest. He lay on the ground, trembling, his body spasming. From on high there was a distant screaming and Clarinda knew without question that it was Evanna.

"Which one is this, Thulsa?" said one of the Mandraques.

"Who cares?" Thulsa stepped forward, brought his sword around and down. It sliced through Xeri's neck in one sweep with such force that his head skidded across the sewer floor and ricocheted off the leg of one of the Mandraques. He let out a coarse laugh and kicked it as if it were a ball. The others joined in, batting his head back and forth until Thulsa shouted for them to cease such frivolities.

"Did Evanna," and he pointed upward, "go that way?"

From the ground, she said, "I have no idea who that is."

He kicked her. Instinctively she rolled up, twisting her body around so as to shield her belly from the impact. She managed to do so, but the pain was still brutal.

"You! And you!" he pointed at two of his soldiers. "Go up after her! Bring her back down here! I want the Piri to be able to see us cut the Firedraque to pieces in front of her!"

The two Mandraques did as they were told, scampering up the hole after the fleeing Firedraque.

Thulsa strode around Clarinda's prostrate form. "So we have a Piri rooting around down here, eh. And how did that come to be?"

"Why are you bothering to talk to me when you're just planning to kill me?"

"Because," he said, and he crouched in front of her and grabbed her hair, pulling her head back. Clarinda cried out. "Mandraques like to play with their food." He noticed her hand with the missing finger. "Are you pre-chewed food, I wonder? That looks like it was bitten off."

"It was."

"Who did it?"

"My mother."

Thulsa tilted his head back and laughed loudly, his guffawing echoing up and down the sewers. "Your mother! Hah! She sounds like an almighty bitch."

And there was more laughter then . . .

. . . but it wasn't his.

It was rich, and thick, and female, and it seemed to be coming from everywhere at once. The Mandraques looked around in confusion, uncertain of the origin.

And then the laughter subsided and a female voice said, "You have *no* idea."

It can't be, thought Clarinda, *oh gods, no, it can't be.*

Into the pale light stepped Sunara Redeye. A mob of Piri moved in behind her, their eyes alive with bloodlust. And looming above them all was Bartolemayne.

"Hello, my love," said Sunara. "Your family has missed you ever so much."

V.

THE ZEFFER THAT HAD TRANSPORTED Arren Kinklash, the two Ocular and Demali had moved far more quickly than the much larger ones. The fact that it was newly energized apparently had helped, plus the fact that it was carrying far fewer individuals upon its surface. Consequently the battle was still going on when Arren's group arrived on the scene.

The advantage of riding a Zeffer in this situation, Arren Kinklash realized, was that it was easy to blend in. There was a small sea of Zeffers hanging in the air in front of them.

He saw the pure pandemonium going on below them. "This is ridiculous," he said. "How the hell are we going to find—"

"There!" shouted Demali. She pointed. "There he is!"

"Oh." He squinted and had to admit that Demali had remarkably sharp eyes. "Are you sure?"

"Definitely. He's the one who's all alone on the Zeffer."

No one else had yet noticed Arren, Demali, Pavan or the two Ocular upon the smaller Zeffer. That was an indication of just how insane the destruction was that was being inflicted upon Perriz.

"We need to maneuver over there so you can get to him," said Demali.

Pavan was studying the distance separating them. "I'm not sure how we're going to manage that. He's going to see us coming. So will the other Zeffers. This Zeffer is smaller than the others. They will easily be able to beat him back, and not let us anywhere near him."

Arren considered their situation and then turned to the Ocular. "Turkin. Berola. Would you care to take me for a brisk run?"

Berola and Turkin looked confused for a moment, but then they realized. Demali and Pavan did not. "What are you—?" began Demali.

Without waiting for her to complete the thought, Berola grabbed Arren under one arm as Turkin sprinted ahead of her. He easily leaped the gap from the Zeffer they were upon to the next one nearest them. Berola was right behind him, also covering the distance with no problem.

The Zeffer naturally was filled with both Serabim and Mandraques. The landing immediately caught their attention. They moved to the attack.

They had no chance.

Turkin slammed through them, an unstoppable juggernaut. He was closer to being a full-grown Ocular than anyone of the other survivors of their race, and when he was in headlong charge, there was nothing alive that could stop him. Serabim and Mandraques were scattered to either side, and Berola was right behind him, carrying Arren under his arm as if he were a parcel that needed to be delivered as hastily as possible. Most of the obstructions were scattered by Turkin, although she was able to use her free hand to slap aside a few lingering obstacles.

They kept going, picking up speed, and they vaulted to the next Zeffer in line between them and Seramali. Seeing them coming, this group was more ready than the previous group had been. It made absolutely no difference. Because there were so many of them upon the Zeffer, they were too crowded to engage in anything resembling proper combat. Clumped together as they were, they were little more than a collection of angry bowling pins and Turkin was the ball plowing through them. The Zeffer sagged under the pounding weight of the stampeding Ocular, causing a lowering in altitude between it and the next Zeffer over. That didn't slow them either. Turkin bounced upward as if he had been sprinting across a trampoline, and Berola followed suit.

The third group of potential opponents, having seen the fate of the previous two, chose the better part of valor. They slammed into each other to get out of the way. Turkin and Berola ignored them, charging across just as they had the previous two.

They landed upon it and, at the far end, was the Serabim who had been identified to them as a target. He was looking down, oblivious of their presence.

Arren came up right behind him and grabbed him from behind. The Serabim, caught completely off guard, was startled to find himself face to face with a Mandraque, but clearly even more shocked to see a couple of Ocular behind him.

"Seramali?"

"Y-yes—?"

"Your daughter sent me to kill you."

A look of confusion passed across his face, and then with a roar Seramali attacked. He batted aside Arren's grip on him as if he were a child and attacked with his claws outstretched.

Arren backpedalled, pulling out his sword. Then he stepped forward quickly, thrusting with his blade. He struck home, driving deep into Seramali's chest. It caused the Serabim to grunt slightly, which made Arren realize that the blade hadn't exactly inflicted the amount of damage that he'd been hoping. Seramali then grabbed the naked blade with his bare paw, yanked it out of the wound, and then twisted. He tore the blade out of Arren's grasp and tossed it aside. The sword slid across the surface of the Zeffer and fell off the far edge, tumbling down toward the streets of Perriz.

Seeing Arren unarmed, Turkin moved to come to his aid, but Berola stopped him. "No," she said. "He made the promise. He would not want us to interfere."

Backing up from the advancing, infuriated Serabim, Arren overheard them and shouted, "Actually, I would have no problem with it at all!"

That was all the invitation that Turkin needed. Seramali leaped toward Arren, and suddenly the towering Ocular was directly in his path. Seramali shifted his target, tried to bring his claws to bear, but Turkin slapped him as if he were swatting a fly. Seramali went down, tried to stand once more, and then a massive foot shoved down upon him, pinning him.

Seeing their leader in dire straits, the Riders of the other Zeffers began to reposition their mounts. The Zeffers responded to their Riders, some moving slightly downward while others moved up, trying to situate themselves so that the creatures' tentacles could be put to good use.

"Coward!" screamed Seramali toward Arren. "Coward, to use Ocular when you're afraid to lose to me!"

"How is using superior weaponry cowardice?" said Arren, sounding reasonable. "It strikes me as simply being smart tactics."

"You want superior weaponry? Take a look around you!"

Arren turned and saw that the Zeffers were moving into position. He saw the threats that the tentacles presented.

"Arren," said Berola nervously, seeing their peril.

"If you're going to kill me," said Seramali defiantly, "then I suggest you do it now. Oh, but wait—if you do, then you'll have no leverage to bargain for your own pathetic lives against the rage of my people. But if, on the other hand, you use me to live, then you won't be able to accomplish your so-called mission on behalf of my late daughter."

"Should I kill him, Arren?" said Turkin. "Tell me what to do."

Arren mentally berated himself. He had thrown himself into this situation without planning ahead, and now he was paying for it.

Suddenly Turkin looked up. "It's the singing again! Pavan is singing!"

And he was right.

And less than a minute later was when the screaming began.

THE SPIRES

I.

"I DON'T WANT ANY PART of it."

Graves was stalking through the streets of the Spires, Trott directly behind him. With the new day aborning, Graves had had plenty of time to think matters through and he knew what he was prepared to do, and what he wasn't prepared to do. "Not any part at all," he said again.

"You're being absurd. You cannot just walk away from your responsibilities."

"And yet, here I am doing so."

"Graves, you can't sail the vessel by yourself. You'll need me. You'll need Ayrburn."

"I'll manage."

"You can't."

"Watch me."

"I won't be able to watch you if you're not here," Trott said, trying to sound reasonable.

They strode along the docks, Trott racing to keep up. "What is the point and purpose of tracking down the few remaining humans and killing them?" said Graves. "It makes no sense. It's vindictive. It's pointless."

"It is the desire of the Overseer."

"The Overseer is an insane creature who was put in charge of us through some mad impulse by the Magisters!"

"And he holds the power of life and death over us. Over all the Twelve Races."

"So you say."

"You've seen what he can do! You saw how easily he disposed

of insurrection! Do you seriously believe he won't be able to do the same to you!"

"This isn't insurrection. This is simply going somewhere else."

"He will reach across the waves and destroy you."

Graves stopped and turned to face him. "There are humans still dwelling beneath the streets of this very city. You know that, I know that. We've left them alone because there seemed no point in destroying them. We've already annihilated their race. There are very few pockets of any humans left, and their mechanical weapons will not work. Our wards have seen to that. So again, why should we just go around needlessly slaughtering them?"

"Because it's our job. And if we don't start presenting some newly dead humans to the Overseer, then it's going to be our asses as well."

"Then let it be your job, because I am taking my ass and returning overseas."

"He will reach across the waters. He will destroy your vessel. He will destroy you."

"Let him do so, then!" said Graves. "Let him do so in one great stroke and it will be over with, rather than killing me bit by bit. Look at me, Trott!" He tapped the silver metal that constituted his face. "Look at what this world is doing to us! What he's doing to us! Stay here with him if you like, but I will have no more of it. You hear? No more!"

The boat was sitting right where he had left it. He climbed up the gangplank while Trott remained on the deck. "And where will you go, eh?" said Trott.

"I'm going to find my brother."

"Gant? You don't know where to look . . ."

"I'm looking for Bottom Feeders and a large blob. It shouldn't be that difficult. I'll just seek out the latest war. There's always a war going on. It's the one thing that the Twelve Races excel at. No art, no invention, none of the finer things in life. But killing each other, that is well within our abilities. We can kill the hell out of each other. Huzzah for us. All hail the mighty Twelve Races. For a while

I thought—"

"You thought what?"

He shook his head. "The girl. Jepp."

"You mean the Fated One?"

Graves nodded. "I thought she was going to be important somehow. I thought perhaps she was somehow going to rid us of the Overseer . . . or, I don't know, pleasure him so that he's not so much of a bastard all the time. Something, anything. We were drawn to her because she was supposed to make a difference. How could we have been that wrong?"

"Maybe we weren't."

"Obviously we were."

"Maybe . . ."

"Maybe what?" said Graves in exasperation.

" . . . she's standing behind you."

"What is that supposed to mean? Maybe she's standing behind you. Maybe she's on the bottom of the ocean. Maybe she's on the moon. This is—"

"No, you don't understand," said Trott, and he was pointing.

Graves turned and looked behind him.

Jepp was standing there. She was rubbing her eyes and yawning, running her fingers through her hair to try and free it from tangles. "Hello again," she said.

Graves stared at her. He could not believe what he was seeing. "How? How is it possible? You . . . you're dead . . ."

"If I am," she said, "then I have nothing to fear, do I? So," and she clapped her hands and rubbed them briskly. "Bring me wherever you wish to bring me, secure in the knowledge that you are speaking to someone who Death had in its embrace and decided to throw back. Oh," and she smiled, "and do you have any more of those delicious bread-type things? I ate the last of them during the night and I'm feeling a bit hungry."

Graves and Trott had nothing to say.

II.

THE TRULLER CAR BUMPED GENTLY to a halt, jolting the passengers into wakefulness.

Initially Eutok had been controlling the speed and direction of the Truller, but he soon came to the realization that it was all preset and needed no handler. So he, along with the Bottom Feeders, had settled in for a trip the length of which none of them knew.

Zerena Foux had spent much of the time glowering at her son. Karsen, for his part, had made absolutely no attempt to engage his mother in any kind of conversation. Taking their cue from the mother and son, the rest likewise were not particularly chatty, save for the demented old Mandraque who seemed quite interested in recounting adventures that he may or may not have ever had and that absolutely no one was interested in.

Most disconcerting was the Piri that seemed to be inhabited by the shapeless blob. Eutok knew precisely what was going on; the blob had done exactly the same thing to Eutok's mother, the queen. The Piri was looking twitchy as a result, and every so often he would look as if he were trying to shake off the blob's influence, but he was having no luck doing so. The blob thing—Gant, his name was— remained firmly in control.

Eutok had endeavored to stay conscious, but even he had been drifting in and out until he was abruptly awakened by the car's cessation of forward movement. The others stirred to wakefulness as well, looking around and trying to figure out where they might be. "Is this it?" Karsen said cautiously.

"I have to think it is."

"The Spires. The heart of the Overseer's territory," said Zerena.

"Would you prefer to go back, mother? I'm quite sure the Piri would be more than happy to see you return."

"Let them come!" declared Rafe Kestor. He tried to pull his sword from his scabbard but it remained stuck within, unwilling to budge. He did not seem to notice. "I shall smite them one by one, or all together if need be! They shall rue the day—"

"Rafe," said Mingo tiredly. "Not now. All right? Just . . . not now." He climbed out of the car and staggered slightly, gripping the side of the tunnel and stretching his legs to get them working once more. The others followed suit.

All save Zerena.

"How are we going to get back?" she said. "The jumpcar is back in Porto. Our lives are back in Porto."

"So perhaps we begin new lives here," said Karsen. "This is a world of possibilities, mother."

"Because of her."

"Yes, Mother, because of her. And if you want to berate me, if you want to upbraid me, then please, for the love of the gods, do it now so that we can get it out of the way and for—"

Her voice unexpectedly soft, she said, "I have no intention of doing either."

That caught him off guard. "You don't?"

She vaulted out of the Truller, landing unsteadily on her feet, experiencing the same lack of feelings in her legs as the others had. "No. I don't," she said as she shook out her legs.

"Dare I ask why?"

"Because," she said, leaning on the Truller, "you stood up to me. I've been waiting for you to become enough of an adult to do that. I may think the reason you have for doing so is a crap one, but at least you did. And I am . . . impressed by that."

"Thank you, Mother," he said.

She kicked him in the genitals.

Karsen went down, gasping, grabbing at them.

Zerena stared down at him. "That's for punching me before." She then turned to Eutok. "All right, Trull. Let's go topside and check out this dump."

Nodding, Eutok headed out the exit of the tunnel. The other Bottom Feeders followed, with Mingo stopping to look down at Karsen and say, "I saw that coming. How could you not have seen that coming?"

Karsen moaned.

The Bottom Feeders slowed at first, giving Karsen sufficient time to recover and catch up with them. Trying to keep the pain out of his voice, he said, "Are you at all capable, Mother, of just issuing a compliment and allowing it to stop there?"

"Apparently not," she said.

The tunnel upward was fairly straightforward. It wasn't packed with additional crossways or intersections; it was a simple ramp that proceeded upward at an incline. "You can tell this was made quite some time ago," said Eutok. "The quality of the digging is far inferior to what we can do now."

"Seems like a hole to me, just like any other hole," said Zerena.

He sniffed in obvious contempt. "Amateur."

"In this, yes, and happily so."

In time the ramp evened out. They kept going and discovered a dead end. The wall was perfectly smooth in front of them. Eutok placed his hands flat against it, searching around.

"What are you doing?"

"Trying to find some manner of trip switch or something that would cause this to move. But I'm not finding any." He glanced at them. "They sealed it."

"To make sure that nobody returned? Or to make sure that no one followed?"

Eutok shrugged at Karsen's question.

"Very well," said Karsen. He hauled out his hammer. "Let's go to work."

He started hitting the wall repeatedly, and Eutok likewise unslung his battle axe. Together they began to pound at the wall. It shook against the assault and resisted at first, but soon huge chunks were flying out of it. The initially slow progress moved along quickly once they really got going, and finally a slam from Karsen's hammer sounded different in its impact from the ones before. When he withdrew the hammer there was a hole in the wall. From that point on it was a matter of minutes to clear enough space in the hole for all of them to pass through.

They stepped out into a different world. It was a large tunnel with a track down the middle that dwarfed the one the Truller car had run down. The walls were thick with ancient dirt. Eutok had removed the three hotstars from the Truller car, reasoning that it would be wasteful to leave them behind. He held one of them up now, suffusing the tunnel in a soft glow. It seemed to go on forever in both directions.

Eutok whistled. "Looks like Morts weren't exactly slouches at making their own tunnels."

"Which way?"

"Your guess is as good as—"

Suddenly they heard distant screams from down the tunnel.

"That's as good an indicator as any," said Karsen.

"For once we agree," said his mother.

Karsen, Eutok, and Rafe Kestor immediately headed in the direction of the screams; the rest of the Bottom Feeders went the other way. Both groups stopped dead when they realized which way the others were going, save for Rafe who kept running toward the screams. There was momentary hesitation, but Rafe's headlong dash toward danger was enough to settle the matter for all concerned, although Zerena was heard to moan loudly as they followed.

They ran as quickly as they could, Karsen having grabbed one of the hotstars from Eutok and now leading the way. The tunnel opened up in front of them, light flooding the far end. They emerged from the tunnel and came upon a scene of absolute horror.

There were dead Morts everywhere.

It was a mix of males and females, young and old. Karsen almost tripped over a youth whose leg appeared covered in a massive bandage. There was a look of permanent surprise upon his face. His body had been broken practically in half. Other humans lay scattered about, similarly smashed and mutilated.

And there were Travelers everywhere. One of them was allowing the dead body of a female Mort to drop from its hands. The Mort was still twitching, but those were just post-death spasms. The life had already fled.

For a moment, Karsen was terrified that Jepp might be among them. He quickly realized that she was not. The relief of that realization gave way to stark terror as the level of their own jeopardy dawned on him.

The Travelers saw them.

"Shit," muttered Eutok, who very nearly did.

The Bottom Feeders and Eutok were frozen in their metaphorical and literal tracks. The Travelers seemed to come together like a large black storm cloud and they approached the intruders.

And Zerena Foux stepped in between her son and the oncoming Travelers and said softly, "I'll die before I let them touch you."

"Yes," said the nearest Traveler. They all stretched out their hands, and a dark and terrible energy began to build within the confines of the tunnel.

"Ayrburn!"

It had been Gant, still clad in the body of the Piri, who had spoken. He strode forward and incredibly, impossibly, the Travelers backed up. Gant walked right up to one of the Travelers and seemed to be studying him with outright curiosity. "That is you, Ayrburn, is it not? Ayrburn the taciturn? Ayrburn the oblique? Ayrburn the sorely irritating?"

The foremost Traveler approached him, stunned. "Gant?"

"The same."

Whispers of Gant's name echoed among the other Travelers as they looked at each other. They appeared confused, which was something that seemed staggeringly mundane for a Traveler.

"You're . . . a Piri now?" said the one he'd addressed as Ayrburn.

"No. Nothing that simple. I'm inhabiting a Piri. Tania turned me into . . ." He looked chagrined. ". . . into nothing I want you to see."

Ayrburn considered his words. "Bitch," he said at last.

"That, my friend, is understating it." He indicated the corpses of the humans that were scattered around the tracks. "And what was the purpose of this? Seems rather a pointless slaughter."

"Overseer."

"The Overseer told you to do this?"

Ayrburn didn't respond. He just tilted his head slightly.

Eutok was finding the entire business just a bit surreal. To him the Travelers had always been these mysterious, unknowable creatures. Yet here was one of the Bottom Feeders having what amounted to a casual conversation with one of these harbingers of death and destruction.

"Well, that is . . . unfortunate," said Gant. "So . . ." He clapped his hands and rubbed them together briskly. "I see that you have been . . . busy. And we have things to attend to. So we will just get out of your way . . ."

"Overseer," said Ayrburn.

"Yes, I'm sure the Overseer has many serious matters that he wants you to see to. So certainly we—"

"You," said Ayrburn, and he pointed, "and them. Now."

The other Travelers slowly spread into a half circle, ringing them. Eutok definitely did not like the way this was shaping up. He tightened his grip on his battle axe and brought it up in a defensive position.

Gant's Piri head immediately snapped around and he looked with great urgency at Eutok. "Don't do it. Don't even think it. None of you," and he addressed all the Bottom Feeders, "even think about it. They want to bring us to the Overseer, and if we resist, they're going to kill us. They will do it quickly and efficiently and without the slightest hesitation."

"Why are they bringing us to him?" said Karsen.

"Because this is his city," said Gant. "Because if you're coming to the Spires, then you're going to have to deal with him. That's the way the world works, and if you were not prepared for that, then you should not have come here in the first place."

"All right," said Karsen. "But I'm going to make it clear to the Overseer that this was entirely my doing. So if he has any complaints with our being here, then I'm the one who should answer for it."

"Yes, I'm sure he'll take that very much to heart before he slaughters all of us," said Mingo.

Rafe Kestor raised his fist defiantly. "I would like to see him try!"

"You may very well get your wish, Rafe," said Zerena.

PERRIZ

I.

EVANNA WOULD NOT STOP SCREAMING and it was beginning to get on Kerda's nerves.

"Oh my gods," Evanna screamed. "Oh my gods, Xeri, oh my gods, he's dead!"

Kerda pulled the hysterical Firedraque over into an alleyway, looking apprehensively toward the Zeffers. "We don't know that! We don't know for sure that he's dead!"

"Oh, yes, he's dead."

It was the amused voice of a Mandraque who had spoken. Kerda looked up and saw that two Mandraques were approaching. They were heavily armed, and they were grinning mirthlessly. Kerda placed herself between the oncoming Mandraques and Evanna, who was still sobbing and screeching. The Mandraque further back had a crossbow with the arrow already in place and ready to fly.

"Thulsa Odomo," said the nearest Mandraque, "cut off his whining head, and then we kicked it around a bit for our amusement. And that is very similar to what is going to happen to you. As for your mighty defender, I'm reasonably sure that a crossbolt in the eye will dispatch her as readily as anyone else."

Evanna had stopped sobbing very suddenly. "You . . . bastards," she said, her voice trembling with fury. "Oh you . . . you heartless bastards. You will be destroyed for this. You will suffer. Oh, how you will suffer."

"Ah yes," said the Mandraque. "The power of the Firedraques. Why not simply ask the gods, with whom you are so close, to simply strike me down from on high . . . ?"

That was the moment that the sword of Arren Kinklash, knocked out of his hand and sent tumbling off a Zeffer, landed with remarkable precision squarely in the skull of the Mandraque holding the crossbow. The Mandraque literally never even knew what hit him. The sword bisected his brain. He staggered and, as his legs collapsed, his finger spasmodically pulled on the trigger of the crossbow. The bolt went wide of its target and landed squarely in the back of the other Mandraque, who let out a high, outraged shriek of pain. He reached around, trying to claw at it, howling a string of profanities.

That was the moment Evanna pushed Kerda to one side. She took a deep breath and let out a jet of flame so bright, so searing, that Kerda had to shield her eye lest she be blinded by it even though she had the lens covering it.

If the Mandraque had been in pain before, Evanna's attack took it to an entirely new level. He went up in flames, screaming, batting at his body, trying in futility to extinguish it. He stumbled, tripping over his own feet and fell. He continued to flail about as the fire eagerly consumed him. Kerda took a step forward to bring her foot down on his head, but Evanna stopped her. "No," she said tersely. "Don't end his suffering. Let him burn."

Kerda did as she was told. They stood there and watched as the Mandraque twisted and flopped around while the fire devoured him. Before long he stopped moving as a plume of black smoke filled the air.

And that was when all hell broke loose from on high.

II.

DEMALI FELT CHILLS RUNNING DOWN her spine as Pavan stood in the middle of the Zeffer and sang. She had never heard him sing before. It was so beautiful that her eyes were tearing up. All the Zeffers were attending to him now. They didn't seem to be responding to their Riders at all.

They began to sing back. The air was filled with beautiful notes, cascading all around, and Demali felt as she was a child again, sprinting through the dizzying paths of the Upper Reaches, her father running behind her and laughing and calling out that he was going to catch her, and when he did he would raise her high and speak her name with such love that she knew she would always be his, and he hers, and the memory caused her to sob all the more.

Then Pavan's voice began to slide up and down the scales. It was a dazzling array of notes, but it sounded like something more to Demali. It almost sounded like . . .

. . . instructions.

That was when the Zeffers began to turn.

They did so in almost leisurely fashion. All the Zeffers, save for the one that Pavan was upon and the one where Arren, the two Ocular and her father were situated, responded in the exact same manner. They started rotating, slowly turning sideways.

Which proved catastrophic for their Riders and the Mandraques who were upon them.

They scrambled around trying to find purchase, but there was nothing for them to hold onto on the surface. Some managed to grab onto the upper edges of the Zeffers as they ponderously, even majestically turned completely sideways. The rest of them skidded, tumbled, and slid right off the huge creatures. The air was discordant, filled with the sounds of Pavan's and the Zeffers' beautiful songs overlayed with the howls and screams of terror as the Riders and the Mandraques tumbled to their deaths hundreds of feet below.

Some were still managing to cling on, batlike, and then the Zeffers continued to turn until they were completely upside down. Their edges fluttered as they did so, and that was sufficient to loosen the holds of the remaining passengers. They lost their grips as well, and the last of the Riders and Mandraques, who had sought to leave a lasting impression on Perriz, managed to achieve their goal. Perriz's streets were awash with blood that would never fully come out, and a number of the plummeting bodies left huge dents and shattered pavement in the streets far below.

Pavan eased down on the notes and slowly the Zeffers righted themselves. Finally the singing subsided and Pavan simply stood there, his face impassive.

"You killed them," she said in wonderment. "You killed all of them. Why . . . why didn't you do that earlier?"

"I was hoping I would not have to. But it seemed . . . unavoidable."

The Zeffer that they were upon was still moving. It was rising through the air, and the other Zeffers were making room for it, as if according it newly acquired respect. Within moments they had drifted to within range of Arren and the others. Seramali was looking at them with wide-eyed wonderment. "You . . . you are alive. The Mandraque was telling the truth. He . . ." Then his voice trailed off as he realized the seriousness of his situation.

"Yes. I am alive. No thanks to you."

"And you want me dead."

"Yes."

"But you could not bring yourself to kill me, and so you sent this Mandraque to do the deed for you."

"Yes. But . . ."

The catch in her voice got Arren's attention. "But what? What do you want, Demali? I honestly have no strong preferences one way or the other."

"I think," said Demali, "that it would be far worse punishment for him to live. To live knowing that all his plans came to naught. That his beloved Riders are dead. That his daughter whom he once loved doesn't care enough about him to kill him. I think those would all be . . . good things."

"So do I," said Pavan.

And then he hummed.

One of the Zeffer's tentacles reached down and casually slapped

Seramali across the chest. The impact knocked him off the Zeffer. He screamed Demali's name as he plummeted to the ground, and only the abrupt impact ended his screech.

"But I think that was a better thing," said Pavan.

"You . . . you killed him," said Turkin.

"He killed my parents."

"And you said earlier that, even though you knew that, you could not bring yourself to kill him."

"Yes. I know. Odd thing, though," he said distantly. "After you kill the first hundred or so, it becomes much easier." He looked to Demali. "I hope you do not hate me for what I've done."

Her face was still wet as she shook her head. "No. No, I . . . I don't. I could never hate you."

But she wasn't sure she believed it.

III.

EVANNA WAS UNAWARE OF THE passage of time. All she knew was that she had been watching the one Mandraque burn, and the next thing she was aware of, she was seeing Arren Kinklash pulling his sword out of the head of the fallen Mandraque. Kerda was hurriedly explaining to him what had happened, and he was nodding and listening as he wiped the blood from his blade. Turkin and Berola were there as well, Berola with a comforting arm around Kerda's shoulder, rubbing the top of her head in a calming manner.

Then he walked over to Evanna and crouched in front of her. "Evanna," he said gently. "Evanna, perhaps he was lying about Xeri . . ."

Evanna shook her head. "No. He was . . . not. I heard Xeri's screams and the awful way they just . . . stopped. He's gone." She paused and then said, "And what of you? Are you gone?"

He nodded. "At least for the time being. The Serabim are going to bring me to Norda. With any luck, Nicrominus will be with her and I'll be able to bring him back to you as well."

Arren then waited for her to give him a whole speech about how he was needed here, especially considering the damage that had been done to the city. "Everything is going to be fine here," he said, anticipating it. "The few surviving Serabim and members of House Odomo are being hunted down, rounded up. They—"

"I want to go with you."

Her response surprised him. "Ex . . . excuse me?"

"There is nothing for me here. Xeri dead. My father gone."

"But your responsibilities—"

"To hell with them. To hell with treaties. If I don't get away from all this death and destruction, I am simply going to go out of my mind. Take me away from this, Arren. Please." She hesitated. "Do not make me beg."

"No. No, not at all," he said gently. He helped her to her feet. "It's going to be fine. We will find your father. And everything is going to be all right."

"Promise?" she said.

"May I die if I am wrong," he said with as much sincerity as he could muster.

IV.

CLARINDA SAT ON THE FLOOR of the sewer, staring at nothing.

She tried not to listen to the steady slurping sounds that were coming from nearby. The screams of the Mandraques as they had been drank alive by the Piri had faded away. Thulsa Odomo had lasted the longest, give him credit for that. He had kept on struggling until Bartolemayne had decided to simplify matters by snapping his neck. A familiar pair of legs stepped into her immediate field of vision. Slowly she looked up. Sunara smiled down at her.

"How?" It took all Clarinda's energy to form the question. "How—?"

"Did I come to be here?" She chuckled at that. "My love . . .

what did you think we were going to do if not find a new home? The Ocular are dead. We could not feed on them anymore, and our people deserve so much better than living the rest of their lives feasting on animals. Oh, make no mistake. When you left, at first I was furious that you had disobeyed me and was taking steps to return you. But soon I realized that I could take advantage of the situation. Especially because you did not understand just how close I was to you in your heart and mind. Even after all this time, you don't quite comprehend the scope of my abilities."

"Scope? I don't . . . none of this . . ."

Then she realized.

Sunara smiled.

"You made me come here," said Clarinda. "You were in my mind. You made me come to Perriz."

"I cannot 'make' you do anything. I could only suggest. But you are my daughter, and so you embraced the suggestion. Because I knew of the sewer system. I knew that, sooner or later, you would wind up here. It is your nature. It was unavoidable. We followed you, my dear. We did not have to stay especially close because I had no trouble keeping track of you," and she tapped the side of her head, "here. And when you found your way through the sewer and emerged, I saw through your eyes, and thus you showed us the way in. Thank you for that. Thank you for," and she indicated their environment, "all of this. We owe this all to you."

"You're going to . . . to stay here?"

"Of course we are, my dear." She took Clarinda's hand in hers. "And no one is going to know we're here. We are going to be very, very careful about that. We are going to emerge at night, at will, find stray Mandraques or Firedraques or Ocular . . . and we will bring them down here, and we will make them last. I allowed my people to devour these," and she indicated the fallen bodies of the Mandraques, "because it has been a good long while since we truly feasted. We will live here forever. And you will have a home here so that you will have a nice, safe environment to come to term with your child. And once he has been brought into the world, we will kill him, and then we will kill you. Or, as an alternative, leave you begging for death and then not giving it to you. If you're a good girl," and she kissed Clarinda on the forehead, "I may leave it up to you."

THE SPIRES

IT WAS EXACTLY AS SHE had seen it.

The place where the Traveler had brought her, the street, the building . . . it was all precisely as she had seen in her dreams. The difference was that here she could smell the air, truly feel the street beneath her feet. She tried to imagine thousands of humans like herself pouring out of the entranceways that were sunken into the sidewalks, but the entire street remained eerily empty and silent. The only ones there were herself, the two Travelers who had found her upon the ship, and several other Travelers who were simply standing there, looking on.

"Is the Overseer going to meet us here?" she said to the Traveler who had brought her there, the one whom she had come to think of as her Traveler.

"Stop talking," he said tonelessly.

"Does he have a name other than 'Overseer?' For that matter, do you have a name? We were together so long, I feel as if—"

"My gods!" he sighed. "You never stop. Don't you understand what's going to happen here, you stupid woman? The Overseer is going to kill you."

"Why would he do that?"

The Traveler who was standing next to him tried to say something to him in that same eerie, whispering manner that she had heard earlier. The Traveler ignored his friend. "Why? There is no why involved. He is the Overseer. Questions such as 'why' do not concern him.'"

"Questions of why concern everyone. Everyone has reasons for what they do."

"If they are bad reasons, what does it matter?"

"It matters," she said softly. "It just . . . it matters. What is your name? I think it's time you told me your name."

"Graves!"

The Traveler jumped as if jolted and he turned toward the voice that had just spoken.

A Piri emerged from one of the stairways that led down into darkness. "Graves!" he said again, and began to run toward the Traveler.

"Gant?" said the Traveler.

"Gant?" echoed Jepp. She couldn't quite understand why this Piri was being addressed as Gant. She knew what Gant looked like, and this certainly was not him.

Then the Piri abruptly staggered and started screaming in pain. His skin began to redden, to blister under the influence of the daylight. and he staggered back toward the stairs, screeching.

More Travelers were now emerging from the stairs, and they were blocking Gant's means of escaping from the glare of the sun.

"Gant!" shouted the Traveler. Jepp forgotten, everything forgotten, he ran toward the Piri, pulling off his cape and hood as he did so. He remained clad entirely in black, but Jepp gasped as she saw him for the first time in the full light of day.

He was beautiful. She had not thought that any living thing could be so beautiful. Long, purple hair framed his face, but the rest of his face looked like living silver that glistened in the light.

He threw the cape and hood over Gant, who collapsed to the street, gasping for breath. "Thank you . . . thank you," Gant managed to gasp.

"Why are you still in that form?"

"I . . . didn't want them to see . . . I didn't—"

That was when Karsen emerged from the darkness.

Jepp could not believe it. It seemed impossible. It had to be impossible. For a moment she thought that she was dreaming. That was the simplest explanation. Her dreams had become so vivid that she was no longer capable of distinguishing the imagining from the reality. She could not even find the breath to say his name, so stunned was she to see him.

It wasn't necessary. He saw her.

He cried out her name and ran toward her. Jepp dashed toward him, calling out to him, and when she drew close enough she literally leaped into his arms. He held her so tight that it threatened to squeeze the life out of her, and at that moment she would not have cared. She would have been content dying in his arms, because there was nowhere else in the whole Damned World she would have preferred to be.

The other Bottom Feeders were emerging as well, with expressions that ranged from surprise to pleasure to annoyance (the last naturally being Zerena.). The Travelers said nothing, although they were taking care to give the one called Graves a wide berth. It was as if they were somehow embarrassed to be anywhere near him, as if he had violated some sort of code of conduct for Travelers.

"How did you get here?" she said to Karsen.

He laughed at that, sounding weary but happy. "It was a lot of work," he said. "But it was worth it."

"If we die, I have to think that diminishes the worth somewhat," said Zerena.

That was when the ground began to shake steadily beneath their feet. Something was coming from a nearby street. Karsen held Jepp tight, but she gently—but firmly—slid his arm off her. "It's going to be all right," she said. "But I have to face him. I have to be strong. There has to be . . ."

"What? Be what?"

"Order," she said. "Things have to be . . . just so. I have to make them just so."

"I don't understand what you're talking about."

"I'm not sure I do either."

The Travelers converged around the Bottom Feeders, Eutok and Jepp. It was clear why that was so: in order to forestall any thought they might give to fleeing.

Slowly, ponderously, the powerful armored figure of the Overseer stepped out into the intersection. He simply stood there for a time, looking at them.

Then, finally, he spoke.

"What have we here?"

No one answered at first. And then Jepp stepped forward, squaring her shoulders, and if she could not look him in the eye, she could at least take a guess as to where his eye might be and look there. "I am Jepp," she said. "I am a human."

"Yes. I know that."

"And I . . ."

"You what?"

She took a deep breath and let it out slowly, tremblingly. She realized that she was being seized with an almost primal urge to flee the scene. She had never heard the term "fight or flight," but if she had, she would have understood how it applied right then.

"I want there to be people again," she said. "People like me. Lots of people like me. I want the streets of this city to be filled with them. So many of them that, no matter which way you look, there are just . . . just people. Lots of them. And I just . . . I don't see why this world can't be big enough for the Twelve Races and human beings. I don't understand why the few humans who remain alive have to be slaves. I don't understand why everyone cannot be free to live their lives."

"You do not understand that? Would you like me to explain it to you?"

"I . . . I wasn't looking for an explanation actually. I just . . ."

"Human have always been slaves, child. Slaves to their desires. Slaves to their sex organs. Slaves to corporations. Slaves to their stupidity. To their greed and arrogance. To their endless, unrelenting pursuit of more and more pointless possessions, or drugs, or mindless entertainment. Corporations enslave employees. Religion enslaves minds and souls. Everywhere you looked, even when mankind was at its height, there was nothing . . . nothing but slavery. And the sick thing—the truly sick thing—is that everyone believed that they were free. They all thought they had free will. They all thought that they were masters of their own destiny, or at least could be if they had enough money or power or sex partners or whatever they needed in order to feel good about themselves. But it was all a joke. Just a big goddamn joke. Do you know what Voltaire said? No, of course you don't. He said that God was a comedian playing to an audience too afraid to laugh. Well, look where we are now, big guy. Look. You killed the audience. Absolutely killed them. Now who's laughing?"

Jepp just stared at him. "I have no idea what you're talking about," she said.

"No. No, of course you don't." He strode toward her, the ground shuddering beneath him.

Karsen's leg brushed up against hers and she could feel that he was trembling. She put a hand on his shoulder reassuringly. "Breathe," she said softly. "Breathe steadily."

"So you want to repopulate the Earth, then? Is that it?"

"The Earth? What's—?"

"My God, is there anyone with a brain left on this planet? How many times am I going to have to explain it! This! Here! This planet! Where you are standing! It's called 'Earth'. All right? Not 'the Damned World.' Earth! Urrrrrrth. Earth! Are we all clear on this?"

Jepp nodded, not knowing what else to do.

"And I am supposed to just do what? Wave my hand and bring humanity back in full force? In case you haven't noticed, I am not humanity's biggest fan. The fewer humans there are, the better. And I would just as soon get rid of the ones we have. Which reminds me, Travelers, did you get rid of the ones who were scurrying around underneath the streets?"

One of the Travelers bowed slightly in a manner that indicated an affirmative.

"Good. There aren't all that many more. A handful out west, I believe, hiding out. Or at least they think they're hiding out. But they'll be found and dealt with. Just as you will be now, my dear . . . Jepp, was it? Yes. Jepp. And these are your . . . dare I say it . . . friends? You will all be dealt with."

"What do you mean?"

"You want to know? Really? All right, then. You have obviously gone to a great deal of effort to come here, and I feel it only right and proper to make it worth your while. And, most importantly, you deserve to have my personal attention. So here is what is going to happen:

"There is going to be a hunt. A huge, magnificent hunt. The lot of you are going to scatter, or stay in one group; it doesn't make any difference to me. I will give you a full day's head start. Go as far as you want. Run as fast as you can. Feel free to breathe a sigh of relief because you think I cannot possibly find you, and pat yourselves on the back for your own cleverness. And then I will hunt you down. I will use all the resources at my command, and I will track you and come after you, and I will kill you. You will all die, because that's just the way life goes in the big city. I will hunt you, Jepp with no last name, would-be savior of humanity. I will hunt you and I will kill you, and your friends, and your little dog, too."

"My little what?"

"Never mind. It's not important. What's important is that humanity never, ever get a toehold on this godforsaken world ever again. You will die, and those who have tried to befriend you will die, and the handful of humans will die, and then—if we're very, very lucky—everything else will follow. Because the late Nicrominus told me that without humans, everything goes dark, and I'm fine with that. And even if it doesn't, well . . . at least this was a way to kill some time.

"Now run, little Jepp with no last name. You and all your friends. Run!"

"No!" said Jepp defiantly. "I'm not going to run. We're not going to run!"

"She doesn't speak for all of us," said Zerena.

"I'm not going to run because humans deserve more than you're willing to give them! They deserve more belief than you're willing to have in them! You all do!" and she turned and shouted to the Travelers. "You don't have to stand by and allow this! You can stand up to him! Together we can accomplish anything!"

"This is your last chance, child. Run. You have until the count of three or you die right now. One—"

"I'm not afraid of you!"

"Two—"

"Humanity will live! I've seen it! And there's nothing you can do to stop it—!"

"Three!"

He advanced on Jepp, his hands outstretched toward her.

There was an explosion of thunder, but it was like no thunder any of them had heard. It was short and abrupt and repeated itself several times.

The Overseer staggered and looked down at his armored body. Three holes had appeared in the chest. Blood was seeping out of them. As if he was studying with great fascination something that had happened to somebody else, he touched one of the holes with his gloved finger. "Teflon bullets. Armor piercing. Has to be. I'll be damned."

A figure was slowly approaching. It was a female Mandraque. She was holding something made of gleaming blue metal in front of her with both hands. Jepp recognized her immediately; she had seen her in a dream.

The Travelers were frozen in place, looking as stunned as anyone else.

"She is right. We should all be free. Oh . . . and you killed New Daddy. You shouldn't have done that. So I gifted myself with this."

"I'll be damned," he said again.

"That's the plan," she said, and fired once more.

The fourth bullet slammed home and the Overseer fell backwards like a great tree and slammed to the pavement.

All was silent for what seemed an eternity. Finally:

"You stupid bitch," Graves said. "You've just destroyed the world."

"Have I?" said Norda Kinklash. "My. How very exciting."

# # #

Don't miss the concluding chapter of

THE HIDDEN EARTH
BOOK THREE
ORDER OF THE CHAOS

ABOUT THE AUTHOR

PETER DAVID is a prolific author whose career, and continued popularity, spans nearly two decades. He has worked in every conceivable media: Television, film, books (fiction, non-fiction and audio), short stories, and comic books, and acquired followings in all of them.

In the literary field, Peter has had over seventy novels published, including numerous appearances on the *New York Times* Bestsellers List. His novels include *Tigerheart, Darkness of the Light, Sir Apropos of Nothing* and the sequel *The Woad to Wuin, Knight Life, Howling Mad*, and the Psi-Man adventure series. He is the co-creator and author of the bestselling *Star Trek: New Frontier* series for Pocket Books, and has also written such Trek novels as *Q-Squared, The Siege, Q-in-Law, Vendetta, I, Q* (with John deLancie), *A Rock and a Hard Place* and *Imzadi*. He produced the three *Babylon 5* Centauri Prime novels, and has also had his short fiction published in such collections as *Shock Rock, Shock Rock II*, and *Otherwere*, as well as *Isaac Asimov's Science Fiction Magazine* and *The Magazine of Fantasy and Science Fiction*.

Peter's comic book resume includes an award-winning twelve-year run on *The Incredible Hulk*, and he has also worked on such varied and popular titles as *Supergirl, Young Justice, Soulsearchers and Company, Aquaman, Spider-Man, Spider-Man 2099, X-Factor, Star Trek, Wolverine, The Phantom, Sachs & Violens, The Dark Tower*, and many others. He has also written comic book related novels, such as *The Incredible Hulk: What Savage Beast*, and co-edited *The Ultimate Hulk* short story collection. Furthermore, his opinion column, "But I Digress . . . ," has been running in the industry trade newspaper *The Comic Buyers's Guide* for nearly a decade, and in that time has been the paper's consistently most popular feature and was also collected into a trade paperback edition.

Peter is also the writer for two popular video games: *Shadow Complex* and *Spider-Man: Edge of Time*.

Peter is the co-creator, with popular science fiction icon Bill Mumy (of *Lost in Space* and *Babylon 5* fame) of the Cable Ace Award-nominated science fiction series *Space Cases*, which ran for two seasons on Nickelodeon. He has written several scripts for the Hugo Award winning TV series *Babylon 5*, and the sequel series, *Crusade*. He has also written several films for Full Moon Entertainment and co-produced two of them, including two installments in the popular *Trancers* series, as well as the science fiction western spoof *Oblivion*, which won the Gold Award at the 1994 Houston International Film Festival for best Theatrical Feature Film, Fantasy/Horror category.

Peter's awards and citations include: the Haxtur Award 1996 (Spain), Best Comic script; OZCon 1995 award (Australia), Favorite International Writer; Comic Buyers Guide 1995 Fan Awards, Favorite writer; Wizard Fan Award Winner 1993; Golden Duck Award for Young Adult Series (*Starfleet Academy*), 1994; UK Comic Art Award, 1993; Will Eisner Comic Industry Award, 1993. He lives in New York with his wife, Kathleen, and his four children, Shana, Gwen, Ariel, and Caroline.

You thought you knew about King Arthur and his knights? Guess again!

Learn here, for the first time, the down-and-dirty royal secrets that plagued Camelot as told by someone who was actually there, and adapted by acclaimed *New York Times* bestseller Peter David. Full of sensationalism, startling secrets and astounding revelations, *The Camelot Papers* is to the realm of Arthur what the Pentagon Papers is to the military: something that all those concerned would rather you didn't see. What are you waiting for?

DuckBob Spinowitz has a problem. It isn't the fact that he has the head of a duck—the abduction was years ago and he's learned to live with it. But now those same aliens are back, and they claim they need his help! Can a man whose only talents are bird calls and bad jokes be expected to save the universe?

No Small Bills is the hilarious new science fiction novel from award-winning, bestselling author Aaron Rosenberg. See why the NOOK Blog called it "an absurdly brilliant romp"—buy a copy and start laughing your tail feathers off today!

At the age of thirty-eight, Zeno Aristos has quit the NYPD but can't figure out what he wants to do with his life. Then someone close to him is kidnapped, and the search leads through a gauntlet of increasingly dark and cryptic forces. The deeper Zeno digs, the more he realizes he's dealing not with an earthly adversary but with an entity steeped in the deepest and most malevolent of ancient mysteries.

In *Fight The Gods*, Friedman takes a major creative step beyond the Star Trek novels, comic books, and television scripts with which his name has become synonymous, and braves the sinister rooftops and mystical back alleys of urban fantasy. Whatever you think you know of him or of his work . . . you ain't seen nothin' yet.

Matt Fisher was a normal boy—until he found the Door. The Door that led to the House. The House whose Doors opened into places all over the world—and into worlds that had been, and would be, and even never were. But Matt wasn't the only one who'd found his way in. Now he had something the man named Twig wanted, something that could sow the seeds to everything's destruction. This first book in the spine-tingling Latchkeys series, written by internationally best-selling author Steven Savile, sets the stage for more adventures with Matt Fisher and the rest of the Latchkeys Kids!

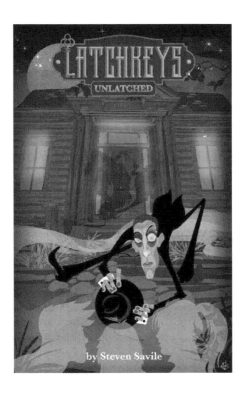

London, 1593. Christopher Marlowe—playwright, spy, and renowned womanizer—is desperately working on what could be his greatest play. Inspiration eludes him, until a chance encounter with a dark temptress rekindles his passion. But something doesn't want him finishing, and it's not just the Queen's Privy Council. Illness and madness rampage through the streets, causing death and mayhem. Can the incandescent playwright stop the chaos before it overwhelms the entire city?

This new occult thriller from bestselling authors Aaron Rosenberg and Steven Savile combines Elizabethan theatre, ancient mythology, and ageless seduction to create a dark, gripping tale that is both as old as time itself and wholly original.

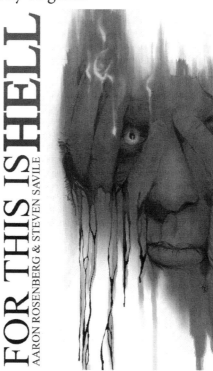

FOR THIS IS HELL

AARON ROSENBERG & STEVEN SAVILE

Athis, an apprentice wizard in the Crimson Keep, isn't the brightest flame in the candelabra. So when he and another apprentice named Belid summon a demon and then panic, trouble ensues—trouble that threatens to snowball wildly out of control. Will they and their fellow student Klaria be able to deal with the consequences before their master finds out? Will the Crimson Keep still be standing when it's all over?

Demon Circle is an original novella from Peter David, Michael Jan Friedman, Bob Greenberger, Glenn Hauman, Aaron Rosenberg, and Howard Weinstein, the writers behind the new author-driven publishing venture Crazy 8 Press. They wrote this story live at ShoreLeave33, and are donating all proceeds to the Comic Book Legal Defense Fund, which protects the First Amendment rights of comic book writers, artists, retailers, and fans.

CRAZY 8 PRESS ™

Peter David
Michael Jan Friedman
Robert Greenberger
Glenn Hauman
Aaron Rosenberg
Howard Weinstein